Terri Nixon was born in Plymou[...] age of nine she moved with her fa[...] fringe of the wild and beautiful Bodmin Moor, wh[...] discovered a love of writing that has stayed with her all her life, and which has inspired her to write several works of fiction based in the area.

She has since moved back to Plymouth with her two sons, and now works in the Faculty of Arts at Plymouth University and engages in a daily battle of wills with a temperamental Vauxhall Astra.

Maid of Oaklands Manor

Terri Nixon

PIATKUS

First published in Great Britain in 2013 by Piatkus
This paperback edition published in 2016 by Piatkus

3 5 7 9 10 8 6 4 2

A CIP catalogue record for this book
is available from the British Library.

ISBN 978-0-349-40103-4

Typeset in Caslon by M Rules
Printed and bound in Great Britain by
Clays Ltd, St Ives plc

Papers used by Piatkus are from well-managed forests
and other responsible sources.

MIX
Paper from
responsible sources
FSC® C104740
www.fsc.org

Piatkus
An imprint of
Little, Brown Book Group
Carmelite House
50 Victoria Embankment
London EC4Y 0DZ

An Hachette UK Company
www.hachette.co.uk

www.piatkus.co.uk

This book is dedicated to the memory of my grandmother Mary Nixon, without whose stories Lizzy Parker would still just be keeping her mouth closed and her hands busy.

Part One

Chapter 1

March 1912

I wasn't always Lizzy. A name may seem an insignificant detail in the tumult of all that was to come, but the change neatly separated the old life from the new and so Lizzy I became, in the sweep of a pen and in the fall of a word from a stranger's lips.

For now though I was still Mary, tired and terrified, and trying to ignore the mounting waves of anxiety that had begun in earnest the moment my feet had touched the platform. I stared at the huge house in the distance and let out a long, shaky breath; this would be my first taste of domestic service beyond helping to bathe my baby brothers, and as if that wasn't enough to bring on the collywobbles I'd be working for the Creswells who, to hear my mother talk, were Cheshire royalty.

Memories of her own service in this very house had been

shared often, and with a mixture of fondness and remembered trepidation. It was all too easy to fall foul of the strict rules, she'd said, but reassured me that busy hands and a firmly closed mouth would see me through the most difficult days.

The train had tipped me out three miles down the road at Breckenhall, and my first glimpse of Oaklands Manor was coloured by grumpiness and exhaustion, but as I drew closer I stopped noticing how my feet hurt inside their tight new shoes, how the handle of Ma's worn leather case cut into my palms, and how the sweat trickled uncomfortably between my shoulder blades despite the coolness of the spring day.

For all its forbidding size the house was beautiful, although it looked as though it might take me another week to reach it up the long, straight avenue that stretched from the road to the front door. Turrets at either end and balconies dotted along the upper two storeys of the Manor broke up what might otherwise have been a rather forbidding appearance, and made it look a little bit like something in a story book. My younger sister Emily would have fallen in love with it immediately, just for that.

To either side of me, glimpsed through the trees that gave the house its name, lay immaculately tended lawns, at least two sizeable ponds, and a summer house that looked big enough to house me, my mother, Emily and the twins comfortably.

At last I reached the end of the avenue where it curved away in two directions, sweeping around in a carriage drive outside the huge front door. I stared at that door, pretending for a moment that Oaklands was mine. Inside I would be greeted with deference, escorted to a light, airy suite of rooms, and then left alone in my private bathroom to soak away the grime of my long journey from the West Country.

Instead I sighed, and turned to follow a narrow path that branched off the main thoroughfare and led around the side of the house. The high wooden gate swung open without any squeaking or creaking, and clicked quietly shut behind me, leaving me standing inside a large, walled garden.

After the modest home in which I'd grown up, with its lovingly tended but tiny vegetable patch and its closely planted gooseberry and blackcurrant bushes, stepping into this garden felt like stepping into another world. Even this early in the year the beds were bursting with green life, and they stretched so far into the distance they might have gone on for ever.

But I didn't want to be marked down as late on my first day, so I pushed aside the temptation to walk down through the rows of budding plants and looked instead for the entrance to the servants' hall. I rounded the corner of the house, expecting to see another neat, straight wall, hopefully with a clearly visible door where I would go to present myself for work. Instead I saw a higgledy-piggledy collection of outhouses and sheds, jutting walls and recesses and several doors of varying sizes, any of which might have been the right one. Or the wrong one.

I stopped in my tracks, searching my memory for some help from all the hours Ma had spent instructing me about etiquette, and in particular the importance of using the correct entrances, but finding none.

Muffled voices from the largest of the outbuildings came as a relief. Crossing the small courtyard I began framing a question in my head so that my voice would come out clearly, and with a confidence I certainly didn't feel. I pushed open the door and froze; my eyes had adjusted far too quickly for comfort and the polite request for assistance died before it reached my lips.

The two people inside the outhouse said nothing either. The man simply removed his hands from inside the young woman's underthings and the woman stood up straight, levering herself off the wall with her elbows and letting her apron and skirts fall back into place.

My mouth was open, but one glance at the narrow face of the young woman was enough to snatch away any urge to speak; she was too far away for me to see her eyes in the gloom, but her jaw was set and her mouth was a thin straight line as she pushed her hair back up under her cap with a single sharp, snapping motion.

I winced, thinking, *Idiot, you've managed to make an enemy before you even set foot in the house.*

Uttering something intended as an apology but which was, in reality, just a wordless mumble, I backed out and waited for my heartbeat to return to normal before making my way back across the yard to the main building. Late or not, there was nothing on earth that would persuade me to go back in there to ask directions. I'd just have to find my own way.

'Right, well, you'll not answer to "Mary" here,' the housekeeper told me a short time later. 'The head housemaid is named Mary so we'll need to find another name for you.'

Mrs Cavendish had a strong Scottish accent, which made

some of her words hard to understand, but her voice was kind enough, although her eyes missed nothing as they swept over me. 'What's your middle name?'

'Elizabeth.' It was all I could do not to bob a curtsey.

'Lizzy then,' she said, noting it down. 'Aye, that'll do fine.'

For seventeen years I'd been Mary Elizabeth Parker, and suddenly I was just Lizzy; it felt as if a part of me had been neatly snicked off – quickly enough so it didn't really hurt, but nevertheless changing the shape of who I was. I turned the new name over in my mind; it was just one more thing to get used to among countless others.

Mrs Cavendish began to outline my basic duties while she examined my hair, fingernails and general appearance. I tried to stand still under the scrutiny, but the bottom of my right foot suddenly began to itch like the devil, and my face seemed to have taken on the task of trying to soothe it from a distance. I could feel my nose wrinkling and my eyebrows dancing, and then my lips twisted inwards until Mrs Cavendish stopped talking and sighed.

'If you've a problem about your person, girl, please see to it. I canna expect you to take in what I'm saying with your face all busy like that.'

Gratefully I eased off my shoe and raked my itching foot down my left shin, for once glad of the rough woollen stockings. The relief must have shown on my face because Mrs Cavendish's own mouth flickered as she tried, unsuccessfully, to hide a smile.

She planted her fists on to her broad hips. 'Well, Lizzy, you're neat and clean enough, I suppose, aside from that sooty smudge on your cheek. You'll meet everyone at supper, but for now you may go and change into your uniform, and then we'll have a wee chat about what's expected of you.'

The room into which Mrs Cavendish ushered me a few minutes later was at the very top of the house, and she was wheezing by the time she threw open the door at the end of a narrow corridor. 'There you go, lass,' she said. 'Now, be quick with your changing, you've a lot of instruction to take note of. This is your first time in service, aye?'

'Yes, Mrs Cavendish.' This time I actually did nod my head more than was necessary, turning it into a sort of almost-bow.

She affected not to notice. 'You've some clothes on the foot of your bed there. Change into the plain dress for supper and make sure your hair is tucked away. All of it, mind. And wash that smudge off your face. Come down to the kitchens as soon as you've done.'

A moment later I was, for the first time I could remember, alone in my own room. I turned around slowly, savouring the moment, taking in the tall wardrobe, the narrow beds, the wooden floor peeking through the thin, worn rug, the cracked jug and basin on the dresser. And, most of all, the silence.

I had craved privacy for so long it seemed barely possible that now I was going to be able to enjoy it, every night, away from the meddling fingers of Emily and the twins ... then it registered: beds. Plural. I peered more closely at a small table in the corner, and this time took in the photograph of a middle-aged couple in a tarnished silver frame, the hairbrush and comb set, and the jumbled collection of hairpins. A horrible thought flashed into my head: what if this other bed belonged to the girl I'd seen in the outhouse?

'Bugger,' I said softly, and despite my trepidation it sounded funny so I said it again, louder. 'Bugger, bugger, *bugger*!'

'I can see you're going to be one to keep an eye on.'

Mortified, I whirled round to see a young woman in the doorway. She was perhaps twenty years old, and dressed in clothes much like those that lay folded at the foot of my bed. And she wasn't, thankfully, the girl from the outhouse. This girl had a rounder, far more pleasant face, and seemed friendly enough despite her words. Her accent was hard to place, but my mother had a friend who originally hailed from Liverpool and the light, musical way she spoke was similar.

She held a small laundry basket perched on one hip and was watching me as if she thought I might add something interesting, but all I could do was blush and try frantically to think of something to say. No words came, so I heeded Ma's advice and kept quiet.

The newcomer moved into the room and dumped the contents of the basket on her bed. 'You're the new girl then,' she said, rather unnecessarily. 'Mary,' she added.

Surprised she knew my name, I just nodded.

'And you are ...' She let it tail off, her eyebrows raised.

For a moment I floundered, then I realised: *she* was Mary, the housemaid Mrs Cavendish had mentioned.

'I'm, um, Lizzy Parker.'

'You don't sound very sure,' Mary said. 'Are you or aren't you?'

'Yes.' I managed to sound certain this time, and in seeking to convince Mary I began to accept the change myself.

She began folding the clothing she had tipped on to the bed, and I glanced at my own new uniform, wishing she would hurry up and go. I was used to undressing in front of my sister, of course, but this was a total stranger, and one who was my superior in the house; the thought of removing my travelling clothes and revealing anything of myself in front of her made my belly shrivel.

Finally she shook her head. 'You can't be precious here, love.' She didn't sound unkind, more amused, but still I felt a flush heat my cheeks.

'It's not that,' I said. 'It's just, well . . .'

'Oh, go on then,' Mary said, and smiled. 'I'll leave y'alone just this once, I've got to stop into Miss Peters's room anyway. But mind, you might be glad of a bit of help when it comes to lacing yourself up and putting all your hair out o' the sight of Eagle-eyes Cavendish.'

When the door had closed behind her I turned again to the neat pile of clothing awaiting my attention. There seemed an awful lot of layers for one person; yards and yards of material, and I would be expected to pay for it out of my wages whether I wanted it or not. Which I didn't.

Some ten minutes later I turned and faced the mirror with my eyes screwed shut, and then opened them to get the full effect. I shut them again immediately, but the image still danced on the inside of my eyelids: short, skinny girl, clothes too big, appalling mess.

I shuddered, then cracked open one eye and had another look. Well, yes, it was undeniably bad, but maybe not as bad as I'd first thought: a tweak of the dress smoothed out a couple of lumps and bumps, and a firm hand either side of the apron pulled it into place so it fell more or less neat down my front. I nudged the discarded corset further under my bed with my foot.

Then came the difficult part. I studied the cap for a moment, and then my hair. The two didn't seem likely to reach an amicable agreement, so I seized a handful of the dark curls that had been the bane of my mother's life – now I knew why – and twisted them around my fingers, then piled the whole lot as close to the top of my head as I could manage. A few experimental jabs with hairpins, and a quick, sweeping movement with the cap, and it was done. It even felt quite safe, as if everything was actually going to stay in place.

Halfway down the stairs I realised I'd been optimistic in that regard, but as long as I didn't sneeze, all would be well. By the time I reached the lower hallway I had revised my opinion downwards still further, and was trying not to make any sudden moves with my head. A sound on the stairs made me turn, hand atop my cap to keep it in place, and I saw Mary, a broad grin on her face.

'Do wi' another pair of hands now, could we?' Before I had chance to reply, she'd put down her basket and whipped the cap off my head.

Immediately everything fell to pieces and she got busy, gathering it all up with firm, practised fingers. 'Oov go' uff luh heh.'

'Pardon?'

She took the hairpins from her mouth. 'You've got lovely hair,' she repeated, as her hands worked deftly to pile it all up again. 'It'll be devilish difficult to keep it neat though, if you don't pin it proper. I'll do it for now, and later on I'll show you how to fix it y'self.'

'You're really kind,' I mumbled, feeling bad about my earlier attitude. In fact I was glad I'd be sharing with her; it seemed I would need more help than I'd realised.

'Norra a local lass then?' Mary asked as she replaced my cap and snugged it down tight.

'No, I'm from Plymouth, I've never been as far up as Cheshire before.'

'And what do you think?'

'It's very . . .' I struggled for the word but could only find 'empty'.

Mary laughed. 'Thought you'd be used to that, coming from the West Country.' She gave me a gentle push in the direction of the kitchen. 'Go on then, Lizzy Parker. Lesson number one: it doesn't do to keep the Cavendish waiting.'

Lesson number one turned out to be the first of a seemingly impossible number of them. Mrs Cavendish sat me down at the big wooden table in the servants' hall and began my instruction, or 'wee chat' as she'd called it. Names and their associated positions within the household whizzed past my ears, some of them taking hold but often followed by the words: 'And this is the most important thing.' This, of course, immediately made me forget what had gone before, and try to concentrate on the next part. Which was in turn followed by something still more vital.

'And if you should see Lady Creswell or any of the family in the course of your duties, which y'should not if you're where y'ought to be, you're not to be noticed,' she said. I blinked. Ma had said I'd be 'invisible' while I worked at Oaklands, but I didn't think I'd actually have to try and shrink into the walls.

Before I could ask Mrs Cavendish to clarify this she had continued: 'And there's no followers allowed.'

'Followers? You mean . . .'

'Ye ken very well what I mean, young lady. You're a comely enough lass, and likely to attract attention for all you're just skin and bone. But if you're seen fraternising with any member of the opposite sex, or, God forbid, found with a visitor in your room, you will leave this house and never return. Is that quite clear?'

Images of a narrow-faced woman and a smirking man in a nearby outhouse mocked everything she had said, but I learned fast. 'Yes, Mrs Cavendish.'

'Right, well, that'll do for now. I can see your head's fair fizzing with everything I've told you. And remember, if you're not sure of anything, don't just guess, ask someone. Far better to be thought simple than wilful.'

It occurred to me there was much my mother hadn't warned me about. Although I knew she'd done her best to prepare me for this position, her own time in service had been long ago and there would have been many changes in the intervening years. Still, her excellent references had led to my being here, and I must learn to make the most of it.

'It's time to lay the table for tea,' Mrs Cavendish said. She followed my surprised glance at the large clock on the mantel. 'Aye, we have it early so's to leave time for preparing the meal for upstairs. We'll be clearing away by four-thirty, but not unless we get a shake on and get started. Come on, now. After supper you'll be helping Ruth in the kitchen.' She looked at the clock again and scowled. 'That's if she ever shows up. She's sailing close to the wind, that one.'

The housekeeper shut her mouth quickly and I gathered she shouldn't have spoken her displeasure aloud, but it made me feel a bit better to know there was someone at least as visible as me in the firing line.

It was after midnight by the time I crawled into my bed that night, and as I slid between the sheets I relished the feel of cool cotton against my hot and swollen feet. My hands were raw and my head thumped with each beat of my pulse. Through heavy eyes I watched Mary winding the alarm clock set for six o'clock, and tried not to count the hours between in case I should suddenly realise there weren't enough.

'You'd generally be finished well before now,' she said kindly. 'It's just bad luck that bl— that poor Ruth wasn't feelin' well, you'd not normally have to cover for her.'

I nodded, and opened my mouth to speak but instead yawned wide enough to unhinge my jaw. Mary smiled and climbed into her bed, checking the clock one last time before bidding me goodnight.

'G'night,' I murmured, and closed my eyes.

When I opened them again it was with a sigh of relief to see I was back in Plymouth, prodding at the unmoving back of my gently snoring sister to get her to turn over and be quiet. Eventually she snuffled and shifted, and the room fell blissfully silent again. I lay in the dark, thinking ahead to the coming day and the simple pleasures it would bring; peace and quiet to do some letter-writing in the morning, and a long walk up across Dartmoor, maybe a picnic with Emily and the twins. The boys could play on the rock at Yelverton, that huge lump of granite and slate stone that always swarmed with children eager to show off their climbing skills; Adie and Albert were getting braver every time we went there, and Emily and I would stand together, holding hands and trying not to squeeze each other's fingers too tightly with fear as we watched our four-year-old brothers fiercely compete.

I might make time to visit Father's grave too, and tell him which of the spring flowers had bloomed early this year; he had always been interested in moorland flora, had told me it was because he spent so much of his time underground that it helped him to think of all the colour and the life going on above his head while he worked.

All in all my day would be full, fresh and rewarding, and bring pleasure to all of us in one way or another. I smiled in the darkness and closed my eyes ...

Within seconds they were open again. Mary snapped off the harsh jangling of the clock and rubbed her hands over her face. 'Time to get going, Lizzy.'

I rose on to my elbows, coming back to reality with a hollow sense of dread. The dream fell away from me in wispy fragments far too quickly but it was best not to try and hold on to the bright, comforting pieces that remained; they would only serve to contrast with my new life all the more horribly.

There was no time for Mary to teach me the rudiments of securing my hair, so once more she fixed it for me herself and made sure I arrived in the kitchens promptly, half an hour after my first full day had begun.

My first job was to stoke the fire in the range for hot water. That wasn't too bad since the cinders were still hot, but to my dismay I found the next task was emptying the female

15

servants' chamber pots, and then cleaning them. The smell was rank and stale, and I gagged the first couple of times, although after that I learned to hold my breath until I'd finished scrubbing the china with my vinegar-soaked rag. When all that was done I turned my attention to drawing water in preparation for scrubbing the pantry.

'You'd better 'ave kept your bleedin' mouth shut!'

I jumped and turned around, knowing already who I'd see. So this must be the elusive Ruth. Just my luck she had turned out to be the kitchen maid.

'I've said nothing to anyone,' I said, turning back to my bucket to hide the fear I was certain must have shown in my face – I could feel my heart speeding up uncomfortably with it.

'Good thing too. What's your name?'

'Lizzy Parker.'

'Oh, yeah, the new scullery maid. You sound funny, where you from?'

'Plymouth.' Just saying the name made me shake with a new surge of homesickness.

'Bloody hell, what are you doing all the way up here? Don't they want you down there no more?'

I faced her again, hoping to draw on my family connection to the house. 'My mother worked here a long time ago. Upstairs.'

But Ruth wasn't listening; she glanced over her shoulder into the kitchen. 'Right, Miss Lizzy Nosy Parker, listen here. I'm Ruth Wilkins. I answer to Mrs Hannah the cook, and *you* answer to *me*. Understand?'

I flinched as her sharp finger poked me hard in the shoulder, but managed to keep my voice calm. 'Yes.'

16

'Good. I'm not going to be kitchen maid for long, got higher plans. So if you plays your cards right you might be in with a chance at my job eventually.'

'What plans have you got?' Not that I cared, but I already knew I was going to be deeply relieved when this girl moved on, so the sooner the better.

'Never you mind. Just remember you need to keep me on your side. And if you happen to see something you didn't ought to 'ave seen, you keep it to yourself. You won't get no thanks, nor make no friends, being a tattle-tale.'

We both knew I had already seen enough to get her dismissed, and I hadn't 'tattled' yet. I just gave a small nod and picked my full bucket out of the sink, hoping my trembling hands weren't too obvious.

Ruth began preparing early-morning tea for the upper servants, and now and again I caught her looking over as if assessing the effect of her words on me. *Keep your mouth closed, and your hands busy, and you'll stay out of trouble*, Ma had said. It was good advice; I didn't trust Ruth Wilkins one little bit.

Chapter 2

After dinner I found myself with what I already recognised as a rare moment of peace. The morning had passed in a blur of pots and pans and morning prayers, and to my relief Ruth had vanished as soon as the meal was over. She'd run me ragged all morning, and always with the sort of smile on her face that wasn't really like a smile at all.

Craving a breath of fresh air I stepped outside into the yard, and as I closed the door behind me I heard voices coming from around the corner. One of them I recognised immediately; the flat, Cockney drawl had been haranguing me constantly for the past six hours. The other must belong to the man she'd been with in the outhouse yesterday. He would probably be one of the upper servants or a driver.

Whoever and whatever he was, he wasn't happy about something, and his voice had dropped to little more than a hiss. 'It's only a matter of months, Ruth. You'd better get yourself up that ladder and in full view of those that matter.'

'I can't help it. You keep me out all hours, then I get in trouble and no one trusts me!'

'All right then, from now on until you're where you need to be, we lay off.'

Ruth's tone turned pleading. 'What, altogether? C'mon, Frank, we don't 'ave to go that far.'

'We do if you're going to get out of that kitchen and up those stairs. Besides, we can't risk anything with that new girl skulking about.'

'Don't pay the scullion no mind, I've got her where I can keep an eye on her, she won't dare cross me.'

My hand clenched and I winced as the chapped skin tightened over my knuckles. The fact that Ruth was probably right did nothing to lessen the anger I felt at her words.

She was speaking again. 'Well, what about one last time then?' A pause, then her voice took on a low, singsong tone. 'Oh, Frankie, you know you want what I've got 'ere for you.'

I felt my face flame as I realised what was going on, again, just a few feet away – this time out in the open, in the herb garden. What must it be like to have such feelings for someone that you were prepared to take that kind of risk? In all my seventeen years I had never taken so much as a strong fancy to anyone, and yet here was Ruth throwing herself at this unknown man, shamelessly begging him to continue with what they had been doing yesterday.

The rule about followers clearly held no fear for these two or else they must be confident everyone else was occupied, but with their attitude they were sure to get caught eventually and then Ruth would be dismissed. It would almost be worth risking her wrath just to ensure that happened. I went back into the house where, lost in this pleasant thought, I bumped into Mary coming out of the scullery.

Instantly my mouth dropped open, about to tell her what I'd seen and heard, but I clamped it shut again. Mary seemed nice, but I didn't know her well enough yet to trust that she wouldn't go straight to Ruth and warn her she'd been over-heard.

'What on earth happened?' she said. 'You look like you've lost a penny and found sixpence!'

I shook my head. 'It's nothing,' I said. 'Only relieved to have got the morning out of the way without breaking anything.'

'Hmm.' She frowned, clearly not believing a word of it. She seemed about to say more, but time and task were at odds and we both hurried back to our stations to begin the afternoon's work.

The brief meeting gave me much to think about, though, and I was glad I hadn't blurted out my discovery of Ruth's indiscretions. As I scrubbed the pots from our own dinner, I watched the girl in question working angelically alongside Mrs Hannah, as if butter wouldn't melt in her mouth, and pondered the identity of her secret lover. He couldn't be anyone special to be going after Ruth Wilkins, I decided; she wasn't a likeable sort of person at all, even if she was enviably good at her job.

Conversation between the others had been carrying on in a mostly undecipherable but comforting hum. I caught the odd word, now and again a laugh, or an exclamation of dismay when something broke or clattered to the stone floor, but mostly it was calm background noise as my mind wandered around the unfamiliar corners of my new environment.

Then the noise stopped, all at once, and I looked up to see why. A tall, broadly built older gentleman in a very smart suit had strolled in, with such an air of command about him that I'd have thought Lord Henry Creswell himself had come to visit if I hadn't known he'd died long ago, during the war.

'Mr Dodsworth,' Mrs Cavendish said, nodding to him. 'Will Mr Carlisle be joining Her Ladyship for dinner again?'

'He will.' The butler took off his hat and laid it on the table, and Mrs Cavendish immediately removed it and hung it on the rack by the door. It had the feel of an old routine; Mr Dodsworth didn't even blink. I thought back to Mrs Cavendish's instructions and remembered these two were equal in status, which would explain why she wasn't suddenly the hardest-working person in the room, as everyone else was trying to be.

Mrs Cavendish sniffed. 'Why Her Ladyship insists on entertaining a man of such questionable morals, I couldn't say.'

'He's a perfectly respectable gentleman, and a war hero,' Mr Dodsworth protested mildly, and again I had the feeling they'd been through this before. I smiled as I turned back to my work, keeping their conversation on the top level of the other noises; it couldn't hurt to learn as much as possible about the family for whom I was working, and their friends and acquaintances.

This Mr Carlisle, for example; I couldn't immediately work out his relationship to the household, but my initial assumption that he was somehow connected romantically to Lady Creswell was soon dispelled.

'Will he be bringing a lady friend this time?' Mrs Cavendish wanted to know.

'Not that I'm aware,' Mr Dodsworth said. 'Mr Carlisle is staying a few days, as usual, and there have been no requests to have a maid on hand, or another room prepared.'

'Well, why couldn't Her Ladyship have told me about him at the meeting this morning?' Mrs Cavendish grumbled.

I thought the cook should be the one who was more inconvenienced, and said so, very quietly, but Mrs Hannah only shrugged. 'I always make sure there's more than enough; Lady Creswell runs a prestigious house, and if it's not Mr Carlisle popping in on an hour's notice it'll be someone else.'

Listening to the varying opinions of the kitchen staff, that began flying the minute Mr Dodsworth was called away, I deduced that Mr Carlisle was, by turns, a shy but friendly man, a secret womaniser, a popular, polite and extremely eligible bachelor and an unwelcome hanger-on. The one thing everyone seemed to agree on was that he had been a close friend of Lord Henry Creswell, now deceased, and that the two of them had made a striking if mismatched pair; Mr Carlisle was not, by those same accounts, a man born to the privileged life he now led.

Mrs Cavendish was of the firm opinion he was making a nuisance of himself with Her Ladyship, while Mrs Hannah pointed out that Lady Creswell could quite easily refuse him hospitality if she so chose, and that Mr Carlisle was almost family in any case. He sounded mysterious and exciting, and if he really were a war hero I would have loved to learn what he had done to earn the label.

Mary came into the kitchen in the midst of the discussion, and, still caught up in curiosity, I asked her what she thought, since she must have seen him often.

22

She dismissed the question immediately, with an uncharacteristic frown. 'I have better things to do with my time than speculate about the comings and goings of house guests. And so do you,' she added pointedly. I nodded. Mary was fast becoming my mentor in all things, and if she thought I should be quiet on a subject, then quiet I would be, although she was not usually so abrupt in her advice. I knew her mother had been unwell of late, though, so perhaps concern was shortening Mary's patience. I'd have been the same.

Besides, there was little time to dwell on thoughts of the intriguing Mr Carlisle. My days were filled with work, with listening to instruction, and with gradually coming to know which of my fellow servants were to be relied upon, or avoided.

Ruth and Mary were complete opposites, yet there existed between them a sort of grudging respect. Ruth was an excellent kitchen maid, despite her general character flaws, and in turn she knew Mary was in daily contact with the family, however one-sided the contact, and Ruth had clear designs in the same direction.

Mrs Creswell's maid, Miss Peters, rarely showed her face in the kitchens, but I saw her now and again as she took her dessert with Mrs Cavendish and Mr Dodsworth. She seemed nice enough, not stuck up as I'd thought she might be, although she spared no words for me, of course. Emma Bird was the second housemaid, a bright, cheerful girl a year or so older than me. She didn't seem at all wary of Ruth, and I watched her often, hoping to uncover the secret. I liked Emma, she was friendly and helpful whenever our paths crossed.

Mrs Cavendish was as she had appeared on my first day; kind enough but, brisk and efficient herself, she had little patience for the slip-ups and mishaps of others. She spent most of the time in her office attending to household business, but her appearance in the kitchens was enough to make me clumsy with nerves. More than once I caught her looking over at me when something had slipped in the sink and caused a clatter, ready with a sharp word no doubt, but luckily I hadn't broken anything. Yet.

And then there was the discovery that Ruth hadn't been fraternising with another servant after all, so I no longer needed to listen carefully to the voices around me to satisfy my curiosity as to which of us was breaking the rules so blatantly.

I'd been working at Oaklands about a month, and was on my knees in the back doorway cleaning up a spill, when the familiar voice spoke above me. 'Move aside, girl, some of us have business to attend to.'

I started. So this was Frank then ... he had quite a self-important tone about him. I glanced up and saw not a stable boy or a driver but the butcher from Breckenhall, a box balanced on his shoulder. Normally safely ensconced in the scullery at this time, I hadn't been in attendance during the daily delivery of fresh produce before. My face heated as I remembered the way I'd seen him last, with his hands up Ruth's skirts, and I couldn't look at him directly for fear he'd recognise me too, and make some remark.

As I rose from my knees I saw a younger man behind him. He wasn't what I'd have called handsome, not tall like his companion either, but he had dimples and sparkly blue eyes that I was surprised to see were directed at me. I paused, unsure whether I should acknowledge this, but the butcher barked at me again to move.

I bent to lift my bucket out of the way and, in my confusion and embarrassment, stepped on my own skirt and sloshed some of the grey water over the shiny shoes of the impatient tradesman in front of me. He cursed, and my ears burned at the sound of it even as I muttered my apologies.

A shove from behind sent me stumbling against the door jamb and Ruth's voice cut across over my head. 'Don't worry, Mr Markham, she'll pay to get your shoes cleaned.'

'No, she won't,' the younger man said. 'Don't be so horrible, Ruth.' I looked gratefully at him and he winked. 'Don't listen to her, she's just a bully.' Horrified both by him and for him, I looked back at Ruth who, to my surprise, didn't seem angry at all.

'Well, she should,' she amended. Then she changed tack and flicked her cloth at the butcher. 'Stop makin' such a fuss. You're like an old lady.'

In the ensuing jumble of conversation, I seized my bucket and scrubbing brush and returned to the kitchens, still lifted by the boy's friendly smile and fearless intervention on my behalf.

For a long time that day my mind dwelled on Ruth's indiscretions and how long it would be before she was discovered and sent away, but those wonderings were pushed firmly to the back of my mind as news from the world beyond started drifting down to the kitchens, bringing word of the English-built steamship that had met with a terrible accident on her first voyage.

It had sailed from Southampton less than a week ago, bound for America. Everyone had been talking about the glamorous passengers, their exciting destination, and the privilege of making the journey on the *Titanic*'s maiden voyage. But word was now coming in that she had struck something, possibly an iceberg, and no one knew what had happened then to the ship that had been heralded as the last word in luxury and opulence.

Some were even saying she was safe and being towed to Halifax. That struck me as odd because Halifax was right in the middle of the country, miles from the sea. I mentioned this to Mary as we stepped out for a bit of air before preparing tea in the servants' hall.

She looked at me blankly for a moment and then laughed. 'It won't be Halifax in Yorkshire, daft lass. There's a place by that name in Canada too, right on the coast. That'll be where they're taking her.'

'Do you know everything?' I asked, full of admiration.

She shook her head, still smiling. 'No, pet, but I've learned a lot about other parts of the world. I always wanted to travel.' She stared out over the garden as though she were seeing the rolling seas instead of rows of carrots and cabbages not yet grown. 'One day, I want to go to Australia, and maybe even New Zealand. Certainly to America ...' She tailed off, her expression saddened. 'What a shame, such a beautiful ship. I hope she isn't too badly damaged.'

'I heard Mr Dodsworth say she collided with an iceberg, but icebergs are huge. Why couldn't the sailors have seen it and just turned away?'

'I suppose we won't know until they talk to the officers.'

We were silent for a moment, thinking about how it must have felt to be so far from home and at the mercy of an icy sea.

26

'Were any of the Creswell family on board?' I said, as we straightened our aprons ready to go back indoors.

'I don't think so. If they were I'm sure their servants would have been quick enough to tell us they were going too; a trip like that would be something to boast about.'

Mary tucked a stray hair back under my cap. I'd learned how to do it myself by now, but it was never as neat as when she did it. 'Don't worry, lovey. I'm sure the ship is safe, like they say. All we can do is wait and see what the newspapers say tomorrow.'

But of course the *Titanic* wasn't safe. Nor were more than a thousand of her passengers, aristocracy and servants alike. The news shook even the most talkative of the staff into silence and we all worked in a state of numbed shock. Meals were consumed, laundry washed and folded, floors scrubbed. Life went on, but the hand of uncertainty had touched every one of us as we considered all those other ordinary people, just like us, snuffed out before the sun rose on a cold grey dawn, and never seen again.

Chapter 3

After I'd been at the manor for two months I'd earned a day off, although in reality it amounted to little more than half a day. I'd carried out my early-morning duties in the kitchen, and I'd still be expected to lay the table for the servants' tea at four, but the time in between was mine and it felt like a week.

'What are you going to do, have you decided?' Mary asked.

'Decided? I've thought of nothing else!' I picked up my brush and pulled it through my hair, enjoying the freedom of feeling it lying thick and heavy on my shoulders. 'I'm going to walk into Breckenhall, I have letters to post, and then it'll be so lovely just to wander around and see everything. I didn't have time when I arrived.'

'You'll enjoy it, I know. And as long you're going that way you might do me a favour at the same time?'

'Of course.'

'I need to check the times of trains to Liverpool in case

they've changed. Would you be able to get me a timetable book from the station?'

My heart jolted. 'Are you leaving?'

'No,' she said, and smiled at my obvious relief. 'I'll be gone for about a month, though. My mother's having an operation. Only a small one, but she'll need my help while she recovers.' Mary saw my crestfallen expression and patted my arm. 'You'll be fine, lovey, and I'll write to you while I'm away.'

Although I knew she would do as she'd promised, still I felt a shadow pass over this long-awaited day. Mary was my salvation in that enormous house, the one person I knew I could go to whenever Ruth's constant sniping wore me down. She always turned things around so we ended up giggling about Ruth's shameless fawning over Mrs Hannah. And I'd even ended up telling her about Frank Markham, only to discover she'd known for months.

'Ruth lets him push her on,' she said. 'He's only using her, and the sooner she finds that out the better.'

'Using her for what?' Then I blushed, thinking I'd guessed what she meant.

Mary laughed. 'Not that! He's a man of the world, doesn't need a scrawny little kitchen maid to ... well, anyway, no. I think it's a little more complicated than that. But don't ask me to go any further. It's only hearsay and nothing I'd want my name associated with if it ever got out.'

And with that I'd had to be content.

Closing the wooden gate of the kitchen garden behind me, I realised I hadn't even set foot in the world this side of it since the moment I'd arrived. I took a deep breath and held it, wondering if the air would taste different. It didn't, of course; there was just more of it.

As I made my way down the avenue I glanced back at the front door, remembering how I'd imagined passing through it into welcoming arms, being taken upstairs to bright, clean rooms, and soaking in a deep bath full of scented bubbles. The notion made me smile now, being so much more aware of the vast chasm between my life and theirs, and I was relieved that the envy I felt was not tainted with bitterness but with a more natural appreciation of how life might be lived instead.

Grateful as I was for my position, it was so good to be out! Seeing hedges and fields instead of the undersides of tables and the insides of chamber pots, sky and birds instead of four walls and a sink. It was a warm day and I loosened my coat as I walked, wishing I'd left it behind, but it was a relief to be able to swing my arms freely, with my letters and my purse tucked away in my pockets.

In Breckenhall I attended to my own business quickly, and once the letters were posted I turned my attention to the rest of the town. Wandering through the streets, looking at the elegant houses that stood contentedly alongside little cottages such as I was more accustomed to, I found myself thinking of my family far away in Plymouth.

My mother would be peeling vegetables for a stew despite the weather, I knew; there was nearly always a pot of some kind bubbling on the stove. Adie and Albert would no doubt be getting under her feet, and Emily would be curled up in a chair with her nose in a book. I swallowed a surge of homesickness and determinedly counted my blessings instead.

I had a job, a good friend, a kindly employer – although Mrs Hannah was the one to whom I answered in the kitchen, I always thought of Mrs Cavendish as fulfilling that role – and here I was in the sunshine, healthy in mind and body, and with time at last to enjoy the day.

I gazed through the window of a tea shop, at those lucky ones who sat inside the cool, pretty room, nibbling sandwiches and cakes. One day after I'd saved some of my earnings I might do the same. For a moment I allowed my mind to play with the romantic picture of myself sitting opposite someone special, watching him over the rim of my teacup and knowing his smile, whoever he was, was for me alone.

Then I caught sight of the church clock and realised I would have to walk very quickly if I were to collect Mary's train timetable and be back at Oaklands by four o'clock. It was so warm in the sun I'd be lucky not to get overheated on the way and have to stop and rest, making me later still.

In my hurry I almost tripped up, and in order to avoid doing so again I had my head down in concentration, studying the uneven pavement as I walked quickly to the station, and, to my horror, straight into a man standing by the stationmaster's office.

'Whoa! Slow down, love!' He put out a hand to steady me, gripping my arm.

I flushed in embarrassment, but his accent was similar to Mary's and that simple fact put me more at ease. 'I'm terribly sorry, sir, I was in a bit of a rush.' I looked up to see if he was cross. He was, but not with me; he was looking past me at the railway track. I noticed he was very pleasant-looking, and quite casually dressed in shirt-sleeves and plain trousers so that it was difficult for me to tell if he was gentry or working class. In either case he would be my superior, and I had almost sent him flying.

'If you're worried about missing the train, don't be,' he said. 'It's late, as usual.'

'I'm not catching the train, thank you, sir. I just need to collect a book of train times to Liverpool to take back to my friend.'

'Liverpool, eh?' the man said, fishing in his pocket. 'You have to change at Chester. Here, take mine. I know it by heart now anyway.'

'Oh, I couldn't—'

'You could, and you will.' The man studied my face for a moment, dark eyebrows drawing down in a frown. 'You look a bit hot and bothered, love, don't you think you ought to sit down?'

'I'm afraid I don't have time,' I said, taking the timetable with a grateful smile. It was very used-looking, but still quite readable. 'Thanks ever so much, sir. I have to get back to work, I'll be in trouble if I'm late.'

'All right then, but don't walk too fast. The sun will soon get to you. How far are you going?'

'To Oaklands Manor, sir.'

'Oh, you work at Oaklands? Well then, that's another problem solved. Hop in.'

I stared at him, confused, and then noticed he was gesturing at a motor car parked haphazardly behind the fence. Surely he was teasing?

But he nodded at the car and then at me. 'As soon as Miss Evangeline arrives I'll be taking her back to Oaklands and we would pass you along the road anyway. May as well save us the bother of stopping to offer you help.'

Miss Evangeline! The daughter of the house. I'd never even seen her and here we were at the station at the same time. If this man was in fact her chauffeur, despite his casual attire, I was sure he wasn't even permitted to make the offer of a ride. The heiress to the Creswell fortune would likely be annoyed to find herself sharing her drive home with the very lowest of her household's servants, but there was no doubt I had dawdled too long and I *would* be horribly late unless I accepted.

Miss Evangeline's chauffeur smiled, his irritation at the lateness of his mistress's train visibly fading. 'Go on,' he said gently.

I took a hesitant step towards the motor car with its shining red and black trim, gleaming as if it had never been driven along a dusty, dirty road in its life. I noticed there was a silver ornament on the front but resisted the urge to touch it as I climbed into the back seat, the springs squeaking under me. It smelled like polish and leather, with a hint of something unfamiliar; probably the fuel the car used, very different from that of the train on which I'd travelled for the first time just two months ago. Although it wasn't such a comforting smell there was something powerful and compelling about it.

I was trembling from head to foot already. How would it feel when the motor actually began moving? But my shaking was mostly due to excitement at the previously unthinkable fact that I was even sitting here.

I looked back over at the chauffeur, who was glaring at the empty platform again, and with his attention elsewhere I had time to appreciate his square-shouldered poise and the bold, strong features clearly outlined in the bright sunlight. He really was quite handsome, clean-shaven and with dark hair that looked almost as difficult to control as my own. Despite his higher position his behaviour towards me was comfortably informal, and his easy smile had melted away most of my nervousness, for the time being at least.

When the train had come and gone, and the steam had drifted away from the platform, I caught my first glimpse of Miss Evangeline Creswell. She seemed quite childlike still, although we were the same age. She clamped one hand to her head as the breeze threatened to take her hat off, and the other hand clutched at my benefactor's arm while she bounced eagerly on her toes.

'Oh, you must let me, please!'

'Absolutely not. Your mother would never allow me to set foot in the house again if anyone were to see you. And as for what she would do to *you*, well—'

'Then we shall keep each other's secret.'

'We shall do nothing of the sort. And you don't know how to drive anyway.'

'Oh, don't I?'

'Evie ...' The man's voice held a warning tone, and at the same moment I realised that he was more than a chauffeur, Miss Evangeline confirmed it.

'For your information, Uncle Jack, I've been driving a good deal whilst in London.'

'Why did you have to tell me that?' he groaned. 'Now I can't pretend any more that I'd no idea.'

'You knew?' She sounded disappointed.

'I'd heard,' he said, leading the way to the car where I sat, frozen. 'But if your mother knew she'd have you confined to your rooms until you turn sixty.'

'Then it's a good thing I know you won't tell her,' said the girl. 'Besides, someone who dresses as you do can't possibly tell tales to my mother and expect them to be believed.'

'What's wrong with the way I dress?' He sounded amused.

'Honestly, you *never* wear the right clothes! It's why I love you, of course.' Then she caught sight of me and her china-blue eyes widened. 'Hello, whoever you are. Uncle Jack, have you been out collecting waifs and strays, or are you going to tell me this is your latest conquest?'

My face was heating up unbearably and my stomach knotting with returning nerves. As young as she was, this girl had the power to have me dismissed with a single word.

'Don't be ridiculous,' her uncle said. 'You should know who this is, she works for you after all. In fact, I'm taking her back to work now.'

Miss Evangeline frowned, assessing me properly for the first time. 'I've never seen you before, and I do know the staff rather well. Unlike my mother.' She said this last to her uncle, with a defensive edge to her voice.

'I'm n-new.' I was surprised I had a voice to stammer with. 'I've only been at Oaklands for two months.'

'Well then,' Miss Evangeline turned to her uncle, 'you see? For all your disapproval, this girl began work after I'd already left for London.' She turned back to me. 'You're very pretty, but you're a skinny thing. We must make sure Mrs Hannah feeds you up. What's your name?'

'Mar— Lizzy.'

'Mare Lizzy?' Miss Evangeline said, eyebrows raised. 'Well, Mare Lizzy, I know how words are thrown around in the kitchens, and when they're caught they're often fumbled. I'd hate for anyone to be under the mistaken impression I'd gone against my mother's wishes whilst in London.'

'Of course not,' I said quickly, sensing the reprieve and grasping at it. 'I'm sure I shan't remember a thing about our meeting once I'm back at work.' Heart thudding, I let my eyes meet hers and they held for a moment.

Then Miss Evangeline smiled. 'I have a feeling I can trust you, Mare Lizzy.'

'I'm just Lizzy,' I said.

'I know that, silly,' she said. 'Uncle Jack, did my luggage arrive safely?'

'It did. I believe Peters has already unpacked it for you.'

'Good old Alice, it's not as if she isn't busy enough with Mother. Now, if we don't hurry I shall be late for tea, and Just Lizzy will be late for work.'

'I'm not the one standing around gossiping,' he said. 'And I do wish you wouldn't call me Uncle Jack, it makes me feel ancient.'

'You are ancient,' she retorted, and winked at me before climbing into the front seat. Luckily not the one with the driving controls.

The drive home was something quite spectacular, skimming along the dusty road, bits of leafy hedgerow flicking against the wing mirrors and snapping off on the glass screen before the front two seats. I felt both exhilarated and terrified. We were certainly not travelling at what might be called a sedate pace, but Miss Evangeline kept urging her uncle on to greater speeds.

'I went much faster than this in the Surrey countryside,' she cried. 'Come on, let's fly!'

Heaven knows what would have happened had he given in to her wish to drive part of the way.

From my place in the back seat I found my eyes constantly drawn to him, noticing how his eyes crinkled at the corners whenever Miss Evangeline told him off for dawdling, and the way his hair curled into the nape of his neck, worn longer than was currently the fashion and clearly not tamed by oil. He laughed often, glancing round at his niece now and again, affording me a clearer look at his strong jawline and short, straight nose. I found my breathing becoming more shallow the longer I looked at him, and made myself turn instead to the spectacle of the countryside flashing by.

When we drew up at the bottom of the long avenue, Miss Evangeline made him stop. The car slowed to a halt, and as the engine purred beneath us she turned to me, her expression apologetic.

'Lizzy, I don't want to sound mean but I really think it might be better if you walked from here. Mother will hear the approach of the car, if she hasn't already, and will certainly come to meet us at the door.' She hesitated, then shrugged. 'She doesn't approve of family and servants mixing, I'm afraid. Terribly old-fashioned, of course, but I must respect her wishes.'

'When you're in her house at least,' I said without thinking, and those baby-blue eyes, almost hidden under cascading golden curls, opened so wide it was a miracle they stayed in her head. My heart shrivelled and I felt myself shrink with embarrassment. Damn my traitorous mouth.

Miss Evangeline turned to face front again, her back suddenly rigid. Her uncle kept his eyes on the glass screen, and I could see his hands gripping the steering wheel although we were stationary. He must have been cursing the moment we met.

Miss Evangeline's voice was cool when she replied, all trace of friendliness gone, 'You'd better go quickly, I'm sure you have duties to attend to.'

I shuffled gracelessly across the shiny leather back seat and pushed open the door. 'Thank you very much for the ride, sir.'

'Not at all,' he said, but his voice too was clipped and formal. I stumbled as I got out of the car, I couldn't get away from them quickly enough. Nor they me, judging by the speed with which the car began moving again the moment my feet were on the road.

What hurt most was the intimate sound of their mingled laughter wafting back to me over the chuntering of the engine, fading with the dust from the tyres as I began the long walk behind them up to the house. What a story she would have to tell her friends, even if she couldn't tell her mother. I could scarcely believe I had been so foolish; I had instinctively liked the girl, who had behaved towards me in a manner that was completely different from the way I'd thought someone in her position would act towards her servants. But in the end a servant was all I was. I had been given the chance to make my mark and had ruined everything; to them I was 'just Lizzy', and I must never forget it again.

I told no one about my meeting with Miss Evangeline, but couldn't help listening with greater interest whenever her name was mentioned. She was generally thought of as shy, even timid, and it was hard not to chime in to the contrary whenever I heard her described as such.

But, mingled with the odd sense of privilege I felt to have glimpsed the real girl, there was the remembered shame of our encounter, although often I could ease this by recalling instead the thrill of the ride in her uncle's car. If I closed my eyes I could still feel the hard thrum of the wheels on the road, and the wind that had blown my hair back to stream out behind me – never mind that afterwards it had taken almost an hour to comb the tangles out, and I'd had to abandon the effort or be late for work after all. I would have given almost anything to be able to do it again.

It seemed only natural that, while thinking of the way my blood had raced in time with the engine, my memory also recreated the view from the rear seat: of a man with a straight back, clad in a white shirt with sleeves rolled back in casual manner to reveal strong, tanned forearms, and long-fingered hands that rested on the wheel, effortlessly guiding the motor along the lanes. As sickening as it was acknowledging Miss Evangeline's low opinion of me, it was equally so to know that I had also made myself look snippy, rude and ungrateful to her uncle. Remembering his dark-blue eyes and that unexpectedly warm smile, I thought perhaps I was starting to understand a little of what made Ruth speak to Mr Markham the way she had ... the understanding was at once shocking and exciting, but it made my disappointment in myself all the more intense.

Mary was grateful for the timetable, even in its creased and crumpled state, and was soon busy making plans for her trip home. I couldn't shake off the niggling thought that she might never return, and kept seeking assurances from her to the contrary; I relied on her for so much that I didn't know how I would cope if she were to leave for ever.

I liked her dry way of talking, too. Her accent didn't sound as if it could ever be used to convey harsh words and was friendly and musical, whereas Miss Evangeline's uncle's was flatter, fainter, as if he'd spent years trying to cover it up but now and again he forgot. When he had coolly dismissed me from his car, of course, he had sounded anything *but* friendly.

On the day she left Mary accompanied me out to the yard on my break. 'Right then, Lizzy, I need to tell you something really important and you've got to pay attention, all right?'

I looked over my shoulder but no one had followed us out. 'All right.'

'This business with Ruth and Mr Markham … I'm a bit concerned you're dwelling on it too much, and that's going to get you into trouble. So I'm going to tell you what it's all about and you've got to swear – *swear*, mind you – that you'll tell nobody else. Are you any good at keeping secrets?'

'Of course,' I said, and nearly disqualified myself by telling her I knew a secret about Miss Evangeline that would get her into awful trouble if it got out. I held my tongue and listened instead.

'As you know, Miss Evangeline will turn eighteen in a couple of months.'

I nodded. 'Her birthday's not long before mine.'

'When she turns eighteen and becomes Miss Creswell, there's more important goings-on than a change of formal address. And that's what's behind Ruth and her ambitions to be noticed by those above stairs.'

'What is?'

'When Miss Creswell is eighteen she's going to be allowed, or rather expected, to take her own maid. Ruth is determined to be the one she chooses.'

'Oh, but they'll hate each other,' I said, and then went on quickly, 'I mean, from what I've heard, Miss Evangeline is such a shy girl she wouldn't appreciate someone as bossy as Ruth.'

'Well then, if she's too soft in the head to take control of her own business perhaps someone like Ruth is just what she needs. I'm sure Lady Creswell will have plenty to say on the matter in any case.'

'And that's it, is it?' I felt a bit disappointed, after all the possibilities that had gone through my head.

'That's it as far as Ruth's concerned, yes. But there's the small matter of what Mr Markham's after and why *he's* so keen Ruth should become closer to the Creswells.'

I brightened immediately. 'What's that then?'

'On Miss Creswell's birthday she will be presented with the Kalteng Star. Do you know what that is?'

'No, what is it?'

'It's a blue diamond, said to be worth nearly a million pounds.'

'Oh!' I felt the path tilt under my feet. 'That's quite a birthday present.'

'It's not really a present, it's more her birthright. Lord Henry's ancestor John Creswell mined it in Borneo at the turn of the last century, and it's been passed down to the daughters or granddaughters of the family ever since. It's been held in trust for Miss Evangeline until she's old enough to be presented at court. She'll be one of the richest young women in the country by the time the Season begins next May.'

'How do you know all this?' My head still buzzed with imaginings of what such a valuable jewel would look like.

'Everyone knows about it, it's no secret. I expect your ma knows of it too, if you ask her. If Ruth is chosen as maid to such an easily led girl as Miss Evangeline, she'll be set for life. And Frank Markham with her, no doubt.'

'Will Mr Markham marry Ruth then?'

'Who knows? He's young enough to make that likely, not yet thirty. It wouldn't be a scandal if he did. But he'll want for nothing that she doesn't want for, that's certain enough.'

'No wonder they're so careful not to get caught out.' They were clever in the way they behaved in public: ignoring each other would have seemed rude or suspicious so they appeared to be good friends instead, allowing a certain amount of banter to disguise the true extent of their relationship.

'No doubt she'll be first choice if references are asked for,' Mary said. 'And you,' she patted my arm, smiling, 'are shaping up nicely in that kitchen. So keep up the good work, and keep your head down.'

'Keep your mouth closed and your hands busy,' I murmured.

'What's that?'

'Oh, nothing. Just something Ma used to say.'

'She sounds a wise woman.'

'She is.' I boosted myself on to the large iron milk churn that sat permanently under the kitchen window. 'I wish you didn't have to go away.'

'I'd like to say "so do I", but frankly I'll be glad to see the back of this place, even if it's only for a month. Don't worry, it'll fly by. I'll be back messin' up our room in no time.'

But after wishing for so long for a room to myself, I had never felt so lonely as on that first night when I wound the clock and set it on my own bedside table. Talk of becoming kitchen maid eventually was all well and good, but then I'd have to move out of this room and I'd see even less of Mary. I missed her already, and wrote as often as I could find the time.

Dear Mary,

I must say, Ruth is behaving impeccably. Her work is so good even Mr Dodsworth has noted her and she is actually being nicer to me! (It's probably just in case someone is watching or listening, but I don't mind the reason as it makes my life so much easier.)

I'm positive you're right and she'll be chosen for Miss Evangeline. I'd even go a bit further and say she deserves the job. However I broke a plate yesterday, and both Mrs Hannah and Mrs Cavendish gave me such identical looks of annoyance, I'm sorry to say my taking up the position of kitchen maid is unlikely. Plus, of course, the cost will be stopped out of my wage.

My pen hovered over the paper as I remembering the incident with toe-curling clarity. I'd been delighted to be given the upstairs china to clean for the first time and, aware of being watched, my hands had been shaking as I scrubbed at a stubborn streak of gravy. The plate had slipped from them and crashed to the bottom of the stone sink, breaking into three large pieces. That the women's annoyed looks had held no sur-prise only added to my shame.

I shook my head and continued my letter, thinking how unfair it was that a single mistake was likely to see me remain a scullery maid just when the perfect chance for promotion might have presented itself. Except it wasn't just one mistake, it seemed to be one after another, and then, as always, I was washed over by the awful memory of overstepping even the generous mark drawn by Miss Evangeline and her uncle.

Mary's reply, when it came, put my whining to shame.

Dear Lizzy,

I'm sorry to hear things aren't going as well as we'd hoped. I'm afraid I have more bad news. My mother passed away this week and I must stay here a little longer until the legalities of her will are completed.

Lady Creswell has been very kind, and has given me leave to attend to matters here for as long as it takes. I hope to return before Miss Evangeline's birthday celebrations. Meanwhile, keep working well and I am sure you will eventually progress from scullery maid to kitchen maid, and from there, who knows? You're a good girl and Mrs Cavendish knows it.

Take care, and I will be back before you know it.

Your friend always,

Mary

I thought about my own mother, so far away, and tried to imag-ine how it would feel to know I would never see her again. Since the death of my father she had been everything to us, as Mary's mother had to her, and the thought of losing her was painful in a way I had never allowed myself to contemplate. My heart ached for Mary's loss and I made myself promise that once she returned I would be a different person. I would be the one who could be relied upon, for once.

With Mary's sad news still uppermost in my mind, I returned to the kitchen to discover my general clumsiness had further-reaching consequences than I had imagined.

'You're to sort out the shelves in the spare linen room,' Ruth told me with poorly concealed pleasure. 'Mrs Cavendish said you're more trouble than—'

'She did not!' Will said, making me start. I hadn't seen him at first, behind the refrigerator door, and presumably Ruth hadn't either. 'She just said it might be a good thing, since Mary's not here, for someone to help Alice out.' He closed the refrigerator and grinned at me, ignoring Ruth's scowl. 'She'll be back in a few minutes to take you up.'

'Why don't you mind your own business, Will Davies?' Ruth grumbled, but again the butcher boy's easy charm had smoothed over what might have become a bruising encounter, and I gave him a grateful smile. Besides, it would actually be nice to be alone with my thoughts for a while, punishment or not.

I soon found myself following Mrs Cavendish down a long corridor on the first floor. I was carrying a bucket of water and a brush, but despite this felt much lighter in spirit. She stopped outside a recessed door at the very end and placed the paraffin lamp on the floor while she selected the right key.

'Now,' she explained, 'this room holds the table linen and bedding we don't use all the time, so it's a little neglected. We need extra for Miss Evangeline's birthday party, and Alice and Emma will want it made ready to iron after lunch.'

She pushed open the door and lifted the lamp inside so I could see properly. My heart sank. Thoughts of a pleasant hour or two spent folding napkins were immediately dashed; this would be an exhausting task and take all the rest of the morning, by which time I would barely be able to lift my arms, let alone scrub the pots.

Mrs Cavendish set the lamp just inside the door on the floor. 'We'll need at least three of the larger cloths, and all the napkins. The rest just needs to be tidied up. Come down for your dinner when you've done.'

Left to myself, I put the bucket of water and brush down and, ignoring the ghostly shadows the lamp threw on the strangely shaped bundles, began to pull crumpled napkins from a shelf. Remembering Ma's advice, I sprinkled water from the brush on them and rolled the linen tight, stacking everything neatly behind me in the corridor. Soon I'd settled more happily into the work; at least I was out of reach of Ruth's sharp tongue here.

I was almost at the end of the first shelf when it happened: one of the larger tablecloths, caught up midway by the pile next to it, resisted my attempt to take it off the shelf. I gave it a quick tug, and took a step backward.

I felt my foot strike something, and a moment later it grew horribly bright, and the shadows I had become accustomed to changed beyond recognition. I whipped my head around, already knowing what I would see; the lamp had tipped on to my neat pile of rolled napkins and cloths, and the top two were ablaze, with flames licking both up and down as they rolled off the pile and on to the floor.

I heard the shriek before I realised I was going to make it, and seized the bucket, dumping its contents on the flames and watching with passionate relief as they sizzled out. My heart thumped painfully. An acrid smell reached deep into my nose and throat and made me cough, but worst of all was the sight of the smouldering, blackened cloths, the frilly-edged holes that went through at least three layers, and the rest of the pile drenched with water and daubed with flecks of soot.

I stared, as if by wishing fervently I could make it all pristine white again and cause the puddles and the holes to disappear. It was a relief when my eyes blurred, but of course when I blinked it was all still exactly the same. Without thinking beyond the next minute or two, I grabbed the acrid-smelling rolled napkins, and the now-extinguished lamp, and bundled them back inside the laundry store.

Sitting in the dark, breathing in the horrible scent of another failure, I felt a deep longing for home and kindness; my sister would have laughed at me, then helped me clean it all up, and Ma would have shouted for a minute, then hugged me and told me she was at least glad I hadn't been hurt. Who was there to do that here? Only Mary, and she was miles away.

I felt tears prickling in the back of my nose, and stinging my eyes. I told myself it was just the smell, but I knew better. After a moment of trying to hold back the sobs I realised it didn't matter; no one would hear me, and the awful pressure in my chest was begging for release. I put my forehead on to my folded arms and began to cry.

Footsteps outside the door cut through the soft sounds I was making. I raised my head. The relief of giving my emotions free rein was cut short in a gasp of dismay. I'd hoped for some time to think, to come up with a way of lessening my crime,

47

possibly even washing the linen in secret, but if Mrs Cavendish saw everything in all its soggy, blackened glory there would be no hope for me.

I held my breath, and in the silence heard a suspicious-sounding sniff from outside, then a louder one, and then the door was pushed open. The light from the window in the hallway was weak, but it was enough to make me blink and look away, wiping my eyes on my sleeve.

Instead of Mrs Cavendish's, I heard a male voice, familiar-sounding but mystified. 'Are you all right? I can smell burning. What on earth's happened here?' I turned back, and Miss Evangeline's uncle Jack peered closer and recognised me. His mouth twitched. 'It's Lizzy, isn't it?'

I nodded, and started to try and explain, but the sympathetic look that crossed his face undid all my carefully rebuilt composure, and all that came out was another sob. He held out his hand and, when I bemusedly placed mine in it, pulled me to my feet.

'You shouldn't be sitting here breathing all this sooty air,' he said. 'Come next door and we'll work out what to do for the best.'

Still bewildered, I let him lead me out of the linen room, and stood shaking while he pulled the door closed and locked it. It did seem odd he should have a key, but the brief time I had to wonder at it passed as he placed a hand in the small of my back and steered me towards the next room, where he had clearly just come from. It was a study, and the sunlight streaming through the long window showed me it was rarely used; dust tickled my nose, but it was such a welcome change from the bitter air inside the linen room that I didn't care.

Jack leaned against the large desk, arms folded. He had been ready to laugh at the absurdity of his discovery, I was sure, but my tears had obviously given him pause and that compassionate look was lingering around his eyes. I remembered how kind he'd been at the station, and how I'd repaid that kindness with what had seemed the most awful cheek. Mortification took hold once again; I didn't deserve his understanding.

'I'm so sorry,' I began, but he held up one hand.

'I've no doubt about that. You don't have to go through all that rigmarole, not with me. What I want to know is, how are we going to get you out of this mess?' He studied me for a moment. 'Here, you're in shock. This'll help.'

He went around behind the desk and, to my amazement, unscrewed the cap on a whisky bottle and poured generous measures into two tumblers. He handed one of them to me, and met my eyes with one of those smiles that had shortened my breath before. It did again.

'You've got a sooty smudge,' he said, echoing Mrs Cavendish's words on my first day. I attended to it as best I could without benefit of a mirror then raised the glass to my lips, blinking as the whisky fumes stung my eyes. I pretended to drink. The merest touch of the liquor numbed my lips, and I wished that I dared to drink the entire glassful down; perhaps it would numb the rest of me too and I would stop feeling this lurking fear at the thought of owning up to what I'd done.

When I lowered the glass again Jack was just doing the same, although in his case the level in his glass had gone down by half. He gestured to one of the easy chairs by the fireplace. 'Come and sit down, love.'

He sat opposite me, and leaned forward with his elbows resting on his knees. 'It's not just what happened in there that's bothering you, is it?' His voice was quiet and low, soothing. I shook my head, and only then felt able to look up at him properly. His eyes were lit by the same shaft of sunlight that showed up the dust in the room, and seemed bluer than ever, surrounded by their thick lashes. His eyebrows were straight, dark lines that gave his face a faintly stern air. I also noticed a scar on the side of his neck I hadn't seen before, and felt a wholly unexpected flicker of protective anger; how could anyone hurt such a kind and friendly man?

He looked back at me with concern, unaware of my indignation. 'What's really the matter, Lizzy?'

Under the gentle weight of his insistence I told him Mary's news, and how badly I felt for her.

'She's such a good friend, such a hard worker, and she's having a terrible time of it. Her mother has just died suddenly.'

Shock flashed across his face, then he immediately looked sympathetic. 'That's …' He broke off and shook his head. 'That's horrible, poor Mary.'

'It is. And she's always so sweet and kind to me, even when I make such awful mistakes.' I told him how I was always doing things wrong and couldn't understand why; at home I was never so clumsy. 'My mother was so proud when I got this job. She loved working here, but I suppose she wasn't away from her family at the time,' I said. 'She gave me lots of advice, though, and I do try to remember it, but it's hard sometimes.'

'So your parents were from this area originally?'

'Yes. My father worked in the salt mine at Winsford, but it closed down. He and my mother decided to begin married life with a new start in the West Country, so they moved to Devon, where I was born, and he got work there. He ... he was killed three years ago in a mining accident.'

'That must have been awful, for all of you,' Jack said quietly, and touched my hand. 'I'm so sorry.'

'Thank you,' I said, trying not to imagine what it would feel like if that hand had instead touched my cheek. I felt my face grow warm at the thought, and sought an escape from my discomfiture.

'What about you?' I asked. 'You don't sound as though you were born here either.' I wondered, for a moment, if I were breaching more rules of etiquette, but he saw my sudden hesitation and smiled.

'I shouldn't think your mother had any advice for you, did she, as to how you should behave when sequestered in a study with a strange man, after setting the linen room on fire?'

That made me laugh, and I shook my head. 'Not that I can remember. I'm sorry if I've stepped too far beyond what's polite.'

'Not at all. It's only fair I should tell you a little about myself in return. Not that there's much to tell: I grew up in Liverpool, as you can probably tell, and I have an older sister, Diane, who lives in Scotland now. My parents were hard-working and respectable, they taught me to live by the same values. When I was seventeen my friend Arthur and I got jobs as navvies, building the ship canal. It was hard work, but fun ...' His thoughts drifted a moment, then he shrugged. 'A bit later I joined the army and moved away, and now I work in the diplomatic service, which is why I travel such a lot. My parents both died several years ago but I still go back home when I can. It's a great city.'

For him to be Miss Evangeline's uncle then, it must be Lady Creswell he was related to rather than Lord Henry. I puzzled for a moment over how Lady Creswell had come to marry a lord if she came from the same humble beginnings as Jack, but felt it would have been too much to ask. 'I'm sorry about your parents,' I said instead.

'That's kind of you,' he said, and a silence fell while I cast about for something else to say, something to take the edge off the worry that was once again gnawing at me. Finally I decided I must face it.

'About the linen,' I began, and he sat back and crossed one leg over the other, eyebrows raised slightly as if in anticipation of entertainment. It was so much easier to talk when I could see the light of amusement in his eyes, and as I came to the end of my explanation his lips twitched again. I found a smile creeping across my own face in answer; he had a way of making problems like mine seem trivial and easily solved.

'I realise it all sounds too silly for words but I don't know how I'm going to tell Mrs Cavendish.' I stood up, suddenly realising I'd made another mistake. 'I'm so sorry, I shouldn't be sitting here like this, complaining to you!'

He rose too. 'I'm the one who told you to sit,' he reminded me. He was standing very close now and I could see how tall he was; my eyes were level with the middle of his chest. One of his hands hovered over my shoulder for a moment, then dropped back to his side. 'Take a moment to compose yourself. We'll think about what's to be done.'

'I can't expect you to put yourself out for me,' I protested. 'This was my doing.'

'And providence clearly sent me along at just the right

moment. If there's one thing I've learned over the years, it's never to argue with providence. Now, sit back down and finish your drink.'

I did so, reluctant to leave the room and his immensely comforting presence.

'I trust you weren't late for work that day we gave you a ride back?' he said after another pause.

I smiled, grateful for the change of subject. 'No, I wasn't, thank you. But it was such a marvellous experience!' I said with renewed enthusiasm. 'I would happily have put up with having my wages docked if I had been late. I had the devil of a job trying to straighten my hair afterwards, though,' I added, and he laughed.

'I can imagine. From what I remember it's quite long, your hair. You'll have to wear a scarf next time.'

'Oh, there won't be a next time,' I said, a tingle running through me at the realisation he'd noticed enough about me to remember my hair. 'But my brothers will be so excited to hear about it.'

'How many brothers do you have?'

And just like that he managed to get me talking about my family again, and as I did so I felt myself relaxing. His interest didn't seem at all feigned, and it was hard not to respond to the way those indigo eyes rested on mine, and to the faint smile that occasionally lightened his face.

As I talked my gaze fell on a photograph on one of the small tables. It showed two men in army uniform, clearly the best of friends despite their evident difference in rank. The taller man was Jack, the other must be Lord Henry Creswell, Evie's father. Along with that thought came the realisation: Jack was not Evie's uncle at all, he must be the mysterious Mr Carlisle I'd heard talk of. The war hero.

Jack followed my line of sight and the light died from his eyes. I felt the warmth go out of the room at the same time.

'How did you two meet?' I matched my soft questioning tone to his, in the hope it would prompt the same, easy response as his had from me, but it didn't. Jack's answer was short.

'We fought in the same war, as you see.' He rose again and finished his drink in one mouthful. I put my half-full glass on the table, cursing my wandering gaze for drawing his attention to something that was clearly still painful to him.

But then he took a deep breath and blew it out, lifting his unruly dark hair away from his brow. I remembered Evie's teasing him about his lack of conformity to fashion, and decided I was as glad of it as she was. It made him seem so much more approachable.

'I'm sorry,' he said, 'that sounded rude. I don't mean to be, it's just . . . it's difficult.'

'I understand. I shouldn't have been so forward,' I said, stumbling over my words in my anxiety to reassure him it wouldn't happen again.

He shook his head. 'Not your fault. Anyway,' he went on, all briskness now, 'let's go back into that room and see if we can't rearrange things so as to avoid any unpleasantness, shall we?' But despite his assurances to the contrary I knew I had touched a nerve, and could have kicked myself for my own clumsiness. Without another word I followed him out of the study.

Inside the cramped laundry room his height and vitality seemed more apparent than ever. He lifted piles of huge, lace-trimmed tablecloths as though they weighed no more than the napkins. He picked up the burned ones and placed them right at the very back, with a promise to retrieve them later when he could hide them in his luggage.

Finally he took a fresh pile of unblemished ones and ushered me back out into the hall. 'We'll just fold these, and that will be plenty for Evie's party.'

We? He was actually going to help fold the linen as well? My already rising regard for him soared. I turned away discreetly and spat as quietly as I could to moisten my apron and wipe my sooty fingers, and although he knew exactly what I was doing he didn't draw attention to it.

He shook out the snowy linen of a tablecloth, and as it floated out between us I realised I'd never have been able to get a good fold on it by myself; it was enormous, and weighed so much more than I'd expected. Holding two corners each we stepped in to match them, and as I passed my end to Jack I felt his fingers close on mine. It was not the first occasion on which we'd touched but it felt different this time; a tremor ran between us and I stepped away quickly, leaving him fumbling for the corners to avoid dropping the cloth in a heap.

'I'm sorry,' I said, moving in to help again, but this time it was he who backed away, leaving me feeling strangely empty, as if the space between us had just grown far wider than it really had.

We worked in silence for a few minutes more, and by then we had a respectable pile of cloths to add to those in daily use. Of course there had been no water left in the bucket to sprinkle on them, but Jack had rolled them very tightly, far more so than I could have done.

'You'd better go back downstairs now,' he said at length. 'But don't forget to wash your face first.' He kept glancing down the hall to make sure no one was coming, and I grew more and more aware of the absurdity of the situation; as unconventional as Jack Carlisle was, helping a scullery maid do her job would take a lot of explaining.

As he put the newly folded and rolled linen at the front of the little room, ready for Alice and Emma to take, I tried to think of a way of thanking him that sounded heartfelt but not gushing. He had done so much more than ease a difficult situation for me. My job was now safe of course, and that was something for which I could never sufficiently thank him, but just as importantly, I no longer felt quite so lonely in this huge house without Mary.

'I just want to say,' I began, aware of how utterly inadequate it would sound, 'I know how it ... how you shouldn't have ...'

'Lizzy, listen,' Jack broke in, and pondered for a moment whether to speak further before deciding to push on. 'I come from a working-class family, as I said. I don't dress the way the Creswells expect me to, I often don't talk the way they expect me to, and I certainly don't act the way they expect me to. Nevertheless, I'm accepted. Because of Henry. You're a hard worker, I've seen that, and you're an intelligent and ...' he stopped, then went on '... an intelligent and respectful girl.'

I felt the heat in my cheeks again, but this time it was fuelled by pleasure at his words. I wondered what he had been about to say before he changed his mind, but he was speaking again and his voice was earnest.

'You mustn't ever feel you're not worth our time or our gratitude,' he said. 'I know how it is downstairs. How you're told to stay silent and out of sight. That's all well and good when other people are around, there has to be some order after all. But remember, I'm no better than you are, not by birth, not by occupation and certainly not by character. Do you understand?'

I nodded, his face blurring a little until I blinked to clear my eyes. 'Thank you,' I whispered, not trusting myself to say any more.

He handed me the bucket. 'Now, you'd better go and have your dinner,' he said, and stooped to pick up the brush. Careful not to touch him again, I took it from his hand and walked back up the hallway to the top of the servants' stairs, on legs that shook so badly I wondered how strange it must look to him. When I glanced back, however, the corridor was empty.

I didn't stop to consider the depth of my disappointment for fear of what that would reveal about the direction my heart was taking, but it would not be long before I realised there could be no denying it even to myself.

Chapter 4

23 August 1912

'Raspberries!' Mrs Hannah exclaimed, her voice cutting across the busy kitchen, and we all looked around. Duties on the Friday morning, the day of Miss Evangeline's birthday, had begun a good hour before the usual time, and I had been swilling out chamber pots and stoking fires well before six o'clock. The night before had been a late one too, as preparations got underway as far in advance as possible, and we were all more than a little heavy-eyed despite the industrious bustle and the sense of heightened importance to the day.

Now, Mrs Hannah was checking through her list, ticking things off with a thick stub of pencil. 'Ruth, you need to go down to the canes.'

'But I can't!' the kitchen maid wailed. 'I might be called at any minute to move upstairs!'

'It'll be a long time before you get that call,' Mrs Hannah

pointed out somewhat archly, but her gaze began travelling across the room in search of alternatives and I saw a chance to prove my worth.

I raised a hand. 'I'll do it.'

Mrs Hannah looked at me for a long moment, and then nodded. 'Well, I don't suppose as you could do much damage picking a bit of fruit,' she allowed at last.

I was used, by now, to the universal assumption that I was bound to cause problems, but her words stung nevertheless. Still, grateful for the chance to get outside in the warm morning air, I quickly slipped into my outdoor shoes, hoping Ruth wouldn't change her mind, although it didn't seem likely since she was more interested in keeping one eye on the door for Mr Dodsworth.

Basket in hand, I wandered down through the rows of vegetables towards the fruit cages, remembering my first glimpse of the walled gardens and the urge I'd felt then to do exactly this. I enjoyed the feel of the sun and the warm summer breeze on my skin, and the flicker of pride and relief that came with knowing precisely what was expected of me and being able to provide it. As I approached the raspberry canes, I heard talking and stopped. Thank goodness I knew Ruth was safely back in the kitchen or I'd have been sure I'd stumbled upon her and Frank Markham again. Instead I recognised the soft, Irish tones of the gardener, Joe the hall boy's father, and my attention slipped away again.

I bent to my task, plucking the soft, furry fruit, and popping the occasional one into my mouth if it looked particularly juicy. Happy in my work, Mr Shackleton's voice humming faintly on the other side of the canes by the wall, I let my mind wander

59

and, as it had done frequently lately, found it settling on a tall man with dark hair and dark-blue eyes, a smile of surprising sweetness on such a strong face.

For a moment I thought my imagination was playing tricks on me because the next voice I heard belonged to that same man. I straightened up from where I had been parting the canes to check for ripe fruit further in, and turned my head to lessen the sound of the breeze flapping at the edges of my cap. I'd not been mistaken. I immediately let go of the canes and felt my heart pick up pace, sending a pleasant flutter through my chest.

He was there, just a few feet away. His voice – low, and to my ears a little sad – drifted through the fruit canes and washed me with a sudden longing to see him. Without giving myself time to think, I picked up my basket and marched around the cage in time to see Mr Shackleton taking a small spade back from Jack Carlisle, who was pressing the earth with one elegantly shod foot.

They both looked up, the newly planted tree between them, and I was both surprised and thrilled to see the bright, unguarded smile on Jack's face. It was wiped away immediately, before Mr Shackleton could see it, but there was no denying it had been there. Warmth pooled in the pit of my stomach and I tried hard to keep my own smile vague and aimed at Mr Shackleton.

'I'm so glad I found you,' I said to the gardener, and gestured at the wooden box of tools by his side, relieved to have seized on a reason why I had strayed from my task. 'I wonder if you have anything I can use to cut back some of the canes?'

But fate was either heavily in my favour or else determined

to send me further into turmoil because the elderly Irishman shook his head. 'Not here, but there are some secateurs in my shed.'

'Oh, thank you,' I said, reluctant to leave but happy to have the memory of Jack's smile, however brief, to hold on to. I nodded a polite farewell to them both but Jack spoke up.

'Mr Shackleton, surely it's not safe for the young lady to go poking around in your shed? All manner of sharp objects in there, I should think, and quite dangerous if you don't know where to look.'

Mr Shackleton looked embarrassed. 'Of course, Mr Carlisle, sir. I'll fetch them out to the miss.' He turned to me and smiled. 'Mr Carlisle's after plantin' another apple tree, first one's doing ever s'well, perhaps he'd like to tell y'about it while I go for the cutters.'

He shuffled off up the garden, and my stomach twisted into knots as I realised Jack and I were alone. He had been working hard in the August heat. His jacket was off and hung over the handle of a long-tined fork stuck in the ground, his open-throated shirt was pasted against his chest in places, where he had sweated through it. As I glanced away quickly the sun seemed to radiate a burst of added warmth. I longed for a breeze to cool my skin but none came, and the silence stretched.

Defeating the very purpose for which I'd approached the men, I could not look at Jack again. Instead I admired the fresh, spindly-looking tree, and clasped the basket of fruit tightly to my chest as he came over to stand beside me.

'I was just helping Mr Shackleton,' he said, sounding, to my surprise, a little embarrassed. 'We didn't have a garden when I was growing up. Or even a window box.'

City life was familiar to me and it was nice to think he must have had a similar upbringing, although we'd been lucky enough to live near the outskirts and had made thrifty use of a good-sized garden.

He moved closer and I kept my eyes on the new planting, still agonisingly aware of him. 'Mr Shackleton said you'd planted one before?' My voice had begun to shake, and I thought I would have to stop talking, but he didn't appear to notice.

He gestured to another tree, close to the wall, several years older and with its branches already bearing set fruit. 'I planted that one for Henry the year he . . .' Jack's own voice trembled then, and he cleared his throat '. . . the year he died.'

Only then was I able to look up at him. His eyes were fixed on Henry's tree, growing strong with its roots deep in Oaklands soil. The regret and sorrow on his face made me want to reach out to him, but what then? Touch his face? His hand? I looked at the soil ground into his skin, and at the lean strength of him. He didn't look like a gentleman playing at gardening, he looked like a hard worker, and as if he were no stranger to that work whether it was in a garden or anywhere else.

I wondered what it would be like to feel those hands on my own skin, and was only mildly perturbed to find my imagination turning then to what it would be like to be drawn against the firm muscles clearly outlined beneath his damp shirt. As if he had heard my thoughts he turned to look at me. His mouth opened slightly but he seemed to find it as hard as I did to form any words. I sensed, with a sinking sensation, that he was about to leave instead.

'Why is the tree hidden away down here?' I asked quickly. Anything to make him stay.

He settled back into a more comfortable stance. 'It's hard to explain,' he said, and I put my basket down, happy to wait while he gathered his thoughts. It seemed that, out here, there was no social divide between us at all, and it was strange to think that in a few minutes I would be back in the kitchen and he would more than likely be drinking tea with Lady Creswell and her daughter. Here, at the bottom of the garden, in the shade of one of the giant oaks that grew on the other side of the wall, we were equal as we could never be anywhere else, not even in Lord Creswell's study. I never wanted to leave.

Jack sighed then and I looked back at him, jolted by the melancholy that tugged his straight, dark brows into a frown. 'I suppose the only way I can explain it is that the house, the pictures, the little plaque in his study, that memorial by the front gate ... those are for his family, and for visitors. This,' he gestured at the tree, 'is what I wanted for him, and what he would have wanted for himself. He loved this part of the garden, much more than all that out there.' He gave me a crooked little smile as he waved at the wall and the magnificent grounds beyond. 'A lot of people would be surprised by that, but we talked about it a lot when we were in Africa. He told me then he'd teach me how to make things grow.' Jack's smile deepened a little, but there was more than a tinge of sadness to it. 'I think his main concern was growing fruit for home-made wine,' he confided, and I returned his smile.

Footfalls, and heavy, nasal breathing told me Mr Shackleton was coming back down the path, and I couldn't decide whether I was disappointed or relieved; Jack's presence was disturbing and exciting, forbidden and yet perfectly, naturally, right. I wanted to stay out here with him, but I was terrified of the way he was making me feel – as if any control I had on my emotions was slipping away with every further word that passed between us.

I stepped forward to look more closely at Henry's memorial and felt Jack's warmth as we crossed on the narrow path. There was a package lying at the foot of the tree, a small, paper-wrapped rectangle, but I didn't ask about it, couldn't bring myself to speak again.

Instead I looked at the tough little apple tree, ten years in the growing and planted in the midst of Jack's grief. I reached out to touch the trunk as if I could draw off some of that pain and ease it, and as I stepped back I realised Jack had moved to stand close behind me; my foot knocked his and I stumbled, but his hand was strong and steady at my waist. I twisted to thank him but his hand stayed there, now in the small of my back, and I saw the pulse quicken below the clean angle of his jaw. He drew a breath to speak, but Mr Shackleton rounded the fruit cage and Jack let me go abruptly. My own pulse was pounding in every part of me, and my legs were barely able to support my weight as I bent to pick up my basket.

'There you go, miss,' Mr Shackleton said. 'These'll do the job fine, but they can be a bit stiff so just you let me know if you need any help.'

I took the secateurs with thanks, and bade both men good-bye without looking at Jack, then walked back to where I'd been working, on trembling legs. I tried to focus on the job and all else that needed to be done that day, but my head was filled with images of dark-blue eyes and muddy hands, of the glisten of sweat along the wide sweep of his collarbone, and of thick dark hair, tumbling over a forehead furrowed with thoughts I couldn't read.

Returning to the kitchen with the fruit, I saw that the activity there had increased further. Later on, guests would begin arriving for the Saturday to Monday that would neatly bracket Miss Evangeline's birthday celebration. Fortunately, many of them would have their own servants to attend them. But this in turn caused complications, not the least of them accommodation.

I had retreated to my room to change my dress after accidentally dousing it in smelly water when I saw another bed, a small put-me-up, had been set in the corner. I eyed it nervously, with the nasty feeling I knew who else would be sleeping in here, and it wasn't long before my fears were confirmed; as I readjusted my apron the door opened and Ruth walked in.

She looked at me dismissively then dropped her bag on Mary's bed. 'This'll do me.'

'You can't sleep there,' I said at once. 'Mary will be back this afternoon.'

'Then I'll have your bed.' She saw my expression and sighed. 'Look, I'm higher ranked than you, it's only right you should have the smallest bed. Besides, it'll only be for one night.'

'What about tomorrow and Sunday?'

'Don't you worry, I'll be on the other side of the house by then.'

She was right, of course; although tomorrow was the big

party, today was the day Miss Evangeline became Miss Creswell. Today she would celebrate with her family and friends, and today she would take her own maid.

As I shifted my clothes to the foot of the smaller bed I wondered who would be named as kitchen maid once Ruth had moved on, and wished yet again it could have been me. The job really wasn't much better than my own but it was one step up the seemingly interminable ladder to a position of responsibility. And it would have been nice to have someone wash out *my* chamber pot for a change.

Back downstairs the talk was all of the Kalteng Star. Had anyone seen it? Was it as beautiful as they said? How much was it worth? How much longer would it stay in the Creswell family? And when conversation eventually moved on it didn't move far.

'No doubt Mr Carlisle will be trying to get his hands on it,' Mrs Cavendish offered at one point, after checking Mr Dodsworth was safely out of earshot. 'Likely as not he'll set his sights on the daughter now, rather than the mother.'

Her words struck me breathless, although I knew it should have come as no surprise; Jack and Miss Evangeline were not related after all, and remembering the fun they seemed to have in other's company, and their shared attitudes to social convention, I could see how they might be drawn to one another. The reminder cut deep, and I tried to take heart from Mrs Hannah's reply.

'Miss Evangeline is far too young to be taking up with Mr Carlisle, he's been like a father to her.'

'Nevertheless she's a pretty girl, and he's a man when all's said and done, and a very dashing one,' Mrs Cavendish put in.

'And they do spend an awful lot of time together when he's here. Which seems to be a lot more often lately, come to think of it.'

Mrs Hannah scowled. 'Nonsense, he's an honourable gentleman. You do him no credit.'

I desperately wanted to add my agreement, but managed to keep silent as I hovered around the table clearing up after the cook's preparations. She and Ruth were cutting and dicing, mixing and covering, working on so many different dishes it was as if there were five people busy instead of two. I concentrated on sweeping up vegetable cuttings and putting them out for compost, and making sure the clean knives and muslin coverings were ready before anyone had to ask. Things were going well and Mrs Hannah kept smiling her thanks, raising my hopes a little for the furthering of my career.

'Mr Carlisle has confirmed his attendance at last,' Mr Dodsworth said, putting his hat down on the table. Mrs Cavendish at once swept it wordlessly away and put it on the stand in the corner. Although I was used to this pantomime by now it still made me smile. 'And I'll thank you to keep your opinions to yourself, Mrs Cavendish.' So he had heard, after all. 'He is a friend to Lady Creswell and nothing more, just as he was to Lord Henry, God rest his soul.'

'Aye, well, so you say.' Mrs Cavendish spoke mildly enough, but an arched eyebrow told me she wasn't the slightest bit convinced. She changed the subject. 'So, Ruth, ye haven't had the call yet?'

'Call?' Ruth said, frowning at the list of ingredients on the table in front of her.

'To see Lady Creswell. Your promotion, aye?'

67

'Oh! No, not yet. Mr Dodsworth, have you heard anything?'

'I might have,' he said with an air of mystery, then relented. 'I haven't been told anything official, but I do overhear things, as you know.'

He winked, and Ruth gave a shriek of such excitement that I actually glimpsed something in her I could come to tolerate. She flushed and bit her lip, and tried to concentrate on slicing her carrots paper-thin, but I could see her hands shaking. Naturally I was as eager for her call as she was; it would signal the end of her reign over me, and perhaps then I would be able to work to my proper abilities, unhampered by nerves.

'Congratulations,' I ventured, and for the first time since I'd arrived, she actually smiled distractedly at me although she didn't speak. I wasn't even sure she realised who'd congratulated her.

'Who will take over your job then, Ruth?' Mr Dodsworth asked.

All eyes turned to me but Mrs Cavendish quickly put that idea to bed. 'Someone who can handle best china without breaking it, I hope,' she said, and my hopes crashed once more. Then, to my surprise, she patted me on the shoulder. 'You'll learn, lassie, in time.'

And so the day marched on. Ruth jumped every time someone came into the kitchen, expecting her summons to Lady Creswell's rooms at any moment; the house thrummed with tension and gossip in equal measure; staff both household and visiting came and went, the visitors introducing themselves and generally getting in the way; and I was busier than I'd ever been, keeping the cooking area clean for Mrs Hannah and Ruth.

Will Davies and Mr Markham arrived just as Ruth and I were clearing our own dishes from the kitchen table. I was glad to see Will; we had become quite good friends and he always stood between Ruth and me if he could. The others were in the servants' hall, and I could see Mr Markham looking at Ruth with a clear question in his expression.

I decided to be charitable and put him out of his misery. 'Ruth, I'm so glad you've been chosen for Miss Creswell's maid,' I said, and saw the satisfied tightening of Mr Markham's mouth.

'Congratulations, Miss Wilkins,' he said politely.

She lifted her chin in acknowledgement, and her speech became awkwardly formal. 'Thank you, Fr ... Mr Markham. Of course, this means I'll no longer pass the time of day with you, as our duties will see us in different parts of the house.'

'Well then, perhaps our paths will cross while you are out and about with your mistress,' Mr Markham said.

Will stood behind him, and his expression wasn't what I'd expected at all. He appeared both surprised and, for once, miserable. Surely he wasn't yearning after her too? Ruth was a hard, cold one and would stamp all over his cheery nature, he must know that.

I kept my tone bright. 'Good news, isn't it, Will?'

'Um, yes,' he said. Then forced a smile that looked as if someone were complimenting him and standing on his foot at the same time. 'Congratulations, Ruth, Miss Creswell will be lucky to have you.' He turned back to me and his expression cleared. 'And what about you, Lizzy? Does this mean you'll be taking Ruth's place alongside Mrs Hannah?'

Ruth snorted and I glared at her, my fledgling tolerance wiped away. 'No, Mrs Cavendish has told me quite plainly it will not, so I'm afraid you're stuck with me getting under your feet a little longer.'

He laughed and I was pleased to note it sounded more natural than his somewhat strangled congratulations. 'Very glad I am to hear it, too.'

Mary arrived a few minutes after two, and gave me a brief hug before vanishing upstairs to change. I didn't see her for the rest of the afternoon, but it was comforting enough to know she was once more in the house and I would have the chance to talk to her later.

The family's meal was to be served earlier than usual today, in order for an informal supper to be taken with the first arrivals. Consequently our own meal was also taken early, and quickly, so we could prepare Miss Creswell's birthday dinner in good time. By three o'clock I was clearing away the plates and stacking them to be washed.

Ruth still hadn't been summoned to Lady Creswell's rooms but she constantly checked her appearance in the back of a silver spoon, making sure she was available to go at a moment's notice. I envied her so much, it was useless to pretend otherwise. I could have done that job perfectly well, given half the chance.

'You'll get there,' said a voice at my elbow, and I turned in relief.

'Oh, Mary, I'm so sorry about your mother,' I said. She looked older, and very tired, and she wouldn't be entitled to a holiday for some time after having been away for so long.

She brushed aside my condolences, but I could see she was

touched and blinking back tears. 'I've heard Ruth will be Miss Creswell's maid,' she said, and I noticed her accent had become stronger during the time she'd been away. 'Lady Creswell was talking about it to Miss Evangeline earlier. Miss Creswell, I should say. It looks very much as though you are going to be doing double duties for a little while, until they find a replacement kitchen maid.'

I groaned. 'I shall never get a rest.'

'Well, think of it this way,' Mary said encouragingly, 'you'll have the chance now to prove how good you are. By the way, why are your night-clothes on the small bed, and whose are those on yours?'

I told her about Ruth, and she sighed. 'She shouldn't have made you swap beds, but it's sometimes better to accept with good grace what you can't change. You'll have your day. Now hurry up with those plates, you'll be wanted soon enough when Ruth gets her call. We'll talk later.'

I was determined to prove Mrs Cavendish wrong, which is no doubt what she'd had in mind, and worked harder than I had ever worked before. It was while I was on my knees scrubbing the inside of one of the huge ovens that I realised talk had dropped off. With my head inside the oven it was hard to place voices or hear words, but I grew aware that, instead of the familiar hum of many people talking at once, there were only two in conversation.

Curious, I pulled my head and shoulders back into the room and felt my belly flip over; Jack Carlisle was once again where he ought not to have been, this time in the kitchen.

'He's attending to matters in the dining room,' Mrs Cavendish was saying. Clearly then Jack had come looking for Mr Dodsworth, but he was looking around with great interest at the goings-on and preparations for Miss Creswell's party.

'Thank you, Mrs Cavendish,' Jack said, and then he caught sight of me. I couldn't duck away again without seeming rude, so I remained kneeling back on my haunches and his gaze moved on around the room. I felt the weight of it on me still; he had paused at me, I knew it, and although I much preferred him muddy and breeze-blown to this, the epitome of smart respectability, the sight of him was enough to speed up my heart until I could almost hear it.

I became horribly aware of the messy picture I must make; up to my grimy elbows in grease, with my hair flopping out of my cap as usual to lie, sweaty and dark, across my cheek, and my apron blackened and splashed with dirty water again. I still felt the warmth of his hand on my waist, and wondered if he had looked at me now and wondered what had possessed him to touch me at all. But this was the reality of how I spent my days, and the chasm between us, if it had ever really been forgotten, now yawned wide once again.

When he left he nodded to each member of staff again, saving me for last. I wanted to believe it was because he could then hold me in his mind the way I held him, but he had begun with Mrs Cavendish so I concluded he was merely working down through the ranks. Watching him walk away and back upstairs where he belonged, I vowed to put him from my mind and to concentrate on nothing more than work from that moment on. If only it were that easy; all I could do was promise myself I wouldn't waste my life mourning the loss of something I had never had and which I knew could never be mine.

More gossip filtered in about the guests, much of it once again surrounding Jack after his impromptu visit below stairs. I wondered what he would think if he could hear what was being said about him. Mrs Cavendish seemed to think he was cousin to the devil. I could think of no one less deserving of being branded as such, and found it hard to hold my tongue but managed it with a great effort.

Later, I was washing the last of the dishes and Ruth was working alongside Mrs Hannah; the two of them were putting the finishing touches to Miss Evangeline's birthday cake, to be served at the formal party tomorrow night when the Kalteng Star would be presented.

Ruth still hadn't been called upstairs, and was starting to get annoyed. I knew the signs well enough by now; drawers were slammed, people received short, clipped answers, and her chest fetched heavy sighs that invited the listener to ask what was wrong while her grim face warned against it.

Mrs Hannah kept looking sidelong at her and moving the elaborate cake out of her way as she added whorls of peach-coloured icing around the edges. The way Ruth was going she would end up causing a disaster that would take hours to put right.

'Och, stop fashin', girl,' Mrs Cavendish said at last. 'The family has not long finished supper and there'll be guests to attend to. Matters of the household will wait until later.'

'Yes, of course,' Ruth said. 'I'm sorry.' The meekness of her tone made me regard Mrs Cavendish with renewed respect.

'Ye may not even be called to Her Ladyship until tomorrow,' she added, and with that Ruth had to be content. She followed Mrs Hannah to the pantry to help fetch more ingredients, and I returned my attention to the washing up. The scullery sink was full of freshly plucked birds so I was using the smaller of the main kitchen sinks. It was nice to feel more involved, but I still didn't dare join in conversation.

I lifted a large bowl from the greasy water, and everything happened sickeningly quickly after that: I turned to the table to set the bowl down on a cloth to dry, but my foot slipped in a pool of water and I dropped my burden awkwardly, so that it landed on its bottom edge instead of its base. It began to roll across the wooden surface of the table in a slow, ponderous curve and, with no one now close enough to halt its progress, straight towards the untended birthday cake.

With a cry of horror I lunged after it, but instead of seizing the edge my frantically reaching fingers struck the side and gave the bowl a helpful push onward. The sound the cake made as it hit the floor was like a slap and I squeezed my eyes tight shut, praying that when I opened them I'd be safe in my bed and just awakened from an awful dream.

The kitchen erupted in shrieks and frantic activity, and I felt sick. So sick I believed I might faint. I felt a cool sweat break out on my forehead. It couldn't have happened, not really, that would be too unfair. What had I done to deserve such horrifically bad luck?

From somewhere distant I heard my name, harsh and

furious, on someone's lips. Then I felt my arm seized above the elbow as I was thrust towards the door.

'Neither use nor ornament! Go to your room and pray Lady Creswell is not disposed to have ye dismissed.'

A firm hand pushed me into the hallway at the foot of the stairs, and behind me I heard Ruth's voice saying in tones of poorly concealed delight: 'Stupid scullion!'

I managed not to cry until I heard Mrs Cavendish's sharp retort: 'Silence, girl! It was an accident, nothing more.' Then she added, 'I doubt Her Ladyship will see it that way, though. Yon maid will be lucky to last through tomorrow in this house. Now, fetch a tray.'

I heard Mary come into the room much later. 'Lizzy, are you awake?' Her voice was only a whisper but I could hear the hesitation in it.

I sniffed. 'Yes, I doubt I'll ever sleep again. I keep seeing and hearing it happen over and over.'

The light clicked on and Mary sat on the end of my small, cramped bed. 'You're a daft one,' she said despairingly, and handed me a cotton handkerchief.

I sat up and blew my nose. 'Do you think Lady Creswell really will dismiss me? I mean, I heard Mrs Cavendish say it was an accident, and—'

'It was an accident that will take most of tomorrow to put right. And while Mrs Hannah is doing that, who's going to be doing her other jobs? You have to understand that what you do affects everyone. You may feel small and insignificant, but when something like this happens it causes ripples.'

'Ripples?'

'Well, in this case huge great waves. Think about it: Mrs Hannah won't have Ruth to help her tomorrow, because she will be moving upstairs to attend to Miss Creswell. So Cook's job is already going to be doubly hard. Add to that her having to re-make the cake that took the best part of today to prepare, and the kitchen will be a shambles on the very day it needs to be running at its smoothest. We may be allowed some of Miss Peters's time, but she will mostly be kept busy attending to Lady Creswell.'

'There are other servants staying,' I said, misery piling up again. 'Surely they can help?'

'Certainly not!' Then Mary's tone gentled again. 'Those who are here, and them that arrive tomorrow, are upper servants and here for the sole purpose of attending to their own masters and mistresses. To try to press them into kitchen service to make up for the carelessness of our scullery maid would make this house a talking point for all the wrong reasons.'

'Well then, Lady Creswell won't want to dismiss me, will she?' I heard eager hope in my own voice. 'She'll need all the help she can get.'

Mary sighed and her face flooded with pity. 'Lizzy love, she'll need all the *reliable* help she can get. Your leaving won't affect her at all, but the rest of us will be working like Trojans twice over.'

'Too bloody right!' came a furious voice from the doorway, and Ruth flung her apron on her bed. *My* bed. 'I could skin you alive for what you did today.'

I tried to repeat that it was an accident, but all that came out was a hiccup as my chest hitched and the tears started again. I didn't care about Ruth, but the look of reproach on Mary's face was more than I could bear.

'Shut up,' Ruth said. 'We need to get to sleep. It's going to be another early start in the morning, thanks to you.'

'Oh, hush, Ruth,' Mary said. 'You won't have to work down there for much of the day. By the time breakfast is over you'll be starting in your new position.'

'And thank God for that. I 'eard they was taking on a new scullery maid as of tomorrow lunchtime,' Ruth said. 'Girl name of Martha. One of the Hoskinses. Mr Dodsworth knows them quite well and he recommended her.'

Mary squeezed my arm. 'Yes, I heard that too. I'm sorry, lovey.'

My heart clenched and I suddenly felt quite hollow. I couldn't decide which was worse: the thought of explaining to Ma how I had nothing to show but shame for my time at her beloved Oaklands Manor, or the bleak knowledge that I would never see Jack Carlisle again, not even from a distance.

I tried to smile. 'At least I won't have to stay around here and be shouted at by everyone.' I said this looking pointedly at Ruth, but it was wasted bravado. She had turned her back on the room and all I could see was the hunch of her shoulder as she pulled the covers up to her chin.

When the alarm sounded the next morning it took me a moment to remember what had happened. It wasn't until I opened my eyes and saw the room from a different angle that

77

I remembered Ruth had taken my bed, and from there it all came crashing back. I saw again the painfully slow journey of the bowl, and my own desperate but clumsy fingers giving it the push it needed to take the cake to the floor in a mash of sponge and icing. I felt the grip on my arm sending me from the kitchen in disgrace, and now, in reality, I heard Mary speaking to the top of my head, the only part of me showing as I cowered beneath my thin bed coverings.

'You must dress and present yourself for work, Lizzy.'

'Why?' I couldn't imagine anything worse.

'Because you've not yet been officially dismissed and you must show willing to help whether it's wanted or not. Mrs Cavendish or Mrs Hannah may send you away again for fear of more accidents, but they must be given that choice. Do you understand?'

I sniffed, and let the covers fall. Ruth was beginning her morning routine, and as she turned to the wash basin I could see nervous excitement in her movements. Her mind wasn't allowing her to focus on the task, and her hands moved from jug to towel and back again, then rubbed at her face as if she could remove the smile that kept tugging at her lips.

'I hope you get the call soon, Ruth,' I said. Perhaps, by being generous, I would earn a second chance from whichever of the fates held me in their hands today. She spared me no more than a glance before turning back to the washbowl, but at least I had tried.

'Come on, pet,' Mary said. 'Look sharp, and remember lesson number one.'

It doesn't do to keep the Cavendish waiting . . . I'd been so full of expectations that first day, sure that possibilities for my advancement were just around the corner. Now here I was just five months later, half a day away from the disgrace of a train back home.

I paused in the narrow hall, straining to hear anything that might be being discussed in the kitchen. There were murmurs and the odd raised voice, but none of the talk was about me. I didn't know whether to be relieved or disappointed; at least if they were talking about me I would feel less of a non-person.

I sighed and pushed open the door. It was another early start for everyone, and even busier because of what had happened the day before. Mrs Cavendish was in her office off the kitchen, Mrs Hannah was creating the icing decorations to put in the pantry until they were needed, and Joe Shackleton was stoking the fires to provide hot water. Normally my job.

'Good morning, Mrs Hannah.' I bobbed a curtsey to her as was expected every morning, but this time my knees were trembling so much I almost lost my balance.

'Good morning, Lizzy,' Mrs Hannah replied, but she wouldn't look directly at me.

'Mrs Hannah, the cake ...' I began, but she shook her head.

'No, girl. There's no time to talk. Go and see to the pots, you'll be dealt with in good time. Meanwhile we have a lot to catch up with.'

She bent once more to the intricate little roses she was creating, and I hurried through to the scullery to draw water, eager to escape her quiet reproach and the knowing glances of the others.

As I worked I kept looking around me. Perhaps it was

merely a reaction to the way things had happened for the worst, but I realised I would actually miss Oaklands. Not only Jack and Mary, but most of the people here, as well as the reassuring feeling of being in good, paid work. I'd miss seeing Will too; every friend I'd made here took on a greater importance than they might have at home, and he had been my champion from the start. It was too bad, and very frustrating; as I'd told Jack, I was never such a clumsy oaf at home, but here it was as if something stood against me, ready to push me back every time I tried to step forward.

Then a quiet voice compounded my wretchedness. 'Lizzy, I'm to take you to Her Ladyship now.' I looked around. Mrs Cavendish had just returned from her daily meeting with Lady Creswell, and I felt my heart plummet; so it wasn't to be a strong reprimand, a fine, or even quiet dismissal by Mr Dodsworth. It seemed my calamitous history had brought me to the attention of the head of the house. Perhaps they'd found the burned linen after all . . .

'She has instructed that you should not leave any of your belongings in the kitchen,' Mrs Cavendish went on, 'so make sure you've got your spare apron, and don't forget your outdoor shoes from the hall.'

All eyes followed me as I made my unsteady way across the kitchen and unhooked my clean apron from the rack. I wasn't sure whether I should say my goodbyes, but in the event I couldn't speak anyway and, through a blur of tears, saw a few nods of sympathy. I nodded back and turned to follow Mrs Cavendish up the stairs into the main house.

Chapter 5

I had been up here before but always at the back of a crush of servants as we gathered for morning prayers with the family. I had never even seen Lady Creswell up close, let alone her rooms, and despite the squirming sensation in my stomach I couldn't help staring with ever-widening eyes at everything I passed.

The stairway led up into the back end of the hall. From there all I'd seen before had been the polished wooden floor and the high arches of the ornately decorated ceiling. Now I was able to see the main staircase, richly carpeted and stretching away to the family's rooms upstairs.

On the walls hung pictures of horses, and portraits of Creswells past and present stared down from wide, gilded frames. Even the youngest in this family commanded attention. They all had the same broad brow and finely cut bone structure and they carried an air of complete authority, of knowing their place in society and ensuring anyone who saw them was equally well informed.

One of the pictures was of Lord Henry, who had posed for a family portrait with his wife and two small children, and I recognised Miss Evangeline's impish and barely contained energy even as a small child of perhaps three years. Lord Henry's hand was resting on his wife's shoulder and his eyes were fixed ahead with a calm composure that wasn't quite arrogance.

Lady Lily had been very young then, holding her infant son on her lap with one hand and her daughter's hand with the other. It made me smile to think that in all probability she had been restraining the girl rather than merely making maternal contact, and that her own smile was hiding the strain of keeping her daughter in one place and quiet for more than a minute at a time.

I was brought back to a bleaker present by the echo of our shoes as we crossed the polished floor of the entrance hall, and the distant sounds of activity deeper in the house as guests began rising for their breakfast. My stomach growled at the thought of food. I hadn't yet eaten, although I'd been offered a thick slice of bread as it came out of the oven. The smell had made my mouth water but I knew I'd be unable to chew and would probably choke on it.

Mrs Cavendish stopped outside a door on the far side of the hall, and raised her hand to knock. Before she did so she smiled down at me kindly. 'I'll see ye get a good reference, hen,' she said. 'Don't worry, you'll get other work.'

She knocked. We waited and my heart seemed to have stopped, waiting too.

'Come in,' said a clear voice from within.

Mrs Cavendish opened the heavy door and ushered me in ahead of her. 'Your Ladyship, this is Lizzy Parker, you asked to see her.'

Lady Creswell looked up from the large book that lay open on her desk and I felt a sense of unreality, as though the portrait had come to life in front of me. Her blonde hair was elaborately dressed and, in contrast to the frenzy below stairs, she looked cool and unruffled.

She was sitting before a large picture window, beyond which I could see the wide sweep of the driveway and the very edge of the walled kitchen garden. I recognised it, yet it seemed like a different place altogether, seen from this extraordinary room, the morning room I guessed, judging from the way the August sun beamed through and lit on the various ornaments and photographs on the occasional tables.

'Good morning,' Lady Creswell said.

I dropped a curtsey. 'My Lady.' My voice only shook a tiny bit, for which I was grateful, but I felt as though my limbs were made of paper.

Lady Creswell looked past me at the housekeeper. 'Thank you, Mrs Cavendish, that will be all.'

And then, with the quiet click of the door behind me, I was alone with Lily, Lady Creswell.

The silence in the room while she studied me was so long and deep I could feel it in my bones, but at last she dropped her gaze back to the ledger in front of her and sighed. I felt my insides tighten as I forced myself to stand still and keep my mouth firmly closed. Had I opened it I would have started to beg, and that would have robbed me of the very last shred of dignity I possessed.

Besides, I had brought this down on my own head; I had caused mayhem in the kitchens and forced the other servants to work twice as hard on the very day they could least afford the time. Not to mention setting the linen on fire; the fact they didn't know about that didn't mean I didn't deserve punishment. I would stand here and take any judgement Lady Creswell chose to pass, no matter how awful, and in the long silence my mind was already beginning to consider other possible avenues of employment.

Then she spoke again. 'Do you sew?'

For a moment I thought she'd said *you may go*, and I curtseyed again and almost turned to leave, then blinked instead. 'Begging your pardon, My Lady, do I what?'

'Do you sew? Are you good with a needle?'

I thought back to all the years spent mending my own clothes and those of my family, and nodded. 'I am quite competent.'

'And have you good manners?'

'I've been told so, yes.'

'Do you smoke?'

'No, My Lady.'

'You can read and write, of course?'

'Yes, quite well.'

She looked up at me again, her brow furrowed for a moment. 'Then I suppose I must bow to my daughter's wishes. On a trial basis, of course.'

The room went fuzzy around me. 'Pardon, My Lady?'

'Miss Creswell has requested that you take up the position of her personal maid. From today.'

I was vaguely aware that I was staring at Lady Creswell with what must have been a witless look because she inclined her head slightly and lifted her eyebrows. The movement brought me to my senses and I shook my head, then spoke quickly in case she thought I was refusing.

'Thank you! I'm sorry, I'm just a bit—'

'Surprised? No more than I am, Parker.' This new form of address buzzed inside my head, as if a bumble bee was knocking about in there, and through it I could hear her continuing, 'As far as I'm concerned Ruth Wilkins would be the more sensible choice, but your mother was highly respected by my husband's family, I understand. More importantly, Evangeline has evidently met you and insists she can trust you.' The words had the feel of a question without actually being one.

'I . . . yes, we did meet, once.'

'That appears to have been enough. Evangeline has never been one to ponder too long over life's more important decisions.' Lady Creswell sounded resigned but then her briskness reasserted itself.

'Very well, Parker. You will take up residence in the rooms recently vacated by the governess. Mr Dodsworth will take you there directly.'

'My Lady, I—'

'I'm aware you must be a little overwhelmed but there is no time for that now. Today is, as you know, a very important day, and we are short-staffed in the kitchen.' She cleared her throat in a marked manner, and I flushed. 'As such I shall expect you to help out while Miss Creswell is riding. Kindly change your clothes and report to Mrs Cavendish as soon as you are ready. You will take up your duties later this afternoon when Miss Creswell returns, but you will behave according to your new station from this moment on.'

Lady Creswell pulled at a thick silk rope that hung from the wall beside her, and after a moment the door opened. I turned to see Mr Dodsworth, his face, as ever, giving nothing away. 'My Lady?'

'Escort Parker to her new rooms, if you would, Dodsworth. She's to have the old nursery and workroom.'

His eyebrows went up, but that was the only outward sign of surprise. 'Very good, My Lady.'

'Thank you, Dodsworth,' Lady Creswell said, and finally she smiled at me. 'Good day to you, Parker, and congratulations.'

'My Lady.' I curtseyed again, this time deeper, and with legs that shook almost as much as before but for a very different reason.

As I followed Mr Dodsworth out, further aspects of this extraordinary turn of events kept occurring to me. First there had been the enormous relief that I wasn't being dismissed after all, and the shock and joy at being able to write to my mother and tell her what had happened. Then, as we turned into a long corridor on the first floor, I thought about my new rooms and how they would look, especially compared to what I was used to. Finally the gleeful imp who had so far lain quiet, tapped on the inside of my skull and whispered, 'Think how furious Ruth will be!'

I quietened him at once. There was no ignoring the fact that the girl was a bully, and although part of me couldn't help rejoicing at having bested her, a much bigger and deeper part of me quailed at the thought of what her reaction might be. I wiped my suddenly sweating hands on my apron as we stopped outside the door at the end of the hall, and tried to quell the churning in my stomach that threatened to eclipse the delight I felt in my new appointment.

'Welcome to your new station, Miss Parker,' Mr Dodsworth said, and stepped back as the door swung inward. I gasped before I could stop myself, thoughts of Ruth Wilkins immediately banished. The room was bright, airy and beautifully decorated, clearly a workroom though I could see touches of feminine individuality; frills here, pleats there, ornaments on the mantelpiece, and the curtains secured by neat, buttoned tiebacks.

I stepped into a patch of sunlight that lay across the polished floor and felt the warmth on my skin. There was a door off to one side and I glanced back at Mr Dodsworth. He nodded, so I pushed open the door which led to a small bedroom with another large window ... and just one bed. Yet again tears were threatening and I cleared my throat. Mr Dodsworth said nothing but I heard the door close, very quietly, as he left me to contemplate my new life. It was only as I sat on the bed that full realisation sank in: as maid to Miss Creswell I would see Jack again. Often. The incipient tears turned to a tiny sob of joy, and I fell back and let the smile spread from my heart to my face, and in my mind Jack's own smile, slow and beautiful, rose to answer it.

Half an hour later, different in appearance but still the trembling scullery maid inside, I stood outside the kitchen door once more. By now Mrs Cavendish would know what had happened, whether or not the rest of the staff had been informed. I wondered how she felt about the news, and if she'd at least told Ruth yet.

Just a few hours ago I had stood here listening for the mention of my name on the other side of that door. Now I did so again, but this time bubbling with a mixture of excitement and nervousness. If my position was so much higher, so too were my responsibilities, and all eyes would be on me.

I opened the door.

The first person I saw was Mrs Hannah. She nodded at me, her face giving nothing away. 'Miss Parker,' she said, all politeness. Likely she would wait and see how I conducted myself in my new role before forming an opinion as to whether or not I deserved it.

'Mrs Hannah,' I acknowledged. 'I've come to help with the preparations for Miss Creswell's party.'

'Thank you.' Mrs Hannah lifted a clean apron off the wall. 'You'd better put this on, don't want to go spoiling your nice new uniform.'

I tied the apron, grateful to have something to do with my shaking fingers, and looked around the kitchen. 'Where's Ruth?'

'She went out to the garden for herbs.'

'Does she know?'

'Not yet.'

Excitement turned to apprehension as I kept one eye on the door to the kitchen garden and began peeling vegetables. Soon Mrs Cavendish returned from her paperwork and plucked her own apron from its hook.

'So, Miss Parker, Miss Creswell chose ye specifically?'

'I believe so.'

'On the basis of what?'

'On the basis of a chance meeting earlier this year.'

'And what did ye think of your new mistress?'

I stood straighter. 'I am not prepared to discuss the matter, Mrs Cavendish.'

She held my gaze for a moment, then smiled and some of the tension that had been tightening my shoulders fell away. 'Good girl.'

We both looked up as the back door opened and Ruth came in. She stopped dead as she saw me, not only back in the kitchen, but working alongside Mrs Hannah and wearing the black dress uniform of an upper servant. Her face went carefully blank, then she turned to Mrs Hannah and placed the basket of herbs on the table.

'What's this, fancy dress?' she said, but the tremor in her voice betrayed her fury. 'Do I get to dress up as Mr Dodsworth next?'

I forced a firmness into my voice I certainly did not feel. 'Listen, Ruth ...'

'Don't you "Listen, Ruth" me, you little upstart,' she snapped, and went scarlet as Mrs Cavendish banged her hand on the table.

'Quiet, girl! Any more and you'll report to me in my office at the end of the day.'

I watched as Ruth picked up her apron, her hands also visibly shaking, and tied it before taking up her position opposite me. She said no more, but now and again I caught her looking at me with bewildered resentment, and the old fear returned. But with Mrs Cavendish there and the kitchen buzzing with preparations for the party there was nothing she could say.

Dinner was a new source of taut nerves and potential embarrassment as, for the first time, I took it in the servants' hall with Mrs Hannah and the others. I looked around for Mary's friendly face, but she was busy upstairs and would take her lunch later. Despite feeling her absence keenly, I took a deep breath and told myself it was time to stand more firmly on my own two feet.

It was strange to be served alongside the head cook and other high-ranked staff, and there was one uncertain moment when I took my place on the left of Mr Dodsworth and prepared to sit down, gathering my skirt to do so before catching Mrs Cavendish's famous eagle eye. She gave the tiniest shake of her head, and I paused somewhere between standing and sitting, while Mr Dodsworth took his time about granting us permission to be seated. Just when I thought my legs would give out altogether he nodded, and I sank gratefully on to my chair.

I watched carefully as everyone ate, taking silent instruction and grateful that there was such a lot to discuss that after the first curious exchange of raised eyebrows no one paid me any close attention. Talk of the party, the guests and of the Kalteng diamond and what it represented bounced around the table, but there was no discussion of Miss Evangeline herself. It was a subtle shift but one I noticed immediately; it was her eighteenth birthday after all, which made me wonder what turn the conversation would have taken had I not been present.

When we were finished I moved, from habit, to clear the dishes and felt Mr Dodsworth's hand on my wrist.

'I believe Miss Creswell will shortly be returning from her ride,' he said, looking pointedly at my apron. 'Your assistance has been appreciated by Mrs Cavendish and Mrs Hannah. As it is by me.'

'You're welcome, Mr Dodsworth,' I said, and nodded in turn to the housekeeper and the cook. 'I was very happy to help.' The words sounded odd in my mouth and, as always, I felt the strong urge to curtsey.

A soft knock at the back door put an end to the faintly awkward moment and as I went into the kitchen to drop my soiled apron into the laundry basket I glanced into the scullery. A young girl was standing there in outdoor clothes, her gaze fixed ahead, looking neither up nor down as Mrs Cavendish spoke to her. This must be Martha, the new scullery maid. She looked young, pale and absolutely terrified, so as I passed the door and her gaze instinctively flickered my way, I gave her the biggest, most friendly smile I could muster.

Her eyes went as round as Mrs Hannah's best Willow Pattern plates, and she paled even further, snapping her eyes back to the front. The exchange cast a faint shadow over my happiness; to this girl I was someone to be feared, or at least be wary of, and I wanted to tell her that I had been just like her only a few hours ago. My own first day wasn't so long ago that I had forgotten the feeling of helpless excitement, so liberally dusted with outright terror, and more than anything, just at that moment, I wanted to go to this girl and be to her what Mary had so quickly become to me.

But, of course, that was out of the question. It would simply make life more difficult for the poor girl, with Ruth especially, so I settled for another smile, hoping to convey comfort with it, and then turned away to begin my new life.

Chapter 6

I checked my appearance in the full-length mirror, and tugged my cap straight just as the bell above my door rang. The jangling sound made me jump and my heart stuttered, then an enormous weight seemed to overwhelm my limbs and I found I couldn't move them for what seemed like an age.

Eventually I took a deep breath and pushed the fear aside, picking up the workbasket that lay on the table and feeling its weight in my fingers as an oddly comforting thing; I didn't know if I'd need it, but it seemed prudent to arrive prepared. During the short walk from my own room to Miss Creswell's I suddenly had the horrible thought that maybe this was nothing more than an enormous joke at my expense, repayment for my brazen cheek of four months ago.

I gripped the wicker handle of the basket tight as I stood in the hall, certain I would drop it otherwise. Probably on Miss Creswell's foot. I raised one hand to knock, but before I could the door opened and a pretty pink and flustered face appeared, saw me and broke into a sunny smile.

'Lizzy!' Miss Creswell seized the basket and pulled me into her room, shutting the door. 'I'm so glad Mother allowed me to choose my own maid. We'll have a lot of fun, I think.'

'Miss Creswell, I'm not sure—'

'Oh, you mustn't call me that, not in private anyway, and I'm certainly not going to call you Parker. You must call me Evie.'

I gaped at her. 'I couldn't.'

'You certainly could,' she said, 'and if I'm in charge you have to do as I say, correct?'

'Miss Cresw ... um, Miss Evie ... I don't really know what—'

'Not "*Miss* Evie", just Evie.'

'Like "Just Lizzy"?' I said, and felt a smile creeping up on me despite my nerves. It was impossible not to respond to her enthusiasm.

'Exactly like that.' She caught my hand. 'Listen, I know this is all a bit rushed and probably a big surprise for you, especially after the way we parted, but it's the best thing that can have happened, don't you think?'

'Well, for me it is,' I said, 'but what made you choose me over Ruth? She's far more experienced, and she's—'

'She's a hard-faced madam who only wanted the job because she thinks she's too good for the kitchens,' Evie said. 'Whereas you have something about you that I like. Very much.' She looked me over, frowning, and I grew aware of everything about my person that could possibly be wrong, as if someone were itemising each point; my stockings were crooked; my cap was already back to sitting at its usual attention-defying angle; my shoes needed a clean; my sleeves were too long and turned back in a hurry; no doubt there was a smudge of something on my nose too, the way she was staring.

'Miss Evie,' I began, but she held up one hand. I fell silent and watched while she bit the inside of her lip, concentrating.

'No,' she said at length. 'I can't put my finger on why I chose you, but that proves it.'

'Proves what?'

'If I were able just to pick one thing ... say, for instance, you have a polite manner about you, or you have a sparkly smile, or even that I simply thought you would be an attentive and competent maid ... that would be a good enough reason to suspect I'd made the wrong choice. Not that those things don't apply to you,' she hurried on, 'because I'm sure they do. No,' she pondered, 'it has to be something indefinable for a friendship to work, and happily I have *no* idea why you made such a favourable impression that one time we met.'

'Nor do I, I was unforgivably rude,' I reminded her, and immediately wondered why I couldn't just keep quiet.

Evie's expression cleared. 'Ah, that must be it!' Then she smiled. 'Don't look so worried, I was just teasing, you weren't unforgivably rude at all. The fact is you were right, I *was* being something of a hypocrite. Mother's rules seem so horribly old-fashioned, but obey them I must. At least, as you say, when I am in her house.'

'Then may I ask why Lady Creswell gave you permission to choose me?' I said, curiosity getting the better of my nerves. 'It seems to me I'd be the last person she'd want, and when we spoke she didn't seem happy about it.'

'That would be down to Uncle Jack.'

My heart leaped at the words and I curled my fingers into my palms so she wouldn't see them shaking.

'I told them I didn't want a maid,' Evie went on, 'but Mother insisted, and so he suggested the compromise that I be allowed, within reason, to select my own from the staff.'

'And I'm "within reason"? I'm – was – the lowest of all the servants, and here the shortest length of time too.'

'I told Uncle Jack you'd be perfect, and he didn't take much persuading. He likes you, Lizzy, just as I do. He'd never have given you a ride home in his precious Roller if he didn't.'

'Well, I'm sorry to disagree, but I think he would have.' The words were, once again, out before I'd had time to think.

But again, Evie smiled. 'You see? You have the knack of getting to the point. You're right, of course, Uncle Jack would offer a beggar a lift – and probably buy him dinner into the bargain. And he had only just met you and hadn't had time to form an opinion anyway. But that doesn't change the fact that when we spoke of you again recently, he made his approval quite clear. Funny,' she mused, 'he told us he could sense you had a burning desire to do well. Yes, those were his exact words.'

I choked on a laugh, picturing how he too must have been biting back a grin as he'd said it, but Evie appeared not to notice my reddening face.

'We both had the devil of a job not laughing out loud that day, you know. We managed to hold it in until we had driven away, but it was difficult, let me tell you.' She turned to her wardrobe while I absorbed her words with relief; that sudden stiffness and formality had not been born of shocked anger after all. Laughter bubbled in me then as I pictured Jack's rigid shoulders, and his hands tight on the wheel as he determinedly remained facing front. A burning desire to do well, indeed!

Evie turned back to me, all impatience, and dispelled the image. 'Come along then, I have a party to attend at which I must dazzle everyone. Which means we have preparations to make.'

Before I knew it I was kneeling on a luxuriously soft, deep green circular rug at Evie's feet, teeth clamped on a mouthful of pins. Her chatter had not stopped from the moment she'd pulled me into her room but I still felt a sense of unreality, certain I would wake any moment in my narrow put-me-up bed to find Ruth standing over me, a nasty smile on her face. A pin-prick in the cushion of my thumb finally convinced me I was actually here, and I spat out the pins and sucked the bead of blood away before any of it could be transferred to Evie's light-blue ball gown.

She twisted to see herself in the mirror. 'I feel so grown up,' she said, but she didn't sound as happy about it as I would have expected.

'You are grown up,' I reminded her. 'Eighteen years old now.'

'When are you eighteen, Lizzy?'

'Not for another month. At the end of September.'

'I was born on a Friday, and I'm celebrating my most important birthday on the same day,' she said. 'What day of the week were you born on?'

'Saturday,' I said. 'The twenty-eighth.'

'Fitting,' she observed. 'Saturday's child. You really do work hard for your living. Did you know that originally the rhyme had Thursday's and Saturday's children the other way around?'

'No,' I said, amused at the butterfly mind I was coming to know already.

'I read that somewhere. I wonder if you have far to go as well. Although, interestingly, *Friday's* child used to be "full of woe" instead of Wednesday's, and I'm certainly not that.'

'And how could you be, on such a day?' I said. 'You must be so excited.'

'It's frightening really,' Evie said. 'I think Mother's a little out of sorts about it as well. She's not sure how to talk to me any more, or how much freedom I should have.'

'It must feel strange for her.' I put the final pin in the narrow ribbon of dark-blue velvet. 'Are the two of you close?'

'Not particularly,' my mistress said, twisting the other way. 'She much prefers my little brother Lawrence. That's lovely, thank you. The seamstress did a beautiful job, but I like the tighter fit, and by the time Mother sees it, it will be too late for her to disapprove! Shall I take it off so you can stitch it or is there more to do?'

'Just this bit of lace at the neckline,' I said, standing up. 'If you'll keep still long enough, that is.'

It occurred to me, as Miss Creswell stilled without demur, that I hadn't even flinched after I'd spoken. How quickly we adapt to our new roles in life.

Later, the gown painstakingly stitched to size, I took it back along the landing to Evie's room. Was I supposed actually to dress her or just be there to lend assistance if any were needed? Well, she would soon let me know. This was a situation where we would both be learning as we went and at least I could not be held responsible for my lack of experience. If a young lady chooses a scullery maid to serve her, a scullery maid she gets. It gave me a warm shiver deep inside too, to think that Jack had so readily given his approval to her choice, and I kept remembering Evie's bafflement at his words of recommendation, and smiling even more widely.

There was an air of excitement throughout the whole house. Last night had been busy enough, but tonight was a landmark occasion and Evie was the focus of it, which meant she had to be perfectly presented; anything out of place would be put down to me.

I needn't have worried. Evie seized the gown with a delighted smile and hung it over the door, then sat down at the dressing table and allowed me to dress her hair. She wanted it done simply so she wouldn't have to worry about it during the evening, and that suited me very well. Remembering everything Mary had taught me, I set Evie's blonde curls high, secured with a dozen decorated pins, and finished off with a spray of fine feathers that matched the colour of her new gown.

She stood then, in her heeled shoes, while we puzzled over the layers of corsetry, sorting out between us the order of the undergarments, and laughing as we argued. But when she finally stepped into the circle of the gown on the floor and we pulled it up over her legs, waist and shoulders, the giggling stopped. In silence I fastened the gown at the back, and smoothed the matching silk gloves over her arms, then stepped away.

'How do I look?' Evie said, still smiling, but anxious now.

I could hardly speak. I had begun to forget the differences between us; for a while this afternoon we had simply been two girls of the same age, muddling through together. But now, standing before me in her ball gown with her head high, her long, slender neck bare and awaiting the legendary Kalteng diamond, my mistress was every inch the society lady.

I suddenly felt grubby again, even in my smart new uniform, and was once more aware of the heat beneath my arms, the beads of sweat at my hairline, and my aching fingers, sore from hours of sewing.

'You look beautiful, Miss Creswell.'

'Whatever happened to "Evie"?' she said, a teasing note in her voice. But some of the light had faded from her expression.

'Maybe tomorrow, but tonight you are most definitely Miss Creswell.'

'Lizzy . . .'

'You'll be missed downstairs if we don't hurry things along.' I found a smile for her, and it brought back her own and made me feel better at the sight of it. As long as I didn't let her friendliness fool me into thinking I was more important than I was, I would never have to feel envious of Evie, and this night was hers.

I accompanied her to the top of the stairs, as invisible in my black dress as I'd ever been below stairs. The excitement that had subtly permeated the house earlier now spilled out of every room, and washed over the assembled guests as the new arrivals handed coats and hats to the footmen and Mr Dodsworth, and sought out friends with exclamations of delight.

The entrance hall was filled with vibrant gowns, head-dresses both elegant and outrageous, and vivid waistcoats, according to Evie's pronouncement that there should be as much colour as possible. Jack Carlisle was greeting guests as if he were one of the family, and I noted, rather breathlessly, how well evening clothes suited his tall, strong figure, and how long his legs looked in the impeccably pressed trousers. I had a moment to feel a pang of envy for whichever lucky maid had prepared his clothes for that evening, and then he, along with everyone else, turned to face the stairs as Evie began her descent. Murmurs of surprised approval rose from the guests, and from where I now stood, behind and to the right of my mistress, I could see the curve of her smile. The birthday girl, centre of attention and beautiful, she had every right to smile.

My attention stole back to Jack, and to the pride and pleasure on his face. I couldn't imagine how it would feel to have him look at me like that, and it wouldn't help the tightness in my throat to dwell on it – besides, I still had work to do. As I turned to go to Evie's room I heard her hiss my name, and glanced back. She was standing halfway down the stairs where she could still see me, although no one else could.

'Thank you,' she mouthed, and then she was gone.

100

Chapter 7

I collected Evie's riding clothes and took them downstairs to be brushed or laundered. As I stepped into the service corridor I recognised the figure just ahead of me. 'Mary!'

She turned and smiled. 'Well, well, little Lizzy Parker, how you've soared today!'

'I can still hardly believe it myself. I've just dressed Miss Creswell for her ball and sent her on her way. This morning I was ready to pack my belongings and be away myself.'

'If anyone deserves this chance, it's you,' Mary said. 'You've worked very hard and it hasn't always gone well, but you've not given up. You're meant for higher things, I always knew it.'

I murmured my thanks, suddenly shy in the face of such generosity. 'How is Martha getting on?' I remembered her terrified face, and hoped things were better for her than they had been for me at first.

'Oh, well, Ruth, being in the bad mood she was, behaved in her usual objectionable manner. It was all a bit unpleasant for a while. But Martha turns out to be an exceptional hand with a whisk and has no small talent with an oven.'

'So Ruth needs to look to her laurels.'

'Indeed! So, what did Miss Creswell look like in her ball gown?'

'Absolutely beautiful. The colour suited her so well.'

'Will you be listening to the presentation of the diamond?'

'Of course not, how could I?'

Mary winked. 'The same way as the rest of us. No one minds, providing none of the guests see or hear you. Now, take Miss Creswell's things through, and meet me back here at a quarter to twelve.'

Just before midnight, Mary and I were crouching at the top of the back stairs. Behind us were Emma the second housemaid, and Joe the hall boy, and behind them were Martha Hoskins and Ruth. Their talk was in whispers but I could hear everything that was being said – most of it to do with Evie and her possible suitors now she was 'out' in Society. The constraints on conversation I had observed in the kitchen did not extend to this gathering and Ruth had very little to say that was complimentary, but I was determined not to rise to her baiting.

'Is Mr Carlisle here tonight?' Emma wanted to know. 'I'm sure he would be one of the most eligible bachelors, and as he is well known to the family I should think he—'

'He's far too old, at least thirty-five,' Ruth interrupted. 'He and Lady Creswell are much more of an age.'

'I heard he knows more about Lord Henry's death than he should,' Joe said. His quiet Irish tones were rarely heard downstairs, but here rank had taken a step back and we were just listeners in a stairwell. His calm tone, as much as his words, sent a chill racing through my blood.

'Shut up, Joe!' It was Emma speaking, her voice furious even in a whisper.

'Aye, I'll shut up, but you know there could be truth in it.'

'Don't be absurd,' she said, 'everyone knows Lord Henry died in South Africa.'

'Well, you would believe that,' Ruth said. 'You've had a fancy for Mr Carlisle for years.'

Emma drew in a quick breath, which mercifully hid my own. 'Nonsense,' she said with some heat. 'And you need to stop spreading that sort of gossip as well, Joe. Now hush, or you'll be sent back downstairs.'

'Listen,' Mary said suddenly, and everyone stopped shuffling about and fell silent. From the huge entrance hall, where the guests had gathered, we could hear murmurs and muted clapping, and then a raised voice I recognised at once.

'As you all know, Evangeline was born eighteen years ago in this very house, and I have been privileged to have watched her over the years as she has grown from a harum-scarum headstrong little girl . . .' Jack paused as laughter rippled around the room, then continued, in softer tones '. . . into the graceful, beautiful creature we see in our midst tonight.'

There were murmurs of agreement, and he went on, 'Henry should have been here tonight to make this presentation, but I know he'll be watching from his cloud, bursting with pride and complaining that the wine's the wrong temperature . . .' More laughter, respectfully muted this time.

'But in tribute to his selfless sacrifice I am proud to take his place tonight, and to have been granted the honour of presenting this ...' There were audible gasps of astonishment then. 'The Kalteng Star,' Jack went on, 'discovered in Borneo in 1806 by John Creswell, and upon which the Creswell fortune was built.'

I itched to see it but knew I would at least have the chance later when I helped Evie undress. In the meantime all we could do was listen to the sounds of people moving closer to the diamond, each hoping for a clear view as the chain on which the diamond hung was placed about the Creswell heiress's neck.

'But this is more than an heirloom,' Jack said after a moment. 'It is a symbol of strength and beauty, and a fitting reflection of the spirit of the young lady now wearing it. Ladies and gentlemen, charge your glasses, please. I give you Miss Evangeline Creswell. May she always charm and exasperate in equal proportion.'

'Miss Evangeline Creswell,' echoed the crowd, interspersed with laughter at Evie's audible protest of 'Uncle Jack!'

Mary spoke briskly. 'Right, off with you all, or we're for the high-jump. Lizzy, get away upstairs now. It's been a strange and busy day, and you'll need to be available for Miss Creswell later.'

'Oh, yes,' Ruth said. 'Back you go to your pretty new room and your pretty new life, Lizzy.'

'That'll be Miss Parker to you,' I said, amazed that my voice came out so strongly despite the trembling I felt inside. I heard a gasp and a giggle both at once. I could guess who the former had been, but the latter might have been anyone's. I thought it might have been Martha, and smiled in the darkness of the stairwell; perhaps she wasn't as timid as she'd first seemed and would be able to stand up to Ruth's bullying ways.

Alone in my room, however, the smile soon faded. I lay down, fully clothed on my bed, and turned Joe's words over in my mind. My heart shrank at the certainty I'd heard in the hall boy's voice; he hadn't sounded as if he was merely passing on gossip, though how could he possibly know what had happened in Africa ten years ago? But he didn't seem the type to stir up trouble just for sport, and he'd seemed so certain there was more to Lord Henry's death . . .

The jangling bell pulled me out of what had soon turned into a deep, exhausted sleep filled with images of faceless soldiers and great piles of precious stones. Blearily, not yet sure of my surroundings, I turned my head to locate the source of the sound and saw the bell on the wall emitting its shrill signal. Evie had returned to her room and was summoning me.

I sat up and swung my legs off the bed, surprised to find they had enough strength to carry me out of my room and down the corridor. By the time I reached my mistress's room I was alight with expectation again; now was my chance to see the famous diamond necklace, and I was sure even Ruth would be agog when I described it to the others. Not to mention what Emily and Ma would think when I told them.

I knocked and went in. Evie was sitting at her dressing table pulling the feathers and pins out of her hair, and I moved behind her to help untangle the mess it had become after an evening of energetic dancing. My eyes went straight to the mirror, and to the upper slope of her breast where the Kalteng Star hung. I was so dazzled I could hardly draw breath; no matter how beautiful people said it was, how much it was worth and how prized a possession, nothing had prepared me for the glorious simplicity of it.

A perfect circle, perhaps half the length of my thumb across, it sat flush within a plain gold band, like a pool of water with sunlight rippling across it. Each breath Evie took brought a new combination of light and shadow, the dark, still depths of the stone drawing the eye in as if to discover some ancient secret.

'It's, it's …' I couldn't find the words. Instead I continued drawing the pins from Evie's hair, my gaze constantly drawn back to the liquid beauty of the Kalteng Star.

'I'll tell you what it is, shall I?' Evie said. She reached back and lifted her hair away from her neck, bending forward. 'It's a millstone. Take it off, Lizzy, please. I can't bear to wear it a moment longer.'

Her voice had lost all the girlish excitement of earlier, and she said no more while I fumbled at the catch, with fingers that suddenly felt as thick as Frank Markham's sausages. What on earth could she mean? To be given something so exquisitely breathtaking, quite regardless of its monetary value, and then to wish it away … perhaps she retained a little of the spoiled child within her after all.

I lifted the necklace away and laid it gently on the dressing table in front of her, but she immediately scooped it up and dropped it in the top drawer, which she pushed shut with far more force than was necessary.

'That stone is the cause of more heartache, and sorrow, and more broken relationships than any stupid family arguments or even divorces,' she said. 'I'm supposed to be thrilled, and beg Mother to let me wear it all the time, but the truth is I'm glad

I have to hand it back tomorrow. It can go back in the safe where it belongs, until New Year at least.'

'What a terrible waste.'

'It's not even rightfully mine.'

I wasn't sure if I'd heard correctly. 'Not yours? Then whose is it?'

'It's a long story and I'm too tired tonight, but I'll tell you this much: that stone will not bring happiness. It never has and it never will. I wish I'd been given a motor car instead.'

For a moment my mouth hung open, and Evie laughed, dispelling the gloomy atmosphere. 'Better stop that or you'll catch flies!' She stood up and wriggled her shoulders out of the top of her dress. 'I'm glad it's all over now.'

'But earlier you were so excited.'

She looked wistful as I helped her ease the dress down over her hips to fall at her feet. 'Yes, I was. It was all ahead of me then, an endless night where anything might have happened.'

'And now?'

'Now the night *has* ended. As all nights, however wonderful, eventually must.' She stifled a yawn. 'I don't mean to sound ungrateful. You will come to know me well enough to understand that, I hope. But sometimes all this seems so trivial compared to the real world.'

She stepped out of the silken circle and together we unfastened her corsets, neither of us saying anything. When she was ready for bed, she turned to me. 'I'm telling the absolute truth, Lizzy, when I tell you I wish John Creswell had never set eyes on the Kalteng Star.'

I had no hesitation in believing she was speaking honestly, and before too many months had passed her bleak words had

107

found their harsh echo in my own heart. Beautiful the diamond undoubtedly was, but if it had the power to build fortunes and families, so too could it tear them apart. It could delight, and did, but it could also destroy. And would again.

Chapter 8

After the excitement of Evie's birthday, my own came and went with noticeably less fanfare. But at least there was a package from home with letters from Emily and my mother, and coloured cards from the twins, and I sat on my bed to open it. Amidst regret that my birthday would be spent so far from home, there was delight at my news, and excited suppositions from Emily regarding my new duties.

I smiled and shook my head. She seemed to think it was all parties and giggling together, trying on Evie's clothes and sharing secrets after dark. I'd write to my sister later and put her straight – it was as well she understood what the world of employment was really like, whether as a scullery maid or a lady's maid, and that it wasn't at all as she supposed.

I worked hard for Evie, keeping her room fresh and clean, washing her undergarments and ironing her clothes. I was always on hand to help her dress for family gatherings, clean up after her preparations … and then of course there was the endless mending. Her becoming a young woman seemed to have made no difference to the way she flung herself at life. There were constant tears in dresses or skirts caused by impatient exits from motor cars or train carriages, shoes that required restitching after her seeming inability to walk anywhere at a sedate pace, and holes in coat pockets after she would insist on forcing too much into them rather than carry a bag or purse.

As for sharing secrets, it had happened just once. A week or two after Evie's birthday she had told me something that had obviously been bursting out of her, something she could tell no one else about. Something that weighed heavily on my mind and would not go away.

I had been mending her riding habit, and pushing my needle through the tough material of the jacket had worn deep grooves into my fingers. I stopped to let the soreness ease for a moment, and glanced out of the window down to the driveway, feeling emptiness creep through me; Jack was leaving again, making his farewells as Simon loaded the car. Many people thought it odd that Jack didn't travel with his own servant ... the thought sneaked unbidden into my head that perhaps it was because he had so much to hide, but I pushed the notion away; Joe and his stories had taken up altogether too much of my attention recently. Instead I concentrated on Jack's mannerisms: did he seem eager to be gone, or regretful? More familiar with Evie, or with her mother?

Lady Creswell stepped forward to offer him her cheek, which he duly kissed, but Evie flung herself at him and hugged him tight. I saw him glance at Lady Creswell, and then his arms came around Evie and he kissed the top of her head, which, like mine, barely reached the middle of his chest.

Something unexpected and strong twisted deep inside me at the sight, and I couldn't tear my eyes away from them locked in their tight embrace, utterly innocent yet the bond between them unmistakable. Perhaps it was simply that she missed a father's embrace? But Jack was not her father, and Evie was a woman now ... my heart shrivelled and, from being unable to look away, I suddenly couldn't bear to watch any longer.

When Evie came back upstairs a while later, she came directly to my rooms. Unusual that she should do that, rather than go to her own and ring the bell for me to attend her. I put down the jacket with relief; my fingers felt as if someone had stripped the skin from them.

'I'll be finished with this soon,' I told her, indicating the crumpled riding suit. 'You'll be ready for tomorrow's ride out, don't worry.'

She looked distracted and flushed, and little wonder, but she visibly brightened when I said that. Riding was her favourite pastime ... not least because her mother disapproved of the headlong way she did it.

'Thank you, Lizzy.'

She sat down on my bed, and seemed to come to a decision in that moment, as if removing the weight from her feet had allowed her to release something from her heart. 'Tell me, have you ever loved someone? I don't mean your family, I mean ... well, a man?'

'How do you mean?'

'I don't mean,' she dropped her voice to a whisper, 'not, you know, *loved*, but just ... loved.'

Jack was never far from my thoughts, and he surfaced in

111

them again now, but I shook my head. 'Are you trying to tell me something?' I asked, disconcerted.

'I am in love, and with someone my family would deem completely unsuitable. There!' She smiled with relief. 'I've said it. Out loud, and thankfully to someone who would never breathe a word to anyone. You won't, will you?'

'Of course not!' I assured her, but my heart did that slow twist again. This time it kept twisting, and the pain went all the way through me. I turned away to stare out of the window, feeling the old tightness in the back of my throat that told me tears were all too close. Of all the people I could have borne to see on Jack's arm instead of myself, surely Evie was the best, but it did no good to tell myself that, not when his touch was the one thing I yearned for above all else. Now instead I would have to watch him and Evie growing closer every day.

'So have you?' she persisted.

'Loved someone?'

'Yes!'

I searched my feelings and found the least painful path. 'No, not in that way.' Whatever my racing heart told me when he was near, it was not enough to think of it as love, I knew that much at least. Fascination, undoubtedly. Desire, yes; I had finally accepted the truth of that. But not love. Love was supposed to be glorious and joyful, not leave you with this empty echo of unfulfilled promise. It was certainly not supposed to hurt like this.

'Does this "unsuitable" man love you back?' I asked, somehow keeping my voice steady.

'Yes, he does. He finally told me so yesterday.'

Now I had to walk across the room and pretend to be

searching for something among the mess of my workbasket, just to disguise the way my hands were shaking. 'Why are you smiling so much, if there's no hope for the two of you?' Surely the age gap wasn't that insurmountable? Jack was no more than thirty-five, as Ruth had pointed out.

'Because one day, and I believe it will be soon, things are going to change,' Evie said. She grew serious, a rare occurrence for her, and, as I always did when that sharp intelligence broke through her generally flighty manner, I felt a tiny leap of hope in the pit of my stomach. As if she somehow knew things the rest of us had yet to suspect. It banished, for a moment, the painful thought of helping her dress for her wedding.

'Change?' I ventured.

'Yes! People are starting to think differently, can't you feel it?'

'Differently?'

'Stop repeating what I say, and think about it!' Evie urged. 'People are less concerned about how many buttons they should wear on their coats, and more about who can't afford a coat at all, and why. More about the rest of this enormous world and their place in it. Most of all, how it can be changed for the better.'

'I don't go out in company enough to notice,' I reminded her, 'but I've heard them in the kitchen, talking about votes and suchlike.'

'I'm not just talking about the Suffrage Movement, Lizzy, nor just about women. I'm talking about all of it: society, the way we live ... it's so foolish the way we carry on, and I can feel we're finally learning to stop clinging on to a way of life that's dying.'

'And you're sure that's good?' The tingle of hope in me faded; this sounded a bit frightening.

'It's good because people are starting to make their own

choices,' Evie said. 'They're not going to be bound for ever by the way things have always been. And that means freedom from the stupid rules we live by every day of our lives, an end to accepting it all without question.'

'Like whether or not someone is "unsuitable",' I said, sensing her need to get back to her original point.

'Exactly!'

'Well, let's hope it happens before ...' I didn't finish my sentence: *before he gets too old to be a proper husband to you.*

'Before what?'

'Nothing. I wish you all the best, Evie,' I said, and bent to pick up the riding jacket, adopting a brisk tone. 'Now, if you're not going to tell me any more about your mystery man, I should continue with this.'

'Yes, of course,' she said, getting up to leave. 'Perhaps you could draw me a bath when you've finished?' She paused at the door to look at me, and her serious expression was back. 'This isn't a passing fancy,' she said, and I remembered the embrace by the car and understood.

After she left I sat still, not sewing at all, playing over and over in my head the sight of Jack and Evie locked together, and wishing I could be happy for them. They deserved that much, at least.

The evening of my birthday brought a surprise in the form of a gift from Evie. She waited until I had laid out her clothes for the morning, and then reached under her pillow.

'Happy birthday, Just Lizzy,' she said, holding out a parcel wrapped in the finest paper I had ever seen.

Stunned, I stared at her, and it was a moment before I found my voice. 'You got me a gift?' I stammered. 'But I'm only ... Evie, I—'

'Just take it!' she laughed.

I did. It was soft, and as my shaking fingers closed on the paper it tore a little bit and I could see beyond the tear to a piece of dark-blue material.

'Go on then, you might as well tear the paper right off now,' Evie urged. I could see from the way her eyes stayed on my face that she was as eager for my reaction as I was to see what the parcel held. I was content to stare at the paper for a moment, though: silver and blue stars on a background of blue and silver stripes, all topped off with a silver ribbon tied into an intricate bow. Evie was many things but she was not artistic, this must have taken her hours.

At her impatient urging I turned the parcel over and pulled at the ribbon securing it. It fell open and I caught at the object within, holding it up with a gasp of pleasure.

It was a stole of dark-blue velvet, heavy and soft with a faint smell of rosewater lingering about it. Before I could put it on Evie had seized it and draped it around my shoulders, then turned me to face the mirror. I blinked twice – the first time was to clear the tears that clouded my vision, the second to reassure myself I had done so, and that my eyes were not playing a trick on me – then I stared at my reflection, unable to find any words.

Evie had no such problem. 'Mary Elizabeth Parker, you are quite the young lady,' she said, and smiled. 'You're so pretty, much prettier than you think. The colour of the velvet makes your eyes look even bluer, and your hair was made to rest on something this lovely.' So saying she unpinned my cap and removed it, letting my hair tumble to my shoulders.

'Evie,' I managed at last, in barely a whisper. 'I can't, I don't—'

'You can and you will,' she said. 'Today is a special day for you, you're a woman now. And I hope you will find the love of a good man someday, and that you'll be able to tell people of it, and celebrate it.'

Her voice had turned sad, and I pulled my gaze away from the hypnotising image of myself and, without thinking, threw my arms around her neck, hugging her tight.

Immediately I had done so I drew back, appalled at what I'd done, but she reached out and took my hand, as if it weren't blistered and coarse, as if it hadn't just that afternoon been scrubbing down the bath. As if it were the hand of a true friend.

'You must forgive my little bouts of melancholy,' she said, 'it's just that I miss seeing him. It's hard for us. He can't be here as often as he'd like, and when he is, he has other business to attend to, other people to see.'

'How do you manage to spend any time alone with him, with so many people around all the time?'

'He has duties that often see us in the same place at the same time. Purely by chance, of course,' she said with a little, inward-turned smile. I felt a surge of embarrassed guilt: of course, he'd picked her up from the station after her time in London, and who else had been there spoiling things for them then?

'Still, it must be so hard for you,' I said. 'And for him as well, of course.' I imagined Jack would have many women eager for his attention although it didn't seem fair, or necessary, to voice the thought. 'I don't know what to say about this gift,' I said instead. 'Thank you hardly seems to be enough.'

'Enjoy it, you deserve it.' Evie gestured towards her night clothes. 'Help me get changed now, if you wouldn't mind, and then you can finish for the night. Oh, and I believe your friend Mary has a card for you too.'

'You spoke to Mary?'

Evie winked. 'I speak to all the staff, but don't tell Mother.'

'Oh, I intend to go to Lady Creswell this very minute and inform her of your insupportable behaviour,' I said, rolling my eyes.

This time she laughed outright, and as I prepared myself for bed a little later, the card Mary had made sitting alongside those from my family, I revised what I had been going to say to Emily: working for any other girl my own age might have been as demanding and dull as working for her mother, but Evie Creswell wasn't just any other girl.

The following morning I found myself in the hallway at the back of the house, searching for Joe Shackleton; Evie's riding boots were in need of cleaning before she went out and he was nowhere to be found.

As I glanced around with growing impatience, the outer door opened and Frank Markham stepped in. He shot me a glare for which I couldn't fathom the reason, until I remembered I'd taken the job he'd wanted for Ruth. I raised my chin and scowled back at him, and he abruptly turned towards the kitchen, but not before I'd seen the corners of his mouth lift. That hint of a smile, though suppressed, was gratifying, but I had more important considerations at the moment. Where *was* Joe? I let loose a word that would shame a sailor.

'Well,' a familiar voice said, 'such language! And you an upper servant as well.'

I turned to see Will Davies standing in the doorway, a large box balanced on one shoulder. He grinned and eased his way past me with the delivery. 'Happy birthday for yesterday, by the way.'

I couldn't work out how he knew, then remembered he would have seen Mary. How nice that he should have asked after me. 'Thank you,' I said, accepting a kiss on the cheek. 'And how are you?'

'Ticking along nicely.' But something about the way he said it made me peer at him more closely; the smile was there but he looked tired.

'You look as though you'd benefit from a few days off,' I observed.

'Tell that to Mr Markham.'

My ferocious glare in the direction his employer had taken seemed to bring back some of the light that had been missing from his expression and Will chuckled. 'Not in the best of moods today, then?'

'I'm not normally this bad. I just can't seem to find Joe anywhere, and he has work to do.'

He gestured at the boots in my hand. 'Is Miss Creswell riding out today?'

'She will be if I can get these cleaned. I don't want to upset her so soon after I've begun the job.'

'Give them to me, I'll do them. Can't have you getting into trouble, can we?'

'Are you sure?' I said, hoping there was enough gratitude in my voice to hold him to his offer.

'Absolutely. This is my last job for today, I get Sunday afternoons off. Where does Joe work?'

I pointed to the room off the scullery, where the hall boy had put the family's shoes ready for cleaning. 'In there, the rags and everything are all laid out ready.'

'Right. Just let me take this through to the kitchen,' he patted the box on his shoulder, 'and I'll get to work. Put the boots on the table and get back to your mistress, I'll leave them here in the hall when they're done.'

'Thank you so much, Will,' I said, relieved.

He grinned. 'Call it a late birthday present.'

On my way back up the stairs, I saw Mary.

'You're looking a bit pleased with yourself,' she said. 'What's to do?'

'Nothing really, only I thought I was going to have to let Miss Creswell down but Will stepped in and offered to help.'

'Ah. Nice of him.'

'He said it was a late birthday present,' I said, 'so it's thanks to you actually, for telling him.'

'I haven't seen Will for a good few days,' Mary said, 'and I'm sure I didn't mention it when I did see him. Someone else must have told him.'

I frowned. 'No one else knew. Well, except Miss Creswell, of course.'

We stared at each other in silence for a minute, then Mary took a deep breath. 'We can't take that to mean anything.'

'No.' But everything Evie had told me came back into my mind, one phrase at a time until it all clicked neatly into place.

'She meets him when she's out riding,' I said, working it out as I spoke.

'Lizzy! You can't—'

'It's obvious! Oh, and that's why ...' My words trailed away as more occurred to me.

'That's why what?'

'When Ruth thought she was chosen for this job, Will looked quite shocked, even upset. I thought it was because he had feelings for her and that he was disappointed he wouldn't be seeing her every day any more. But it was because he already knew it was supposed to have been me! Only one person could have told him that. He asked me if she was going riding today, his afternoon off as it so happens, and then offered to clean her boots to ensure she would be!'

Mary glanced over her shoulder, but we were alone on the stairs. 'You can't possibly say anything to anyone else about this,' she warned.

'I won't.' It was too romantic for words, I wouldn't have spoiled it for anything.

It wasn't until I left her and continued to my rooms that the other truth hit me. My heart did a quick double-thump, and no matter how much I told myself it made no difference, that Jack Carlisle was still as far removed from me as the stars, the tingle of something unexpected and sweet started low in my belly and sent silver wires up through my chest. He did not belong to Evie as I'd assumed. Relief swept through me, along with the realisation that I'd been wrong about something else too: fascination and desire aside, I did love him after all.

Chapter 9

I hadn't intended to say anything to Evie about Will. It was meant to be my warm little secret to enjoy when I heard her nonchalantly ask each Sunday afternoon if her riding boots were clean, or her jacket mended. But, as it always has done, my mouth eventually took charge.

I did manage to avoid letting anything slip for a month, but on the penultimate day of October I'd been unable to help myself. I'd been downstairs taking dinner and we hadn't yet retired for dessert so, as usual, I was half-listening to the pleasant drone of Mr Dodsworth's voice as he held forth. But today the rest of my attention was on the scullery, where Ruth and Martha were watching over the family's lunch as they ate. The subject had turned to All Hallows, and Martha was becoming visibly upset by Ruth's insistence that the Manor was haunted.

'And of course you know who'd have a restless spirit, what with him dying so young and all?'

'No, who?'

Ruth's voice dropped to a sinister note. 'Lord Henry, of course. Some say he was killed in cold blood, in't that right, Joe?'

He was passing through on his way to the hallway. 'You both know what I think,' he said, and I shivered but at the same time the thought of Jack made my heart beat a little faster. How would I feel if it turned out he had killed Lord Henry after all?

'There's no proof, though,' Martha said. 'And anyway, even if he *was* murdered, it happened over in Africa.'

'No distance at all to the determined spirit,' Ruth pointed out. 'After all, he don't have to book no place on a ship, nor wait for the tides. And he's got no feet to wear out with walking.'

'But why would he come back?'

'To avenge himself, of course. To tell his family to find out who done him in, and see justice done. He's been heard, in the hallways late at night, a full-grown man weeping like a child.'

I knew she was only trying to scare the girl, but I still felt my throat go tight at the thought of a desperate spirit trying to communicate with those he had loved. As a result, I found myself choking. A firm hand clapped me on the back and I looked up through streaming eyes, to see Mr Dodsworth frowning at me.

'Are you all right, Miss Parker?'

I nodded and wiped my eyes on my napkin. In consequence I missed a good part of the conversation next door while I was showered with advice about chewing my food twenty times before swallowing.

When Mrs Cavendish and the others slid back into their

own discussions, I turned my attention back to the scullery, alerted by the sound of soft sobbing. Martha had her back turned to the main kitchen but I could see her shoulders hitching, while Ruth mopped up the last of the gravy with a hunk of bread.

I heard the scrape of my chair going back before I realised I had risen, and was in the scullery in a few steps, glaring at Ruth. 'Why do you have to be so spiteful?'

Her eyes widened and her gaze slipped past me to where the others were finishing dinner. I followed her line of sight, and the glower on Mrs Cavendish's face was enough to cool my temper. Still, it seemed Ruth would be well advised to stop baiting Martha, for the time being at least.

Instead of going back in to finish my lunch and be berated by the housekeeper, I went out through the back door and sat on the old milk churn. I really should learn to keep out of things that didn't concern me; I felt sorry for Martha but if I kept acting without thinking I was going to lose my own job.

I took a few deep breaths and gradually calmed down. It was time to attend to Evie's ironing while she was at lunch, and the thought of being alone in my light, airy workroom calmed me even further. On rising, however, I came face to face with Ruth, her expression one of absolute fury.

'You've got the devil of a nerve,' she hissed. 'How dare you talk to me like that in front of the scullion?'

I raised my eyes to the window above me and cocked an eyebrow; no doubt every word we spoke would be overheard, deliberately or otherwise. Then I took a few steps away and she followed, plainly as keen to settle this as I was.

'Why don't you just leave her alone?' I said. 'You know she has to go through the corridors alone at night.'

'What's it got to do with you?'

'She's terrified!'

'Look, just because you get to wash Miss Creswell's underthings now, don't make you better than me. And you swannin' in here every day like some little princess . . .' She jerked her head towards the kitchen. 'They laugh at you and all your new airs, d'you know that?'

'I don't care.'

But I did, and it hurt for a moment, until I remembered to whom I was talking and that it probably wasn't true, and then I smiled. That only infuriated Ruth further, and before I could move away her hand had shot out to pinch the back of mine. It was a schoolyard gesture, and I jerked my hand back in astonishment.

Then a laugh slipped out. 'You're just a pathetic little bully!'

'Pathetic, is it?' Ruth said, and this time it was her boot that she led with, connecting smartly with my shin. My temper boiled and I slapped her hard across the face. Her cap slipped, and a bright red mark appeared on her cheek, and the next thing I knew we were grappling, there in the yard. Months of dislike, jealousy and mistrust had finally spilled over, and we each struggled for the upper hand, grunting as we tried to keep anyone from hearing us.

All at once I felt myself pulled backwards and lost my footing, slipping on the wet ground. I glanced over to see Ruth had been flung aside to land face down in the mud. Behind her stood Frank Markham, and I twisted my head to see Will standing over me, not bothering to hide a wide grin.

Frank, on the other hand, looked as though he would have liked to plant his boot in Ruth's behind where she lay, raised on her elbows, glaring up at him. I bit back another laugh as Will helped me up. Such an absurd situation to have been found in, but at least it was by friend rather than foe.

'You'd better not let anyone see you two wrestling out here,' he said.

'Well, she started it, the spiteful little wretch!' I watched Frank helping Ruth to her feet. He held her by the arms to prevent her from lunging straight at me, which was clearly her intention judging from the scowl on her face, and his gaze travelled across the yard to rest on my face. Safely above Ruth's line of sight, he winked at me and I looked away before I could be surprised into smiling.

Will took my arm and steered me away towards the far end of the kitchen yard, leaving Frank to sort out Ruth. 'Lucky we came along when we did,' he pointed out as he watched me rub in vain at the mud on my skirts.

'I'd have shown her a—'

'Lizzy!'

'Well, will you watch out for poor Martha when you can?' I pleaded. 'Ruth's been scaring the life out of her with talk of ghosts and ghouls.'

'It's just All Hallows fun,' Will protested.

'No, it isn't, it's cruel,' I said, growing angry again. 'I'll tell you this, Will Davies, if I hear—'

'All right! I'll watch out for her, don't worry. And Frank will see that Ruth behaves herself, at least for a while, although she's a hot-head, that one.' He raised an eyebrow as he grinned at me. 'No less are you, by the looks of things. Anyway, to change the subject,' he went on hurriedly as he saw my expression, 'how are you getting along in your new job? Your mistress treating you well?'

'Of course she is, you know Evie . . .' I stopped and smiled at him. 'You couldn't resist asking me about her, could you?' He went pale and checked over his shoulder. 'Don't worry,' I told him, 'they've gone.' Will relaxed until I added '. . . into the outhouse', and then he shuddered, making me laugh.

'How long have you known?' he asked. 'Did she tell you right away?'

'She doesn't even know I've worked it out.'

'Then how did you?'

I told him about my first suspicion, when he'd acknowledged my birthday, and then how it had all clicked into place. He grinned when I told him how eager Evie always was to go riding, and his face softened when I told him of the glow in her eyes each time she returned.

'It's hopeless,' he said, 'but you know how she is.'

'She doesn't think it's hopeless,' I reminded him.

'No, she doesn't. And that's what's so incredible. She has all this,' he waved a hand, 'and I'm not even a fully fledged tradesman yet, but she's determined that everything will work out.'

'Do you think she's right?'

He sighed. 'When I'm with her I believe everything she says. If she told me the railway from Breckenhall to London was made out of liquorice, I'd just ask how it tastes.'

'And when you're not with her?' But I already knew what he'd say.

'I *want* to believe her. I wish I could.'

'Don't give up, Will,' I urged.

'Oh, don't worry, I won't. If anyone's worth the uncertainty and the hope, it's Evie.'

'Good!' I shook out my skirts and straightened my apron. 'I'd better get back to her. Do you have any messages?'

'You're going to tell her?'

'I think that's best, don't you? My mouth doesn't seem capable of keeping this one quiet, and if anyone's going to find themselves in the way of it, better it should be the two of you.'

'Very true. Just say . . .' He considered a moment. 'Just tell her I look forward to the next time she rides out.'

He squeezed my arm then pushed past me and crossed the yard, picking up the box he'd dropped in his attempt to stop me from killing Ruth. As I followed him I glanced at the outhouse, remembered his theatrical shudder, and smiled.

Evie's face went as white as Will's had when I told her, and for a moment she couldn't speak. But when I'd convinced her I could be trusted with her secret, she let out a huge sigh of relief. 'You've no idea how good it feels to be able to talk to someone about him at last.'

'Feel free to talk as much as you like,' I said, envious that I was unable to do the same thing. Jack had begun haunting my dreams and waking moments alike; the more I learned of him, his hard-working past and his unquenched grief at Lord Henry's loss, and the more I came to know him through Evie's eyes as well as my own, the more I acknowledged that I had warmed to more than just his physical appeal. It was utterly hopeless, of course, but each time we met I was finding it harder and harder to hide my fascination with his every word and opinion, and often challenged him without thinking. When it was just the three of us our conversations became lively and interesting, and often political, with both Jack and Evie listening to me as an equal, and I learned a great deal more than I would have if I'd kept silent.

During those times, often as we sat in the garden despite the general wetness of the summer, I watched Jack closely and was coming to understand what drew me so completely under his spell; tousled good looks notwithstanding, his manner relaxed utterly when the eyes of the household were off him. He laughed often and freely then, sometimes letting himself go with a great belly laugh that seemed to surprise him as much as it did me.

Now and again during our more intense discussions his eyes would rest on me and his expression would turn faintly speculative, but a remark from Evie would snag his attention again and he'd be off, reminding her that he was far more in touch with the way government worked than she was, as well as with the way its policies were viewed by the lower classes. He seemed at first to expect me to capitulate to his every opinion, given our shared background, but had quickly learned that I needed to be convinced first and that I refused to agree blindly with whatever he said until he had done so.

'The Liberal Welfare Reforms are going to change workers' lives,' he insisted one Sunday morning. 'Lloyd George knows what he's doing, Evie, and your higher taxes are going to make for a more equal Britain.'

'It's not the higher taxes that trouble me,' she said, 'you know that. I'm worried that these measures will not in fact be

129

enough, but will be viewed as such by those who remain unaware of their limitations.'

'Absolutely,' I said. 'The reforms sound wonderful, but perhaps they're just a way of keeping the masses quiet?'

'Quite!' Evie agreed, and we both turned to Jack, who shook his head in exasperation.

'You can't expect reform to happen overnight,' he said, eyes going from one to the other of us with, I was glad to see, no discernible difference in expression. 'And the act for unemployment insurance has been passed now, and that will go a long way towards helping "the masses", as you call them. Which reminds me, Evie. Before you distracted me, your mother actually sent me to tell you it was time for church.'

I rose to accompany her back to the house. Jack stood up too and, for a brief, heart-stopping moment our hands brushed together. We both jerked back as if stung, and as I looked up I saw a fleeting frown touch his features; it seemed almost as if he were in pain. I know I was.

Those discussions were the highlights of my days. I spent a good deal of my spare time talking to Mary and building upon my scant knowledge of the government's policies, so as not to seem foolish in front of either Evie or Jack. When it was just the three of us we would happily argue for hours, but I had to be careful not to forget myself in front of others.

I found myself smiling at the memory of the last time I had done just that: Mr Dodsworth had been quietly setting the table for breakfast, and Evie had asked me for her wrap, ready for an evening out with her mother, Jack and some friends.

When I'd come back downstairs with the wrap, Jack was growing hot under the collar about the Marconi scandal, which was rumbling on, and about which Mary had lectured me in the kind of detail born of outraged sensibilities. Evie had taken the opportunity, as usual, to test Jack's conviction that the government was beyond reproach in the matter.

'Honestly, Uncle Jack, everyone's saying it. They *must* have known the government was going to support the British arm of the company, or why buy so heavily into the American one?'

'Asquith had no part in it,' Jack said firmly. 'There was no inside knowledge when the ministers bought those shares.'

'Even though the Attorney General's brother was running the company?' I'd retorted then, and froze.

Mr Dodsworth had dropped a side-plate in shock, Evie had seized the wrap and buried her face in it, and Jack had suddenly found an interesting fleck of dust on the cuff of his coat sleeve. I'd quickly obeyed Mr Dodsworth's frantic signals for me to apologise immediately and withdraw from the room while he did the same, taking the broken plate with him. I never did discover what Jack thought the Attorney General's brother might have been up to.

'. . . in the yard?'

I started, struggling back to the present. What had we been talking about? Evie was looking at me with a question clear on her face, and I tried to recapture what she might have said but it was no good. 'I'm sorry, what was that?'

'I was asking what you were doing out in the yard? When you saw Will,' she clarified.

I told her about following Ruth, and then, knowing Will would tell her anyway, went on to confess the tussle we'd had.

By the end of the tale I knew I needn't have worried; she was outraged, certainly, but not with me.

'That poor little girl! And she's only been here a month.'

'I know, Ruth really frightened her,' I said, growing cross all over again.

Evie kept her gaze on mine for a moment but her focus had gone far beyond me. 'Well then, I think Miss Wilkins might be due a little fright of her own.'

It was on my lips to ask what on earth Evie was cooking up now, but the mixture of wickedness and anticipation in her expression told me I wouldn't have to wait long to find out.

Chapter 10

Later that evening I was in my workroom, my mind flitting happily from thoughts of home to Oaklands and, inevitably, Jack, when the door opened and Evie poked her head around.

'Lizzy...'

'Evie! What are you—'

She glanced over her shoulder then came into the room and shut the door. 'Are you terribly busy, or might you be able to spare an hour?'

I held up the skirt I was re-hemming. 'I'll have to let you decide. Will you be wanting this in the next two hours?'

'Oh, pfft!' She waved it away. 'Come with me, but make sure you're not seen by anyone. Anyone at all, do you understand?'

'Of course, but why?'

'Just come with me. And bring that.' She pointed at my workbasket.

*

I followed her downstairs, Evie checking ahead to make sure the way was clear. I tagged along behind her, bemused but enjoying myself ... until I found we were in the long corridor at the end of which stood the spare linen room. My heart thumped uncomfortably and I rubbed my fingertips against my skirt as I remembered trying to clean them with my apron. The thought flashed through my mind that perhaps Jack hadn't been able to remove the burned linen after all.

I prayed Evie would stop at one of the first two doors but we kept going, past ornately carved lintels and more paintings. It seemed a shame that such beautiful artwork was largely ignored down here, accompanied only by the dusty smell of disuse, but even that wasn't enough to tear my mind away from the possibility that Evie knew what had happened. She and Jack were close, and he had found the situation – that part of it at least – quite amusing, but still this was Evie's house, not his, and even she would have her limits.

It was with a mixture of dismay and relief that I realised we had stopped outside the third door and Evie took a key from her pocket. 'This is Father's study. No one uses it any more.'

I couldn't admit I knew quite well which room it was, and that someone most certainly *was* using it, and quite recently. 'Why are we here then?' I asked instead.

Her eyes gleamed in the dim light from the hall lamp. 'I'm going to ask Mother if I can have it for my own private study.'

Relief poured over me. 'So you'd like me to clean it up? Mend the curtains?' I gestured at the basket over my arm.

'Oh, no, I'm going to ask someone else to clean it up. And I don't know if they need mending anyway.'

'Then why—'

'Shhh! Come on.' She unlocked the door and ushered me inside, then locked it again behind us. It was pitch-black in the study and I stood very still for fear of bumping into something and causing damage.

There was a hiss, and a flare of light lit Evie's face, rather eerily, as she held up a match. 'This is the last part of the house without proper gas light yet,' she said. 'Father wouldn't hear of it. I think Grandmother Edith managed to pass on her own fears to him, much to Mother's annoyance.' She touched the head of the match to the wick of a paraffin lamp on the table, and a dim glow filled the room, allowing me to look around.

Nothing appeared to have been touched since the last time I was here. With a little ache in my heart I glanced at the two chairs by the dark, empty fireplace, and turned quickly away to look at the room as a whole; apart from the whisky bottle and the two tumblers, now cleaned, there were only one or two other small items to indicate someone had spent any time here. I looked for the picture of Jack and Lord Henry, but it was gone, and I remembered that small, wrapped package I'd seen at the foot of Henry's tree. The ache inside me intensified.

One thing I did notice for the first time was a collection of leather boxes in the corner, criss-crossed tightly with canvas bindings.

Evie followed my glance. 'Father's papers,' she said. 'Mother has no idea what to do with them, even after all this time. Uncle Jack has offered to go through them for her but she still can't bring herself to agree.'

'How are you about ... well, about your father's death?' I asked, curious; she never mentioned him.

Evie shrugged. 'I miss him sometimes, but even when he was alive we didn't see him very much. I have no real memories beyond him coming home, usually with friends, and there being lots of parties we weren't allowed to attend.'

'That's a terrible shame,' I said. My memories of my own father probably numbered only a few more than hers; he'd worked such long days and I was almost always asleep by the time he came home. But those I had were filled with warmth, and a deep regret that I would never be able to tell him of the unexpected happiness I'd found in my work. I hoped he knew, somehow.

I shook off the melancholy thoughts, and instead concentrated on my relief that the escapade with the laundry remained undiscovered.

'Evie, what are we doing here?'

She lifted the basket off my arm and carried it to the table so the light from the lamp fell full on to it. 'We,' she said, hunting about in its contents, 'are going to teach Miss Ruth Wilkins a little lesson.'

'We're what?' I was at once thrilled and horrified. 'We can't! I'll get into awful trouble if anyone finds—'

'They won't,' Evie interrupted. Leaving the basket, she went over to the window and pulled back the curtain a little bit. A second later my heart slammed painfully against my ribs: a man's silhouette had appeared outside the French window, the outline clearly that of a soldier. Just before the scream tore loose I realised it was Will Davies, and I let my breath out, shaky and thin.

Then he waved, and the last of the shock ebbed away as Evie waved back and pushed open the window. After a glance behind him, Will stepped into the room and Evie quickly jerked the curtains back in place. The three of us were finally standing together, for the first time in one place, and I felt a surge of happiness suddenly, as if we were family reunited. The urge to throw my arms around the two of them was almost too much for me so I stepped away instead, folded my arms, and frowned at them both.

'You do realise if someone comes in, or sees the light from out there, we will *all* be in trouble?' I said.

'I know,' Evie smiled, 'isn't it delicious?'

'You're barmy.' Will grinned at her, and as I tried to maintain my disapproval Evie's hand stole into his, and his fingers folded around hers, and I gave up and shook my head, smiling too.

Evie explained her idea. 'We'll tie a piece of thread to the middle of one of the curtains and run it back up to the top . . . secure it with pins along here,' she traced an imaginary line, following the top of the wall until it came to the door, 'and then down, over the door and out into the corridor. Do you have something thin but quite strong in there?' She nodded at my basket.

'I expect so, but—'

'I'm just coming to that,' she shushed me. 'I'm going to ask Ruth to give the room a good dusting tomorrow evening. Ready for me to move in, you see?'

I was beginning to. 'And you're going to arrange for a little surprise from beyond the grave?'

She laughed. 'Isn't *that* delicious!'

'But Lizzy recognised me straight away,' Will pointed out, 'so Ruth will too. And she mustn't see the thread either. Or the

137

pins.' Part of me wished he would manage to persuade Evie it couldn't work, but she was not so easily put off.

'Hmm, yes. Well, we'll just have to trim the wick of the lamp down so there's less light,' Evie said. 'Lizzy, you'll keep watch from down the corridor, maybe tucked into the doorway of the spare linen room next door' – I hoped my blush didn't show as she said that – 'then move into place outside the door as soon as I close it. I'll be in here with Ruth, feeding her imagination until you jerk the curtain aside, just a tiny bit, and Will does his turn. *Then* we'll see who ends up scared to walk the corridors at night.'

It did sound simple, and remembering how my heart had leaped at the sight of Will in that uniform, it would be effective as well.

He clapped his hands together. 'Right! How long should I stay there?'

'Just long enough for her to see you, then I'll distract her while you disappear again. Lizzy can let the curtain fall back and you must return to the summer house and change out of Father's things. We don't want to risk anyone else seeing you, particularly if Ruth screams.'

'Which you hope she will,' I guessed.

Evie's smile became a wicked grin. 'Oh, well, I wouldn't want to scare her *too* much,' she said. 'That would just be mean.'

In the end it went almost perfectly. The following evening Evie asked Mrs Cavendish if she could spare Ruth for half an hour to help out, and a curious but pleased Ruth accompanied her along the corridor to the old study. I was watching from along the hall, unseen or overlooked, it didn't matter which. If Ruth saw me she would simply assume I was working.

Evie played her part perfectly, adopting a shy tone to make her request. 'Mother has said I can have the study now, so I hoped you might help me by doing a little dusting?'

'Of course, Miss Creswell,' Ruth said, bobbing her head and making me snort into my sleeve.

'Thank you so much, Ruth. I'll just show you what I'd like you to do.' Evie gave a little shiver. 'Does it feel cold to you down here?'

'No, miss, not especially. Perhaps there's a window open somewhere?'

'It wasn't a draught, more like an icy sort of a chill. Maybe it's because it's All Hallows Eve.' Evie added a laugh that struck just the right balance between embarrassment and not-quite-convinced dismissal, and I was lost in admiration.

'Oh, I don't believe in ghosts,' Ruth assured her.

'Gosh, don't you? I do.' Evie unlocked the door and led the way into the room. The moment the door clicked shut, I left my hiding place and hurried to take hold of the piece of string we'd tied in place last night. I carefully released it from where it had been wound around a picture hook, listening out for my cue from inside the room.

'There's not much light for workin', Miss Creswell,' Ruth was saying.

'I know. Perhaps later on you can ask Joe to replace the wick. I hope to persuade Mother to put a proper light in here now I'm to use the room.' Evie paused, and then added, 'Mind you, Father would probably turn in his grave. He hated the thought of it.'

'Still, he won't know now, will he?'

I rolled my eyes at the crassness of Ruth's comment, but it stiffened my resolve and I gripped the string more tightly.

Evie's voice took on a wistful tone. 'There has been talk lately of his spirit walking the corridors at night. Perhaps you've heard it?' Ruth, wide-eyed innocence no doubt sitting uncomfortably on her face, must have shaken her head because Evie went on, 'Well, idle gossip no doubt, but actually, as odd as it sounds, I like to think there may be some truth in it. And this room was so important to him, I'm sure there must be unfinished business of his here.'

That was my cue. As hard as I could, I pulled down on the string, seeing in my mind's eye the way it would pull tight up the door, across the ceiling and down the heavy curtain.

There was a gasp, a loud one, from inside the room, and Ruth said in a trembling voice, 'The curtain moved!' Then she gave a wordless shriek and I buried my face in the crook of my elbow.

Evie sounded concerned. 'Ruth, whatever's the matter ... oh, did I knock you? I'm sorry.'

I immediately let go of the string, allowing the curtain to fall back into place while Ruth was distracted. I could hardly believe it had worked so smoothly.

'Tell me,' Evie urged, 'what did you see?'

'There was a man outside, in the garden ... Miss Creswell, don't go over there!'

I heard Evie open the window. 'But look, there's nothing there!'

'Not now there in't, but I swear there was! Dressed up like a soldier an' everything, he was!'

140

'Oh, Ruth!' Evie injected a note of mingled hope and fear into her voice. 'Do you think ... maybe you saw my father?'

'Now wouldn't *that* be something?' The voice in my ear was so close I almost screamed myself, and I whirled around to see Jack Carlisle leaning on the wall beside me.

Chapter 11

His breath fanned my face, and the feelings that rushed through me at that moment were so complex they made me dizzy; there was shock, certainly, quickly followed by tingling warmth, and then terror at being caught . . . along with mortification that, of all people, he should have been the one to catch me.

Jack held a finger to his lips, then grabbed my arm, pulling me the few steps to the linen room and into the deep doorway, standing between me and the corridor.

'Liz . . . Miss Parker, I have no idea what on earth you and Miss Creswell are up to with Ruth,' he looked back towards the study, 'but that little madam is going to be out of there in about ten seconds, and *not* in the sunniest of moods.'

Sure enough the door crashed open, and Jack assumed an air of deep interest in the picture beside his head. I dimly guessed that Ruth had come out, seen him, and hurried off in the opposite direction, but pressed back against the closed door with Jack's body blocking out the rest of the world, I could think of nothing except how it would feel to reach out and trace that glorious jawline to where it met the high collar of his shirt, and then to place my lips against the lightly tanned skin there and feel his pulse match my own.

He looked down at me, and now there was a strange expression on his face. Not anger, thank God not that, but the humour had left his eyes. Then the study door slammed again, and the moment was shattered as Evie saw him and groaned.

'It was just a joke, Uncle Jack. No harm done. Have you seen—'

'She's here,' he said, and took my hand, drawing me out of my hiding place only slightly more gently than he had put me there. 'What in blazes are you two playing at?'

'Nothing terrible,' Evie reiterated. 'And before you go giving Lizzy a telling off, she was only acting under orders.'

'So I imagine.' He became aware he was still holding my hand and let go, but I could feel the warmth of it on my skin regardless.

'Evie, you really must think things through,' Jack said, exasperated. 'Lizzy isn't here to indulge you in your childish pranks.'

'Childish?' she said, affronted, 'I'll have you know it was meticulously planned and executed to perfection.'

'Ruth was being cruel to one of the younger girls yesterday,' I put in. 'And I told Evie about it.'

'And Evie became the great protector,' Jack said. 'Of course, it would have been out of the question for you to take the offender aside and discipline her in the accepted manner.' Evie's eyes met mine and quickly slid away as both our mouths twitched.

Jack saw it and shook his head. He sounded resigned when he spoke. 'Look, both of you, I'm not going to tell anyone about this. That Ruth girl always struck me as a bit of a trouble-maker and I imagine you had your reasons. But I must insist you keep back to your wing of the house now, and don't go skulking around down here.'

'What are you doing here anyway, Uncle Jack?' Evie said suddenly. 'Mother isn't expecting you until tomorrow.'

'Lucky for Lizzy I *was* here,' he said. 'Another few seconds and Ruth would have walked right into her.'

'That would have been awkward,' Evie acknowledged. 'Come on, Lizzy, we need to take down the string before Ruth brings someone back for a ghost-hunt.'

'I'll do it, you go back to your rooms,' Jack said, and I realised he hadn't answered her; what *had* he been doing here? Particularly if Lady Creswell didn't know. And why had he been anywhere near Lord Henry's study at all? Those dark-blue eyes met mine again, their depths suddenly more dangerous than mysterious. Then he blinked slowly and smiled, and the illusion vanished.

I cast a glance back at the doorway as I followed Evie up the corridor, but even as Jack's form dwindled into the distance the smile stayed in the forefront of my mind, eclipsing the questions and the unsettling sense that he was hiding something from me. At least for now.

At the beginning of December Evie suggested a trip into Breckenhall, and arranged for Simon to drive us. Excited to be going out, and even more excited to be in a car again, I dressed carefully for the outing. While I was reaching for my warm scarf, my glance fell instead on my stole. Usually it lay across my feet as I slept, its weight comforting during the cold nights, but it was good to lift it off my bed and tuck it around my shoulders today.

Remembering Evie's words on my birthday, I looked in the mirror and was pleased with what I saw; my coat covered my plain dark dress, and the hat I wore was almost the same shade as the stole. There was a world of difference between Evie and me, but today the division seemed a little bit smaller.

The chauffeur left us outside the post office and took the car back to Oaklands, promising to return in two hours.

'Time for tea and cakes,' Evie said as the car disappeared around the corner. 'And then,' she continued, in that innocent yet conspiratorial way that made me both smile and groan, 'a little visit to Mr Markham's, to pass on a special order from Mrs Hannah.'

So I'd been right. 'What special order might this be?'

'Well, it's quite funny really. I decided this morning that I had a particular longing for some roast chicken. I spoke to Mrs Hannah about it and luckily there was plenty in the pantry. Then, silly me, I realised it wasn't chicken I wanted at all, it was lamb. I felt so bad about being awkward that when Mrs Hannah said we had none in the house, I offered to bring a message to Mr Markham while I was shopping so he could add it to tomorrow's order. Aren't I helpful?'

'Extremely,' I said drily. 'And if I were to offer to take it instead, while you buy your brother's Christmas gift?'

'I would say the fault is mine, so I wouldn't hear of it.'

'Well then, while you're doing that, I'll post these letters home.'

'Oh, no!' The lively pretence dropped away instantly. 'You'll have to talk to Mr Markham while I pass this note to Will.'

I relented. 'All right. Why don't you buy Lawrence's gift while I go in to the post office, and then I'll meet you at the tea shop so we can plan your little ruse.'

She agreed and we went our separate ways. As I paid for the stamps I considered what my mother and Emily would make of the subterfuge in which my days were often drenched now. The romantically minded Emily would be delighted and excited, while Ma would have some sage words of advice to dispense. Emily would demand details, and whatever I didn't tell her she would make up; Ma would shake her head and tell me she didn't want to know anything except that I still had a job. Both of them would be talking about me to the neighbours, which was why I kept my letters frequent but short.

Better they not know of things like the prank we had played on Ruth, which had resulted in her refusing to go alone to the spare linen room. Better still not to know I was party to the illicit romance between my mistress and the butcher's apprentice. And certainly better not to know my heart had been captured by a man some still, foolishly I was sure, believed had been instrumental in the death of the one for whom Ma had worked all those years ago.

The letters were posted. Within a few days my mother would know I *did* still have a job, Emily would know that Evie's new dress for Christmas was a beautiful shade of green, and Adie and Albert would know the farm up the road had a dray horse bigger than our garden shed. They would all know I wished them a Merry Christmas and that I missed them. Everything else I kept to myself.

Half an hour after arriving in town Evie and I sat down to cups of tea as we discussed the real reason behind her suggesting the outing.

'With Orion lame I won't be riding for a while. He'll need to rest at least until the Boxing Day meet,' she said. 'And Will's busier than ever too at this time of year. I just want to hand him this note personally, and hope he brings one for me in return later.'

'And you need me to distract Mr Markham while you do it?'

'It should be quite easy, don't worry. Just give him the order from Mrs Hannah, and ask him some questions about the deliveries over the next few weeks if you have to.'

Evie carefully drew her note out from where she had tucked it inside her glove. 'I wish I could say everything I wanted to on this silly piece of paper.' She straightened her shoulders. 'But at least he'll know how much I wish I could be with him.'

I looked around the tea shop, remembering my first half-holiday and how I'd peered through the window, daydreaming about meeting someone special . . . and less than an hour later I'd met the man who had ultimately settled so deep in my heart, yet who still remained hopelessly out of reach.

Evie left her tea half-finished, and watched with ill-concealed impatience while I took a few hurried sips of my own. 'Do be quick,' she urged, and I replaced the cup in the saucer with a small sigh of regret.

'I'm ready,' I said, and was rewarded with a swift smile as she stood up and seized her coat, leaving me hurrying to catch her up.

Frank Markham's premises lay in the middle of the rows of shops that flanked the town's main street. They were all doing a bustling trade in these weeks leading up to the festive season. Evie handed me Mrs Hannah's order, and gave me a pleading look as we paused outside the door. I interpreted it to mean *do your best*, and nodded.

There was only one customer, looking on with a watchful eye as Mr Markham rang up her purchase, and no sign of Will. I wasn't looking directly at Evie, but I could sense her craning her neck to see if he was bending down behind the counter. However it soon became quite clear he was not in the shop.

The customer responded to some disarming comment from the butcher, collected her package and left. Evie's eyes met mine and widened slightly in encouragement.

'Good morning, Mr Markham,' I said. 'I, uh, I see you're working alone today?' Although phrased as a question and clearly interpreted correctly, Mr Markham did not address it.

'Good morning, Miss . . . Parker, isn't it?'

'That's right.'

'And, of course, Miss Creswell,' he went on, nodding politely in Evie's direction.

I could see she wanted to grit her teeth, but breeding won out and she smiled back at him. 'Good morning, Mr Markham. We've brought an extra order from Mrs Hannah, since we were shopping this morning.'

'Where's Will?' I asked, tired of the charade. 'Does he have the day off?'

Markham grinned at me and winked at Evie. 'That's better, miss, don't be shy. No, Will is out in the back shed cleaning the pantry.'

Evie looked into the bag over her arm. 'Lizzy, I've left my address book in the post office. Would you be so good as to give Mr Markham the order whilst I run and fetch it?'

Before I could acquiesce she had slipped out of the shop, leaving me and Markham alone. I passed over the note on which Mrs Hannah had written her new order, and he took it, allowing his fingers to brush against mine.

I jerked my hand away and took a step back. 'Thank you, Mr Markham. I expect I'll see you soon. Goodbye.'

'Wait a moment, Miss Parker,' he called as I turned to leave. 'Yes?'

His smile still hovered, only now it seemed gentler. 'I can understand your interest in Will, he's a very popular boy.'

'I have no interest in him,' I protested.

'Well, if you say so. But if I may observe, you seem a strong and uncommonly lovely young woman. Perhaps a boy wouldn't be enough for you.' His gaze held mine and, to my horror, I felt a tingling response as his grey eyes narrowed slightly, and the curve of his mouth deepened.

'Perhaps, Miss Parker, what you're really looking for is a man.' His voice dropped. 'Someone to do justice to the wildness in you. I can see it, you know, behind that pretty, shy smile of yours.'

My powers of speech deserted me as I stared at him. I pictured him and Ruth in the outhouse, and for the first time the thought of them together didn't cause me to flinch in disgust but rather she had my sympathy. If she felt about this man the way I did about Jack, who could blame her?

Markham came out from behind the counter but I was frozen to the spot and couldn't have moved if the shop had caught fire. 'May I call you Lizzy?' he murmured, reaching out to caress the stole across my shoulders. Still dazed, I nodded, and caught my breath as his fingers travelled the length of my arm ... I couldn't feel them through the thickness of my coat but the sight of them was hypnotic as they rested on my gloved wrist.

'Lizzy, I think you and I have ... a connection. Wouldn't you say?'

'I don't think so,' I managed, and he laughed, low and soft in my ear, as he bent closer to whisper, 'Don't deny it, angel.'

He straightened and moved away, and the spell was broken. As I reached the door for the second time he spoke my name again and I turned, wary in every nerve. But he simply smiled again, told me he would add the lamb to the main invoice, and went back to his work.

Outside the shop I took a deep breath and blew it out, feeling my hair lift with the force of it. It wasn't difficult to understand what had happened in there: Markham's touch, and softly spoken words, had reminded me of the pulsing excitement Jack aroused in me so effortlessly. But Jack was unreachable, whereas this man had made it clear he was not. I shook my head. I'd have to watch myself around Frank Markham from now on or I'd end up risking my job the same way Ruth had been doing. And with my poor luck, I wouldn't be anywhere near as successful at hiding it.

Thankfully it was only a few minutes before Evie came around the corner, flushed from her own encounter and looking happier than ever.

'He sends his regards,' she said.

I spoke briskly, eager to be gone. 'Good. Will he reply to your note?'

'Yes, by way of a letter to you. Anything addressed to me catches Mother's attention since my coming out, and that would be an end to everything. At least, until I leave home,' she added, reminding me again of her conviction that all would be well for the two of them in the end.

'I'll pass it on as soon as it arrives,' I promised. Watching the glow light her face I reflected that I must have looked the same way for a moment after leaving Frank Markham. He couldn't hold a candle to Jack Carlisle, had none of his easy grace and bold, masculine beauty, but Jack could never be part of my life. Perhaps, then, I should just enjoy Frank's attention while it was mine, and if being admired by him helped dampen my feelings for Jack, so much the better. Anything that diverted my dreams from him could only be helpful in soothing the constant ache I was feeling.

I rarely spent time in the kitchens nowadays, but occasionally I would find myself there when the deliveries arrived, and when Frank looked at me with approval I no longer shied away from it, but met his eyes with a cool appraisal of my own. Why should he be the only one to choose who was worthy of attention and who was not?

Things were easier with Ruth now, too. She had stopped teasing Martha, and Mary told me her behaviour seemed to have taken an inexplicable turn for the better. Having promised Evie to be discreet, I couldn't tell my friend I knew why this was, but I took note and observed a quieter, more reflective Ruth. We would never be friends but we both seemed to have reached the conclusion that it was far too bothersome to keep up hostilities, and as a result when our paths did cross there was a sense of slowly maturing, mutual tolerance.

In all, it was an interesting time, if a busy one, with preparations for Christmas adding to the daily workload. Evie's note from Will arrived and she couldn't suppress a squeal of joy when I gave it to her, though she didn't open it in front of me. Her hunter was recovering but she still insisted he should rest until the hunt gathered on Boxing Day, although I could see she had struggled with the temptation to hack him out gently the previous day, a Sunday. So this letter from Will was more precious than ever, and I could see it in her face as she slid the note into her pocket with trembling fingers.

Envious of her happiness, I went down to the house-keeper's office, where Mrs Cavendish had called me to discuss arrangements for guests at the upcoming Christmas and New Year's Eve parties. It was the day before Christmas Eve and the decorations were up, fires already lit at both ends of the hall, and the sharp smell of pine from the huge Christmas tree hung in the air, making me yearn for my home on the edge of the moors.

Adie and Albert would be old enough to help this year; pushing cloves into oranges and laying them along the window ledge to scent the living room with their heavy spice. Emily would do the tree, our joint and joyful task in years gone by, while our mother got together with her childhood friend to collaborate on the cake-making. Rose would bake them and Ma would decorate them, and between them they would create the most breathtaking icing snow scenes on the most delicious fruit cake I'd ever tasted.

Passing through the great hall, with its tasteful sprays of holly and the crackling sound of the sap from massive logs spitting in the hearths, I felt closer to tears than I had in months. Only the thought that I was likely to run into Ruth stopped me from giving way to the crushing wave of homesickness, and I focused my thoughts instead on what Christmas in a house such as this would be like.

The first party, on Christmas Eve, would be a lavish enough affair no doubt, with extra guests being the most likely reason for Mrs Cavendish calling for me now, but the New Year celebration would host all those guests plus around a hundred in addition. Mary said it was always the most extravagant party for miles around.

I wondered whether Lord Lawrence was still young enough, at fifteen, to bring a relaxation of formalities to the proceedings on Christmas morning; although if it were left to Evie I suspected everyone would remain in their nightwear all day and play games. I smiled at the thought, and it helped ease the pain of missing my own family.

In the kitchens all was smooth-running activity. People crossed the floors carrying huge pots and piles of plates, missing each other by a hair's breadth in the familiar dance of a team long practised. Mrs Cavendish was already in her office and, despite the hillock of paperwork at her elbow, seemed as calm and organised as ever. 'There will be three extra guests arriving tomorrow, so you will divide your time between Miss Creswell and Mrs Constance Harrington 'til Boxing Day. You'll need to fetch extra bedding from the spare linen room and—'

She broke off as the bell jangled above her head, and we both looked up. At the same time I noticed, through the window overlooking the kitchen, that Will and Mr Markham had arrived. Will was carrying the wooden crates as usual, and Markham was checking his paperwork against the contents as they were unloaded into the cold room.

Mrs Cavendish sighed. 'It's Her Ladyship. Wait here 'til I get back, if you would be so good, and tell Mr Markham to leave his invoice. I'll sign it for tomorrow. Unless Mr Dodsworth comes in, of course, then he can do it.'

After only a few minutes, during which time I idly read some of the invoices and notes stacked in neat piles on the desk, I heard footsteps and pretended to be hunting for a pencil.

When I looked up, however, it wasn't Mrs Cavendish returning after all. Instead I saw Frank Markham looking at me with the hint of a smile on his face. 'Good morning, Miss Parker.'

I struggled to keep my voice calm. 'Good morning, Mr Markham. Mrs Cavendish says please leave the invoice, she'll sign it for you to pick up tomorrow.'

'Been called away, has she?'

'She's with Lady Creswell.'

'Ah. She'll be a while then.' His smile broadened and he leaned back against the door, pushing it shut. The click of the latch made me jump and feel horribly vulnerable, but there was a window looking on to the kitchen, I reminded myself, so he couldn't make any serious advances. I really should stop worrying.

I smiled back and forced down my feeling of being trapped.

'I can't sign anything,' I pointed out, standing straighter and pretending I hadn't noticed he'd taken a step closer. My legs trembled and I felt my hands growing clammy, but it wasn't the pleasant sensation it had been before.

'I know that, pet,' he murmured, and came around the desk to where I stood. 'Now, will you just relax and accept the fact that you are going to attract attention whether you like it or not?' His gaze drifted down across my breasts and then rose to meet mine, one eyebrow raised appreciatively. 'You're quite the little beauty under all those drab layers, aren't you? You hide it well, but it seems you've got curves any woman would be proud of.' He stepped closer still and his hand, ostensibly moving to rest on the edge of the desk, brushed my hip.

I turned away, embarrassed, and the movement of my head carried my attention to the window where I saw Ruth staring in at us, her face blank with shock.

Frank's soft laughter warmed my cheek. 'Don't be afraid,' he whispered. 'One of these days, lovely Lizzy Parker, you're going to discover how it feels to be truly wanted and loved, the way you deserve.'

His words echoed my own longing so completely that for a second I believed them. Then it hit me like a shower of cold water. Of course he was playing up to me: as Evie's maid, I was in the position he'd always encouraged Ruth to seek.

'I think you'd better leave,' I said.

He didn't seem annoyed, or even aware I'd seen through his flattery. 'I do have work to be getting on with,' he agreed, and put the invoice in the middle of Mrs Cavendish's blotter. Then, to my relief, he left. He looked back in through the kitchen window as he passed, and raised a hand in farewell, and I was struck cold by the look of pure venom Ruth threw my way before hurrying after him. I swallowed hard; hostilities were resumed, best to keep out of her way for a while.

When Mrs Cavendish had given me the details of my new duties I made my way up to the linen room, the key in my pocket. I passed Lord Henry's study and smiled; after the look Ruth had just given me I appreciated the prank more than ever. But when I got to the doorway in which I'd been pinned and protected by Jack Carlisle's body I felt that sweet pain of longing again. I stood still for a moment, squeezed into the space where he'd pushed me, then closed my eyes.

Lost in reliving the moment, I thought I was hearing again the slam of the study door when Evie had emerged, then I realised it was indeed the same door, but closed more quietly – surreptitiously even. Footsteps followed, leading away to the main hall, and I craned my neck to see out of my hiding place.

There was no mistaking that square breadth of shoulder, the long, easy stride or the way Jack's hair was impatiently raked back, refusing to bow to the current fashion for extreme neatness. He carried a leather briefcase, and as I watched he slipped something into his pocket, presumably the key to Lord Henry's study.

Yet again Jack was somewhere he didn't belong, and I tried to focus on why that might be. But my body was taking the lead and drawing my thoughts away from caring. Instead I closed my eyes again, remembering the clean scent of his soap, and the warmth of his hand holding mine, sending sparks through my blood. I leaned back into the recess, my head resting against the door. His face floated before me, that expression of exasperated humour that had faded into something deeper and more intense ...

'Lizzy?'

I started and opened my eyes. 'Ja— Mr Carlisle. I was ... was just fetching ...' My words tailed away but gestured vaguely over my shoulder at the linen room door. Then, finding the courage from somewhere, I asked, 'Is there something I can help you with?'

'No,' he said, and his eyes cut away from mine. 'I thought I heard something, that's all. So I came back to check, and here you are. Again.'

'Here we both are,' I pointed out softly, when I'd meant to reply in a firm, businesslike way.

He looked back at me and his hand came out, seemingly without forethought, and touched my arm. Stunned, I stared at him and, just for a moment, read utter hopelessness in his expression. Then he smiled, and it was impossible not to smile back despite my sudden breathlessness.

'The burned linen is all gone,' he said, as if nothing had happened between us, 'never again to see the light of day. Or paraffin lamp,' he added, a teasing light sparkling in his eyes but not banishing their bleakness entirely.

'Thank you,' I said with heartfelt gratitude. 'And thank you for not telling Mrs Cavendish, or I might have lost my position altogether.'

'Can't have that, can we?' he said. 'Whoever would Evie get to play her pranks with her if you weren't here?'

His gaze went from me to the doorway in which we stood, the way mine had done a few moments ago. I wondered, with a jolt, if it was actually the same memory as mine that had brought him back to this corner of the house, and not a noise at all; I hadn't made a sound, I was sure of it.

I fixed my eyes somewhere below his chin, breathing faster at the thought, and as I raised them again I was rocked by the realisation that I was right. At the same moment he groaned in surrender and caught my face between his hands. At the touch of our lips it seemed the fizzing in my blood surged right through me, from the tips of my fingers, gripping his waist, to the roots of my hair, imprisoned beneath my cap.

Although I had never kissed anyone in passion before, it felt so natural I had no time to wonder and worry; as the first panicky question flew into my head I thrust it aside, along with all other thoughts, and let myself feel instead. Pressed against him with the thundering of my own heart in my ears, my lips instinctively parted and I felt him sigh and tasted the faint flavour of whisky, fiery and fresh. His tongue touched mine, gentle and hesitant, and I responded, exploring the warmth inside his mouth and then retreating. I gently bit his lip before letting him pull me closer again. As my hands slid around the small of his back, his moved from cupping my face to cradling the back of my head, fingers pressed to the base of my skull as if he was worried I might try to escape.

We remained locked together. All sense of time and propriety had flown away. Only the sound of a door slamming somewhere in the house brought us back to heart-breaking reality. Our lips broke contact slowly, reluctantly, and even then we remained close, foreheads touching as we both struggled to control our breathing.

'Oh, Lizzy,' he said at last, and his voice cracked with the strain of all he'd been feeling. There was nothing I could say,

158

no words were enough; we both knew the situation now, and we also knew, without discussion, how hopeless it was. He kissed me again, but this time it was a brush of his lips against my cheek, and his hand tightened on my shoulder before he turned to go.

I watched him walk away, my whole body alive with the fire he had kindled in it the day we'd first met. Helpless acknowledgement of his power over me swept aside everything I'd tried to tell myself. It wasn't growing up, or even being with a man, that frightened me; it was taking that irrevocable step with anyone other than Jack.

Chapter 12

Pick up the gown; shake it out; lay it flat; sprinkle the water. Steam rose to soak my already sweat-dampened sleeves and brow as I pressed the heavy iron down with a sense of relief: almost done. I blew my curls away from my hot face and worked the point of the iron into the tiny frilled edges of the sleeve. For a long time the pile beside me hadn't seemed to be going down at all, and the short walk to the stove to swap the cooling iron for the hot one was starting to feel like a trek across the Himalayas. But I had finally reached the bottom of the last basket.

How anyone could get through so many clothes in such a short time was something I still couldn't fathom. Of course the Christmas season was a seemingly endless round of parties and gatherings, requiring at least four changes of clothes a day plus evening wear, and even Evie, who I suspected would be far happier in a pair of workman's trousers, was subject to the conventions of Society.

The freshly pressed garments hung along a rail at the side of the room, and I looked over at them with a real sense of achievement. It had taken me eight solid days to mend, launder and iron them, but tonight would mark the end of the insanity and allow me to get back into a proper routine.

Evie had gone downstairs at the last possible moment, beautiful as ever, but playing fretfully with the diamond at her neck.

'I wish I didn't have to wear this,' she'd said. 'Especially tonight.'

'Why especially tonight?'

She shrugged. 'It seems so ostentatious, particularly when there are some less well-to-do relations here.'

'But they know you have it, so wouldn't it be ridiculous if it never saw the light of day? Your relations might feel it wasn't appreciated at all and would be better off in other hands.'

'Yes, I suppose you're right, as always. You have to stop doing that, you know. But your point is very much taken.'

'Because, you know, we can always swap places,' I went on mildly. 'I mean, that gown would fit me, with some very small adjustments, and you could always see to the rest of the ironing.'

Evie shuddered as she looked at the pile. 'Stop it! I give in!'

She had gone downstairs much happier, leaving me to my solitude and the laundry. I only envied her a little bit, and that wasn't for the dancing, or the food, or even the wearing of the Kalteng Star. It was a far more basic longing: downstairs, in the lavishly decorated ballroom of this enormous house, were friends and family, so many people who were glad to see her, and who would, for the most part, have been so even if she wore rags.

And then there was Jack. He had returned from a trip to London earlier in the day, and knowing he was close by, even when I couldn't see him, was both comforting and frustrating. I found it increasingly hard to think back to a time when I had not yearned for his approval, and his touch, with this hopeless intensity, and knowing now that he felt some measure of the same towards me made it a hundred times worse. Like being shown a prize you had missed out on by a whisker instead of a mile. He was downstairs now, no doubt charming even the stoniest of hearts with his friendly manner and easy humour, and I felt the sting of jealousy for everyone who snared his attention, however briefly.

The last dress was finished just after ten o'clock, and I hung it carefully on its padded hanger and hooked it on to the rail with the others. Only then did I allow myself to acknowledge how hot and tired I really was. I picked up the iron to put it away and it suddenly felt almost too heavy to hold, although if there had been another basket waiting I wouldn't have thought twice about tackling it.

How strange that we can keep going, and going, and going, until we know we are finally permitted to stop, and then in that instant even breathing seems too much of an effort and we know we can't possibly do another thing.

I could feel sweat trickling between and beneath my breasts, soaking my dress at the small of my back, and as I raised my arm to brush my curls away again I felt the heaviness of my hair like a hat I would have taken off if only I could. I glanced towards the dark window; after a wet summer we were

162

having an even wetter and windy winter, and the thought of stepping out into it made me break into pleasant, anticipatory shivering.

I hurried downstairs and passed through the kitchens to the back door, vaguely aware of the frantic activity as the cook and her staff worked to replenish the table upstairs, but most of my mind was focused ahead, to the moment when the breeze would touch my skin and the wind lift the hair off my neck.

It was every bit as blissful as I'd dared to hope. There was a light drizzle falling, and as I walked into the garden I turned my face up to the dark sky and sighed with deep pleasure. My skin seemed to open up to receive the moisture, and I rolled my sleeves back and allowed the rain to splash as far up my arms as I could.

When I had cooled down enough that my being outside was by choice rather than urgent necessity, I sat down on the milk churn I'd always retreated to in moments of stress or exhaustion when I worked in the kitchens. I could feel a cold puddle soaking through the seat of my dress but it didn't matter; all that was required from me for now was to be on hand after the party to help Evie undress. There would be plenty of time to change before then.

I eased my hot, aching feet out of my shoes and reached down to remove my stockings, feeling a little laugh bubbling up at the absurdity of it. What was I, a child who wanted to splash in the rain? Well, yes, and why not? I stuffed my rolled-up stockings into the pocket of my apron, and very slowly placed both feet on the wet, muddy ground. It felt delicious.

I couldn't help contrasting the way I was behaving with the formalities of the New Year's Eve ball, taking place just a few yards away, and wondered what Lady Creswell would think if she could see me now. I squelched my toes and let out a laugh, not caring if Mrs Cavendish or Mrs Hannah came out to reprimand me.

I almost didn't hear the voices, but my laughter had subsided to a happy sigh and the wind had dropped, so the sound drifted easily to me from beyond the kitchen garden. The voices were high and clear, the sound of children arguing and, lifting my skirts clear of the mud, I crossed the yard and eased open the wooden door to peer beyond it.

There was a little light spilling from the house on to the grass, but not enough for me to see who was there. I was able to pick out three boys standing under the oak trees where the garden met the parkland, too engrossed in their argument to notice me.

I decided it wasn't my place to interfere, and had turned to go back when I heard one of them yelp. When I looked around again one of the boys was holding his upper arm, and I saw then that he seemed to be younger and that the other two were clearly banding together against him. I hesitated; boys fight, it's what they do. My own twin brothers, close though they were, had a habit of squabbling over the silliest things, but this looked different.

I moved forward, hoping the sight of an adult might send them back towards the house so that I wouldn't have to decide what to do next, but they didn't glance my way. I could hear them clearly now, and quickly identified the smaller boy as Evie's brother Lord Lawrence.

'We didn't steal it! It belongs in our family!' he said hotly.

'It should have come back to us years ago, our grandfather

trouble! I'll try to come back, if I can, but if I can't there'll be a good reason. Remember that.'

It was cold inside the outhouse, and smelled musty. A little light from the main kitchen leaked in through the tiny window, but only served to create eerie shadows. I glanced at the lantern and supply of matches, but immediately rejected that comforting notion. Jack was convinced I'd lose my job if anyone came out to investigate, so a secret this must remain.

Instead I sat on a pile of sacks in the corner and began to take stock of my aches and pains. My throat still felt raw, but the pain was easing. My fingers actually hurt the most: throbbing with each beat of my heart. I fumbled in my apron pocket for my stockings, and used them to dab some of the blood away, but the wool caught on a torn nail and I was only just able to bite back a shriek of pain that might have brought someone out from the kitchens. I shoved the stockings back into my pocket and blew on the tips of my fingers instead.

My face felt swollen and sore, and my lower lip tasted like metal when I ran my tongue across it. Despite this I couldn't help doing it several times, almost giving in to self-pity before my anger rose again.

That horrible boy! What had Jack called him? Wigford? Wingford? Well, whoever he was, he was a bully and a thug; he and Ruth would no doubt get on famously. I tried to remember what they had been talking about before it had come to blows, something about the Creswells being thieves, but as I

169

sat hunched against the wall my nausea worsened and, with my eyes too heavy to keep open, I rested my head on my knees, my bunched up dress softly pillowing my aching face.

I came awake some time later, unsure why. Then I heard someone easing open the outhouse door. Swallowing a moan, I tried to melt into the wall, my mind taking me back to the day I'd arrived, stumbling in on Ruth and Frank Markham in here ... what if New Year's Eve excitement had spread to the staff and a couple of them were taking advantage of the family's preoccupation with the party?

'Lizzy?' The voice was a whisper but I recognised it at once.

There was a flare of light, and a match touched the wick of the lantern. Instinctively my hands flew up to cover my face, but I was dimly aware of the light coming closer. There was silence, then a muttered oath and a chilled hand touched mine, drawing them away from my face.

I looked up and saw Jack flinch. 'I'm all right,' I told him, but while I had slept my mouth had swollen further. At the unfamiliarity of it, and hearing my voice sound so croaky and small, I suddenly burst into tears.

An instant later I was leaning against Jack, feeling his hands on my damp, cold back, patting and rubbing it as if I were a small child. The feeling of security and safety he offered only seemed to make things worse for me; I cried harder, and could hear him murmuring quietly but could not make out the words. It didn't matter.

Gradually my tears subsided to a soft hiccupping, and then it seemed as if the night had shifted. I became aware, properly aware, that this was Jack. *His* arms wrapped around me, his coat buttons pressing into my cheek, his breath stirring the hairs at the crown of my head. I breathed in deeply, praying for the moment to last, not caring that I was cold and uncomfortable as long as he was here with me.

He fell still. His hands had ceased their mindless soothing motion and he'd stopped murmuring soothing words. Abruptly my face flamed, setting my lip throbbing again, and I sat up, away from him.

'I'm so sorry,' I said, and found it was easier to talk now. 'I've caused you no end of trouble tonight. I should go back. What time is it?'

He blinked slowly then checked his pocket watch, leaning away to angle it towards the lamp. 'It's just after one.'

'Oh, no!' I gathered my skirts, wincing at the pain in my fingers. 'Evie!'

'Evie is by no means ready for you yet,' Jack said. 'She's still busy fending off proposals of marriage, or worse.'

'I'm not surprised,' I said, and subsided gratefully. 'She looked so beautiful tonight, a real lady.'

Jack laughed softly. 'Ah, if only they knew her like we know her,' he said, and I felt a rush of pleasure at the secret we shared. Our chuckling mingled in the semi-darkness but as it faded he seemed to remember where he was, and with whom.

Suddenly withdrawn, he was Mr Carlisle again. 'Let me attend to that hand,' he said. He reached out and opened my fingers, hissing between his teeth as he saw them – they looked horrible, caked in dried blood, and I could only guess how dreadful my face looked. 'I'll be back in a few minutes,' he said. 'Don't worry. Just keep quiet and still. Don't go running off.'

He rose to go, and the lantern cast shadows over a face that seemed suddenly harsh and unfamiliar, stifling any temptation I'd felt to laugh at the notion of running anywhere. In the shifting light he was all hard angles, and Joe Shackleton's words of warning echoed in my mind as I watched the square-shouldered frame duck through the doorway; once again I had no trouble believing there was more to Jack Carlisle than first appeared.

The darkness, and my own weariness, began to play tricks on my mind. Why had Jack been out there alone? He had made it sound as if someone was coming, and hurried me back here to keep me out of sight, but what if that had not been to help me avoid discovery as he'd said but rather reasons of his own? What those reasons may be, though, I couldn't guess.

I sat in the dim chill of the outhouse, wondering if he was going to come back at all. Or, worse still, with some means of silencing me.

The door opened again and I stood up quickly, the better to defend myself. The moment I saw Jack's concerned expression, however, I knew I'd been over-reacting. He put down the lantern and box he'd been carrying, and crossed the outhouse in a couple of strides.

'Sit down, Lizzy,' he said, in a voice that brooked no argument. I did as I was told. My torn dress fell away, showing my muddied petticoat, but he made no comment and I decided he must be used to seeing young women in a state of undress, and was too tired and sore to let the notion upset me as it might once have done.

The box he'd brought turned out to be stocked with a covered water bowl, some clean cloths and bandages, and a collection of ointments. I also saw he'd brought my shoes, which he must have picked up on his way across the yard.

Without a word he began dabbing at my lip and carefully wiping away the dried blood that covered my chin. As he rinsed out the cloth I saw the rust colour swirling in the water, and started to feel sick again. I tried not to stare at it. Instead I closed my eyes and concentrated on the sensation of his fingers working to clean my face, and the brush of his breath against my cheek.

There was a pressure on my right leg, at the place where my petticoats showed through the tear in my dress, and I realised his hand was resting there, steadying himself while he crouched to his work. I don't think he even noticed what he'd done or he would certainly have removed it. Warmth radiated through my clothes just above my knee, but the more I thought about the contact, and the small scrap of clothing that separated his hand from my bare flesh, the more that heat seemed to creep upwards.

Feeling abruptly dizzy, I opened my eyes and watched the night's moisture drip from his hair on to his forehead, my eyes tracing the shape of his thick, dark eyebrows, the straight nose and firm, beautifully moulded mouth. The lips that had brought my feelings to life with such tenderness were set in a grim line now.

His movements became slower, and then stopped altogether. 'I can't do any more for you here.' He seemed to have trouble forming his words, and then we both became aware that he was gripping my leg tightly rather than just leaning on it. It seemed there was anger and frustration in that touch, and he snatched his hand away. 'You'd better go now.'

'Yes. And ... thank you.' I felt the loss of contact as I had felt the loss of his warmth earlier, but this ache was more intense, as his touch had been.

'What will you tell everyone?' he asked.

It hardly seemed to matter. I felt like crying again. 'I'll say I slipped in the yard in the dark. No one will worry too much anyway.'

'Of course they will!' he said, his voice harsh and unguarded, and his hand was back at my face, his palm gentle against my cheek. It was the hardest struggle I'd faced yet not to turn and press my lips against it.

He seemed to come out of himself and his hand dropped away again, although this time it was a weary gesture. 'Go on up to your rooms now. Evie will soon be ready for you.'

'Miss Creswell,' I corrected, finding a smile that hurt my heart more than it hurt my bruised mouth.

He was surprised into smiling back, but it was a shadowed smile, tired and joyless. 'Happy New Year, Lizzy,' he said softly. 'I hope nineteen-thirteen brings you all the happiness you deserve.'

'It can't, though, can it?' I said sadly, and by the flickering light I saw my own feelings written clearly on his face.

There was a long silence, and then he shook his head. 'Not for either of us,' he said. 'Just be as happy as you can, and I'll be the same. It's all we can do.' It was the closest we had come to speaking of what lay between us, and in a strange way it helped.

I was halfway up the stairs before I remembered my shoes,

but they would have to wait until morning now. I reached my room without seeing anyone, and turned on the light. The first thing I saw was the neat row of freshly ironed gowns and undergarments ... how long ago it seemed that I had finished the last one with such a sense of achievement. I could feel fresh blood beading on my lip, but as I moved towards my bedroom and the wash basin there my eye lit on a note lying on the ironing board.

> *Dear Lizzy,*
> *I was right about the arguments the necklace might cause, and came to ask if you wouldn't mind taking care of it for me for tonight. However, I find you have gone to see in the New Year with the other staff so I have left it in the top drawer of my dressing table, and ask that you please take it down to the safe first thing in the morning. I will not be calling on you later, you've earned your night off a hundred times over!*
> *Happy New Year, Lizzy, see you in 1913!*
> *E.*

A few minutes later, dabbing at my face with a dampened cloth in the comfort and brightness of my beautiful room, I still felt the warmth and pressure of a hand resting on my knee. With all my heart then, I wished myself back in the cold, damp outhouse with the spiders, the dripping roof and Jack.

When I'd cleaned up as best I could, I eased myself gratefully into bed with the feeling that something was missing, but it took a moment to identify what it was; my stole must have slipped on to the floor. For a moment I thought about climbing out again to pick it up, but I was just too bone weary to care. A glance at the clock showed me it was approaching two o'clock. I would be up at seven; chilly feet would not keep me awake tonight.

Chapter 13

1 January 1913

The sound of scraping and clanking broke through my disjointed dreams, and I raised my head off the pillow to see Emma Bird kneeling at my fireplace. My morning tea was sitting on its tray on the dressing table, but the thought of sipping something hot with my torn mouth made me break out in a sweat.

I raised myself up on my elbows, blinking against an appalling headache that had settled behind my left eye and in the temple on that side. The sound of the sheets rustling alerted Emma to my wakefulness, and she turned with her usual ready smile.

The smile abruptly died. 'Miss Parker! Whatever's happened to you?'

I started to answer, to give my prepared story at least, but overnight my lower lip had swollen so much I could barely open my mouth. I mimed a tumbling motion with my hands, and saw her gaze fix on my bloodied and torn nails.

'You've done all that by falling down?'

I nodded and took a deep breath, forcing my lips apart. 'It was outside,' I managed, and she must have understood me because she glanced towards the window, as if she'd be able to see it happening if she did so.

'Do you want me to fetch someone? Mrs Cavendish maybe?'

I shook my head. The housekeeper was altogether too sharp for my liking and I hadn't got my story fixed right in my head yet, she'd be bound to spot a lie if she questioned me now.

Emma finished making up the fire, casting doubtful glances my way every time she heard me hiss or mutter under my breath as I dressed. Finally she stood up to leave and by then I was able to sip a bit of the cooled tea, thus convincing her all was well. She collected up my dirty clothing, and left. As I bent to put on clean stockings I noticed the mud on my feet. I would have to check the scullery and back hall for grimy footprints, but that would have to wait. For the first time I was glad of the poor lighting in the hall; hopefully I'd be able to get any mess cleaned up before anyone noticed.

I checked my appearance in the mirror before venturing out of my room; my mouth looked puffy and there was a bruise at my temple, but Jack had obviously pulled David away before his fingers had managed to mark my neck. I grew shaky again, thinking how close I had come to real danger.

At half-past seven I was standing in Evie's room, looking at her slumbering form hunched beneath the blankets and trying not to begrudge her the blissful escape of sleep. I laid her tea tray on the bedside table and picked up the discarded gown from the back of the armchair.

'G'morning, Lizzy,' Evie mumbled, from the depths of her bed.

'Morning,' I said, and it came out sounding almost normal. By way of experiment I opened my mouth, relieved not to feel the now-familiar tearing sensation, and flexed my sore fingers. They had protested at every movement first thing that morning, but I had used them enough now that they only throbbed when in direct contact with anything solid. Progress of a sort.

I laid out Evie's day clothes, then remembered her note. 'I'll take the necklace down in a moment,' I told her. 'I'll set the bath running first.'

Once the water was filling the bath I went back into Evie's room. She was sitting up in bed now, and her expression when she saw me properly was even more horrified than Emma's had been.

'Lizzy!' she breathed. 'Did someone hit you?'

'I fell,' I told her, resisting the sudden urge to break down and tell her everything. 'Out in the yard.'

'Your poor mouth ... and your hand! A fall did all that?'

'My hand got caught underneath my basket,' I said, 'and I hit my face on the ground. It was my own fault, I was in a hurry because of the rain. Didn't watch where I was going, my foot caught in my skirts.'

It sounded plausible in my head, but the words came out fragmented and hollow-sounding to my own ears, although not apparently to Evie's. She was out of bed in a moment, examining my fingers and making tiny, distressed noises. Guilt

179

knotted my stomach tight. I hated the necessity for lies, but I would hate to lose my job even more.

'I'm quite all right,' I assured her. 'Your bath will soon be ready. Would you like me to see you into it before I take the necklace down?'

She yawned, sensing my wish to change the subject. 'Oh, yes, please. Honestly – the trouble that thing caused last night, you wouldn't believe it. I got so annoyed with all the pointed comments and sly looks, I barely wore the thing more than two hours.'

'I don't understand how something so beautiful can cause so much bitterness,' I said, shaking out a large towel. 'Is it just jealousy?'

'In a way, but it's far more complicated than that. I'll tell you sometime, but not just now, I can hardly think straight, I'm so tired.'

Once Evie was settled in her bath I went back into the bedroom to collect the necklace. I opened the same drawer I had seen her put it in before, but the diamond wasn't there. Nor was it in any of the others.

I went back through to the small adjoining bathroom. 'Which drawer did you put it in?'

Evie was lying back, almost asleep again. 'Top right,' she murmured through the wash cloth that covered her face.

'No, I've looked there.'

'It's there, just feel around for it. It may have been pushed to the back. You know how I slam the drawer shut sometimes. I was certainly angry enough last night.'

Already knowing it would be in vain, I nevertheless went back to search again. Evie's insistence worried me; she wasn't in the slightest doubt. When I reported back again, confirming the necklace wasn't in any of the drawers, she sat up, frowning.

'Help me out. It must be there, I'll find it.'

Wrapped in a towel, Evie bent closer to the drawer and felt right into the back of it. When she finally accepted the diamond wasn't there, she began turning things over on top of the dresser, becoming more and more frantic.

'I should have put it in the safe last night but I was too eager to get back to the party,' she said. 'Maybe Mother followed me up here and saw it, thought it wasn't safe to leave it and took it down?'

'Surely she would have told you if she had,' I said, and immediately regretted my words as I saw the flicker of hope in her die.

'Perhaps. Or perhaps she simply got swept up in the party again, and forgot,' Evie said, but I could see she no longer believed it.

'Would you like me to go down and check?' I asked gently.

She nodded and looked around for her own personal safe key. 'If you would, yes. I'd go myself, but ...' She gestured to her towel and tried for a smile. It didn't sit well today; her face was too tightly drawn.

On my way down to the safe I saw Mary coming out of the drawing room.

'Happy New Year!' she said, then drew closer and saw my bruised face. 'Lizzy! What—'

'I haven't got time,' I told her quickly. 'I'm all right, don't worry, but the Kalteng Star is missing.'

She drew a shocked breath. 'Are you sure?'

'I'm just going to check the safe now. Evie … Miss Creswell, that is … left it in her room last night, and this morning it's nowhere to be found. She hopes Her Ladyship has taken it to the safe already.'

'Well, best you hurry along then, you can tell me all about it later.' Mary gave me a gentle shove in the direction of the morning room, and hurried off. I knew she wouldn't be one to spread gossip, but perhaps it would be no bad thing if the servants did get to hear about it: maybe one of them had seen something suspicious, or helpful.

The jewellery safe set aside specifically for the diamond was, as I'd suspected, empty. Evie's face crumpled when I told her, and I felt so sorry for her I could have cried myself.

'Perhaps Her Ladyship did move it after all but hasn't yet put it in the safe?' I suggested. 'It might be in her room.'

'No. It's been stolen, I think we both know that,' said Evie, and sat down on her bed, her face in her hands as if blocking out the world would change the blow it had dealt her. Wordless, I laid out her day clothes and helped her dress, and all the while she was asking me the same thing: how would she tell her mother?

In the event that was the least of it. Lady Creswell listened to the stilted tale of the missing necklace and promptly telephoned the police. Evie's room was locked and she joined her family in the drawing room, while all the upper servants were summoned to the lower house to await questioning.

I found Mary in the laundry room. She put down the sheet

she was folding at once. 'What's happening then? And when are you going to tell me what happened to your face?'

'What do you know about the Kalteng Star?' I asked, ignoring the second question. However little she knew, it would still be more than I did.

Mary looked as if she were about to press me for an answer, but obviously sensed she would not get one. 'It's been in the Creswell family since it was discovered – the turn of the last century, I think, eighteen-five or -six. It's passed down to the eldest daughter of each generation, although they don't really own it.'

So Evie had said before, but I was still confused. 'What do you mean, they don't own it?'

'Well, see, John Creswell – the first Lord Creswell who discovered it – gave it to his daughter Catherine when she turned eighteen. Ever since then it's gone to the first daughter, for her lifetime but Creswell's will stipulates they are only its legal guardians.'

'Why?'

'It's that stone he built all this on.' Mary waved her hand to encompass the room and the entire estate surrounding it. 'Wealth breeds wealth. Just having the diamond opened doors to Lord Creswell. Everyone knew of it, and its great value. And because he owes everything to the Star, when the end of the Creswell line comes the stone is to go back to Borneo and its people.'

I shook my head, not for the first time, in admiration of her. 'How on earth did you find all this out?'

'I listen. You know how it is, and I like to know as much about the family I'm working for as I can.'

'So what about when the eldest daughter marries?' I said. 'Do they have to leave the diamond at Oaklands?'

'No, the stone goes with them, and is passed down as before – unless they don't have a daughter. Then it reverts to the Creswells and awaits the birth of a granddaughter or a niece instead. It's the continuation of the Creswell line that determines when the guardianship of the Star is over and the stone should be returned.'

'Didn't John Creswell have any sons?'

'Yes, one. Alexander. Younger brother to Catherine.'

'Well then, why didn't he leave it to Alexander? Keep it in the family.'

Mary smiled. 'You're missing the point, Lizzy. John Creswell didn't want to confine it to just one household. He wanted to increase the extended family's wealth and influence by seeing to it that the eldest daughter was always seen as highly marriageable. But he also wanted to be sure the stone was returned to its rightful origins eventually.'

'So is that why there were arguments about it last night?'

'Were there? Well, you'd know more about that than I would,' Mary said. 'I don't know about any arguments, but I should think having the Wingfields there, and Miss Creswell flaunting the Star—'

'She wasn't flaunting it,' I protested. Then, as the name registered, I exclaimed, 'Oh, the Wingfields!'

'What about them?'

I realised then I couldn't tell Mary what had happened; she would likely be questioned about the disappearance of the stone like the rest of us, and it wouldn't be fair to make her lie. 'Nothing,' I said. 'I just heard the name mentioned last night. So the Kalteng Star passed to them at some point, I take it?'

'Yes, Catherine Creswell married a Wingfield.'

'And subsequently the diamond found its way back to the Creswells, but the Wingfields don't think it should have?' Now the accusations of the boys in the garden made sense to me.

'Exactly. I think it was a Margaret Wingfield who died without having any children, that would have been back in eighteen-eighty or so. Any family connected only by marriage, like the Wingfields, had to have a direct line, mother to daughter so the diamond came back to the Creswell line then. Since there have only been male children up until now it will leave here with Miss Evie when she marries. And that's all I know. Now, for goodness sake tell me how you got those bruises.'

I started to tell the familiar story, but before I'd reached the part about my falling over Mrs Cavendish appeared in the doorway. 'Miss Parker, follow me, please.'

My stomach lurched; her expression was grim, and her reaction to seeing my swollen lip was one of suspicion rather than concern. I glanced back at Mary who smiled, but she had clearly noted Mrs Cavendish's less than friendly demeanour and the smile wavered between encouragement and sympathy. I tried to smile back but terror was tying me in knots and I quickly gave up.

In the morning room a pale and worried-looking Lady Creswell sat on the chaise while an unfamiliar gentlemen took her usual place behind the desk. Mrs Cavendish hadn't uttered a word all the way up the stairs and across the front hall, and the last look she gave me as she closed the door behind her was one of profound disappointment.

Trying to stop myself from shaking head to toe, I cast my eyes around the room, remembering the last time I had stood here and the sense of unreality that had marked the occasion. The same thing was happening again, but this time it was more nightmare than dream. I longed to be able to sit, or even to grasp the back of a chair for support; it was a wonder my legs were holding me upright with my fear and exhaustion growing worse by the minute.

The man sitting behind the desk looked tired too, but seemed quite kind and even smiled at me. 'Good morning, I'm Inspector Bailey. And you are ...' he consulted a sheet of paper on the desk in front of him '... Miss Mary Elizabeth Parker?'

For a moment I wasn't sure myself. Then: 'Yes, sir,' I said.

'I'm going to ask you some questions, Mary.'

'If you please, sir, I'm called Lizzy now.'

'Very well, Lizzy. You are Miss Evangeline Creswell's personal maid?'

'Yes, sir.'

'How long have you worked in the service of Miss Creswell?'

'A few months, sir. Since last August.'

'And before that?'

'I was ... in the kitchens.' I couldn't bring myself to say the words 'scullery maid', not in this room – it reminded me too strongly of how fortunate I was to be here and how easily that might all change.

Inspector Bailey nodded. 'A big leap, for a kitchen girl. What was it that prompted Miss Creswell to ask for you in particular, do you think?'

As best I could without giving away Evie's penchant for fast cars and Jack's indulgent amusement, I told the policeman how I'd accepted a lift home and we had discovered we shared the same sense of humour.

'And did you know Miss Creswell would be in Breckenhall that day?' he asked.

'No, sir. I'd only been here a few weeks. It was the first time I'd seen Ev— Miss Creswell. She'd been in London.'

'So you deny engineering the meeting in order to create a favourable impression on her?'

I stared at him, struggling to find the right words. 'I never would have thought of such a thing!' I managed at last. He kept his shrewd brown eyes on mine for a moment, seemingly to satisfy himself I was telling the truth.

'Perhaps you could explain how you came by the cut on your face?' he said then, pen poised to write.

'I tripped in the yard,' I told him. 'I'd gone out to collect some flowers for Evie's room for the morning—'

'Flowers? In December?'

'We have Winter Beauty honeysuckle growing at the edge of the kitchen garden,' I told him truthfully. 'I thought it would be a nice smell for her to wake up to.'

'So you went downstairs at what time?'

'After I'd finished the ironing, sir. A little before half-past ten, I think.'

'You went out at half-past ten at night to pick flowers? How could you have seen what you were doing?'

'There's enough light from the kitchen windows. I've done it before.'

Again, perfectly true, and flower collecting was the only

reason I could think of for having had a basket with me under which I could have trapped my hand.

Inspector Bailey was writing all this down. 'And you tripped?'

'Yes, sir. I was in a hurry because of the rain, and my foot caught in my skirt. When I went down my hand got caught under the basket, so I couldn't stop my face from hitting the ground.'

'Why didn't you let it go?'

'Beg pardon, sir?'

'Miss Parker, if you were falling, surely your first instinct would have been to let go of the basket. To drop it,' he clarified, seeing my blank expression and misinterpreting it; in fact I was frantically searching my mind for some reason why I wouldn't have done just that. Might I have been holding the basket awkwardly? And if I said so, would he ask me to demonstrate? It also crossed my mind that having a ready answer might make it seem as though I'd given it too much thought.

In the end I just shook my head. 'I don't know, sir. It all happened so fast.'

His gaze held mine for a moment longer than was comfortable, then he looked down at what he had written. 'So you damaged your hand, and your face, falling in the yard?'

'Yes.'

'And you saw no one else out there? No one who could come to your aid?'

'No. They were all busy in the kitchens.'

'Still, wouldn't it have been prudent to seek help for your injuries on your return to the house?'

I thought fast again, feeling sweat dampening my dress. 'I didn't like to disturb them, they had a lot to do, so I thought it best if I just went and lay down. I didn't realise at the time quite how badly I'd hurt myself.'

'Very commendable. So you returned to your room shortly after ten-thirty, and remained there for the rest of the night?'

'Yes, sir.'

There was a pause while the inspector shuffled his papers around and peered closely at one sheet, upon which I could see an indecipherable scrawl. 'How shortly after ten-thirty, would you say?'

My heart stuttered at his tone; it was sharper and suddenly a lot less friendly. 'Only a few minutes I should say, sir,' I said, struggling to sound straightforward and unconcerned. I had to exonerate myself from any suggestion I'd been out later than that.

'That *is* interesting,' Bailey said. He didn't elaborate, and I felt the tension tightening to the point where I had to speak or scream.

'What is interesting in that, sir?'

He studied me, eyes narrowed. 'Interesting in that Miss Creswell claims she was in your room at ten-forty, writing you a note, and that you were most assuredly not there at that time.'

This time my heart actually skipped several beats. 'Well, perhaps I was mistaken about the exact time.'

Inspector Bailey smiled suddenly. 'Perhaps,' he said. 'Easily done after all, a busy girl like you.'

I calmed down again, and for a moment I wondered why I was putting myself through this – wouldn't it have been far easier to tell the truth? It was certainly tempting but Jack had said if I did that I'd be sacked immediately. Better to sit tight and stick to my story until this business with the missing necklace was over. That way I would at least keep my job.

'May I go now, sir?' I ventured, unnerved again by the way he kept re-reading the notes he'd made of Evie's interview.

Bailey put down his sheaf of papers and folded his hands on the desk in front of him. His eyes met mine again, and I fought not to squirm. 'Yes, Miss Parker, you may go. For now.'

Chapter 14

As both Evie and I had been questioned, I was allowed to return to attending her as usual. She was sitting by the window but turned eagerly to me as I came in. I had never seen her so upset.

'No one's blaming you, surely?' I said. 'It wasn't your fault.'

Evie shook her head, and her eyes slid away from meeting mine. 'The police found the note,' she said quietly. 'I left it in your room, and of course they've searched in there. It said exactly where the necklace was left.'

'You don't think I took it?' She shook her head but my heart turned over at the sight of her confusion; if Evie didn't believe me then who else could I turn to? Immediately my mind presented me with the only answer. He'd helped me more than once; would he help me now?

As if echoing my fervent wish Evie burst out, 'I wish Uncle Jack were here! He'd know exactly what to do.'

'He's not here?' I was surprised to hear my voice sounding close to normal despite the sudden tightness of my throat.

'He had to leave early last night, to go back to Liverpool.'

'I thought he was at the party?'

'Yes, but only for a while. He caught the ten o'clock train from Breckenhall. If he'd stayed, maybe he could have stopped all the gossip and I wouldn't have felt I had to take the stupid diamond off!' Her voice rose, cracking in her agitation, and I felt as if my own head was cracking along with it. Jack had lied, and not just to those at the party: everything he'd said to me out there on the lawn was a lie. He'd been protecting himself, not my job. The thought flashed through my mind that he might even have been the thief, but as Evie's words sank in I realised it was only after he'd left that she'd been driven to take it off.

So he had come back to the house in secret for *some* reason, which meant there was very little chance I could rely on him as a witness. My spirits plummeted further. I had to convince Evie of my innocence; I couldn't bear the way she was looking at me.

'I have to tell you something,' I said. She looked at me, stricken, and I went on quickly, 'I didn't steal your necklace, I promise. But I haven't been entirely truthful either.'

'All right,' Evie said, but the wariness that crept into her expression hurt me badly. She came closer and sat on the edge of the bed, waiting.

'I was outside last night, just as I said, but I didn't fall over.'

'Then how did you hurt yourself?'

'I got caught up in ...' I took a deep breath, aware that by telling her this I might be throwing everything away for no reason. 'In a fight. With some boys.'

Her face went slack with astonishment. 'Boys? What boys? Where?'

I explained how I'd gone outside to cool down, about hearing the voices and seeing the three boys out on the lawn beneath the trees, and how I'd recognised one of them. 'It was your brother.'

She frowned. '*Lawrence* was out there?'

'Yes. And the other two were taunting him about ... well, I didn't know what it was about, at the time, but it must have been about the necklace.'

'And then what happened? How did the fight start?'

I told her, and when I came to the part where my fingernails had been ripped on David Wingfield's coat, I showed her my hand again. 'Then he knocked me backwards and ... I must have banged my head on the ground or one of the tree roots.' There was no sense in accusing the boy of anything more violent, I realised. It was only likely to cause him to deny the whole story when confronted. 'Anyway, I think I must have fainted because when I opened my eyes everyone had gone. Seeing me like that probably scared them.'

Evie was pacing about now, more angry than upset. 'And what happened then?'

I decided a version of the truth was better than another outright lie. 'I hid in the outhouse until everyone had gone to bed.'

'But why? You should have had those cuts seen to immediately!'

'Evie, if anyone found out I'd been *out* there, let alone fighting with guests of your family, I would have been sacked on the spot!'

'Nonsense! Perhaps if you were a scullery maid still, but why would you think that?'

I shook my head helplessly. 'If I can be sacked over a silly kitchen accident or if someone caught me in a clinch with ... I don't know, Billy the stable boy ... why wouldn't I be dismissed over assaulting a house guest?'

'Yes, put like that I see how it looks,' she agreed. 'Well, I would have stuck up for you. In fact, I will. You must know I'll have to tell the police about this, if only to clear your name. Because I really believe they think you stole the Kalteng Star.'

'And you?' I asked, in a small voice, dreading her answer. 'Do you think I did?'

'Of course not,' she said more gently, rubbing my arm. 'And neither will they, once they've questioned those Wingfield brats.'

'But I still have no alibi,' I said. 'No one saw me after that, not until this morning.'

'Still, you have to go to the police now and tell them the truth,' Evie said. 'It's the only way to make sense of your story.'

I wrapped my arms around myself to try and calm the trembling. 'But then they'll know me to be a liar.'

'If you explain you were worried for your future here, I'm sure they'll understand. And if you do it before they talk to the Wingfields it's bound to be looked upon more favourably.'

She was right, and I could still do it without bringing Jack's name into it. Maybe one day I would find out what he had been doing at the house, and then wish I hadn't, but at the moment I owed him my life and, until I knew the full story, keeping quiet was the least I could do for him in return.

I sat before Inspector Bailey again later in the day. I was so tired now I could barely keep my eyes open, but I had to think clearly and keep to my story. Evie had been wonderful and I felt badly about deceiving her, but if Jack had wanted her to know he was at the house he would have told her. Unless she was keeping his secret too?

I closed my eyes against the headache that hammered away at my temples; it was all too much, I was growing dizzy trying to understand it all. The surface of the desk before Bailey seemed much more cluttered now, reflecting the turmoil in my mind; piles of written notes, a package wrapped in brown paper – presumably the policeman's lunch, he must have been expecting a long day – and diagrams and drawings of the layout of the house and grounds.

'So, you now claim you weren't in your room at all, but in the outhouse recovering from an illicit brawl on the front lawn,' Bailey mused as he wrote.

I flinched, and glanced over at Lady Creswell, whose expression was unreadable. 'Yes,' I said.

'A brawl involving Lord Lawrence Creswell, and two visitors from the Wingfield branch of the family.'

'I didn't know who they were until it was too late, sir. I just saw two bigger boys picking on a little one. It didn't seem fair.'

'No, indeed. Lady Creswell, I think Miss Parker is to be commended, don't you, for helping your son?'

I couldn't tell what she thought on the matter, but in any case I had no time to study her reaction; Inspector Bailey was talking again. 'So when we question all three boys, they will tell us the same thing?'

'Yes, sir. And all this happened at about half-past ten. I saw a light on in Miss Creswell's room at that time. It must have been when she was taking off the necklace.'

'Immediately prior to leaving the note in your room,' Bailey clarified, and I nodded.

He smiled. 'Miss Parker, you are to be commended further, I think.' My answering smile was wiped off my face a second later as he went on, 'You are surely one of the most skilled and consummate liars it's ever been my misfortune to encounter.'

The shock of it was like a slap. 'I ... I don't understand ...'

'I have questioned everyone who was at the party at the likely time of the theft, *including* those three boys, and not one of them has reported any such fight taking place. They did not leave the house all evening.'

I gaped at him, then stammered, 'Well, sir, perhaps they were scared because they'd done wrong—'

'Not even Lord Lawrence Creswell. And he did no wrong, did he? He'd have no reason to pretend to be anywhere else.'

'But it's the truth!'

'I'm coming to the conclusion that your notion of the truth must be taken with a very large pinch of salt.'

I couldn't think of a single thing to say in reply. Bailey sat back and regarded me with stony indifference. Then he reached out and unwrapped the brown paper package, which turned out not to be his lunch after all. I was surprised instead to see inside it my precious blue stole, muddied and crushed.

'Where did you find that?' I asked.

Bailey withdrew it from my eager reach. 'Were you wearing it when you got involved in this fight you mentioned?'

'No. I noticed it wasn't on my bed when I got back, but I thought it had dropped on to the floor and was too tired to look for it.'

'It was found in the kitchen garden, by one of my officers.'

'I wasn't wearing it! I hardly ever wear it out of the house. And I was hot from the ironing, why would I have been wearing something like that?'

'Precisely my point. I am sceptical of your claim that you went outside merely to cool off.'

I was growing desperate now. 'But the ironing—'

'We only have your word that you were working that late, Miss Parker.'

I stared at him in dismay, but he barely lifted his head from over his stack of notes. With an absent wave of his hand towards the door I was once again dismissed.

'I just don't know what to do, Evie,' I said. My fingers throbbed with each movement and I'd lost count of the times I'd stuck myself with the needle, but I'd dismissed her suggestion we should leave the mending until later; the normality of it was soothing somehow despite the discomfort in my fingers.

'The police are speaking to Clarissa Wingfield now,' Evie said. 'Try not to worry, they'll find the real thief.'

'Who's Clarissa Wingfield?'

'She's David and Robert's mother. I don't like her one bit,

but she'll know what her boys were up to at least. I've never known a woman with a tighter rein on her children.'

'Oh, good!' I felt the heavy blanket of despair lift a little. 'I wish I'd told the truth at the start.'

'Well, I understand why you didn't,' Evie said. 'If you didn't *need* to tell them you were fighting on the lawn—'

'You make it sound so horrible,' I said, able to smile at last. 'I was saving your little brother from a beating!'

'I know, and I'm sure he's grateful. Actually you'll be surprised to hear he's the same age as the elder brother, David, but the Wingfields come from burly stock and they seem much older; their grandfather, Samuel, is big too, and still very strong for his age. Those boys will have put the fear of God into poor Lawrence, he's not the bravest of soldiers. If they tell him to keep quiet, he'll keep quiet. Don't worry, though, if Clarissa has no luck *I'll* make sure Lawrence at least tells the truth.' Her tone was determined, but I recalled Jack's equally fierce warning to the Wingfield boy and reflected that I might well need Evie's help to get Lawrence's testimony. Even if it was his word against his cousins'.

'Well, I'm glad their mother is being questioned,' I said. 'I hope Lawrence won't be bullied into lying, though.'

'No, he's not a coward, not really, just young for his age and not very worldly. Comes of growing up without a father, I suppose. Or even much of a father figure.'

I heard my voice thicken as I asked, 'What about Mr Carlisle?'

'Well, as you've seen, he's rarely here for more than a day or two at a time, although lately he does seem to have been here rather more. That's not how it's been for the past ten years. But why should he be anyway? This is not his home, after all, and Mother says he only comes here because he feels bad about Father.'

My heart lurched, remembering Joe's story and how that jarred with the existence of the sturdy little tree hidden away at the bottom of the garden. 'Why should he feel bad? It wasn't his fault, was it?'

'He feels he should have been able to help Father. I keep telling him, it was war! Terrible things happen. He shouldn't punish himself.'

I let out my breath slowly in relief. 'Hasn't he a family to go to?'

'He travels such a lot,' Evie said, 'the one woman he was with long enough to form an attachment to ended up marrying someone else while he was away in Africa or somewhere. Well, you know her, Constance Harrington, who you looked after at Christmas.'

I remembered, glad I hadn't known at the time. 'She's very pretty. Beautiful actually.'

'Yes, she is. Clearly Jack thought so too; they were engaged for a year before she broke it off.'

I just stopped myself from expressing surprise that any woman would give Jack up so easily, and instead made a word-less little half-interested noise and concentrated on my pinning.

'I do actually like Constance, despite her breaking his heart,' Evie went on. 'And despite her being a Wingfield, of course.'

'She's a Wingfield too?' I said, trying not to dwell on the fact of Jack having his heart broken by another woman, especially the calm, elegant beauty I'd met just over a week ago.

'By birth, yes. She's sister to Matthew Wingfield. Hates his wife, though. That's Clarissa. You should see the two of them together, Lizzy. Daggers drawn but all camouflaged under this wonderful, icy politeness – it's a perfect scream!'

'So Clarissa dislikes Constance as much as Constance dislikes her?' I was starting to quite like the sound of this Clarissa; not only would she help prove my innocence, but she had taken against Jack's former fiancée too.

'Between you and me, I think Clarissa is jealous of Constance's great good fortune in marrying the handsome Doctor Harrington. And, of course, Constance is a real Wingfield by blood, whereas Clarissa is just a Latchbrook who made a lucky match. Oddly, though, it's Clarissa who gets on better with Samuel. He's not a nice person at all but he certainly approves of Matthew's choice of wife.'

'And Matthew is his son?' It was hard to keep the relationships straight in my head, but it took my mind off everything else, and I welcomed the normality of our conversation.

'Yes. Matthew is lovely. Quiet, but very kind. He would do anything to help anyone. He lacks much of a sense of humour but you can't hold that against him. Heaven only knows how he and Clarissa ended up together, I can only assume he was too timid to turn her away! His other sister, Susannah, sadly died a long time ago.'

'So Constance and Matthew are more like their mother?'

'I should say so, thank goodness; Lydia's a little mouse. Constance is much younger than Matthew as well, so she's the baby, really.'

I worked in a strangely contented silence while Evie told me more about Jack's wonderful fiancée, who had made no secret of her wish that he had chosen a regular job instead of one that took him overseas so much. In that much, at least, she had my sympathy.

Eventually, however, the conversation came back to the grim and frightening present.

'Have they spoken to Mary yet?' Evie asked.

'I don't know, I've not seen her since this morning.' Mary would speak on my behalf, I knew that, but anything she had to say could only be in support of my character; we hadn't seen each other at all the previous night.

'I think I heard Mother say the kitchen staff were next on Inspector Bailey's list,' Evie said. 'That shouldn't take long. They were all so busy no one would have seen anything but food and dishwater all night.'

'Well, one good thing will come of talking to them,' I said, putting in the last pin. I stood up and stretched to ease the ache in my back. 'They'll be able to tell him I wasn't wearing the stole when I went out.'

Evie looked troubled. 'Will they, though? Do you think they'd remember?'

'They would if they'd seen it,' I said. 'It's not something I'd be likely to be wearing with my uniform, is it?'

As I spoke my spirits lifted further, and, reluctant to be brought low again, I urged Evie to change the subject. She told me more about the Women's Suffrage Movement with which she had become involved, much to her mother's disapproval, and I listened with half an ear while the rest of my attention strained for the sound of a car arriving on the front driveway.

But Jack would be away for some time, and my disappointment was mingled with relief. It was as well he was out of sight, and I would have hated him to hear the rumours that I was a thief, but I was constantly surprised by how flat I felt when he wasn't around. I dreaded the day he would arrive with a new woman in tow, someone who would hold his arm, and his heart, and would wordlessly, unknowingly, rob me of all my cherished dreams.

Just the knowledge that he was in the house had always given my working days an undercurrent of pleasure and anticipation, but now I wished he was here so I could warn him it might be discovered that he had been at the house long after he was supposed to have left. I didn't want to dwell on the reason why; it wasn't only unknown, faceless women who could shatter my dreams.

A knock at the door brought my own attention fully back to the moment, and I opened it to see Inspector Bailey, Lady Creswell and a uniformed policeman, all staring straight at me and all grim-faced.

Bailey laid his hand on my arm and I froze from the inside out. 'Mary Elizabeth Parker, you are under arrest for the theft of a necklace containing the diamond known as the Kalteng Star.'

Chapter 15

After that it all became one short, brutal nightmare of blurred faces, questions, and an awful, aching sense of loss. One moment I had been talking to Evie, letting her enthusiasm and optimism lift me out of the fear that had gripped me since Bailey first questioned me, and the next, it seemed, I stood alone in the dock at the courthouse in Chester.

Of what had happened in between I had no clear recollection. All I could remember was Evie's shocked gasp at my arrest, and her voice calling after me as I was led away down the hall, 'I believe you, Lizzy! And I'll help you!'

But she hadn't been able to help, and now I would be lucky if she still held my words to be true in her own heart, no matter what she had said then. I could hardly blame her, given the stories that had emerged about that awful night.

Ruth Wilkins, her expression carefully hiding all the spite it generally reflected, had stood there in front of the jury and calmly lied her way through her testimony.

'Mary asked me to go and find Park ... the defendant ...

since we was short-handed in the kitchen, and her mistress was at the party,' she said. That alone made me cross; did they think I'd been sitting down with a book?

'And did you find her?' the prosecutor asked.

'No, sir. I went into her workroom and she wun't there.'

'Did you check her bedroom?'

'I knocked but there was no answer, and I didn't think she'd be in there anyway, since it weren't knockin' off time yet. I went back down to the kitchen.'

'And?'

Ruth cleared her throat, and darted a glance at me. 'And I seen her just goin' out the back door, so I followed her.'

'Did anyone else see her?'

'Not so far as I know, they was all pretty busy, sir.'

I would have put my year's wages on a bet that she was lying, but of course I couldn't be sure. Not yet.

'And what did you see, when you followed Miss Parker outside?'

'I seen her standing by the gate, the one that goes out to the main garden.'

'Was she alone?'

'No, sir. There was a man. I din't recognise him, it was darker over there.'

I drew a slow, shaky breath – I didn't think she had seen me when I'd originally gone out, but it was possible she *had* seen me by the back gate later, with Jack: although her overall story was a lie, it might well have been made up of a selection of disjointed truths.

'Miss Wilkins, did anything strike you as odd about Miss Parker's behaviour?'

'She did seem a bit anxious, sir. She din't look too happy to be with the man by the gate.'

'And can you tell me what she was wearing?'

'Her uniform, sir.'

'Nothing else?'

She shook her head, and relief thundered through me; no mention of the blue stole.

'And was she carrying anything?'

'I seen her take something out of her apron pocket, wrapped in something soft.'

'Soft like velvet, perhaps?'

This time the look she gave me struck cold in my heart. 'Yes, sir. Maybe like velvet.'

I gripped the wooden rail in front of me, every part of me wanting to scream that she was lying, but I knew I could never prove it. All I could do was hope the story was torn apart by further questioning and more truthful testimony.

'What did Miss Parker do with this object she took from her pocket?'

'She gave it to the man, and then I went back in. It was cold, and besides they looked as if they might be arguing. I din't like to interfere.'

Bless her black heart ...

'And that is the last you saw of Miss Parker on the evening of December the thirty-first last year?'

'It is, sir.'

'No more questions, Your Honour.'

The judge turned to my defence counsel. 'Do you have any questions for this witness?'

Counsel bobbed up in his seat. 'No, Your Honour.'

205

'Very well. The witness may step down.'

Before Ruth did so, she very publicly shot me a helpless 'I'm sorry' look, and raised her shoulders in a shrug of faux-regret. At that moment it was as well we were separated by court officials: my throbbing hands curled into fists, and my teeth were grinding so hard against each other I half-expected to feel them splinter in my gums.

The next witness was Evie, who spoke warmly of me, of my hard work and my general character, but who could not, in all conscience, account for my whereabouts that night.

'I wrote the note, left it on her ironing table, and went back downstairs,' she said.

'And you didn't see Parker at all between her dressing you for the party and rousing you the next morning with your tea?'

Evie's apologetic look was at least genuine. 'No.'

'Thank you, Miss Creswell, you may step down.'

And then it was the turn of Clarissa Wingfield. She took the oath, a tall woman with elaborately dressed hair and a gown so nipped in at the waist I wondered how she could breathe.

But she plainly had enough breath to seal my fate. 'I understand there had been some taunting in respect of Miss Creswell's jewellery,' she said in a clear, accentless voice that carried right across the courtroom without any necessity to raise it at all. I might have been impressed by her bearing had I not been listening to an even bigger pack of lies than those spouted by the hateful Ruth Wilkins.

'I followed her from the party, she seemed upset.' At this, her voice softened and she turned sympathetic eyes on Evie, who sat close by with her mother. 'I thought perhaps to comfort her.'

'Who was doing the taunting, Mrs Wingfield?' the official asked.

'To my shame, I confess that my sons were partly to blame for Miss Creswell's distress,' Clarissa said, and cast her gaze downwards. I frowned, sensing something nasty in the offing.

The prosecutor continued, 'So you sought to redress the insults by offering comfort. I see. And how did Miss Creswell react to this offer?'

'I didn't see her. I reached the top of the stairs but saw Miss Parker instead, going towards Miss Creswell's room. I'd heard they got along terribly well, and thought her better equipped to deal with the situation.'

This was too much for me. 'But I didn't go anywhere near Evie's room!' I protested.

'Silence,' the judge reproved, and I caught Evie's stricken look.

'Please, Your Honour, I never did. I was—'

'Be quiet, Miss Parker, or you will be held in contempt,' the judge said, and I subsided, my heart hammering in fear. Surely these lies would be exposed?

'And when you went back downstairs,' the prosecutor continued, 'did you find your sons David and Robert in the house?'

'Yes, Your Honour, I did.'

'Was there anything in their appearance or demeanour to suggest they had been fighting?'

'No. They had clearly made up their quarrel with Lord Lawrence and were all playing billiards together.'

'No mud on their clothes. No ...' he consulted his notes '... torn clothing?'

'Nothing,' Clarissa said, her voice firm. She didn't look at me once.

Mary took the stand to attest to my honesty and good character, but this was immediately thrown into question by the fact that I had initially lied to the police when questioned. She cast me a look of dismay and was quickly dismissed.

Mrs Cavendish said she had seen me hurrying through the kitchen, that I had seemed flustered and hot, and that I hadn't returned at once. At first I took this to be a good thing; it was the truth at least. She hadn't seen the blue stole, but then Ruth had already testified that I had removed it from my pocket. However the housekeeper then admitted she had been called upstairs shortly afterwards, and so could not say with any certainty whether I'd come back in. I could have wept, but instead stared dry-eyed as the questions were asked, answered, and gradually built their impenetrable wall of evidence around me.

All through the trial I felt my longing for Jack increasing; just seeing him would give me strength, I knew that much, and several times I came close to blurting out his name as a witness, but each time I did I remembered he had saved my life. I must do what I could to repay that, and trust in the justice system to prove my innocence.

There was always the hope that he would be called, and, seeing my terrible situation, would at least admit to having returned to the house and broken up the fight. But although his name was mentioned, and I started to shake in anticipation, it was only as having been a guest at the party. Many people had seen him leave well before ten o'clock, and he was in consequence discounted as a possible witness to the theft.

As the questioning turned away from him, and back on to what Ruth had seen by the gate, I realised she hadn't seen Jack at all. He would have noticed her standing by the kitchen door, surely, even if I hadn't been seeing too well myself at that point. No, it was a complete fabrication on her part and I wondered if, had I not been the unwilling object of Frank Markham's attention at Christmas, her story would have been the same. But I would never know.

'And so, Miss Parker, we are led to believe that you stole the diamond necklace under the orders of this mysterious gentleman. Will you not identify him? You owe him nothing. After all, he *has* left you facing this rather discordant music all alone.'

'There was no gentleman,' I insisted, and now my throat was tight with tears. 'I just went out to get some air!'

'And you broke up a fight between three strapping young men?'

'They were only boys! I know it sounds—'

'Thank you, Miss Parker.'

The defence rose. 'Your Honour, I would like to call Lord Lawrence Creswell.'

Lawrence! Evie must have been able to talk to him after all . . . I could have hugged the boy. He stood opposite me but did not look in my direction as the questions were asked. He confessed that, yes, he and the Wingfields *had* quarrelled and that their argument had spilled out from the billiard room into the garden.

'We were scared to say so before,' he said, sounding far younger than his fifteen years. 'We weren't supposed to go outside. Afterwards I went and got changed, and gave Robert some spare clothes too. The muddy ones are hidden in my room.'

With each word my heart lifted a little higher, and I could feel the joy creeping over my face as the story unravelled. I met Evie's and Mary's eyes and they sent me their own smiles of relief and delight, and then I turned my attention back to Lawrence ... and went cold all over.

'I heard Robert say "Get off him!" and David did, and I just ran away.'

'No!' I cried. 'I was the one who said that!' I tried to remember if I'd mentioned it in any of my interrogations, but it hadn't seemed important at the time and had doubtless been forgotten in my desperation to prove how I had come by my injuries. Now it sounded as though I were seizing on a piece of the boys' story I could use for my own convenience, and the defence counsel glanced at me, frowning before he continued. 'Did you see anyone apart from your cousins? Did you, perhaps, look back as you ran away and see a third person by the trees? Think very carefully, now,' he addressed the witness.

'No, sir. I just realised David had stopped hitting me, and I got up and ran before he could start again.'

'And the voice that told him to get off, *could* that have been a female voice rather than a male one?'

'Well, Robert's voice is ...' Lawrence stopped and looked down at his feet, embarrassed. 'Everyone knows he sounds like a girl, sir, sometimes.'

Everyone except me, I thought with rising despair.

Having done the job of the prosecution, albeit unwittingly, Lawrence was then dismissed, and with him my last hope. I was drowning again.

Robert made a brief appearance, but while I believed Lawrence had been telling the truth and really hadn't been aware of my presence, Robert had clearly been carefully schooled in what to say. His voice confirmed Lawrence's assertion that he sounded like a girl when scared; he was clearly terrified now as he mumbled his way through his testimony, describing how he had pulled his brother David off Lawrence and let the smaller boy go free.

Then it was David's turn, and he echoed his younger brother's story almost word for word. He even contrived to send an annoyed glance Robert's way as he described how his best coat had been torn after he'd only worn it once.

And then I was called again. I stood determined to break apart the Wingfields' version of events, and once again bitterly regretted I hadn't mentioned that first, angry shout; it was my only real proof I'd been there, since it was the only sound I'd made while Lord Lawrence had still been within earshot.

But when my barrister asked about it I could only shake my head. 'I know I didn't mention it before but it's the truth. And it was me who pulled him off Lord Lawrence too. I twisted his ear and made him angry, which was when he hit me.' I gestured to my still-swollen lip.

'But none of the boys admit to having seen you there, how do you explain that?'

I agreed that Lawrence might not have seen me, but did not hold back in implying that David had manipulated both his brother and the truth.

The prosecutor stood up to cross-examine me then. 'Why would they lie, Miss Parker?'

'And why would I?' I countered. 'I must have been there, or how would I know they'd been fighting at all since they kept it so secret?'

From the corner of my eye I was aware of several people sitting forward with sudden interest, and allowed myself another glimmer of hope, but that was quickly extinguished too.

'Your rooms, and those of Miss Creswell, are on the same side of the house, is that correct?'

I was momentarily taken aback by this change of tack. 'Yes,' I said, after a moment's pause.

'Ah. Very nice views, I gather, from the front of the house. Right down the avenue, and . . .' counsel smiled, but it was the smile of a shark '. . . across the gardens. Gardens accessed from the French windows that open directly from the billiard room downstairs.'

'I wasn't in my room!' I protested again, but hopelessness was draining the last of my strength.

'Very well, let us assume you *were* out in the yard and overheard the fighting. Tell us again; you ran across the wet grass towards the trees?'

'Yes.'

'Where were your shoes and stockings at this time, Miss Parker?'

'My . . .?'

'I'll remind you. Your shoes were discovered in the outhouse, your stockings found, by Miss Emma Bird, in your apron pocket. Somewhat bloodied.'

'Oh. Yes, I took them off, my feet were hot.' It sounded utterly implausible now, and I cursed the impulse that had made me do it, but it was too late. Far, far too late.

'The blood was from after the fight. I used the stockings to wipe my fingers on,' I added.

The prosecutor frowned. 'I submit to this court that you saw

212

the note from your mistress, took the opportunity to steal the diamond, and arranged to meet someone who could remove it from the premises.'

'But who? And how could I have arranged that? No one knew Ev— Miss Creswell was going to take it off until halfway through the party.'

'Oaklands Manor is equipped with a telephone, is it not?'

'But I've never used one of those in my life! I wouldn't know how.'

'So you say.' He dismissed this with a wave. 'Miss Parker, I put it to you that yourself and the unknown gentleman had relations of a physical nature in the outhouse. After which you argued, perhaps because this had been your first time, and you used the rolled-up stockings to, shall we say, *tidy* yourself afterwards.'

Shock at the mere thought of it was enough to stop my breath, but now the prosecutor was re-stating his theory, which put the accusation of illicit coupling firmly in the background.

'You stole the diamond under this man's direction, and you have concealed his identity either out of loyalty or from fear of reprisal.'

'No, that's not true.' I managed to keep my voice steady with an effort, but I could feel everything slipping away. It occurred to me that even if I now broke down and named Jack as the man who'd saved me, I would be shouted down, disbelieved – everyone thought he'd left the party, and his distinctive motor car had not been observed again.

I was on my own.

*

213

As the judge passed sentence the room grew dark around me and I fought wave after wave of shivering nausea. How could this be happening? I listened, fighting not to cry out in my own defence as the judge spoke about this being 'no petty crime, not the theft of food, nor of clothing, that might be understandable, but the wilful and materialistic grasping at a family heirloom of great value, for no other purpose than personal gain'.

Fat tears poured down my cheeks as I heard the words: 'Ten years' penal servitude, to be served at Holloway Women's Prison in London. Take her down.'

I stepped from the dock on trembling legs, the warder's hand on my arm part restraint, part support, and just before I began the final descent of the wooden stairs to the cells below I cast about in desperation for a friendly face. Ruth was staring at me, stunned, but turned away quickly as our eyes met. I saw Mrs Cavendish and Mrs Hannah, and even Frank Markham was there, but there was no sign of Will. And none, of course, of Jack.

Then I caught sight of Evie's pale, anguished face, and beside her Mary, who defied etiquette and put her arm around the younger woman. They both kept their eyes on me as I was ushered down, and their faces mirrored my own disbelief and shock.

Theirs were the last faces I looked fully upon until my arrival at Holloway some ten hours later, and passing through the gate into the grimness that lay beyond, I held tight to the memory. As the shadow of the prison walls fell over my face, a dark spot began to creep towards the centre of my heart and, hopeless and bleak-spirited, I let it spread. Only when I felt it threaten to eclipse the brief joy of working for Evie, and of knowing Jack, Will and Mary, did I close myself off to the darkness. Whatever awaited me in prison, that tiny glimmer of light must not be extinguished.

Part Two

Chapter 16

28 September 1916

The day I turned twenty-two is a day I shall never forget. Much of what I endured inside Holloway Prison is locked away in the darkest recesses of my mind and I shall never forget that either, but this day would prove to be one of the most exhilarating, tiring, enlightening and puzzling of my life, and the speed with which I spun back and forth between these emotions left me breathless.

It began early for me, as always, and with the same sense of grim determination not to bow to the misery that had been my constant companion within the prison walls. After all, I had been shut up here for three and a half years, and had twice that again before me. People came and went around me, some young and scared as I had been, some already hardened by life and accepting their punishment as just; others, perhaps victims of circumstance, were openly guilty, but

219

bewildered by the way their lives had slid so swiftly into this nightmare.

Many claimed injustice, and who knew which of them to believe? It didn't matter anyway. Innocent or not, here we were, and here we would stay until the law said otherwise. I had long since stopped bemoaning the cruel twists of fate that had brought me here; I'd learned it only angered the other prisoners, and had grown to share their frustration and annoyance when newcomers wailed and wept, believing their own innocence to matter more than anyone else's.

On arrival I had been ushered into a reception room with five other women, two of whom had already struck up an alliance of sorts and were promising to look out for one another in the dark days to come. They fell into miserable silence as the wardress barked 'Quiet!' and stared at the floor, not daring to speak again. I felt icy despair creeping over me with every shuffle of someone else's feet, every sigh, every whimper from the youngest girl, who was trying to stifle her sobs but doing a poor job.

The remaining two women were clearly old hands and knew what to expect; they remained straight-backed, with their heads up, eyes meeting those of the wardress with something that seemed like belligerence but might have been mere bravado. I was to learn that those two were often mistaken for one another, and to use them frequently myself.

Upon being taken to the doctor I was instructed to undress. I had balked at undressing before Mary on my first day at Oaklands, but this order made my insides cramp with terror. But undress I did, and was subjected to the indignity of a thorough search, then questioned about my age and general state of health before being taken for my bath.

By the time I had realised the wardress was to watch this too, the last shreds of bashfulness were falling away from me. As I dried myself under her dispassionate gaze I turned my back, and found I was then able at least to stand upright. I turned my thoughts to my friends, and to Jack, and in the strange, aching warmth of missing them I managed to struggle through the terror of the next hour or so.

Dressed in prison uniform of rough brown serge and a simple white cap, I stumbled along in over-large shoes to my cell, in the wake of a different wardress. She gave me some bed-sheets, and offered me a toothbrush and a bible and a couple of other small books; a hymn book, I noticed, and one on cleanliness.

She then handed me a yellow badge, upon which were scratched some numbers and a letter: 24.D2.

'That's you from now on,' she said. 'Those there are your cell and block number. You'll be known as Twenty-four while you're here.'

Twenty-four. Another new name for another new life. I thought of Evie and her laughing, deliberate misunderstandings, and would have given anything to hear her call me Just Lizzy again. Somehow I held back the sob that cramped my neck and jaw until the wardress had locked the door, and then I collapsed on to the plank bed and gave in to misery until, drained and hot-eyed, I fell into a sleep filled with terrifying dreams.

My first full day had begun all too soon afterwards, and it set the tone for the next three and a half years. Getting up at five-thirty was nothing new, and my time in the scullery stood me in good stead for cleaning my cell, but the breakfast we were

221

given left a hollow growl of hunger in our bellies as we worked; there was far too long between the tea and chunk of bread they gave us then and our evening meal, and even that was sparse and not nearly nutritious enough. I could have swum in the amount of tea we were given, though, presumably to fill us up so there were fewer complaints of hunger.

Apart from chapel, our day's work and exercise were undertaken in compulsory silence; I looked out for the two women who had sworn comradeship and mutual protection in the reception cell, and saw they now no longer even looked at one another.

If this saddened me, then all the more so did my realisation of the terrible injustices heaped on the women of the Suffragette Movement Evie had championed. Sent to scrub one of these prisoners' cells on my second day, I was horrified and revolted by the evidence of her having been forcibly fed, yet the prisoner, Sylvia Pankhurst, watched me work with a look of intense pity on her face, as if it were I who had been so terribly wronged.

The strength of these women, and their determination not to bow under the weight of their beliefs, helped me through some of the worst experiences of my incarceration. When I had been at Holloway for a week I was allowed to take another bath. Afterwards, shivering in the January chill and pulling my clothes on over still-wet skin, I heard footsteps, and worked faster so as not to hold up the next person in the queue, but I didn't bother to straighten the stripes on my stockings; without garters to hold them up they would only slip askew again anyway. Finished, I reached for my cap.

'Oh, don't cover up all that smashin' hair on my account,' a voice said, and it sounded so much like Ruth's, both in accent and in tone, that my blood froze. When I looked around I saw a much older woman, overweight; surprisingly, though, her pallor and poor skin proclaimed her to be a long-time inmate of the prison. She was looking at me as if I had crawled out from behind the skirting with the rats.

'I'll be out of your way in a moment,' I said, and reached up to put on my cap. To my shock, her heavy hand whipped out and seized it instead, tearing it from my grasp and flinging it over my head. It landed in the bath and floated there, an incongruous white island in the grey water.

A strange, calm fury settled on me. I deliberately turned my back on the woman and lifted the sopping cap out of the water, dismayed but not in the least surprised to feel a hand in the middle of my back, shoving me against the edge of the tub. I stumbled to my knees and struck the bath with my ribs. My whole side flared with pain, but it wasn't until I felt her seize my hair and shove my head forward that I cried out.

My face was plunged into the chilly water and it took every bit of strength I possessed to resist the urge to draw breath and scream again. Instead I went limp, and the grip on my hair slackened immediately, my attacker caught unawares by the ease of her victory. I kicked blindly backwards and felt my stockinged foot connect with a plump knee beneath a thick dress, and the woman stumbled and let go of me altogether.

Raising my dripping head from the bath I leaped up and around, wrenching my neck but being rewarded by the wet slapping sound my cap made as I hit the startled woman full in the face with it.

'Leave me alone!' I yelled, and although my anger was in the forefront, there was terror there too, lending my voice an added strength; it would have been so easy for her to have

223

finished me, and put me back in the bath to make it seem like just another despair-driven suicide. She still might.

Trembling and feeling sick at the thought, I waited to see if she would strike me again, but she just looked at me with extreme dislike. 'You want to watch yourself,' she said. 'One of these days I'm going to cut that hair right off your snooty little head. And maybe your ears with it. Then you wouldn't look quite such the pert and pretty little princess, would you?'

So that was it. Her own features were ill-defined and doughy, her hair wispy and grey, and she had simply decided I didn't deserve to be any different. Perhaps I didn't, but the way she had chosen to express her jealousy was frightening, and next time it might have a very different outcome.

For a moment I toyed with the idea of cutting my hair myself, even shaving it right off, if it would mean I'd be left alone, but then I compared her bullying mentality with the cool courage of so many of the women here, fighting for the rights of this wretch as much as any woman's. I owed them, at least, and from somewhere deep down I found the steel I had always hoped to possess.

'You touch me again and you'll be sorry,' I said. I had no idea what I would do, but just hearing the words from my own lips, as full of false bravado as they were, gave me the courage to look her in the eye without flinching. She glared back at me for a long moment and I knew it wasn't over, but I picked up my blue-and-white apron, straight-backed and bold, and walked past her and out of the room. She let me go. This time.

And so the months had stretched into years. So much time, and many equally unpleasant encounters, but with each one I grew a little less afraid. Equally, though, I grew more tired and more depressed, until I faced each day wondering how I would find the strength to see it to the end, whole and in my right mind.

Mary had written to me without fail each month, her notes full of news both good and bad, some funny and some of bleaker, sadder things – these letters often arrived bundled together all at once after several contactless months, but the dates written on them told me I had been in her thoughts throughout.

Evie had also written diligently, and one of her earliest letters I had read over and over, her hope and excitement rolling off the paper and into my heart.

Dearest Lizzy,

I have written to Uncle Jack in the hope he may help to secure your release. I don't know how, but he does seem to know some terribly important people. I await his response, but will write to you immediately as soon as I hear he is on his way, for I am sure he soon will be!

Yr loving friend,

Evie

I held this letter close to my heart for a long, trembling time, as if I could make a reply come from Jack all the sooner simply by the strength of my longing. I slept with it under my pillow for weeks, drawing strength from it, using it to drive me forward through each interminable day and each cold, achingly lonely night.

One piece of news, coming from both Evie and Mary and arriving on the same day, had surprised me less than it might have done. Mary had sounded the more shocked in her letter.

Dear Lizzy,

I find myself writing to you with astonishing news: immediately
upon our return to Oaklands following your trial, Lady
Creswell appointed Ruth Wilkins as her daughter's maid. I can't
think that Evie was happy about it, but she remained in shock
for some time after your departure, and had little heart for a
fight. (Unusual, I know!)

> *But the scandal of it is that a mere month or two later Ruth*
> *got put in the family way, and was dismissed . . .*

Evie's letter was just as simple, and an image of her sitting at
her writing table, a scowl on her pretty features as she composed it, made me smile for once in my benighted existence.

Dear Lizzy.

Mother has done it again! Her judgement of character is so poor
I can only wonder at her friendship with Uncle Jack. Can you
believe she insisted I accept Ruth Wilkins as my companion, as if
she could fill your shoes? In any case, that little wretch has
shown her true worth, and managed to get herself pregnant. Of
course, she didn't get herself pregnant at all, but you understand
my meaning!

> *She has naturally been sacked, and I intend to name your*
> *friend Mary as my chosen maid. This will annoy Mrs*
> *Cavendish, of course, as a good housemaid is hard to come by –*
> *but a good lady's maid even harder, as we have found out!*

> *I miss you so much, and will do everything in my rather*
> *limited power to see you are released as soon as possible from*
> *this ridiculous charge.*

But nothing apparently had been heard of Jack Carlisle, and while I still held on to a tiny glimmer of hope, his absence, and Evie's worry over it, cast a shadow blacker than ever over my heart. If she had dismissed it without comment I might have attributed this disappearance to habit; that Jack had taken up travelling again and this was the way he usually conducted his life. But Evie was growing more and more concerned and so, therefore, was I.

Then, one day in early 1914, she wrote again and I saw the words dance in front of my eyes, blurred by my tears of relief:

Darling Lizzy,

Uncle Jack is well! I have received a letter from him, rather a hurried one, but he tells me he is back in Africa, and quite safe! (Although the letter has, for some reason, been routed through Serbia, as the postmark shows, which is probably why it has only now arrived.) I'm afraid that this means he will not be able to go to the government on your behalf after all, being so far away, I'm so sorry. But I promise, nothing *will prevent me writing again and again to ask for his help and advice.'*

Yrs ever,

E.

But the fact that he was in no position to overturn my conviction faded in importance next to this confirmation of Jack's continued safety. A weight lifted from my heart as I read the first four words over and over again. Naturally it hurt that he had not cared enough for me to risk whatever secret he had been keeping that night, or worse, that he had not come back to help, even when he'd learned of my arrest. But he had not been obliged to do so, had not asked me to help him by concealing his presence on that night, and despite the way he'd acted, and those softly spoken words with which we'd parted in the first bleak moments of 1913, he had never professed any lasting feelings for me. I told myself I had no right to expect anything more of him.

There was another question that troubled me occasionally, but I stamped on it every time it surfaced because if I ever discovered any truth in the darkest of my suspicions, it might destroy the very last piece of me I still recognised, the piece that wasn't Twenty-four but still Just Lizzy.

Instead I read those words again: *Uncle Jack is well!* And just knowing he was alive, somewhere out there in the vast world beyond these prison walls, was enough to keep at bay the stinging sense of betrayal that kept threatening to undermine my present happiness. And he might yet help me.

Evie's letters, and her accounts of all she was doing to secure my release, continued until war broke out, whereupon she instantly, predictably, launched herself into the thick of things.

I had memorised her last letter. Not deliberately, but from having read it so many times I could recall every crease, every smudge and every word.

Dearest Lizzy,
I know Mary has been keeping you abreast of the progress of this awful war, and you will have heard something of it from those you now live with [typical Evie, not to say the word 'prisoner' even once during her writings], *but I am unsure if she has told you of my news and so I write to share it with you now.*

228

I have decided, much to Mother's absolute fury – although I must suppose that it is largely due to fear for my safety – that I am going to become what they call a VAD. This stands for Voluntary Aid Detachment and, while I am sure I do not have the temperament for nursing, I believe I can put my skills to good use as an ambulance driver. If he were here Uncle Jack would have to stop berating me for my driving habits at last!

This means I will soon be travelling to Belgium. It also means, my dear friend, that once I am gone from England my letters home may be few and far between.

There was more, of course: her concern for my well-being, along with news I *had* already heard from Mary – that Joe Shackleton, along with Billy Duncan the stable boy and Andrew Moore the second footman, had signed up to join the military. And, to my dismay, that Will had done the same ... news which had brought home to me the truth of the seemingly distant conflict in a way nothing else had.

Evie, an heiress with the temperament of a mischievous schoolchild and the heart of a lion, had completed her Red Cross training and left England even before her letter reached me in Holloway, so by the time I was reading it she was facing shells, bullets and gas, and other horrors I couldn't imagine.

In almost my every waking moment since war broke out I had been thinking about those I had known at my two homes, in Plymouth and Cheshire. My brothers Adie and Albert were thankfully far too young to join up, and unless the war lasted another twelve years they wouldn't have to do so. Everyone said it would be over by Christmas anyway. But there were others I had known from Plymouth, men and boys who would have been quick to join the cause. I would never know what had happened to them, if they lived or were lost – it seemed disrespectful to the memory of such sacrifice somehow.

Naturally the one person on whom my thoughts rested more than any other when I considered our fighting men was Jack. No one, not even Evie, had mentioned him again in their correspondence to me. After all, they had no notion of the nature of our acquaintance, but I knew that as an experienced soldier he would have gone immediately to the front lines. I prayed for his safety every night, and my heart guarded that secret, bright spot at its centre that had been my happiest self, reminding me that life had once been full of love, laughter and excitement, and that one day it might be so again.

In September 1916, on my twenty-second birthday, I joined the other women at exercise after the usual bland and insufficient breakfast, nodding to those I had some form of acquaintance with, ignoring those I hadn't. It hadn't taken long for me to understand the way things worked and, just as I had adapted to a new life and a new name at Oaklands, I had adapted here. As Twenty-four, rather than Lizzy, I was only a little ashamed to admit that I had become one of those very people I had been so wary of at first: distant, cold, unwilling to speak beyond what was necessary. In short, I had hardened over these past three and a half years, and although part of me regretted that, it had turned out to be the saving of me.

Exercise hour was almost over, and I was feeling more tired than usual and quite shivery. Another of the frequent chills to which we were prone was setting in, but I swallowed a sigh of weary acceptance as I was called back inside early and led by a wardress to the governor's office. Two hours later, dizzy at the speed with which it had all happened, I was at the main gate to the prison, clutching my small case of belongings and listening to the familiar cold clanking of keys. But this time it was the song of freedom they sang.

The official notification had poured over me like warm water: *released, witness, alibi* ... why it had taken so long they couldn't say, but evidently I was now free to engage legal advice and seek redress for wrongful conviction. It was the word 'free' that finally convinced me of what was happening, and by the time I had ordered my whirling thoughts and realised the Wingfield boys must finally have come forward and told the truth, I had been in my cell collecting my things.

There was no one here I wanted to speak to or would even be allowed to share my news with, no one I knew who would be honestly glad for me, so I packed my change of clothes, my hairbrush and my letters, and ignored the stares of silent, resentful speculation all around me. Instead, I concentrated on the thought that had begun to glow in my mind like a beacon of hope as I went through the process of release. Those boys would not have come forward voluntarily: David hated me, and Robert was led by his elder brother in all things. Lord Lawrence had run away the moment I'd arrived and hadn't looked back to recognise his saviour or to see mine. So someone the Wingfield boys either feared or respected had put pressure upon them to admit the truth, and the only other person who knew for certain that I had been there was Jack Carlisle.

At the thought of his name, spoken inside my head in his own low, lightly accented voice, I felt the glowing beacon brighten until it felt as if its light would fill my whole body and must be shining out through my eyes. It had taken a long time, but Jack had finally put right the terrible wrong he had done me. With luck I would see him once again, and maybe have the chance to forgive him to his face instead of in my dreams.

The warden dropped the keys as they grew slippery with rain, and I bit my lip so as not to exclaim aloud in my frantic need to step through this final barrier. Being so close to freedom, every second seemed like an hour to me ... how on earth would I react if someone laid a hand on my shoulder now and told me it had all been a mistake? My heart hammering with the sudden certainty it would happen, I turned quickly, fully expecting to see the hand already reaching towards me and only noticing how violently my legs were shaking when I saw empty air instead.

The key finally found the lock and turned, and then I was outside the prison walls. As on my long-ago first half-day holiday I had somehow expected the air to taste different, and this time it did. It seemed a breeze had sprung up expressly to blow away the city grime that hung in the air sticking to skin and hair and clothes, and I turned into it with gratitude, and a wide smile that felt as if it would split my face in two. Even the drizzle felt good.

I hadn't realised my eyes were closed, and was happily drifting in my unexpected, and therefore even sweeter, freedom until a hand landed on my arm and jerked me back.

'Happy birthday, Lizzy.'

That voice, heard so often in my head, now lodged in my

heart as if it had always been there. My eyes searched Jack's face, seeing tiredness and deep remorse, but also the unmistakable reflection of my own feelings. Before I knew what I was doing I had lashed out, striking him hard across the face, the force of it burning my hand. Angered beyond belief, I curled that same hand into a fist and brought it down on his chest, needing him to feel the pain of betrayal as I did, to understand some of what I couldn't put into words.

He grabbed my wrist, my name urgent on his lips, and I subsided, dry-eyed and confused at the intensity of my rage. I didn't know where it had come from or how long it had lain quiet inside me, but now he was here, the man who had saved my life and then left me to wish it gone ... the line between love and hate had blurred until they were inseparable.

We stared at one another, both breathing hard in the silence that had fallen. How could any words be enough to lend further weight to what was already passing between us? After a while my heart ceased its thundering, although an insistent throb had set up behind my eyes. As the silence stretched between us I searched for a way to demand the explanations we both needed, but tension began to creep back and the right words to say remained beyond my grasp. Then Jack pulled me to him and I felt his lips press against the top of my head.

I recoiled, thoughts of where I had just come from suddenly uppermost. 'Don't! Please.'

'Lizzy, I—'

'Can we go?'

'Yes, I'm sorry. Of course.' He kept looking around him, as if he expected someone to come and drag me back inside, and since that same feeling hadn't left me either we were both in a hurry to leave. We reached the car, a different and much older one than I remembered, and he held open the door for me.

'We'll talk. I'll explain everything.'

I didn't argue, because wanting to forgive him wasn't enough, I had to understand before I could even begin to take a step towards that. He put his hands on my shoulders to guide me into the car, and cast one last look around before stooping to wind the starter. I wondered who or what he was looking for, but then the engine rumbled and I was briefly back at Breckenhall station in the bright summer sun, until Jack once more climbed into the driver's seat and then we were off.

We soon left the prison behind, and were winding through the streets of Islington. I gazed out of the rain-swept window as we went, relishing the sight of people moving about their lives in freedom. Not many smiles to see but, equally, none of the grey, downcast faces I'd lived among, and been one of, for the past three and a half years.

I found my voice, it sounded weak and quite rough, and I cleared my throat, wincing at the grating sensation I felt. 'Where are we going?'

'To get you something to eat, a bath, some fresh clothing, and to have a long talk. In that order. Then I'll take you wherever you want to go.'

It all sounded so heavenly I didn't even argue that the bath must come first. I was starting to feel queasy again; the excitement, the sudden, quite frightening sense of freedom, and the fizzing mixture of rage and relief all combined with the motion of the car and left me feeling unsettled and unwell.

I closed my eyes and that helped so I rested my head as best

I could against the hard seat and let tiredness slip through me, claiming me fully before we were ten minutes into our journey.

When I awoke it was because the car had drawn to a halt. I sat up, disorientated, but my vision couldn't keep up with the speed of my movement and the resulting dizziness made me break out in a cool sweat.

Jack frowned in concern. 'What's wrong, love?'

'I'm, I just ...' I shook my head, which proved to be a mistake. I swayed in my seat and put a hand out to steady myself on the dashboard. 'I'll be all right in a minute.'

Through streaming eyes, I squinted at the steep steps that led to a front door. They looked as if they needed not only a coat of paint, but possibly replacing.

'Is this where you live?' I asked, but my voice sounded as if it were coming from a long way away. My head was pounding and I could feel sweat prickling along my brow despite the cold. He started to answer but I didn't hear the words, and then the dashboard seemed to move towards my face until someone caught hold of me and I breathed in against damp wool before letting myself sink gratefully into the black hole that beckoned.

Chapter 17

There was a weak sun struggling through the window, matched by my own weak struggle to appreciate it. The bed on which I lay was small and extremely comfortable, and a glance to one side showed me a jug of water on a small table. It looked fresh; there was none of the cloudy, slightly bubbly look water gets when it has stood too long and you know it's going to taste horrible. Not that I would have cared what it tasted like just at that moment. Beside the jug stood a glass tumbler but I already knew it was hopeless to think I'd be able to pour.

Glancing down I realised I was still fully clothed under the single sheet, but my grubby skirt was rucked up about my hips, probably due to a feverish, restless sleep. After a brief examination of my own physical state – wobbly, sniffly and with a headache that could fell a giant, but thankfully whole and alert – I took stock of my surroundings beyond the bed and the tantalisingly inaccessible water jug.

The room was small, but neat enough. Just the bed and side table, a small cupboard, a dresser and a door that looked as though it might lead to a fire escape; it was clearly a hotel room, probably very cheap, but for all its basic furnishings at least it was not governed by yelling warders, or populated by rats and cursing inmates, nor was it maintained by scowling servants who looked down on me like a flea-ridden dog. All of which made it a palace to my mind.

I managed to raise myself to a sitting position, and when my head had stopped spinning I pulled back the sheet and carefully swung my legs over the side of the bed, my eyes on the water jug, my mouth feeling dryer by the second as I imagined how wonderful the water would feel trickling down my scratchy throat.

'Oh, no, you don't!'

The voice from the doorway made me yelp and swing my head around, something I regretted instantly as a new throbbing started up in the base of my skull. Jack closed the door behind him, and in two strides had crossed the narrow room and seized the discarded sheets, holding them high so I could get my legs back underneath.

I did so quickly, aware they were naked to mid-thigh. My face felt hot and it wasn't simply the residue of fever; his closeness to my bare skin had caused a wave of warmth I didn't even want to deny, but I couldn't help wondering if I'd dreamed the pent-up passion I'd sensed between us the last time Jack was at Oaklands. His attitude now seemed more that of a stern parent, and for a second I had a glimpse of how he must have been with Evie as she was growing up.

The thought made me smile, despite everything, and when

Jack saw it he smiled back, although a puzzled frown still creased his brow. He didn't ask questions, however, just tucked the eiderdown tight around me, and made me lean forward while he plumped my pillows.

When he had me settled he poured half a tumblerful of water and gave it to me. 'Drink it slowly,' he warned. I obeyed, and it went some way towards eclipsing the pounding headache and the feeling that my bones had been replaced by India rubber.

'You're not well enough to travel tonight,' he said. 'You can have the bed, I'll sleep in—'

'Why didn't you help me?' I blurted.

There was a silence that drew on and on, and I could see he was looking for the right words rather than excuses, so I gave him time. But in vain.

'I can't tell you,' he said at last, his voice almost too quiet for me to hear. That it was also filled with regret did nothing to allay the surge of bewildered anger that choked off my reply before I could utter it. He reached for my hand but I pulled it away.

He looked at me helplessly. 'I promise you I will, but ... I can't just yet.' Hearing the emptiness of his words he shook his head violently. He stood up and went over to the window and gazed out of it.

'I know it's not enough,' he said, turning back to me, 'but I can at least tell you I wasn't supposed to be at Oaklands that night, not beyond ten o'clock anyway. But I had to come back for something.'

'The necklace?' My voice came out small and weak, my deepest fears finally voiced.

'The ...' He stared at me, his mouth halfway open in surprise. 'No! Lizzy, is that what you thought? I swear to you, I had nothing to do with the theft of that diamond, I didn't even know about it until ... No!'

I took a deep, shaky breath, relieved beyond measure that I hadn't gone to prison in his place. Seeing this, he took one more glance out of the window and then returned to sit on the edge of the bed. This time when he went to take my hand I let him. It lay there, limp and small, almost engulfed in his long fingers.

'Sweetheart, listen,' he said, looking down at our clasped hands as if they held the answer to how to reach me. 'Something happened that night, and it meant I couldn't return to Oaklands for ... for a very long time.' He sighed, then raised his eyes to mine, and I fought a jolt of longing as that deep blue gaze swept me back to Henry Creswell's study, and the kindness I had found there. But Jack's next words dashed the memory with their blatant ring of untruth.

'Would you believe me if I told you I didn't even know the Star had gone missing until earlier this year?'

'No,' I said bluntly. How could he not have known? It would have been in all the newspapers, and Evie's and Lady Creswell's letters must have conveyed the story to him.

'Well, it's true,' said Jack. His eyes held mine, and as I stared into their depths I saw them grow brighter. Then he blinked, breaking the momentary connection between us.

'You must have known,' I said, pleading for honesty from him. 'Africa isn't another world ... you sent that letter to Evie!'

'I wasn't in Africa,' he said, and let go of my hand. 'That's something else I can't explain just yet.'

'Then where were you?'

He didn't answer but stood up again and folded his arms across his chest as if trying to warm himself. I studied him, sipping my water to give me time to gather my thoughts. When I spoke my voice shook with emotion. 'Can you at least tell me how you managed to get me released from prison?'

He relaxed a little. 'Yes, I can do that much,' he said. 'I only hope you understand I would have done it sooner had I known . . .' He broke off and stared in the opposite direction, and when he looked round the brightness was back in his eyes. 'I would have moved mountains to get you out of there,' he said quietly. 'I'd have done anything. Anything at all.'

'And yet you didn't.' I hated myself for the coldness that crept back into my voice, but his continued refusal to trust me with his secrets was eclipsing the joy I felt at being with him. His insistence that he hadn't known about my prison sentence was worse. 'Just tell me,' I said tiredly, and he nodded.

'All right. We both know David held the key to your alibi,' he said. 'But he knew better than to implicate me so it was easier to cut us both out of the story.'

'Yes, I understand that,' I said. 'Why is he so scared of you, though?'

'It's not me he's scared of, it's his mother and grandfather. Samuel wouldn't have cared about you in the least, I'm sorry to say, but he'd have been furious that David had risked the family name. So, I threatened to tell them what David had done.'

'I heard that,' I said.

'I'm sorry,' Jack said, and now there was shame in his voice. 'I thought you were still unconscious at that point.'

'I know. I wondered why you said it, at the time. Then I realised you weren't trying to protect me after all. You were protecting yourself.'

Jack's face clouded over. 'I had no idea it was all going to turn out the way it did, or I'd have done things differently.'

'You were telling me about David Wingfield?' I prompted, not wanting to hear any more excuses, not while he was sitting so close to me, sending my thoughts tumbling and twisting in a whirl of longing and mistrust.

He nodded. 'Did you hear there was an Act of Parliament passed earlier this year, to make military service compulsory?'

'No, I hadn't realised.'

'In January. Between the ages of eighteen and forty one, if you're single and able-bodied and not in a reserved occupation.' Jack gave a wry smile. 'It turns out that, as frightened as David is of his mother, he's even more frightened of being sent to the Front. I was able to persuade him the War Office would hold back his call-up papers, and guarantee there'd be no charge of perjury, if he owned up to the truth. Or at least your part in it. The important part.'

'But how did you manage to arrange all that?'

He looked at me for a moment, then shrugged. 'I work for the government.' He reached out and took the glass out of my hand. 'You're looking tired, you need to rest.'

'So you're not a soldier again?' I persisted.

'No.'

I closed my eyes and murmured, 'I'm glad.'

Jack stilled. 'Are you?' he asked quietly.

I opened my eyes again, and caught my breath; his face was almost touching mine as he leaned across to replace the glass on the bedside table. I could see every individual eyelash, and a tiny pockmark at the corner of his right eye, and as my gaze dropped I saw again the ragged scar that ran across his neck.

Before I realised what I was doing I had raised my hand and touched the scar, following its rough curve from the base of his skull to where it puckered away midway down the front of his throat. He did not move, and my touch was the briefest and lightest of contact, but as I let my hand fall I could still feel the tingling in my fingertips.

I felt a shudder run through him, and he turned his head slightly so that his temple rested against mine. We didn't speak, nor look at each other, but I knew my pounding heart had found an echo in his; I could feel it. Our faces lifted at the same time and the increasingly firm pressure of his head moved from temple to cheek to jaw, and then his hands gripped the back of my head and gently moved me away.

He studied me for a moment; I had never seen a man cry but it seemed Jack was close to it then. 'I've let you down,' he whispered. 'I could have killed you, letting you stay in there.'

I didn't answer; we both knew it was the truth, but here between us now was a truth just as strong, and far more immediate. 'Tell me tomorrow,' I managed to say, before his lips came down on mine.

The kiss was rough, urgent, and the sensation of his teeth against my lips hurt at first. But as his hands moved restlessly in my hair and I melted under the touch, I relaxed and my lips parted. Then we were equal; he was no longer kissing me, we were exploring each other with lips and tongue and breath ... my hands rose from the bed to encircle his waist, and when we finally broke apart I dipped my head to the strong column of his throat, pressing my lips to the smooth skin there and giving silent, passionate thanks for the life that flowed through him.

He bent his own head to the back of my neck, his warm breath sending shivers down into the pit of my stomach. We remained locked together, the stolen, wasted years eroded now by touch, and taste, and this unexpectedly fierce longing to be closer still.

He slid his arms around me, holding me close, and I rested my face against his chest, loving the feel of his strong heartbeat under my cheek, and then he gently tilted my face up, searching my eyes for the forgiveness I so desperately wanted to give him. Because I knew it wasn't there, I closed my eyes and kissed him again instead, and in the slump of his shoulders I knew he understood. Still his mouth remained pressed to mine, his lips mobile and giving, his hands cupping my face and stroking my jaw with both tenderness and sorrow.

This time when the kiss ended we looked steadily at one another without speaking. My own desire was unmistakably reflected in his eyes, but no matter how badly my body wanted his, I couldn't give myself to him.

'I'm sorry,' I said, to fill the silence.

He reached out and gently traced the curve of my cheek with one finger. 'You've nothing to be sorry for.'

'I hope I can understand, and learn to trust you again

someday.' My voice was quiet, and I could see the last, faint hope fade from his expression. 'Jack, I just need to—'

'To sleep,' he said softly. 'I promise I'll tell you more tomorrow.'

He kissed my forehead and left me then, and it seemed the room was darker without him although it was still early afternoon. I lay back, feeling the low throb of a headache returning, and the scratching in the back of my throat that heralded the beginnings of what might be a very nasty chill. But I'd had them in prison and fought them off, and at least here I was sleeping in a warm bed with heavy covers, and ... my old prison clothes.

I sat up carefully and looked about for the small case I'd brought with me. It was sitting on the floor beside the door I'd assumed to lead to a fire escape, though perhaps it didn't after all. I eased the sheet back and tried once more to put my weight on my shaking legs – this time I was able to do so and and discovered the door led to a small bathroom.

While I washed, it struck me; unlike the bedroom, which was empty but for a bed, chair and wardrobe, this room was fully kitted out for a male occupant. Shaving equipment, soap, a burgundy-coloured flannel over the bath, and a dressing gown in rich blue hanging on the back of the door: this hotel room was Jack's home. The home of a traveller. How long would he stay this time?

Pushing the sobering thought aside, I undressed and fell back into bed with a sigh of relief. Unable to face the thought of trying to unravel Jack's half-stories, I had planned instead to lie awake, counting every blessing with which I suddenly found myself endowed. There were so many, but before I'd thought further than the letter I would write home tomorrow, I had fallen into the most blissful sleep I had known since leaving there a lifetime ago, as a young girl named Mary.

The chapel bells were ringing stridently, and I came awake blinking and uncertain. How had I slept through breakfast? Then a click from across the room brought everything into focus, and I remembered Holloway was only a memory for me now. I looked up to see Jack close the door and cross quickly to the ringing telephone.

I shook my head to dismiss the apologetic look he gave me, and climbed out of bed again and went into the bathroom. Today I would find out more about him, I vowed. Even if he couldn't tell me everything yet, it might be enough to help me reach a kind of understanding and, from there, forgiveness. There were so many questions, not least of them why he hadn't known I was in prison . . . if he'd been telling the truth. Time would tell.

I made myself comfortable, and then borrowed his tooth-brush; it felt wonderful to be thoroughly clean again and I dressed quickly in the spare clothes I had brought with me from prison. The blouse drifted loosely about my spare frame, and with no belt the skirt slipped down from my waist to hang off my hip bones, but at least I was clean and decent when I went back into the bedroom.

Jack had replaced the telephone receiver. He tried to smile at me, but failed. Clearly he had decided that blurting out what he had to say was the only way to tell me. 'I have to go again,' he said.

I looked at him, suddenly numb. 'Go where?'

'I can't tell you. I'm so sorry, Lizzy.'

'You promised,' I said. My voice was trembling, but it was anger that gripped me now. Once again he was filling my world with lies. 'You promised to tell me—'

'And I will!' He came closer, his eyes pleading for understanding, but I stepped back, my hands clenched at my sides. He persisted, taking one frozen hand and trying to uncurl the fingers. 'It's complicated. You know I work for the government, and that phone call was . . . look, I've been thinking about it all night, how to tell you, but we need more time if I'm going to explain it properly.'

I nodded, outwardly calm, but feeling my insides squirm and roll nauseatingly. 'And you don't have that time.'

'All I can tell you just now is that you did more good than you realised by protecting me that night. And not just for my sake.'

'You told me I'd lose my job,' I reminded him in a low, bitter voice. '*That's* why I didn't tell the truth right away, and why the police labelled me a liar because of it.'

'If I'd known . . .'

'Stop it!'

He swallowed hard. 'I'm sorry. And I want you to understand I'm aware of just how much I owe you for keeping my name out of it, even when you told them about the fight.'

'You'd saved my life,' I said, 'I felt indebted to you. I hadn't realised you were lying just to save yourself.' I saw the barb sink home. He flinched.

'Please, Lizzy, I know I don't have any right, but I'm going to ask you to trust me a little longer.' He took both my hands

246

then, but I immediately wrenched them away and his fingers closed on empty air, the knuckles white.

'How am I supposed to explain my release without mentioning you?'

'You can mention me. I wrote to Evie as soon as I got back to England and found the letters she'd written to me after it all happened. I told her I would do everything I could to help you. That I'd start by going to David and making him tell the truth.' Jack's brow creased in an urgent frown. 'But whatever you do say, it's *imperative* they believe I've been in Africa all this time. Please?'

I nodded. He'd known I would, of course. I swallowed the sickening feeling of having been manipulated again, and tried not to sound desperate as I asked, 'Where will I go?'

Jack pushed my hair away from my face. His fingers were so gentle it was a struggle not to lean against him and let him comfort me. 'I could buy you a train ticket home to Plymouth, if you like? I'd love nothing better than to drive you myself, but . . . I have to go to Downing Street.'

'Not Plymouth,' I said. 'I'll just be a financial burden. Not to mention an embarrassment.' I hugged myself against the chill creeping steadily through me. 'I'll go to Oaklands. Maybe Mary can speak for me and convince Lady Creswell to give me a job.' Even going back to being a scullery maid would be welcome now.

'I shouldn't be away too long, and I'll come and get you as soon as I'm back,' Jack said. 'I promise . . .' He saw my expression and added, 'I'll write a note to Lily myself. I'm certain she'll let you stay there while you regain your strength.'

He started to write the note immediately, taking a piece of

headed paper from a stack on the dresser, and I tried not to dwell on his eagerness to help me on my way, and the suspicion that, rather than a desire to help me, the note was simply a way of absolving himself from further guilt.

After a hurried breakfast, Jack drove me to the railway station. I was feeling heavy-headed and queasy again, even the single piece of toast I'd eaten weighed heavy in my stomach, a result of being unable to chew. I felt as if I might be ill at any minute, and compounding my misery was the way Jack looked at me. It might have been easier if he had been cold, aloof, regretted our moment of intimacy and sent me packing from his hotel alone, but his eyes rarely left me except to glance at the road, and although he spoke little his voice was tinged with regret.

He saw me on to the train, and put money in my pocket for a taxi from Breckenhall to Oaklands. Finally I studied his face as he held me at arm's length and he returned my intense gaze as if he were storing up memories just as I was. Then the whistle sounded, and he pulled me into a tight hug before stepping from the carriage and out of my life.

As he became a blurred shape dwindling into the distance I closed my eyes and held on to the memory of his dark-blue eyes locked on to mine, his lips forming the words 'I'm sorry', and told myself he would honour his promise to tell me the truth one day.

But our farewell had held a note of finality that I couldn't shake off.

Chapter 18

I lay against pillows plumped by a worriedly attentive Mary, and forced a smile to ease her strained expression.

'Thank you,' I tried to say, but found I had no voice left. My throat was scraped raw and my chest rattled horribly when I took too deep a breath, prompting more coughing that pulled at my insides and made my eyes water.

Mary smoothed the hair away from my forehead, and I felt the chill of the room cooling the sweat on my exposed skin. I shivered, and she immediately tucked the blanket around me more thoroughly. 'Don't try to speak, pet.'

Just the sound of her voice, familiar and kind, set the ever-ready tears trembling on my lashes. To prevent them falling and distressing both of us further, I closed my eyes and concentrated on shallow breaths that granted me at least a few moments' respite from the coughing.

Discovering I had already been here for three days had been something of a shock; it seemed only this morning Jack had put me on the train. I had decided to walk from Breckenhall rather than use his money to take a taxi. After all, who knew when I would have any again? It had proved to be a foolish choice.

But despite the way my head swam and my stomach rolled, I had been immeasurably lifted in spirit to see Oaklands Manor before me, as peaceful and beautiful as it always had been. The war had not visibly touched it, nor had the turmoil and upheaval within the family. The grey walls and high, turreted towers gazed out impassively across well-tended lawns, and the big front door stood firm against anything the world could hurl at it. Nothing could touch the serenity of this house from without, yet I suspected that inside I would find a different place from the one I remembered.

It had all happened very quickly; I had gone around to the kitchen garden and raised my hand to knock at the side door before I paused, not sure what my reception would be. I hesitated a moment longer and then fate intervened; the door opened and Mary stood there, her eyes wide and her mouth falling open. I tried to say hello, but all that came out was a strangled sob and she dropped her steaming mug of tea just in time to catch me as I stumbled into her arms.

Mary had hugged me tight, then glanced over her shoulder and drawn me quickly inside. Wordlessly, knowing she would hear everything in good time, she ushered me up the back stairs to the servants' quarters and into the room we had shared, locking the door behind her. Less than five minutes after my arrival, I was sitting on the bed where I had slept as a scullery maid, a lifetime ago.

Just to be in this room again, smelling the faintly musty

smell of the carpet mixed with laundry soap, was to slide back to the moment we had met and the first words she had heard from my lips. I had learned far worse language in the intervening years, especially in Holloway, but still remembered my own feeling of horror as I realised I'd been overheard. How trivial it all seemed now.

And how dearly familiar she looked, still wearing that motherly, affectionate but exasperated look that had been her normal expression the entire time we'd worked together.

'Right then,' she had said, sitting on her own bed. 'Are you going to tell me what happened or am I going to have to guess? Again.'

I'd started to tell her how I'd been called to the governor's office on the morning of my birthday, but as I did so I felt myself growing alternately hot and icy, and my chest began to feel as if it were full of feathers and bubbles. Mary stopped me mid-sentence and ordered me to bed. I went gratefully, slipping beneath the covers and assuring her I would be just as right as rain after a good night's sleep.

Three days later the fever finally slackened its grip, leaving me weak and exhausted but with a new, if cautious, optimism about my situation. It appeared to be late in the evening when I woke; the curtains were tightly shut, Mary was filling the glass beside my bed with water from a jug, and I swallowed past a lump in my throat as I acknowledged the similarities, and differences, of waking in Jack's room.

In the dim light, I took a moment to study the changes the past three and a half years had wrought in my friend. She had always seemed larger than life to me, a substitute for my mother, filling my narrow horizons with her comforting

251

presence and reliability. Now I could see her for the lovely young woman she really was. Tiredness and care only added character to her sweet-natured face, and the roundness of her cheeks gave her what seemed like a perpetual smile, curving her lips and lifting the corners of her eyes.

Her hair was, as always, tucked neatly beneath her cap, but I could see the rich, deep red colour hinted at by her finely shaped eyebrows. She must only be twenty-five to my twenty-two, and I realised I should now look beyond her competence and maternal firmness and be grateful for the friend she had always been to me. I thanked her for the water. I could tell she was still desperate to hear my news, but I needed a more natural sleep than the shallow, semi-delirium through which I had drifted these past days.

I closed my eyes, but there was something I had to know before I gave in to the softness of the pillow. 'How is Evie?'

'She's well. Hush now.'

'And Will?'

When no answer came I opened my eyes again, fighting the pull of sleep. 'Mary?'

'Go to sleep, Lizzy. We'll talk tomorrow.'

Her tone was gentle, as always, but her evasive words pierced my heart like shards of glass.

'He went missing,' Mary told me the next day as she sponged me clean after my fever. 'Sometime in the summer. The last Evie heard from him was a letter he'd written at a place called Bazentin-le-Petit. She tells me he'd written of a sure victory, but no more has been heard of him since.'

'Do you think he's dead?' The word almost stuck in my throat but I forced it out, past lips that had felt numb from the moment Mary had begun talking.

She tucked some hair back behind my ear, and dipped her washcloth into the basin on the bedside table. I didn't know what her silence meant, and the longer it continued the more my stomach twisted, as if her pronouncement either way would be the truth of it.

Finally she shook her head. 'I hope to God he wasn't, but I'm sure you know that isn't the only consideration.'

'Desertion then?' For which he would face a firing squad ... the thought sent a chill through my already aching bones.

'To be honest I'm not sure which would be worse for Evie,' Mary said, voicing my own feelings. 'She goes searching for him whenever she can, and she has people looking out for him at all the dressing stations and field hospitals, but it's a dangerous place to be travelling and she can't use an official vehicle, they're all needed. She can't get near the trenches without her ambulance, and when she *is* at the Front she's too busy getting the Tommies out.'

I wondered bleakly if hope that might ultimately lead to grief wasn't even more damaging. Evie, so certain of finding her love alive, might not be able to withstand the grief of losing him again should she discover he was dead.

'What of the others we knew?'

'Billy Duncan died at Ypres in the first year,' Mary said quietly. I recalled little Billy's cheerful face, pink from exertion whenever I saw him, his hands constantly chapped and raw from their work in the stables. Deep sorrow cut through me, and I sensed more to come. I was right.

'Joe was serving with him. He wrote from the hospital to tell us what had happened.' Mary took a deep breath and dipped her flannel again. 'Not long after, he returned to the Front, but was killed in May last year. Gas attack.'

I felt the sick feeling of loss once more. 'Oh, poor Joe ... And poor Mr Shackleton, too.'

We both fell to silence, each lost in our own thoughts. Tempering my sadness at the loss of Billy and Joe, however, was the relief that Jack had not been called upon to serve again, and I clung tight to the knowledge that, as a diplomat, he would at least remain safe for the duration.

Mary picked the washcloth out of the water and applied it to the back of my neck. 'So, my girl, what about you?'

'What about me?'

'Well, I assume you'll be needing work. I found the letter to Lady Creswell in your pocket.' Her expression told me she had also seen who had written it, and that she was not best pleased. I couldn't understand why. After all, she hadn't known Jack was the one person who might have saved me from prison.

'It was so good of Mr Carlisle to speak to David on my behalf. And then to write that letter,' I probed. Mary didn't answer, so I went on, 'Did you realise he was in the diplomatic service?'

'No.' Mary's lips tightened, and she reflexively squeezed the flannel. Cooling water trickled down my back and I flinched. 'I knew he was in a reserved occupation, though,' she said, not bothering to hide the contempt in her voice.

'He was a soldier before,' I said, 'and a good one. Surely he'd have signed up if he could?'

'I'm certain if he'd pushed hard enough, such an experienced and physically able man would have been welcomed back to active duty,' Mary said, 'but being some terribly important paper-shuffler for the government, he obviously had higher priorities than serving alongside his countrymen. It was good of him finally to have helped you prove your innocence, but that man's not to be trusted, believe me.'

I realised now there was no point in telling her how close Jack and I had become, although it had occurred to me more than once that I might have dreamed the whole thing in my state of delirium; I had only a couple of pounds and that letter of recommendation to prove I had spent any time in his company at all.

I had read the note on the train, by turns smiling and fighting back tears at the sight of the large, looping scrawl, proclaiming my good character and his certainty that his dear friend Lily would see fit to redress some of the wrong that had been done to me.

I wished I could see it again now, but couldn't ask Mary for it in case she noticed my expression as I read it. 'Will you please give the note to Lady Creswell?' I asked instead.

'Of course I will,' Mary said, 'but first you must get properly well. I know you, and you're not to try and run before you can walk.'

'I'm not sure I could do either at the moment,' I admitted, accepting the thin dressing gown she draped around my shoulders with a little shiver of gratitude. 'When does Evie come home?'

'I don't know,' Mary said. 'We may not see her for a good while yet. She's in great demand and wrote to say that as soon as her tour of duty allowed her a break she was going back to France. Your own letter from her is likely waiting for you at Holloway.'

'What can we do to help?' I said at once, sitting up straight again.

Mary pushed me back. '*We*,' she emphasised, 'can do nothing at all until you are back to full strength and earning a wage.'

'And then what?'

She looked at me for a long while, and I could see doubt in her eyes although she answered me with a smile. 'Who knows? By then the war may be over, Will Davies home safe and sound, and Evie once more driving her mother and the rest of us to distraction.'

But, to judge from the stories we heard daily, the campaign was growing bleaker, more hopeless and more terrifying than ever; although battles, large and small, were being won on the different fronts, the toll on lives was horrific. And, of course, for every young man lost on a far-distant field, a family at home was torn apart.

The Creswells were not immune from the fear either: adding to the worry of Evie's activities, young Lawrence had joined up as soon as he'd turned eighteen, and the last we had heard he was at Courcelette, manning one of the new tanks of which Haig was so enamoured. Slow and lumbering, and hideously dangerous, these beasts of the battlefield were nevertheless impressive to look at and I couldn't help thinking how eager the always adventurous Evie must be to climb into one. Certainly her brother had proved he shared some of her fascination with driving and machinery.

At Oaklands I was kept away from the kitchens until Mary had taken her chance to speak to Lady Creswell on my behalf. Because of this I didn't see another familiar face for almost a week, and during this time of isolation my longing for the sight of Jack, and the sound of his voice, became almost painful. I had only to close my eyes and I could see the amused quirk of his lips as he'd found me crouched in the sooty darkness of the linen cupboard, or the clear intensity of his gaze that day in the walled garden. I could remember almost every discussion we'd ever had, with and without Evie, and worst of all I could feel the last warm touch of his hand at my cheek as he stepped off the train.

Perhaps if I didn't love him I could brush aside his betrayal with the same sense of 'what's done is done' as I now brushed aside the lies told by Clarissa Wingfield and her brood. But I did love him. His passion, his humour, his youthful grief, his innate gentleness and instinct for sorrow in others. Even his politics, or at least his fervent belief in them. That long week gave me time to analyse my feelings, to examine them, and maybe to find something that might ease him away from the place he occupied in my heart. But by the end of it Jack was still there, as firmly and deeply entrenched as ever.

Mary came to me one grey October afternoon as I sat on my bed, flicking yet again through a copy of her favourite *National Geographic*. 'Lady Creswell has asked to see you in the morning room, so let's make sure you're presentable.'

With a stomach-tightening mixture of excitement and nerves, much like the day I had arrived here, I stood still while Mary fussed over my hair and the clothes I'd borrowed from her, tugging my belt straight and checking my teeth.

'You'll do,' she said at last, and led me down the back stairs.

We stood outside the room while I took a single deep, calming breath. In this room my life had previously taken two startlingly different turns. Would today mark a third? I stared at the door, wondering in which direction I would be going next, and as Mary squeezed my shoulder and left I had to force myself not to run after her. But there was no sense in putting it off: Lady Creswell had already made her decision, and whatever the result, I would adapt. Again.

Chapter 19

I knocked on the door, and while I waited reminded myself, although with little conviction, that I was the one who had been wronged. When Lady Creswell called me in I noticed immediately that she was not the only person in the room. Another lady stood by the window, studying me far more closely than politeness permitted me to study her; she remained an outline only while I turned my attention to Lily Creswell.

'My Lady,' I said, bobbing a quick curtsey.

'Miss Parker,' she responded, and cleared her throat in a faintly embarrassed way. 'I understand there was a rather awful miscarriage of justice regarding the Kalteng Star.'

Rather awful indeed. 'I didn't steal it, My Lady.'

'And yet the police and the courts proved otherwise.'

'Yes, but they weren't in possession of all the facts. My Lady,' I added quickly.

She gave me a long look, and then nodded. 'I hope you understand I was as much swept up by circumstance as you were. The police were informed, they investigated and found your story wanting. I do not apologise for their actions, or for David Wingfield's lies. I do, however, wish to convey my own pleasure in seeing you again, and my regret that it took so long to uncover the truth.'

I nodded my thanks. 'Has the diamond been found?'

'No, sadly not.' Lady Creswell sat forward, dismissing the subject. 'I'm told you are seeking to return to work here.'

'Yes, My Lady,' I said, and forced myself to stop there.

'You must realise I can't possibly employ you?'

For a moment I stared at her, then I found my voice again. 'But you have word from a reliable source that I was found innocent.'

'Yes, that "reliable source" seems to speak highly of you, once again,' Lady Creswell said, and glanced at the woman by the window. I took a moment to regard her more closely since Lady Creswell seemed to have included her deliberately; once she stepped away from the window and back into the room I recognised her immediately. Tall, dressed like visiting royalty and with features a portrait painter would love: sharply defined and clear, with large, slanting eyes and hair perfectly cut in the new, short style. Constance Harrington.

While during that bygone Christmas she had barely looked at me, now she seemed intent on doing the opposite and I found it extremely disconcerting, though I had no time to wonder at it.

'May I please ask why you have ignored Mr Carlisle's character reference?' I asked Her Ladyship, giving the hastily scribbled note a new official credence by my choice of words. Or so I hoped.

'I haven't ignored it,' Lady Creswell said, and unbent a little. 'My dear girl, you worked diligently and well, aside from one or two, shall we say, *unfortunate* occurrences, and my daughter valued you highly as her personal maid. But you must see there is no position for you here. Miss Creswell is away ...' Her Ladyship's countenance clouded slightly and I saw Mrs Harrington place a comforting hand on her shoulder. 'And I have had to release several staff of far greater seniority than you held since the outbreak of the war. I cannot possibly be seen to extend employment to you having done that.'

'But you said yourself, I worked well for you. I'll do anything!'

'There is no job here for you, Miss Parker. I'm sorry.'

'Lady Creswell, I have nowhere to go,' I said, and heard the tremor in my voice that signalled defeat. I hated that sound.

Mrs Harrington stepped forward. 'Lily, my dear, perhaps Miss Parker might be prevailed upon to wait outside for a moment. I have a suggestion that might help us all.' Her eyes never left my face, and it was a relief to turn away at Lady Creswell's bidding and leave the room.

Out in the main hall I struggled to regain some semblance of calm; I had a feeling I might need it when I was called back in. If there was a solution, I would grasp it no matter what; I had no choice.

A door opened at the far end of the hall and Mr Dodsworth, as upright and regal as ever, came out of the library. His ever-watchful eye automatically flicked to left and right as he crossed to the dining room. As he caught sight of me I saw his composure not only slip, but fall about him with an almost audible clatter.

'Lizzy!' He looked past me at the closed door, and hurried across. 'What on earth are you doing here? I thought you were ...' He floundered and I felt a little sorry for him; he had always been very kind to me.

'The police know I didn't steal that diamond, Mr Dodsworth.'

'I never believed for one moment that you did,' he said, and there was sincerity in his voice. 'But there can't be any work for you here,' he said, echoing Lady Creswell's doleful news. 'Emma Bird was let go, as was Martha who took your old job in the scullery. And of course Ruth was ... well, we are a skeleton staff here now, since the war.'

'I understand,' I said, 'but Lady Creswell is entertaining a guest and that lady seems to think she may be able to help.'

Mr Dodsworth looked at the morning-room door. 'Let's hope so,' he said. 'Now then, I have duties to attend to in the dining room.' He made to leave, but turned back. 'I'm very happy your name has been cleared, Lizzy,' he said, and to my astonishment gave my hand a quick squeeze. Then he was gone, and my first meeting with the household I had been terrified of seeing again was over, leaving me with a mounting feeling of optimism.

I barely had time to smile in relief before Lady Creswell summoned me back in. I entered, still wearing a smile. It seemed to disconcert the two women slightly; no doubt they had imagined me chewing my nails in hope and anxiety.

'Miss Parker, thank you for waiting,' Lady Creswell said, and pushed right ahead with no further preamble. 'In March next year, subject to successful interview of course, you are invited to take up the position of nurse to Doctor and Mrs Harrington's third child.'

Mrs Harrington took her cue and stepped forward, holding out one slim hand to me.

'I'm very pleased to offer you an interview, Lizzy. Quite aside from the time you attended on me as a guest, I have heard much in your favour despite what you may think.'

In something of a daze I shook her hand. 'I am grateful, Mrs Harrington,' I said, 'but I have to tell you, I have very little experience with babies.'

Mrs Harrington smiled. 'Nor does any young mother the first time she handles one,' she said. 'From what Lily tells me, you have a fine character and a sincere determination to do a good job.' I glanced at Lady Creswell in surprise, but she gave nothing away. 'The rest I can help you with: I have two older children, as Lily says. Their care will, of course, also form part of your duties although they are away at school much of the time. Will you come for the interview?'

'Yes! Yes, please, Mrs Harrington,' I amended, almost laughing in my relief.

She smiled. 'Good. I'm sure it will be nothing more than a formality. I came here to try and steal Emma from Lady Creswell, only to learn she had been let go some time ago. Your situation, while awful for you, has turned to my advantage, and hopefully yours.'

Yet again I stood in that room with the heady sense that my life was veering in a direction I could never have imagined. 'I accept with thanks,' I said. 'I do have two very young brothers, and I helped my mother with them when I lived at home.'

'There you are, you see?' Mrs Harrington said. 'I will send for you in a week or two when John and Freddie are home from school – your train fare to Chester will be paid, of course.

You may spend the day with us and see if you and the boys can agree with one another.'

'In the meantime,' Lady Creswell put in, 'you may stay here and work for your keep, but you'll receive no wages. And I do not wish it known outside this house that you are staying here. Is that understood?'

'Of course, My Lady,' I said, feeling the smile stretch into a grin despite my attempts to remain decorous. Lady Creswell sat back, satisfied. 'Then it's settled. If all goes well Mrs Harrington will be in touch just before the child's due date.'

As I closed the door behind me and stood in the huge hall of Oaklands Manor, the absurdity of the idea that I would soon be going to work for Jack's former fiancée struck me, and I had to clamp my hand over my mouth to hold in the sudden yelp of relieved laughter. As I did so, I wondered if all the good things Constance had heard about me had come from Lady Creswell after all, and the thought that perhaps Jack might have intervened gave me a rush of sudden warmth that I seized and held on to in the ache of missing him.

Less than a week later I was coming in from the henhouse with my basket of warm, feather-stuck treasure when I almost dropped it on the stone floor of the kitchen.

Evie smiled. 'Hello, Lizzy.' Mary plucked the basket from my fingers, and I felt the smile on my face grow wide enough to crack it, then Evie and I were embracing like sisters.

It would be easy to say the intervening years fell away, that's what I had longed for, but they didn't. They lay between us like an unknown country, full of secrets and mysteries and people unknown to each other.

'It's so lovely to see you again,' Evie said, still hugging me tight. 'I thought of you so often, and what you must have been through.'

I shook my head. 'To be honest, the more I've heard of this war, the more I've come to think I had the lucky side of it.' I drew back and looked her over. She had changed, of course, we all had. Older and hopefully wiser, certainly stronger, but I wasn't prepared for the new bleakness I could see in her eyes, despite her smile.

She saw my expression, and patted my hand where it lay on her forearm. 'Don't despair, Just Lizzy. I'm still the same old Evie, I promise.'

'But you have new cares now.'

She glanced at Mary, then back at me. The kitchen was empty but for us; Mr Dodsworth had the morning off and Mrs Cavendish and Mrs Hannah were upstairs with Lady Creswell discussing the dinner plans for the week.

'I see Mary has told you of Will's ... well, his unexplained absence,' Evie said, satisfied we were alone.

'She told me he was missing in action.'

'Missing, yes.'

'You are sure he is alive then?' I couldn't prevent the note of hope from entering my own voice – she had done it again; she had only to venture a supposition, and I believed every word to be the unvarnished truth.

'I'm certain of it. I would have heard had he been presumed dead, but his regiment don't believe he is either.'

'Surely he didn't desert his post?'

Evie shrugged. 'I would sooner believe him a coward than dead.'

'Will is no coward,' Mary said, placing two steaming mugs on the table and returning to fetch a third. 'I've heard stories of men leaving the trenches in such a state of shock it affects them like a physical injury.'

'And I've seen it with my own eyes,' Evie added, her expression sombre. 'Those Tommies are in absolute hell, and there are simply not enough ambulances to get them out.'

We sat warming our hands on the tea, and Evie, still gloved against the chill of the kitchen, withdrew a much-folded letter from her pocket.

'Here's the last word Will sent,' she said, passing it across to me. I opened it up carefully, mindful of the cheap paper, and of the letter's value to her that extended beyond measure.

14 July 1916

My darling Evie,
We are dug in at a place called Bazentin-le-Petit, having enjoyed an easy victory in this and Bazentin-le-Grand, and are resting while we await further orders. If our COs are to be believed I will be able write again very soon, and at length. Hopefully without the censor stamping all over it either! We are optimistic at last, and I have only a few minutes, and little ink, but wanted to tell you again that you have been my heart's constant companion throughout this war.

There was a little more but I handed the letter back to her, sensing it was of a personal nature. 'He seems confident of success,' I said. 'I can't imagine he would leave of his own accord.'

'Exactly,' Evie said. She looked at the letter again and smiled, and I noticed her tracing a faded crest on the top of the paper with the tip of one finger.

'What's that?'

'We sneaked this paper from our hotel room the night before Will left for France,' she said. I reflected that, not too long ago, I might have blushed at the thought of what would have happened in that room. But now I felt only gratitude that they had found a way to be together, despite their different backgrounds. Evie had been right all along.

'What of his family?' I asked. 'Did Will write to them as he wrote to you?'

'Not nearly so often; they were never close. That's why he left home at such a young age and came to Cheshire, so I suppose I should be glad of it.'

'And what do they say?'

She shrugged. 'I have no idea. I'm not sure they even know, or care, that he's missing.'

'But the authorities would have written to them, surely, as his next of kin?'

'They wrote to me. I have the telegram somewhere in my things.'

'I don't understand, they wouldn't write to you unless ...' Then I understood, and felt my mouth curve into a broad smile as she peeled off her gloves. On her left hand a simple, cheaply made gold band gleamed like a fairy-tale promise of happy endings.

'Our honeymoon,' she said, tapping the crest at the top of the paper again. 'I think a few pieces of cheap hotel paper might have been included in the cost of the room, don't you?'

'I do,' I agreed, still smiling. It was perfect – how could it have been otherwise, with those two? 'But why didn't you tell me in your letter?'

'We agreed to keep it a secret,' she said. 'I'm sorry, Lizzy, I was desperate to share the news with you of all people, but we had heard that letters to prison are opened and anyone might have read it. Mother would have been mortified if anyone else had found out, and she was already distraught at my leaving. I couldn't put that on her plate as well. It took her an awfully long time to come around to it.'

Evie re-folded the letter and tucked it back into her pocket. 'So,' she said, clearly eager to turn the conversation away from what must hurt too deeply for me to contemplate, 'the ghastly Wingfield boys, or whichever one of them remains at home, finally decided to tell the truth!'

As we discussed David's change of heart, and Evie sang Jack's praises, I reflected on how we had both defied convention with the men we had chosen. But still, even knowing she might sympathise, it would be a little like telling her I had fallen in love with her father; I couldn't even bring myself to confess I'd spent the night with Jack, despite the innocence of it. She and Mary both assumed he had put me straight on to a train, and I didn't disabuse them of that notion.

'It's funny how war changes things you wouldn't expect it to,' Evie mused a little later. We had fallen to discussing the way the big houses were being run now; so few staff, and old attitudes falling by the wayside as necessity superseded tradition. 'Even when we don't see the fighting close at hand, it still affects the way we think and work.'

'I do feel differently about my work now,' Mary put in. 'In the past year or so I've felt more as if I am actually helping, rather than going through tired old routine for form's sake.'

'And is that reflected in the way my family and the other staff treat you?' Evie asked curiously.

'Well, some people will never change.' We all smiled, no doubt with thoughts of Mrs Cavendish and Mr Dodsworth leaping to our minds. 'But, yes.' Mary nodded. 'I feel far more valued.'

'So here we are, equals at last,' I said.

Evie sighed in mock exasperation. 'We were always equals, Lizzy Parker. Didn't I spend much of my time telling you that?'

'Oh, good grief, yes,' I grumbled. 'Hours and *hours,* how could I have forgotten?' I rolled my eyes and feigned exhaustion, which started us off laughing again, out of all proportion to the humour of the situation, but it was the long-missed sound of freedom and friendship, and we relished it all the more for that.

That was how we were when Lady Creswell opened the door.

Chapter 20

Silence fell like a brick on a marble floor. All three of us sat up straight but daren't look at each other for fear of collapsing into giggles again; it was as if we were naughty children caught misbehaving at school, rather than three grown women, and one of us the daughter of the house.

None of us could remember Lady Creswell setting foot in the kitchen before, never mind finding the three of us there in a state of such familiarity, so there was no precedent for this. We waited, hardly breathing, for her reaction. Her gaze drifted over me, and lingered on Evie for a moment before moving on. 'Mary, I should like you to attend me this afternoon, if you please. Peters is unwell and has taken to her bed.'

'Of course, My Lady,' Mary said, bobbing as close to a curtsey as she could manage from a seated position. She stood quickly, realising this, and bobbed again.

As the door closed behind her mother, Evie sagged back in her chair. 'How on earth does she still manage to make me feel like this?' she said. 'And how odd that she never even greeted me. It's the first time she's seen me since I got back.'

'It's why she came down here, though,' I said. 'She must have realised where you would be.'

'What makes you think that?'

I gestured at the row of bells on the wall. 'If she had really only wanted to summon Mary, she would have rung.' The bell above Lady Creswell's name had not so much as trembled or we would certainly all have jumped. 'Honestly, Evie! She clearly wanted to see you, but didn't want it to look as though she'd had to come looking.'

Evie groaned, and laid her head on the table. 'You're right. I wanted to see you first but I shouldn't have been so impatient.'

'Best mend it then,' Mary said with a smile. 'Maybe you'll be forgiven by tea-time.'

With Mary finishing her duties upstairs, and Evie doing her best to soothe her mother's ruffled feathers before taking a bath, I carried my basket out to the herb garden. This was my favourite chore of the day, although soon it would be time to bring the less hardy plants indoors for the winter and I would have little excuse to be outside in the fresh air.

Wandering down the long path, enjoying the sensation of a brisk wind on my face, I unlocked the little box of special thoughts and memories I held deep in my mind for times just like this. They all emerged: my mother; my late father; Emily; Adie and Albert ... and even, finally, Jack Carlisle. I gave them free rein in my thoughts, and the mingled memories I held of each of them warmed me as I crouched beside the parsley and began cutting.

The joyful and very long letter I had sent home, explaining my release and my intention to visit as soon as possible, had no doubt been devoured by Emily and read to the twins. I liked to think of my mother sitting down at the end of the day with a cup of tea and a few minutes to herself to read my words.

But Jack ... my heart clenched in longing as he took his step forward into the light that shone now just for him. What was he doing? Where was he? How long would it be before he returned? Oaklands was beautiful, but without Jack it was like a song without a singer, a window without a view, a book without words. I felt his absence more keenly than ever out here, so close to the trees he had planted, and decided that as soon as I had finished with the herbs I must see them again, to touch them, as if I could somehow bring him closer by doing so.

'Where the 'ell did *you* spring from?'

Startled, I swung around, slicing off the top of the parsley plant and knocking the basket over. Ruth Wilkins stood there, whisking me instantly back to the times she had confronted me in this very garden for one imagined misdemeanour or another. Except now she gripped the wrist of a grubby-looking toddler who kept jerking to free herself, to no avail.

I stood up, my heart racing despite telling myself Ruth had no power over me now. 'I could ask you the same,' I said, keeping my voice cool with an effort. Her expression, one of nervous wariness, lent me added assurance and I drew myself up taller, straightening my back and squaring my shoulders; if my time at Oaklands had served me well at Holloway, so the reverse was true now, and if my limbs were trembling, and my heart thumping, Ruth needn't know.

I glared at her. 'Well?'

'You're meant to be in prison,' she said. 'You escaped or what?'

'Hardly,' I said. 'My innocence was proven, despite your best efforts.' I was surprised to see a flash of guilt in her expression, but she didn't give voice to it.

Instead she shrugged. 'I never thought you'd get ten years,' was all she would say. As an apology it was woefully inadequate, but it was still more than I'd expected.

'So why are you here? If you're looking for work, you'll have to look somewhere else.'

She glanced at the little girl. 'I in't looking for work, what would I do with a job now?'

'Ah, yes, you have new responsibilities,' I said. 'I'm sure he is a worthy provider.' Except I'd heard Frank had turned her away the moment she'd confronted him with her predicament, and felt a flicker of remorse at my own barb.

But I didn't give voice to it.

'Go away, Ruth,' I said instead. 'No one here wants to see you.'

'They might when I tell 'em why I've come. And so will you.'

'I doubt it.'

'I've got stuff you'll want to hear,' she insisted.

I could feel curiosity warring with my desire for her to be gone. 'Why would I care about anything you've got to say?'

'Because it's to do with that diamond, and who really stole it. Don't worry, there's no one else in the kitchen, I checked. I in't that stupid.'

I regarded her steadily for a moment, my expression bland despite the sudden interest kindled in me by her words. 'You can come in, but only for a minute.'

'Don't worry, we've got better places to go,' Ruth said, defensive and angry. She shouldered past me, pulling the little girl along behind her.

The child promptly burst into loud sobs, which rose to shrieks as I picked up my basket and followed them both into the kitchen. Although the sound made me wince I felt sorry for the little girl, both for her impoverished situation and her poor luck in having Ruth for a mother. I found a crust of bread, which I smothered in honey and gave to the child to chew.

Then I faced Ruth grimly. 'Right, what do you want?'

'Blimey, if you ain't grown teeth at last,' she said, and there was an edge of admiration in her voice I had never heard before. I wasn't fooled, she was not here to pay compliments.

'Get on with it,' I said shortly.

'Get Miss Creswell down and I will.'

I blinked. 'You want Evie?'

'Well, you don't think I'm here for the good of my ever-lasting soul, do you? I came here soon as I 'eard she was back. I assume *you* don't have nothing to pay me with.' Her expression, as she looked me over, was so cold it was easy to forget she was in no position to pass judgement.

I left her alone in the kitchen; I didn't much mind if she helped herself to food, and it was a relief to discover I did have some empathy left after all.

Upstairs I knocked on Evie's door. Aware her mother might be close by, I spoke formally at first. 'Miss Creswell?'

'In the bath!' she called back.

My eagerness to hear what Ruth had to say got the better of me, and I pushed open the door and hissed, 'Come down to the kitchen. Hurry!'

Back downstairs I found Ruth feeding more bread to her little girl. She didn't bother to hide the fact that her shabby coat was stuffed with a whole cooked chicken, and I didn't bother to acknowledge it.

We sat in silence until Evie arrived, dragging a comb through her wet hair, a question dying on her lips as she saw who sat at the table. She looked at me, eyebrows raised.

I folded my arms. 'Apparently Wilkins here has something of great import to tell us, regarding the whereabouts of your birthright.'

'You know where the necklace is?' Evie frowned. 'That doesn't surprise me in the slightest. So, where is it?'

'I never said I knew where it was,' Ruth said, 'just that I thought you might like to know who took it.'

'Right then, let's hear it,' Evie said, sitting down and continuing to comb her hair. She sounded calm, and gave every appearance of merely getting something dull and necessary out of the way, but I knew her too well; the pulse in her neck was beating fast and her hand gripped the comb far more tightly than even her tangled hair demanded.

'First there's the little matter of what you're going to give me in return,' Ruth said.

Evie pointed at her bulging coat with the comb. 'I could *not* call the police and have you arrested for stealing food.'

'Arrested for a chicken?' Ruth snorted, but she looked wary.

Evie leaned forward, her light-blue eyes turning hard.

'There's a war on, you know. Not to mention a little matter of trespass; you no longer work nor live here.'

'She let me in.' Ruth jerked her thumb at me.

I pretended to be deep in thought for a moment, then slowly shook my head. 'No, I think I'd remember that. And while we're about it, you'd better make sure no one catches you with that silver serving spoon.'

'What spoon?'

'This one,' I said, and gave her a bright smile as I handed the little girl a spoon to play with.

The child, immediately captivated by her own reflection in the metal, then discovered it was an even better toy when banged on the edge of the table. She happily did so, while Ruth contemplated her position and realised she had over-played her hand.

'You'll let me keep the chicken?' she said at last.

'I'll even let your daughter keep the spoon,' Evie said. 'Now, you were saying?'

Ruth looked at her for a moment with narrowed eyes. 'You know who stole the necklace?'

I nodded. 'Obviously it was you.'

'Yeah. But I don't know where it is now,' she added quickly, as both Evie and I immediately began voicing questions. 'An' I never done it for m'self anyway. What would I do with some-thing like that? Couldn't sell it, could I? No, I done it for someone I thought would take care of me, but he was a no-good bastard and he never meant a word of what he said.' She looked at her daughter as she said this, and I fought back another unexpected glimmer of pity.

'It doesn't matter why you did it,' I said, my voice hard. 'You stood there in court, and you lied, and because of you I spent three and a half years of my life in the worst hell you could imagine.'

Her expression turned to one of bitterest scorn. 'You think *you* went through hell? You want to try birthin' a child in a cow shed, and gettin' back to work the next day. And you want to know what that work was?'

'I can guess,' I said, but this time there was no pity in my heart for what she had become. There was some for the child who, if she lived long enough, would almost certainly follow her mother's path. 'It must have been terrible,' I conceded.

'You don't know nothin',' Ruth said. 'You ain't got a clue, you never did.'

'Ruth, *fascinating* as all this is,' Evie put in, though managing to sound utterly bored, 'we just need to know what you did with the Kalteng Star.'

Ruth shrugged. 'What I said in court, about goin' looking for Lizzy to help in the kitchens? Well, that was the truth,' she said. 'Only when I seen you weren't there, and I seen Miss Creswell's note instead, I realised this was my chance. Frank knew about the diamond. He was the one pushing me to get upstairs work so's I had a better chance of nickin' it.'

I remembered the overheard conversations, and nodded. 'Go on,' I said coldly.

'Well, before I went to Miss Creswell's room, I thought I'd have a little look at what *should* have been my bedroom.' She shot me a venomous look. 'And then I seen that blue scarf.'

My velvet stole. I held my breath, knowing what was coming next.

'I couldn't see how come *you* was so precious to have such

a thing,' Ruth said, 'so I took it. I din't even know why at the time, but then, when I got the necklace from Miss Creswell's room, I wrapped it in the scarf. I hung on to it for that night, I knew no one was gunna miss it right away. Then, next mornin' when Frank delivered the specials, I caught up to him in the garden and he made sure the scarf got dropped in the mud. So's everyone would think it was you who'd done it.'

I shook my head in disgust. 'And did he pat you on the head like a good doggy for bringing it?'

'You don't know how it was,' Ruth snapped. 'He 'ad a right to that stone! More right than her!' She jerked her head at Evie, who stared in puzzlement.

'What "right"?'

Ruth smirked. 'Frank Markham is a Wingfield.'

'A Wingfield? How—'

'He's a legit'mate one an' all. He's really Frank McKrevie, Susannah's son. Ah.' She nodded at Evie's expression. 'Now you're getting it.'

I looked to Evie to explain. Eyes still wide with surprise, she did so. 'Susannah Wingfield would have inherited the Star, if it hadn't been for Lord John's stipulation that it must return to the Creswell vault as soon as the mother to daughter line was broken.'

'Susannah?' I frowned, trying to remember. 'Oh, that's the one who died, isn't it? Samuel's older daughter?'

'That's her,' Ruth said. 'She'd have been set for life.'

'Samuel has always resented that clause, and made no secret of it,' Evie said. 'He couldn't see why the Creswells should be permitted to extend the inheritance to a granddaughter or niece, if they weren't allowed to do the same.'

'Well, he's right, why should they?' Ruth said. 'Got as much right to it as your lot,' she said to Evie, who didn't look as annoyed as I expected, or even felt on her behalf.

'Rubbish!' I said. 'It wasn't a Wingfield who discovered it, so why should they have the same claim? They were lucky to have had it as long as they did.'

Evie sighed. 'I know. But much as I hate to say it I can't help feeling Samuel has a point. It's only a moral right, not a legal one but it's still a right, of sorts. After all it wasn't Susannah's fault her aunt died childless.'

'Exactly,' Ruth said. 'So bein' all rebellious, and to pay her parents back for not 'anging on to the diamond for her, Susannah married Ballentyne McKrevie. The Wingfields have hated the McKrevies for generations, for some reason or other.'

'The Wingfields don't seem to get on with anyone much,' I observed drily.

Ruth ignored me. 'Samuel disowned her. She had a son but died in childbirth, and McKrevie had the boy adopted. By Harold and Jessica Markham.'

'Frank,' I said, my head swimming under all these names but latching on to the only one that mattered at the moment.

'Frank,' Ruth confirmed. 'So now maybe you can see why he was like he was? Not only was he kicked out of one of the richest families in the country, he also 'ad to hang around and watch the ones who'd stolen his birthright lordin' it over everyone. His mother should've inherited that stone, then she'd never have run off with McKrevie.'

'But then Frank wouldn't have been born,' I pointed out.

'It don't matter who the kid would have been, the thing is if she'd married anyone but a McKrevie the Wingfields

279

would've accepted any kid of hers when she died, and that's all there is to it.'

'So . . . you stole the diamond because you felt the *Wingfields* should have had it?' Evie said, disbelief and scorn in her voice now.

'Look, I don't care who has the bleedin' thing,' Ruth said. 'I took it because I was stupid enough to believe Frank when he told me it was gunna pay for our future. Turns out he just wanted it 'cos he thought it would buy him back into the family. Pathetic. As if they'd have him.' She looked at me. 'You know he was never interested in you?'

I avoided Evie's astonished gaze. 'Of course. *I* was never silly enough to believe he had any interest in anything but the Star.'

'You hoped, though, for a time, din't you? Just like me,' Ruth said, and there was a trace of understanding in her expression.

'No,' I said firmly, 'I put up with him, that's all.'

She gave me a long look, and just as I was about to speak, to break the painful silence, she stood up. 'Right. I don't care what you do with what I've told you. If you get the book thrown at 'im or what, it's no more'n he deserves. But I'll say you're lyin' if I get so much as a knock on *my* door.'

I stood too, and met her stare. But although she had no way of knowing it, and although I had since bested nastier, and stronger, people than her, I still felt the vestiges of that old, sick fear in the pit of my stomach. Her eyes were like chipped slate, and, thin though she was, those arms were all wiry muscle.

But she was more concerned with Frank and his comeuppance. 'He deserves whatever he gets,' she said. 'In fact, I 'ope he cops it in the trenches.' I saw Evie flinch, and knowing she had first-hand experience of exactly what that might mean, hated Ruth even more for saying it.

Throwing one last poisonous look at me, she grabbed the little girl's hand and marched her out through the back door. I heard their voices, a mingled symphony of wailing and scolding, until they faded away into the distance and we were alone again.

I turned to Evie. 'What do we do now? We know who has the diamond, do we go to the police?'

'Well, we know Markham persuaded Ruth to steal it,' Evie pointed out, 'but we don't know if he's still got it.' She shook her head. 'Do you remember the night I wore it for the first time? I told you then it would bring nothing but unhappiness, and wished I'd been given a motor car instead.'

'I remember,' I said, smiling despite all that had happened since. 'I bet I wish that more than you do.' My tone was light, teasing, but Evie's expression was one of such misery I regretted it instantly.

'If only I could take back my stupid decision to put the necklace in my room,' she said, 'all this would never have happened.'

For the first time it occurred to me that she must have held on to that guilt for all these years. 'But you can't possibly think what happened was your fault,' I said. 'You might as well say that if I hadn't come to work at Oaklands, I would never have crossed knives with Ruth to begin with. And how far back do we go when apportioning blame anyway?'

Evie sighed. 'You're right, but I still wish I had ignored it all, like the grown woman I so proudly professed myself to be.'

'It was just childish jealousy on their part,' I reminded her, 'and you were stung by it. Of course you would want to remove something that was making you the butt of their malice. I'd have done exactly the same.'

'Never let anything ruin a party,' Evie said, and smiled a little sadly. 'It's funny how one's priorities are arranged and rearranged throughout life. Not so long ago I would have gone straight to Frank Markham, police at my heels, and made the most enormous racket until the stone was recovered. But that would purely have been in the cause of releasing you from prison.'

'And now?'

'You're here, and I quite simply couldn't care less about that necklace. I have far more important concerns, like the where-abouts of my husband.'

It sounded very strange, that word on her lips, but the instant she had spoken I felt her pain and went to hold her. She bowed her head, still wet from her bath, and rested it against me, taking what little comfort I was able to give. Evie didn't cry but I felt her take a deep breath, and I didn't say anything for fear of upsetting her further.

Eventually she straightened up and gave me a rather weak, but genuine smile. 'What would I do without you?' she said, and I shook my head.

'I just wish there was something I could do to help,' I said. 'How will you ever find out where Will is?'

'I'll do what I should have done as soon as he disappeared,' she said. 'I'll ask Uncle Jack.'

Instantly my heart rose in my chest and I felt such a surge of heat in my cheeks I had to turn away under the guise of rinsing my freshly collected herbs at the sink. 'Will he be able to help, do you think?'

I couldn't tell if my voice sounded as tight to Evie as it did to me, but if it did she didn't mention it. 'I don't know. He has ...' she tailed off and I turned back to see her shrug '... friends in fairly high places, he's proved that. I think he used them, as well as David, to help get you out of prison.'

I pretended surprise for a moment, but Evie only looked back at me knowingly.

'I think so too,' I admitted. She had clearly worked a good deal of it out. 'But that is what you were hoping for so it's no surprise.'

'No, the only surprise is why he's barely written to me at all. I've had three letters in as many years. Very short ones, none of them acknowledging anything I'd said to him in mine. I was so disappointed he never even mentioned my marriage, when he was one of the few people I could speak to about it quite openly. Then he wrote to say that he didn't receive my letters until he'd returned from his secondment two months ago, but that he was going to do his best for you.'

'Evie, what does Ja— Mr Carlisle actually do? I've heard he's a diplomat but I don't know what that means. And Mary says—' Remembering her disapproval, I tailed off but it was too late.

'Mary says what?' We both turned as Mary herself came in. She was looking tired and a little out of sorts, and I hesitated to turn the conversation in a direction that would place Jack in a poor light once again.

'You were telling me that Mr Carlisle is in a reserved occupation,' I said carefully.

Mary glanced at Evie. 'So he is,' she said, 'but I didn't say I knew what that job entailed.' To my relief, she dismissed the subject with a little wave. 'Anyway, you'll never guess who Mrs Hannah saw beetling down the drive just a few minutes ago, bold as brass and with a child hanging on her coat?'

'Ruth Wilkins!' Evie and I both said together. We told her the purpose of Ruth's visit and Mary was comfortingly furious.

'That little whippet!' she said. 'The very nerve of her, demanding payment for her own crimes!'

'Well, she did have some interesting news in return,' Evie said, and by the time she'd finished explaining Markham's parentage, Mary's eyes might have been on stalks.

'Well,' she said, 'that does go some way towards explaining what he hoped to do with such a distinctive stone. He could never have sold it, but giving it to the Wingfields ... that's understandable, at least.'

'If unforgivable,' I added pointedly. 'So will you write to Mr Carlisle?' I asked Evie, eager now to turn the conversation back to Jack, as if talking about him might conjure him in a more solid form than that in which he constantly inhabited my thoughts.

'I will. I have only a day or two before I have to return to Belgium, but that will be long enough to get a message to him. With his connections abroad he should know where to start, at least.'

'You must trust him very deeply?' I said, glancing at Mary, who looked away, tight-lipped. 'I mean, if he finds out Will has deserted won't he be obliged to report it to the War Office or something?'

'I do trust him,' Evie said firmly. 'He's the closest thing I have to a father, and he has treated me like family ever since my own died. He would never betray Will, it would be like betraying me.'

Again I looked at Mary, who busied herself stacking dishes by the sink. I couldn't understand why she was so convinced Jack was untrustworthy; she hadn't joined in the speculation that night on the stairwell when Joe had made his solemn pronouncement, but neither had she defended him. And, I remembered now, she'd cut me short the one time I'd asked her directly about him. I wondered if she actually believed him to be not merely a coward but a murderer as rumour suggested.

'I'm glad you have somewhere to turn,' I said to Evie, reluctant to pursue the thought.

She nodded. 'I'm going to write to him now. He always says to send letters directly to his office in London if it's urgent, and this certainly counts as that so I hope he's there and not in Liverpool. Perhaps you could post it when you go to the village tomorrow, Lizzy?'

'Of course.' It had been on the tip of my tongue to say I knew Jack wasn't in Liverpool as of just over a week ago, but I stopped myself in time.

Concealing the truth from my closest friend was going to prove one of the most difficult things I had ever done, and I wasn't sure how long I could keep it up. I daily fought back disappointment after the post had arrived with no word from Jack, and only the memory of his promise to tell me everything kept me from utter despair. I felt sure that, once he had done so, I would be able to accept and embrace the love for him that I was trying hopelessly to deny.

Evie went back upstairs to finish dressing, and then Mrs

Cavendish and Mrs Hannah returned and I was unable to ask Mary any more about her suspicions. We worked in silence until she had finished with the dishes, and when she went out into the garden I found an excuse to follow.

Dusk had fallen. I found her sitting on my old milk churn, her coat wrapped around her against the evening chill.

Not knowing how to broach the subject casually, I just came out with it. 'Why do you mistrust Jack Carlisle so much?'

She wasn't as surprised as she might have been. 'Why do you care so much?' she countered.

Her response wrong-footed me, and I hesitated. 'I worry that Evie is placing too much trust in him, and that Will may suffer as a result,' I said eventually. It sounded somewhat lame to my own ears but Mary appeared to accept this.

She stood up and led me down the path, away from the permanently open kitchen window and any interested eavesdroppers. The rain was falling in a fast drizzle and I hadn't thought to pick up my own coat; I shivered and pulled the sleeves of my dress down over my hands, but soon forgot my physical discomfort.

'I mistrust him because he covers himself in mystery and lies. He travels alone, and too often. He has no wife and nor has he ever had—'

'He was engaged once,' I put in. 'To one of the Wingfields.'

'Yes, I remember the engagement to Constance. But what happened then?'

'He joined the army.'

She shook her head. 'Many people joined the army, Lizzy, but they didn't turn into men of mist and shadows because of it.'

Mist and shadows ... yes, that described Jack to an extent, but I couldn't help feeling Mary's suspicions were built on the same flimsy material.

'So he travels a lot. What of it? And why should he have a servant with him if he doesn't want one?'

'It was expected of him by Society. Before,' Mary reminded me, that one small word covering so much that had happened since Jack had first come into the Creswells' lives. 'Although not so much now, I grant you. And then there is the question of his "reserved" occupation.'

'Government work. It has to be done,' I said, hearing impatience in my own voice. I was tired of hearing Jack dismissed as a coward, but it was preferable to the other stories I'd heard. I took a deep breath. 'Mary, those rumours about Lord Henry ...'

She stopped walking but didn't turn around. Instead she pretended to examine the leaves on one of the blackcurrant bushes beside the path.

'Do you believe them?' I persisted, forcing myself to speak the words aloud. 'Do you believe Jack ... Mr Carlisle ... could have murdered him?'

'Yes.'

The simple word dropped like a stone into my heart. If she had only hesitated, or shrugged, or seemed in some way to express reluctance, it might have hurt less; but there was clearly no doubt in her mind at all. I couldn't think of a single thing to say. I struggled for some calm, searching question that would give her pause to reconsider her belief. I even tried to bring my own confusion and suspicions to the fore so I might understand better, but all I could think of was the gentleness of his hands, his rare, beautiful smile and his fierce protection of those for whom he cared.

'I don't,' I said. 'I don't believe it for a single moment.'

'Why not?' Mary said. She looked hard at me and I could have sworn she could see my thoughts, and my memories, but she could only know what I chose to tell her.

'Because of how he is with Evie,' I said. 'He couldn't face her day after day, could he, knowing he had killed her father?' I gestured to the end of the garden. 'He even planted a tree in Lord Henry's memory!'

She glanced down the darkening path with a flicker of surprise, but then shook her head. 'Think about it,' she said. 'Why else do you suppose Mr Carlisle has been coming here all these years? Why take on Lord Henry's children as if they were his own, and why take such good care of a family with no formal connection to him whatsoever?'

'Because Lord Henry was his best friend.'

'No! It's because of guilt.'

'But *why* are you so sure of this?' I cried, unable to help myself. Mary had always been such a source of strength to me, always right, always certain. How could she have got this so wrong?

She caught me by the shoulders. 'Lizzy, I understand, and I'm sorry.'

'You understand what?'

'I've seen the way you light up when his name is mentioned; he's a very attractive man, and he's mysterious too, and that makes him exciting. I know he can be gentle when he's with Evie, he saved you from more time in prison, and even wrote a note to help you find work, but—'

'You think I have a fancy for Jack Carlisle?' I managed, pushing the memory of our kiss firmly away in case she could read my expression after all.

'I know you do,' she said, more gently now. 'And I'm certain you feel you know him better than most of us. But please, listen to me, he's not to be trusted. We've all heard things, but I *know* him to be capable of murder.'

There was a chill forming in the pit of my stomach, and the coldness was spreading through me. Mary glanced at the darkening sky, believing it to be the cause of my sudden shivering. 'Come back inside, lovey,' she said.

'*How* do you know?' I said, stepping back out of her concerned reach.

She folded her arms across her chest and glanced over her shoulder as if worried we might be overheard. 'All right, I'll tell you,' she said. 'I wasn't going to, I couldn't see the need, but it worries me that you're so attracted to him. Come inside where it's warm, I'll make us a cup of cocoa and tell you everything.'

Chapter 21

Up in our bedroom, the door shut tight and locked against
interruptions, Mary and I sipped hot cocoa for a while before
she spoke.

Finally she took a deep breath. 'You'll have noticed we
come from the same town,' she began, and I nodded. 'Well,
that's no coincidence. Jack Carlisle and my dad, Arthur, were
best friends when they were boys, and when they got older
they worked together on the construction of the Manchester
ship canal.' I started at that, remembering how he'd told me
the same thing but had neglected to mention that his friend
had been Mary's father. I felt the first icy drip of doubt.

'Dad was two years older,' Mary went on, 'and Jack looked
up to him, admired him, I suppose. Anyway, Jack had a girlfriend, Jean. It was nothing too serious, but the trouble was
Jean admired my dad too, and, rogue that he was, he didn't dis-
courage her.'

'Was she the same age as Jack?'

'A year younger. Children, really. But Dad was a bit of a silver-tongued devil, by all accounts, including his own.'

'And this Jean started seeing Arthur without Jack knowing?' I settled on to my bed, part of me forgetting this was real life and relaxing into the story for its own sake.

'Not exactly, but Dad managed to sweet-talk her into spending the night of her sixteenth birthday with him while Jack was away. The trouble was, she became pregnant—'

'Oh!' I exclaimed, 'Jean's – was – your mother?' No wonder Jack had looked shocked at the news of her death. I was about to mention that, but Mary was talking again.

'Granddad made her marry Arthur in secret, before anyone found out.'

'Poor Jack.' The words were out before I had chance to check them, and Mary's expression told me I'd have done far better to have remained silent.

'Yes, *poor Jack* found out, obviously,' she said, her voice cold. 'They were at work on the canal when someone congratulated Dad, and Jack was so furious he swung out and blacked Dad's eye. That might have been an end to it, honour satisfied, except they were standing on the edge of the construction road. Dad fell and broke his leg, couldn't work for six months and lost his job, and my mother had to go out to work up until the day before I was born. Dad drank himself insensible every night out of guilt because he couldn't provide for his family. Yes, poor Jack.'

'But he was just a child! You said so yourself.'

'Seventeen is old enough to know better. And he looked and acted older, from what my mother said. It was one of the things she liked about him.' Mary sighed and put down her

291

cocoa mug. 'The truth is, he shatters people's lives and then has to spend the rest of his days picking up the pieces. He did the same with us as he's doing with Evie and Lawrence.'

'How do you mean?'

'He left after the fight, and no one heard from him for a long time. Does that sound familiar?' She didn't wait for a reply and I had none to give. 'Then, out of the blue, he came back to visit,' she went on. 'I was about ten at the time and had no idea who he was, but I'd seen him arrive from my bedroom window and was thinking how exciting it all was, how handsome he looked and how mysterious he seemed.' She looked at me pointedly, but I gave no acknowledgement.

'He spent some time in the kitchen with my mother, but I couldn't hear what they were saying so when he went out to my dad's shed I followed him. I listened outside and heard them talking. It was the first time I'd heard the reason Dad had lost his job, and to be honest I was just relieved it wasn't his fault after all.'

'But it was an accident.' I heard the tremor in my voice as I tried to imagine the man I knew in such a violent situation. Somehow it had been easy, even exciting in a way, to imagine him facing down enemy soldiers, but this ... this was different.

Mary nodded. 'I do understand that much. Dad forgave him, and a few years later when he was on his death bed from the drink, Jack told him he had secured me a good job in an excellent house. He said he owed us a living of some kind.'

'So *he* got you this job?'

'I couldn't afford to refuse it, but he did, yes.'

As he'd done for me after leaving Holloway. I swallowed

hard. 'But if your father forgave Jack, and he's tried to make amends, why do you still hate him so much?'

She sighed. 'Lizzy pet, I don't *hate* him, not any more. I did, for a long time, but even then, deep down under all the complicated layers of loyalty and love, I realised my Dad was as much to blame. Possibly more so.'

'So then why—'

'You asked me if I thought he was capable of murder. Specifically if I think he was capable of killing his best friend. Well, now you know why I said yes. I realise it was a moment of passion that led to my dad's fall, but I also know that if Jack had been in his right mind he'd never have lashed out while they were standing so close to the edge. And a man who can lose his mind so quickly and so completely in the heat of anger is more than capable of harming someone, or even killing them. I'm not saying he wouldn't feel remorse for it after, but he could do it.'

'But do you think he *actually* did it?' I persisted. 'I mean, I'm capable of jumping out of that window, but I wouldn't actually do it.'

Mary smiled a little then, and it helped ease the awkwardness between us. 'Now *that* I might pay good money to see,' she said. Then she sobered again. 'I see the way he is with Evie, and although he never looks twice at me here I remember his kindness towards me was much the same. It reeked of guilt.'

'But does that mean it has the same origin?' I was desperate, now, to find the light in this dark, dark story.

Mary looked away. 'When my father was dying, and Jack was talking to him – they were both a little drunk – he said

293

something I have never forgotten, and it wasn't until years later when I heard the rumours that I put the two things together. Dad had said something along the lines of what a good friend Jack had proven to be over the years, despite the fight they'd had, and Jack replied that if being a good friend required killing those you love, then he was the best friend a man could hope for. Dad protested that it wasn't Jack who had killed him, but now I realise Jack was talking about someone else.'

'So you don't *know* he was talking about Lord Henry, you just suspect it?'

'No, I don't know for absolute certain, only he knows that. But I am sure enough, deep down.'

We sat in our tiny top-floor bedroom, listening to the wind rustle in the trees outside, our drinks cooling in the chilly air, and the faint sound of activity from the rest of the house drifting in under the door. It seemed a hundred miles away.

'Lizzy,' Mary said at last. 'Those feelings you have will fade, I promise.'

'What feelings?' Truthfully, there were so many different threads of emotion wrapping around each other and tying me up in knots, I couldn't have separated one from the other if I'd tried, and it seemed easier not to.

'Your attraction to Jack, your refusal to accept that, in all probability, he has killed. Beyond the requirements and duties of war, I mean.'

I didn't answer but put down my mug and began changing for bed. I felt sick, trembling with uncertainty and fear, and hoped Mary would see I couldn't bear to speak any more, and wouldn't probe any further into my feelings. I wondered if she had felt the same herself, and perhaps that was how she had read me so easily; but whether or not she now fully believed Jack capable of such wickedness, nothing less than a confession from the man himself would convince me he had done something as terrible, as unforgivable, as murder.

The following morning I rose early, and was dressed and downstairs even before Mary.

'You're in a mighty hurry this morning,' Mrs Cavendish remarked.

'I want to catch the first post,' I said, pulling on my coat. Evie's letter was waiting in the pocket, and I brushed it with my fingers as I added the shopping list Mrs Hannah passed me.

It gave me a painful twist inside to think Jack's hands would soon be on this same letter, and I wondered if I should try and slip a little note of my own in with it. But the envelope was sealed and if I didn't hurry I would miss the early post. Every hour was vital.

Finally I was on my way, mumbling Mrs Hannah's instructions to myself, and before too long I was passing houses and shops rather than fields and barns. The autumn wind was picking up the scent of the soil and I could smell the damp earthiness of it until I was properly in town, where the scents changed to those of engine fuel, chimney smoke, and the occasional drift of sweet bakery wares. All were still a source of pleasure after the stale stench of Holloway, and I had vowed never again to take even the most unpleasant of outdoor smells for granted.

It was while I was preparing to post Evie's letter, and simultaneously casting about trying to trace the origin of one particularly appetising smell of warm ginger biscuits, that I caught sight of him. My heart stopped and my stomach flipped over, and I nearly dropped the letter in the wet road.

'Jack?' I whispered aloud. He was across the road from me, standing in the alleyway between two shops, almost hidden in the shadows there. I looked around, trying to spot who he might be hiding from, but could only see a few people hurrying by with umbrellas and none of them were paying him the slightest bit of attention. Someone in one of the cars then? Or even myself?

As I watched it became clear that he was looking for someone while trying to remain hidden, but it was pointless trying to work out what was going on. I debated the wisdom of simply dropping the letter into the box as if I hadn't seen him against taking this opportunity to hasten the process along by handing it to him now. Even if he didn't want to see me he would welcome anything that came from Evie.

There was no choice; Will's safety, his life, might depend upon how quickly Jack was able to put some of those government friends of his to work on finding him. Besides, that was *Jack* over there, so close . . .

I shoved the letter back in my pocket, quickly crossed the road and stopped a few feet from the alleyway. No longer able to see his face, I wondered suddenly if I'd only imagined it was him. It was possible; I'd conjured him up so many times during the long, lonely days and nights, what if I'd done it again?

Then I rounded the corner and almost burst into tears at the relief of seeing him, and more so at seeing the expression on his face.

'Lizzy,' he sighed. 'Thank God, I was ...' He broke off and took my hand, and with one last glance past me at the street he pulled me into the alleyway and around the back of the shop.

Once we were concealed there he seized my face between his gloved hands, studied me intently for a long, burning moment and then kissed me with such fierce intensity I thought I would never draw breath again. I dropped my basket, heedless of the puddles, and let my arms slide beneath his open coat and wrap themselves tight around his waist.

The warmth and reality of him, the familiar smell of wet wool from his coat and the feel of his rapid heartbeat against my own, drove away all other thoughts. We remained locked together while he kissed my forehead, my temple, my jaw, and finally reclaimed my lips once more.

'I've missed you more than you would ever believe,' he said when we at last broke apart. 'I'm so sorry, I'm always doing this to you. I had to leave, but I couldn't write to you without the risk of someone telling Lily. I've been desperate to see you.'

I smiled. 'You've been looking for me?' Then, remembering his furtive behaviour, my smile faded. 'And hiding from someone else, it seems.'

'From everyone else,' he corrected. 'I'm too well known here. If I were to be recognised someone would engage me in conversation, and word would get around that I'm in the area.'

'And is that bad?'

'I'm not supposed to be here,' he told me, and seemed poised to say more, but stopped.

More secrets. It hurt. 'I have to give you this,' I said,

withdrawing the letter. 'It's from Evie, and it's important. I wanted to put a note of my own in, but I didn't have time if I wanted to catch the post.'

'Well, I'd much rather have you here in person,' he said, smiling and taking the letter.

I eyed him, feeling suspicious again. 'How did you know I would be?'

'Would be what?'

'Here. In person. Today. You can't have been skulking around Breckenhall every day in the hopes I'd come into town.'

He looked away at my sharp, interrogative tone. 'No. I was … watching someone else. I'd hoped to see you, of course, but I didn't really think I would.'

Someone else. Frank Markham perhaps. Was his declaration of disinterest in the Kalteng Star another lie? I felt my forehead tighten and the dull headache that was all that remained of my illness intensified, making me wince. He saw it and frowned, interpreting it as disbelief.

'I know I've promised to tell you everything, but—'

'But you're not supposed to be here,' I offered flatly. 'And where are you supposed to be?'

'I can't tell you at the moment.' His voice was filled with regret, but he was already distancing himself.

'When can you?'

'Soon, I promise.'

'Mist and shadows,' I murmured, and even managed a thin laugh.

'What?'

'It's how Mary described you. You know Mary Deegan, don't you?'

298

Was it my imagination or did his eyes glance away momentarily as I emphasised her family name?

'Mary,' he mused. 'She's a housemaid, isn't she? I think I know the girl you mean. I've never spoken to her, though. I always got her and Alice Peters muddled.'

The lie was blatant and I recoiled. 'Oh? Did you put Miss Peters's father in hospital as well?' My words were like icicles forming in the air between us. They froze the hand he had stretched out to draw me to him once more. It dropped back to his side.

'You don't know what you're talking about,' he said calmly.

'I know you cost a man his livelihood, and put his family through hell,' I said, my throat so tight I could barely get the words out. 'Or was *Mary* lying to me too?'

'Lizzy, you can't—'

'Is it *true?*'

'Stop it!' he shouted. Then continued quietly, after a cautious look around us in the deserted lane, 'Yes, it's true. There was a fight, I lost control of myself. Arthur Deegan lost his job and turned to drink because of what *I* did to him.' He glared at me, his expression dark and defensive. 'There, now you know, does it make you happy?'

'No!' But I'd had to do it, to wipe out my fairy-tale picture of this man as perfect and replace it with the truth. 'Why didn't you tell me this before?'

'Because it's something that has haunted me for years, something I've never been able to put behind me, and because it has nothing to do with how I feel about you,' Jack said, but his voice was still angry, robbing the words of the comfort they should have given me.

'What happened between Arthur and me was in the past, and yes, I might have instigated it but he was older than me, bigger than me, and, when all's said and done, it was a fair fight.'

'And what about Henry Creswell,' I said, before I could stop myself. 'Was that a fair fight too?'

The colour drained from Jack's face. 'What?' he whispered.

'Mary thinks you killed him. And she's not the only one; they all argue about you below stairs,' I told him, my voice rising with swiftly approaching hysteria. 'He was your friend too, so did you kill him, Jack? Tell me!'

'Yes! All right. Yes ...' He took a step towards me and I felt the wall at my back and the icy rush of terror in my veins. He opened his mouth to say more, but something inside me took over and I ducked beneath his arm, taking advantage of his momentary confusion to push him hard into the wall. He stumbled, taken by surprise, and I ran as fast as I could through the alley to the main street.

I heard him behind me, hissing my name with urgency, but remembered his reluctance to be seen in the town and forced myself not to panic. Instead I walked quickly into the nearest shop and pretended to browse the display of buttons and ribbons on the counter, until my heart had stopped its ferocious racing.

All the while my mind was twisting and turning, hearing his confession echoing again and again. He had killed Evie's father. Jack Carlisle was a murderer ... the pain was like a physical blow, and in my extreme terror I felt my throat close up.

'Miss? Are you all right?' The shopkeeper was looking

worried, but also as though she would rather I take my obvious distress somewhere her customers would not be subjected to it.

'I . . . I just feel a little faint,' I said. 'Would it be all right if I sat down here for a while?'

'Of course. Would you like a drink of water?' Now the shop-keeper was able to display a caring side she seemed happy to accommodate me. It would give me time to work out what to do, and I nodded gratefully as I was escorted to a chair in the corner of the shop.

While the assistant fetched some water from the back I anxiously scanned the street outside. Jack would not risk being seen coming after me, nor would he come to Oaklands; whatever his reasons for staying hidden, they were evidently one of the few genuine things about him.

His secrecy, and the lies he had told, gnawed at me until I felt sick and it was at least twenty minutes before I felt safe enough to leave the shop. To my relief one of the first people I saw was Mr Dodsworth, coming out of the tea shop on the corner of the main road.

I hurried up to him. 'Mr Dodsworth, could I ride with you back to Oaklands, please?'

'Of course.' He looked around furtively as he said it, and it was all I could do not to let out a hysterical laugh as I compared the deception of the butler pretending I no longer worked at Oaklands, with that of the man who had saved my life and then pretend he hadn't murdered his best friend. 'I have one or two errands to attend to first, but I shall be happy to drive you back in half an hour,' he said, satisfied no one had seen or heard our conversation.

'That's perfect. I have some instructions from Mrs Hannah,' I said. I was amazed to find such trivialities had remained in my head after all the turmoil of the past half an hour. I went about my errands with a fast-thudding heart, and my eyes never still for a moment as they constantly checked alleyways and shop doorways.

But Jack had, once again, disappeared.

Chapter 22

Two days later Evie left to return to her post with the Red Cross. I could see her attention slipping away from us gradually, the closer the time came for her departure, and it was like seeing a favourite painting fading in front of my eyes. I knew Will was uppermost in her thoughts, and that the rest of them were taken up with preparations for the horrors she would encounter in a very short time, but still I wished, selfishly, for some sign of her old spark to hold on to while she was gone.

'I'll see you again very soon, Lizzy,' she promised as we hugged goodbye.

'I do hope Mr Carlisle can help find Will,' Mary added, and I caught her eye. I hadn't told either of them I'd seen him in the village, it seemed easier and safer not to; they would have asked so many questions, I was bound to have blurted out something best kept to myself.

'He'll certainly do everything he can, I know,' Evie said. 'And that will have to be enough or I'd go mad thinking about it all. One thing about driving that blessed ambulance in the dark –

303

there's no room for any distraction, or the dressing stations would be filled with victims of my driving and no room for the poor Tommies!'

There was the old spark, albeit a small glimmer. I held on to it gratefully.

As soon as Evie had left to catch her train, Mary disappeared to our room, leaving me in the kitchen with Mrs Cavendish and Mrs Hannah, both of whom had plenty of jobs that needed doing. So it was that I didn't see my friend again until late that night when I climbed the stairs barely able to put one foot in front of the other for tiredness.

My thoughts were constantly occupied as well; since Jack's horrifying revelation I had been unable to put it to the back of my mind. Everything I did, everything I said, and every waking thought had had to push their way past that new knowledge, and I struggled to concentrate on anything else.

I wondered if Constance Wingfield had suspected him of such violence, and if that was, in part, why she had broken off their engagement. Lord Henry had died a good five years later, but maybe Jack had shown a flash of his true colours to her, or she had discovered what he had done to Arthur Deegan.

I glanced up at the top of the staircase, sensing someone standing there. Mary saw me and hesitated then stepped aside in the narrow hallway at the top, allowing me to pass. She was wearing her coat.

'Are you going out?' I asked in surprise. It was almost

eleven o'clock, hardly the time for a pleasure jaunt, and she was due to start work at six in the morning.

'I just needed a bit of fresh air,' she said. 'I have a headache, thought it might help.'

The prospect of fresh air against my tired eyes sharpened my own appetite for the cool October night. 'Do you want some company?'

'No!' she said quickly, and I looked at her, eyebrows raised. 'You're tired, and you have an early start.'

'So do you.'

'*I'm* not still getting over a nasty bout of the 'flu,' she reminded me. 'Now go on to bed and I'll see you in the morning.'

She seemed so eager to be gone that I gave up and watched her hurry down the stairs. Perhaps she had a man waiting? The thought made me smile. In our room I began undressing but had only got as far as removing my apron when I saw the envelope tucked beneath the brush and comb set on Mary's dresser. Guilty but curious, I drew it out and saw immediately that it was empty. The writing on the front read only: *Mary, The Kitchens, Oaklands Manor*.

She probably had the letter with her, which would teach me a lesson for being so nosy. Still, it had served the purpose of focusing my mind on something positive and happy for a few minutes. Then I looked at her bed. More specifically the pillow. Would she . . . ?

'Oh, Mary, you're not at all good at this,' I said with a satisfied sigh, and withdrew the folded piece of paper. 'Now, let's see who your new beau is.'

I opened the letter and froze, my fingers tightening convulsively and tearing the edge of the paper.

Dear Mary,

You and I must talk, it's vitally important. Come to the summer house in the grounds at eleven o'clock on Thursday night. Tell no one – our secret cannot be discovered at any cost.

Yours,

Jack Carlisle

Breathless, I read the short, neatly printed note again. The initial spurt of black jealousy at the thought of a secret liaison between Jack and Mary passed in an instant, to be replaced with a cold, creeping fear.

Mary knew Jack had murdered Henry Creswell, and now Jack knew she knew. Because Lizzy Parker had opened her enormous mouth and told him. My eyes were drawn back to the words *our secret cannot be discovered at any cost.*

'Oh, Mary, no …'

I didn't stop to change into outdoor shoes, I ran. Down the narrow staircase, past the great hall, down the back stairs to the now-dark kitchens, and out into the yard. The wind snatched at my breath and tugged the cap off my head as I stumbled in the darkness towards the garden gate.

Once through it, I had to stand still for a moment to get my bearings, and as I did I saw the deeper shadow against the darkness of the garden, moving towards the faint light that was only visible from the pathway around the walled garden where I stood. Mary.

I debated whether to shout to her, but I would have to do so quite loudly in order to make her hear me, and I didn't want to alert anyone else. I had a second to wonder why I was still protecting Jack after all I'd discovered, and put that together with the flash of intense jealousy I'd felt just a few minutes before; I would never understand my own fickle heart and its twists and turns.

I stopped again before I'd taken more than two steps closer to the summer house. In my mind I reviewed the letter once more, and then compared it with the note I'd seen him write with my own eyes, and which I had read and re-read, and come to know in its every loop and flourish.

This time I did shout out, and I saw the shadowy figure turn. But she didn't stop. Instead she hurried onward and I followed, running on through the darkness, hoping for a clear passage with no protruding roots to bring me down.

The previous days' rain had softened the ground, my indoor shoes offered little in the way of sturdiness, and more than once I felt my feet slide in patches of grass worn down to mud, stopping my breath for an instant each time. As I rounded the wall, the summer house loomed in front of me and a faint, flickering light from inside threw a ghostly glow on to the bushes by the door. I was just in time to see the door close and a large figure move across it, shutting Mary in.

With my heart pounding from more than my late-night run through the grounds, I moved closer to the door and listened.

'. . . longer hair when I saw you before. Admittedly that was from a distance,' the man was saying.

Mary's voice was thinner than usual and higher; she was clearly scared. 'Why did you use a false name to lure me here?'

'I would have thought that was obvious,' he said. 'Who else would you have agreed to meet but the man with whom you're in love?'

There was a long pause filled with the sound of thunder

that was raging in my head. My thoughts flashed back to our conversation about Mary's family and Jack's connection with it, how she had known him since childhood ... I had been so naïve.

All this flew through my mind in the moment it took for Mary to respond, 'In *love*? He's a coward and a bully, and very likely a murderer into the bargain! How dare you associate me with such a man!'

'Come now, Mary,' the man said. 'I saw the two of you. You were angry at first, I grant you that, but I saw him kiss you before you got, quite willingly, into his car! I followed you to his hotel, and when a young lady spends the night with a ...well, I hesitate to use the word "gentleman" ... in such a place, we can only draw one conclusion.'

'I'm telling you, I have *never* spent a night in a hotel, not with Jack Carlisle nor with anyone else!'

Through the pain of betrayal I realised she was so angry she no longer sounded scared and that lent an air of truthfulness to her words. I began to doubt my own convictions, and those of the stranger in the summer house.

'I saw you,' he repeated patiently. 'The way he carried you in was touching, I must say. Rather like a married couple crossing the threshold for the first time.'

I saw him move then, his shadow leaping in the light from the lamp as he stepped away from the door. 'It's a pity you cut your hair,' he mused, and now I had to strain to catch his words but Mary's still came out loud and clear in her anger.

'I haven't cut my hair!' she snapped. 'And I have never been carried, nor embraced, by Jack Carli—' Her voice trailed away as if catching herself out in a lie, and that, more than anything, convinced me she was not in love with Jack after all: it was the resurrection of an old memory that had made her falter rather than the covering up of a new one.

At the same time a light went on in my head and, without stopping to sort out all the confused thoughts it illuminated, I pushed open the door and stepped into the musty-smelling summer house.

'I think you have the wrong Mary,' I said.

Chapter 23

The man turned, startled by my sudden entry, and it was almost comical the way he looked from me to Mary and back again, but no one was smiling.

I glared back, putting on a show of defiance despite the churning I felt inside. 'Who are you?'

'I might ask the same question.' Then he took in my long hair, torn loose from its cap and pins by the wind. 'Ah, yes. This is more like it. Carlisle's whore, I presume?'

Mary's eyes widened in shock as the truth sank in. '*You* spent the night in a hotel with Jack?'

'I'll explain later,' I said. 'Who's this man?'

'But—'

'Samuel Wingfield,' he interrupted. He moved behind me to block the door again, although neither of us had made any move towards it; Mary was too stunned, and I too curious. So this was the infamous Wingfield Patriarch?

'What did you want to see me about, Mr Wingfield?' I said, keeping my voice firm.

He frowned. 'I didn't realise there were two Marys working at Oaklands,' he said, frowning. 'I'd only heard of one.'

'My name is Mary, but I'm known as Lizzy, so no, most people aren't aware there are two of us,' I said. 'How did you even know I was back here? Lady Creswell didn't want anyone to know, and I saw no one in town who knows me, or would think to mention me to you.'

'Overheard a conversation between my wife and my daughter. I understand you're going to be attending my new grandchild,' he said, and sounded even less pleased than I was about the new connection between us. I found myself having second thoughts about wanting to work for Constance, but at least she lived in Chester with her husband and not with the rest of the Wingfields.

'Mr Wingfield, it's been a long day, I suggest you say what you've come here to say, and then leave before someone realises we're both missing from the house and comes to find us.'

'Oh, I don't think that's very likely, do you?' Wingfield took a step forward and laid a hand on my arm.

Instantly all my bravado melted: that touch brought home to me the realisation that I didn't know this man, couldn't predict how he would react to being goaded, and still had no idea why he was here. He was a big man as well, old enough to be my grandfather but burly and strong, and a good six feet in height against my five feet two.

He spoke quietly, though. 'You're still close to Miss Evangeline Creswell.'

I blinked in surprise; I didn't know what I had expected but it wasn't this. 'She's a good friend,' I said carefully.

'Such a pity about the butcher's boy she was sweet on.'

My fingers clenched. 'What do you know about him?'

'I know the situation for young Davies is rather desperate.' The hand on my arm tightened and I tried to pull away, but the strength of his grip made me gasp in pain.

'Lizzy!' I heard Mary take a step towards us but we both knew she could do nothing to help.

'You're hurting my arm,' I said, keeping a tight lid on the panic that threatened to take control.

'I'm well aware of that,' Wingfield said. He smiled again, but there was no more warmth in it than you would have found in the smile of a crocodile. 'I need to be sure you're going to listen to me.'

'I'll listen,' I said, and had an impulse yet again to thank my years in Holloway that there were no tears for Wingfield to enjoy. Instead I fixed him with a look of dislike, and raised my eyebrows for him to continue.

He nodded. 'Very well then. Thanks to a superb network of informants, the details of which I needn't trouble you with, I know exactly where young Mr Davies is currently sheltering. Hoping to avoid detection and thus the firing squad, no doubt.'

Despite the jolt that went through me at his words I kept my face stony. Will was alive . . .

Wingfield's smile widened and I could almost swear I heard the swish of a scaly tail. 'What's so unusual about this knowledge, Miss Parker, is that Mr Davies himself knows less than I do.'

312

'Mr Wingfield,' I said impatiently, 'for all your boasting about your informants, you didn't even know *my* name! How can I believe you have anything of substance to tell me?'

'Quiet! Just listen.'

'Then get on with it, and stop talking in riddles.'

Wingfield's expression tightened, and so did the fingers that dug into my arm, but I was ready for it this time and didn't make a sound.

'Davies was last seen after the victory at Bazentin-le-Petit, but had disappeared *before* the first assault on the next objective later that same day. High Wood,' he clarified, on seeing my mystified expression. 'A disaster, by all accounts, and the attack on that particular line had apparently been delayed for several hours.'

'I don't—'

'Which gave the Germans extra time to fortify it. Suspicious, don't you think?'

I drew in a shocked breath at the implication. 'If you believe Will had something to do with it then you don't know nearly as much about him as you think.'

'I know enough,' Wingfield said mildly. 'Enough to send the authorities after him with all the information they need to find him and bring him to justice, either as a spy or a coward.'

'Justice!' My temper flared again, laced with a steadily increasing fear. 'He'll be killed! What has he ever done to you?'

'Oh, I've nothing against the young man personally,' Wingfield said. 'By all accounts he's a fine soldier, and good chap all round. He's suffering from shock and has no memory of who he is, or how he came to be, well, where he is now.'

'Then why . . . what . . .'

Wingfield waited for a moment while I floundered, then said, 'I can see you are at a loss, so I'll set it out for you in a neat little line. I have information *you* would very much like, both for yourself and for your friend Evangeline. You, on the other hand, have something of far greater value.'

'What?' I frowned, still confused.

He leaned in close, his breath hot on my face. 'The Kalteng Star.'

'What?' I said again, this time incredulous. 'I haven't!'

'Oh, Miss Parker, please! Would we have gone to all the trouble of arranging your release from prison if we believed that? You may no longer possess it yourself, but you know who does, and you're going to get it for me.'

'But I never stole it to begin with!' I cried. 'I can't give you what I never had!' Somewhere in the back of my head an urgent voice was whispering: *Jack arranged your release . . . didn't he?*

'Lizzy, it's time to tell the truth,' Mary said suddenly.

Shock rippled through me as I looked around at her. She seemed to be staring very hard at me. Her brows came together as if she was trying to project her thoughts, and in the unsteady lamplight she appeared like something from a dark fairy-tale; a ghoul trying to reach into my mind and bend me to its will.

'But you know I—'

'The truth, Lizzy! After all, Mr Wingfield *knows* you stole it, or he wouldn't be here offering this chance to rescue Will.'

'You gave it to Jack Carlisle,' Wingfield said, his voice hard. 'And you needn't look so horrified, of course we know. He was the man with whom you were seen at the gate on the night of the party.'

'Jack ... Mr Carlisle left much earlier, even before Evie took off the necklace,' I said, but could hear the lack of conviction in my own voice and it was no surprise to see Wingfield shaking his head.

'Yes, he left, and made sure plenty of people saw him do so. But he came back ...' He paused, frowning, then resumed quickly. 'And you saw him, and took the opportunity to give him what he'd been after all these years.'

I stared, utterly confused. 'I don't understand. All these years?'

'Why else do you suppose he has been so involved in the welfare of the Creswell family, when he was more closely tied to ours?' Wingfield said, his frown turning to a scowl. 'Carlisle has been after that diamond since Constance first told him about it. And his becoming a "father figure" to Lily's daughter had nothing to do with his friendship with Henry, and everything to do with biding his time until Evangeline was eighteen years old.'

'But what has this got to do with me?'

'My daughter-in-law Clarissa has always taken a keen interest in young Evangeline,' Wingfield said. 'Understandable, what with her being the heiress to a fortune that should have been ours.' His eyes bored into mine and I found it hard not to flinch away. 'She couldn't help noticing how Carlisle encouraged the friendship between you girls, and we realised as soon as Evangeline chose you for her maid – a notion that Carlisle endorsed to Lily – that you were perfectly placed to steal the necklace and pass it to him. He hid it extremely well, and then left you to face prison. Persuading my grandson to tell the truth was a gesture made too late; you might have died in there. You owe him nothing, Miss Parker.'

'He's right, Lizzy,' Mary urged.

'You should pay attention to your friend,' Wingfield said, but although he let go of my arm at last it was clear I would not be leaving until he had my promise of co-operation.

'Why should I trust you?' I said, the freedom giving me a little of my courage back. I moved away, but fought the urge to rub at my arm where I could still feel the hard pressure of his fingers. 'If I had the diamond, or knew where it was, do you suppose for one minute I would just hand it over on *your* word?' I gave it all the scornful emphasis I could muster, and saw his brow darken.

'You're not as stupid as you appear,' he said, but there was no admiration in his tone. He reached into his coat pocket and brought out a leather wallet which he flipped open. From one of the many pockets he withdrew a photograph and handed it to me.

I stepped closer to the paraffin lamp and held the picture up, feeling my stomach drop away. It was grainy and dark, but unmistakable: Will Davies, the boy I had last seen all smiles, dimples and impish mischief, sat huddled in the corner of what appeared to be an outhouse or barn of some kind. He was still in his uniform, muddied and too big for him, and blank-faced as he stared uncomprehendingly up at whoever had taken the photograph. There was a darker patch on his face that I took to be mud at first, but might have been blood, it was impossible to tell.

Wingfield was studying my reaction. 'Perhaps you need a

little more incentive,' he said, his voice deceptively soft. 'You have two days to consider how much the life of your friend means to you, two days to admit you really have no choice. In short, two days to find Carlisle and get the diamond off him.' That cold smile was directed at me again. 'I'm sure someone like *you* knows how to persuade a man like that.'

I felt cold, all over and right through. 'And what happens if I can't?'

'Then I will go to the War Office with names, map references and more photographic evidence. William Stanley Davies, erstwhile of the Thirty-Third Division, will face court martial before the week is out. We both know what will happen then.'

'How can you do all this?' I whispered. Helplessness swept over me, robbing me of my ability to maintain the thin veneer of scorn and dislike.

'That does not concern you. All you need to consider is that, without your co-operation, a very bewildered young man is soon going to find himself with a white square pinned to his chest. I believe this is where you and I part company. For now, at least.'

I couldn't help myself: 'You're nothing but a thief!'

Wingfield grabbed my wrist and jerked me towards him. 'I advise you not to make so free with your insults, my girl. After all, it's only thanks to my grandson that you're walking free today – if he had decided not to corroborate your story after all, you'd still be locked up with the other thieves and whores.'

I twisted in his grip. 'The vilest of them is still worth a hundred of you,' I said, low and fierce. 'They would never have traded a boy's life against a rock that did not belong to them in the first place.'

'And what do *you* know of its history?' Wingfield snapped, suddenly losing patience. He seemed about to elaborate on his claim to the diamond, but instead pushed me towards the door. 'Two days.'

Mary and I stood close together on the wet grass while Samuel Wingfield strode away through the shadowy garden, a tall figure flickering in and out of patches of thin moonlight until he vanished from view altogether.

Mary turned to me, her mouth already open, but I started walking back to the house. She hurried after me, no doubt with questions falling over themselves to be voiced while I slowly, painstakingly, untangled my confused thoughts.

Back in our room we faced each other, neither of us knowing where to start. In the end we both spoke at once.

'Do you really believe I stole the diamond?'

'Did you spend the night with Jack Carlisle?'

I gave a bitter laugh. 'Well, it's plain to see where our different priorities lie on this.'

'Oh, Lizzy, of course I don't believe you stole it,' Mary said. She came over and, to my surprise, put her arms around me. The relief was so great I felt tears prickling in my eyes.

We stood in silence for a minute, then Mary led me to my bed and we both sat down, trying to form our questions more constructively.

'We both know Wingfield had the story more or less right,' Mary began, and held up her hand as I started to protest, 'but he had the wrong two people.'

I nodded. 'Then why did you ...' Belatedly it came to me why she had spoken as she did, and I shook my head. 'Of course, I understand now. I was just so outraged, it didn't sink in.'

'Well, I tried to spell it out for you,' Mary said. 'It's our only chance to save Will from the firing squad.'

I looked at her squarely. 'All right, I've had my question answered. Now it's your turn, ask away.'

'Lizzy, I don't want to come across like your keeper, or your superior, or even like a jealous friend ... but why didn't you tell me about you and Mr Carlisle? When did you spend the night with him? Was it only the once? Have you seen him since?'

'I said one question!' But I couldn't help smiling. For the most part it was with relief that I was at last able to talk about it, though I no longer knew where to start.

Mary waited patiently while I tried to identify the moment I was first drawn to Jack, and when I found it I discovered it had been, not that time in Lord Henry's study, as I'd suspected, but on the very first day we met, when he'd offered me a lift back from Breckenhall station.

I told her everything, from that day onward, and took some time in the telling; every word was like a weight rolling off me, eased by the calm certainty of my continued love for him.

Mary listened in silence, tensing when I told her how he'd come for me at the prison, and how he'd taken me back to his hotel. I told her how we'd kissed and saw her hands twist together, only relaxing when I explained how he'd left me to sleep alone in his bed. I even told her how he'd persuaded David Wingfield to tell the truth, and it seemed, for once, she appreciated the use of his government connections despite the questions of morality it raised.

319

When I reached the revelations about Jack's violent past, I expected my own remembered terror to push aside the feelings of warmth and closeness to him that the rest of the story had evoked in me, but nothing had changed and I felt a passionate relief for that.

'And so now he believes I'm frightened of him,' I finished.

'You should be,' Mary said. Her face was as white as her knuckles now. 'He actually *admitted* he killed Lord Creswell!'

'There must have been something important at stake,' I insisted. 'I know him, Mary.'

'You do not!' she said harshly. 'What could possibly be important enough for that? He has taken advantage of you from the very beginning.'

'He saved my life,' I reminded her.

She looked at me with exasperation, and then sighed. 'Perhaps this evening has held enough excitement,' she said. 'We'll talk more in the morning.'

'Only about what's important,' I said. 'We'll talk about how we're going to get into Frank Markham's place, how we're going to find the diamond ... and about what's for afternoon tea.' I saw a small, flickering smile at that, and she nodded. 'But,' I went on softly, 'we won't talk about Jack Carlisle, all right?'

She rose then and went to her bed, and I went to mine, although I don't believe either of us slept well that night.

Chapter 24

The following morning, true to her word, Mary did not mention my liaison with Jack nor his revelations regarding Henry Creswell.

As soon as the upstairs breakfast was cleared she came to find me and drew me aside, out of earshot of Mrs Hannah. 'Meet me as soon as you can after dinner, in the outhouse by the herb garden, and we'll talk.'

'Ruth told us Markham is still away fighting,' I said, 'so we just need to find a way of getting into his house without being seen.'

'I'll give it some thought,' she agreed, and that was all we had time to say before Mrs Cavendish came back down from her meeting with Lady Creswell and told Mary she was required upstairs.

Her duties with Lady Creswell meant her dinner was taken later than mine, and she found it more difficult to get away. I found myself alone in the outhouse, memories assailing me with every glance I took around its chilly interior.

In the corner, replacing the pile of old sacks on which I had sat waiting for Jack, was a collection of garden implements – I reflected that if they had been there that night I might well have been scared enough to run him through with a pitchfork.

I closed my eyes as I remembered the gentleness of his touch on my hot, bruised flesh. We had become so close then; the fear, the strangeness and the urgency of the night had removed, briefly, the difference in our stations, and the mutual attraction was hard to brush aside. Hard, but not impossible and the realisation of its hopelessness between us had hurt far worse than my physical injuries.

I jumped as the door opened, and at last Mary came in. 'Sorry,' she said. 'Lady Creswell was getting in a flap planning a dinner party tonight. With all the Wingfields, and Constance and Doctor Harrington along with a friend of theirs.' She paused. 'And one other person.'

I brushed aside these details. 'It's all right,' I said. 'I was just ...' I trailed away, remembering my own promise not to talk of Jack. 'I was remembering my first day, walking in on Ruth and Frank,' I finished, somewhat lamely.

Mary arched her eyebrows and I knew she didn't believe me, but she dismissed the subject in favour of what was important.

'Right, then. Markham lives above his premises and the only way to get in is through the shop itself. You can't get in from the yard at the back.'

'Well, that's no good. The shop fronts on to the main street. Someone will notice if we're loitering about there after dark.'

'I've thought about this. What if we go just before closing, and then one of us distracts Martin, the apprentice, while the other quickly goes through the door behind the counter?'

'That might work,' I said, feeling my heart speed up with an odd sort of excitement. 'It's a very bold plan, though. What if we're caught?'

'The new apprentice is nice enough,' Mary said. 'We've passed the time of day often, and know each other quite well now. Even if he catches us, he's not going to call the police or anything.'

'Well then,' I said, 'if you've already struck up an acquaintance with him, it's best if you distract him and I try and get into Frank's place to search for the necklace.'

'You can come down and let me in as soon as Martin has gone,' Mary said, 'and then we'll have all night to search undisturbed.'

I nodded, then frowned. 'What if he's hidden it somewhere else? He probably has by now.'

'In that case,' she said, 'we'll just have to think of something else. We might find a clue to where it is, and gain some time with Samuel Wingfield that way. For now, though, this is the best chance we have.'

'It's going to be hard to get away in time to reach town before the shops close,' I pointed out, hating to pour more cold water on the plan, though it did seem fraught with problems.

'You leave that to me,' Mary said. 'Just be ready to leave by four o'clock this afternoon.'

By three forty-five I was waiting in our room, clothed in my outdoor dress and shoes, and with my coat over my arm. I couldn't help viewing the evening ahead with a touch of excitement despite the gravity of the situation, but when Mary came in I was dismayed to see she had been crying.

Wordless, she kicked off her house shoes and slipped into outdoor boots, then picked up her coat. To my shame I just stood there, utterly astonished, so much so that the words to ask what was wrong just wouldn't form.

It was only as I followed her down the back stairs and couldn't see her face that I felt able to ask: 'Mary, what is it? What's happened?'

'It's not important,' she said, and after a sniff went on, 'I'll tell you while we walk. But not here.'

Not important. So that ruled out the grimmest of news: the death of a family member or friend. But whatever it was had broken through Mary's usually tough exterior and I wasn't used to seeing that. She kept ahead of me, hurrying with her head down and her hat pulled firmly around her face, and it wasn't until we were safely on the road to Breckenhall, out of the confines of Oaklands Manor, that I felt able to grab her arm and pull her to a halt.

'Tell me what's wrong!'

She sighed. 'I think I've done something extremely stupid.'

We continued walking, and as the afternoon darkened and we drew closer to town she told me what had happened that afternoon.

Lady Creswell had interrupted her while she was ironing a dress for tonight's dinner party as it appeared there was a still more urgent job to be done: the morning room was in need of a thorough clean.

Mary had been puzzled, but had obediently taken her

324

cleaning trolley to the morning room. I had watched her work before, and I could see it all in my mind's eye as she described how she had carried out her duties; every nook and cranny dusted, every surface polished, every ornament replaced exactly.

Then had come the most physically demanding part of the job: cleaning the carpet. I knew Mary was thorough, so it came as no surprise to hear she had gone to the rug in the centre of the room and lifted it aside in order to clean beneath it.

It was a heavy rug, I remembered it well; oval in shape and nearly as long as two people laid end-to-end. A difficult task for two housemaids working together, for Mary alone it would have been an enormous struggle, yet she worked at it until she had moved it sufficiently to allow her to clean beneath.

But as she'd hefted the last part of the rug to one side and turned towards her carpet beater, her attention had been drawn to something in the middle of the floor. A piece of white paper, printed with whorls and ornate lettering . . . a five-pound note.

'I realised straight away what it meant,' Mary said as we walked on through the deepening dusk. 'I've heard Lord Griffiths and his household had experienced problems with a light-fingered maid.'

'Surely Lady Creswell doesn't think you a thief?' I protested. 'More likely it was to test the thoroughness of your work, don't you think?'

'Then why not leave something else beneath, like a note of thanks?' Mary said, and I saw she was right and understood her distress; to realise your employer felt the need to test you in such a way was a terrible notion, highly insulting and upsetting. I understood it all too well.

'What did you do?'

Mary stopped in the road and turned to me, and now there was a lopsided smile on her face. 'The only thing I could do, of course. I took the money to Lady Creswell, explained that someone must have accidentally pulled back the rug, carelessly laid the money beneath it and then replaced it.'

The laughter that bubbled out of me fell into silence as she went on, 'And then I told her she would have my notice first thing in the morning.'

'Mary! What did you do that for? What will you do now?'

We were just coming into the main street of the town, and she glanced around. 'It looks as though we might be just in time,' she mused. Then she turned to me. 'What will I do? Well, perhaps I will follow in Evie's footsteps and become a VAD, although I think nursing is more my forte than driving an ambulance. Far better to contribute to the war effort than to spend my most productive and healthy days cleaning carpets and ironing dresses.'

'I will miss you,' I told her sadly. Part of me rejoiced in her strength, that she could just give up her job and try something so new and dangerous, seemingly without a qualm, but the rest of me felt the foundations of my life shake beneath my feet. I needed her, I always had.

'And I will miss you,' she said. 'But you'll have your own new job to think about before too long. We'll talk about this later. For now let's just make sure we get to Markham's shop before it closes.'

The butcher's shop owned and run, in peacetime at least, by Frank Markham lay a short distance up the street. Some shops were already closed but many, mostly those with fresh produce, stayed open a little longer in order to sell their stock while it was still at its best.

Markham's was open, but through the window we could see a tall, thin young man stacking empty meat trays in the large porcelain sink ready for washing.

'Very well, this is what we'll do,' Mary said, and I was grateful she was taking charge. 'We'll go in together. That way Martin will see you but he'll pay no real attention. I'll engage him in some conversation or other, and draw his attention while you creep in behind the counter. You'll have to be very quick, and get through that door into the back as quietly as possible. I'll wait outside. If you can't find the diamond you can come down and let me in to help, but not until it's fully dark.'

'What if we get caught?'

'We won't, I'm sure.' I heard echoes of Evie in that blithe certainty, but this was too serious to leave to chance, and to the hope that Fate eyed us favourably.

'But what if we do?'

'All right,' she said, and pursed her lips. 'Listen, then. If you are caught behind the counter before you are able to get through the door, just say you thought you heard a cat trapped upstairs in Frank's rooms. Martin likes cats, he'll appreciate your concern.'

We looked at each other for a moment, both taking a deep breath at the same time, and then Mary pushed open the door.

The bell gave a loud jangle and the apprentice – Will's replacement, I realised with a pang – looked up.

'Mary,' he said, with obvious pleasure. 'Lovely to see you!'

I hovered by the door and acknowledged Martin's less

familiar but polite greeting with a smile of my own, pretending to examine the pictures of Frank Markham that hung on
the wall: 'Your Friendly Family Butcher'. Well, he'd been
friendly for certain. A small, reluctant smile tugged at my lips
as I remembered his extravagant compliments.

Mary went right into the shop and made a great show of
looking at the few pork chops left on the trays in the window.
Predictably enough, given the fact he was clearly smitten,
Martin put down his empty trays and went over to see if she
needed help. The limp that had kept him from enlisting was
quite noticeable, and I wondered if he, like so many others,
looked upon it as a blow rather than a blessing. I thought that
perhaps Mary held the latter view, at least there could be no
accusations of cowardice here.

She began asking him questions about the meat: was it fresh
today; was it reserved for anyone; would it be cheaper since
the shop was due to close soon; would there be bigger ones
tomorrow ... I was so taken by her inventiveness that it took
a moment for me to realise my opportunity was slipping away.

When Martin leaned into the window space to pick up the
tray of cutlets at Mary's request, I dodged around the counter.
Crouching down, I realised I would not be able to tell from
here if it was safe to open the connecting door, and my heart
began hammering so hard I could feel it in the roots of my hair.

'Where did your friend go?' Martin asked suddenly.

'Oh, she's probably gone outside. She hates the smell of raw
meat,' Mary said. As soon as the words were out of her mouth
I became aware of the sickly sweet, clean-but-not-clean smell,
and wrinkled my nose against it. 'Now, those sausages in the
far corner ... no, that tray there. Next one over ...'

I pushed open the door just wide enough to slide through. I would not know until a shout went up whether I was safe or not, and decided it would be better not to close the door fully in case it clicked; hopefully Martin would think he'd left it ajar himself.

I waited, breathing as slowly as I could, which was still too fast, and wiped my sweating hands on my coat. There was no shout, just continued conversation from the shop, and Mary giving little laughs – I could imagine a playful touch on Martin's arm accompanying those laughs, and there was very little about her performance that was manufactured. I shook my head and smiled. '*The apprentice is nice enough'? Mary, my girl, I think there is more to this 'passing the time of day' than you're willing to admit.*

I looked around me in the semi-darkness, and saw there was nothing else on the ground floor except storage space, so I moved stealthily towards the narrow, carpeted staircase that led up to the main living quarters above the shop.

Just before I put my foot on the first stair, however, I stopped: Martin would be sure to hear movement above him if I just blundered on up to Frank's rooms and starting moving things about. I should wait until the shop was closed and empty before making my way upstairs. I hoped Martin would have no reason to come back into the hallway or storage room before he left.

To lessen the chance of discovery I wedged myself into the small space beneath the stairs, among the collection of boots and coats. The smell of mildew caught me unawares and I held the bridge of my nose between thumb and forefinger, and concentrated on not sneezing for a moment. Then, when the immediate danger had passed, I dragged my handkerchief from my pocket. Another of Ma's pieces of good advice, always to carry one, but I imagined she'd had a very different idea of the situation in which it might become useful.

It must have only been a few minutes yet it felt like an hour or more before I heard the unmistakable sounds of a shop shutting for the day. Eventually I heard the bell of the cash register and the metallic rattle of coins being dropped into a bag, and realised it was likely that Martin would have to come back here after all, to put the takings in the safe.

Frantic, I cast around for something to hide me and in desperation seized a large overcoat and draped it over my head as I sank to my heels against the wall. The smell inside the coat was rank and sweaty, and the rough, unlined material scratched at my skin, but I hardly dared breathe, let alone move, as footsteps came and went along the short passageway, past my hiding place to the store-room at the back of the building.

I remained hidden this way until I was absolutely certain Martin had left for the day, and then I stood up and removed the coat with a sigh of thanks. Seconds later my heart jumped into my mouth as a familiar voice said, 'What the *hell* are you doing here?'

Chapter 25

Mute with terror I stared at Frank Markham, who glared back at me with cold grey eyes. 'Well?'

I found my voice, but couldn't manage more than, 'I was just . . .' before I found myself unable to continue. No matter how scared I had been that Martin might find me, I would have given anything for it to be his bewildered young face peering into mine now instead of this one. I shoved the handkerchief back into my coat pocket as Markham's right hand shot out and gripped my arm.

'After my takings, were you? Upstairs, now, you little thief.'

'Please, Mr Markham, I haven't taken anything, I'm not here to steal—'

'Now!'

Markham yanked me out of my hiding place and I saw why he was at home and no longer fighting: his left arm now ended just below the elbow.

He saw me glance at his stump, and smiled tightly. 'Don't

think this means you can make a break for it,' he warned, 'or you'd be badly mistaken.'

'How did it happen?' I asked, not to stall him but because I actually felt badly for him despite everything. He didn't answer, but pushed me ahead of him up the stairs.

In his rooms above the shop, with the harsh overhead gaslight on, I could see he looked exhausted, sick and in pain, and felt another wave of sympathy for him. I opened my mouth to say something but it was only at that point he recognised me.

'Lizzy? I thought you were in prison!'

Sympathy drained from me. 'It's no thanks to you and your girlfriend that I'm not,' I said. 'You put her up to it, after all.'

There was no point in arguing his innocence, and thankfully he didn't try. 'I never thought you'd get sent down for so long,' he admitted, then frowned. 'Ten years, wasn't it? How come you're out already then?'

I smiled, keeping it as cold as I could. '*Someone* has a conscience and owned up to the truth.'

He paled. 'Not Ruth?'

'It doesn't matter who,' I said. 'Don't worry, they don't know who did steal the Star, only that it couldn't have been me.'

He looked relieved at that. 'So what are you doing here?'

I decided the truth would be the only thing he would believe, so that's what I told him. When I'd finished I searched his face for some sign of understanding; this was the life of his former apprentice at stake and, one would assume, they'd been friends of sorts.

'It's not for me, it could save a life. *Will's* life,' I urged. 'Please, Mr Markham, I know this stone means a lot to you—'

'You have no idea,' he said, and his voice was bleak now as he turned away and stared out of the window at the blackness beyond.

'Yes, I have, Ruth told me. She said you were going to use it to get back in with the Wingfield family.'

'*My* family,' he corrected, without looking back at me. 'Did she also tell you I was turned away, even after I did what they wanted?'

'Yes. I'm sorry. But I really need—'

'I haven't got it!' he snapped. 'Ruth knows I haven't, that's the reason she left me.'

'*She* left *you*?' I said, frowning. 'That's not the way she tells it. She said you turned her out.' But the most important thing now was that I found I believed him when he said he didn't have the Kalteng Star. I felt hollow and fearful, all confidence in any prospect of Will's safe return draining away.

'I would never have turned her out,' Markham said. He came back to stand in front of me, his expression strangely earnest, as if he desperately wanted to be believed. 'As soon as she realised I wasn't going to be a Wingfield again after all, she left.'

'Taking your daughter.'

'Amy,' Markham said, his voice cracking.

I remembered how the child's tearful, grubby face had been transformed by the delight she'd felt in the silver spoon, and hoped Ruth hadn't sold it too quickly. 'Why would she leave when she had nowhere to go?' I asked, genuinely puzzled. I was forgetting, for the moment, that Mary waited for me downstairs.

'She did have somewhere to go at first,' Markham said. 'She has some kind of family in London – that's where Mrs

Cavendish found her. She'd been friends with Ruth's mother. The mother died when Ruth was twelve, and Mrs Cavendish brought her back to Oaklands to live and work. But there are others still there who'd have had her back.'

'So when she was sacked she went home to London?' I tried once again to battle a pang of sympathy as Ruth's story unfolded, but it was getting harder.

'For a while, yes. Then when the ... when Amy was born she came to me with her hand out. Apparently her own family didn't want the disgrace of the child either so she felt justified in stealing from them the train fare back to Cheshire. I told her I hadn't got the diamond any more, and what's more I wasn't being accepted back into my own family, and she turned poisonous.' He shrugged. 'You know what she can be like. She said she had some other bloke who'd look after her, and that Amy wasn't even mine.'

'And you believed her?'

'I didn't believe the bit about Amy,' he said, and I saw the ghost of a smile at the corners of his eyes. 'She was too much like me to doubt for a second I'd helped make her.'

'But you believed Ruth had another man?'

'Pimp, more like,' Markham said. 'At least she'd make some money working for him, but I was waiting for my battle orders. She knew I'd be no good as a provider, over in France somewhere with not even the stone for security.'

'Mr Markham ... Frank ... you said you don't have the Star any more, so where is it?'

'Clarissa Wingfield's got it.'

For a moment I let that sink in, then shook my head. 'No, that can't be right. Samuel Wingfield, your grandfather,' I realised, somewhat dazed, 'is the one who's after it. He'd know if it was already in his house, wouldn't he?'

'Not likely!' Markham said. 'Clarissa came to me years back, told me my only chance of coming back to the family was to bring her the stone. Told me to get in with someone on the Oaklands staff, but that it was to remain just between the two of us.'

'But what can she do with a jewel that famous? She can't add it to the Wingfield family wealth, and she can't sell it.'

'Not in this country,' Markham agreed. 'But if she's able to get it to Amsterdam and cut down, she's laughing.'

'How long has she had it?' I asked.

'About a year, I gave it to her just before I joined up. She'll be waiting for the end of the war if she's got any sense.'

'If it ever does end.'

He looked down at the stump of his arm. 'Yeah. If.'

'What happened?' I asked softly.

He looked taken aback by my question, then shrugged. 'Wound turned septic. Wasn't a bad wound. A Blighty one, at least.'

'A what?'

'A sniper picked me off while I was fixing the wire in front of our trench, but he only hit my wrist. A minor wound, but enough to get me sent home—'

'To Blighty,' I finished. It made sense now.

'Yes. But first, stuck in the wet and the dirt ...' He shrugged. 'We were being shelled by the time I made it back, and it took so long to get me down the line. Even longer at the casualty clearing station. Too late to stop the infection spreading.'

335

'I'm sorry,' I murmured, not knowing what else to say, and Frank Markham nodded his thanks.

I glanced at the dark window and felt my own hands start to shake again. Listening to him talk of Amy, and of his injury, I'd felt the fear falling away momentarily. It was returning now as I considered what he might do to prevent the truth reaching the police.

My voice shook as I asked, 'Mr Markham, will you let me go?'

He looked at me, puzzled. 'Of course I . . .' Then realisation dawned. 'I'm no monster,' he said quietly. 'You're right. Clarissa used me, and I used Ruth and tried to do the same to you. The only good thing to come out of all this mess was Amy.' He sighed. 'If you see Ruth, will you tell her I'm back and I want to see the baby?'

I nodded, privately sure I would never see her again but relieved beyond measure that I would soon be out of this dismal room. Markham studied me for a moment, as if he could see in my face what I was thinking, but he didn't argue. He said no more as he led me back downstairs, but as I stood in the doorway he caught hold of my wrist and I felt my heart leap in renewed fear.

He gave a sad little smile and let go immediately. 'I'm sorry for what we did to you, Lizzy,' he said. 'I hope you've got a good life now, in spite of everything.'

He stepped back inside the shop and closed the door, leaving me with the memory of a brash, confident tradesman who had turned, almost overnight, into this broken man with no life to speak of. And no family.

*

It wasn't until the bell's harsh jangling had fallen back into silence that I allowed myself to breathe easily again. The night air was cold but so fresh I took great draughts of it, clearing the taste of mildew and fear from my mouth.

'Lizzy!'

I jumped. Mary stood half in shadow but I didn't need to see her face to sense the question she wanted to ask. I shook my head and we turned to begin our walk back to Oaklands, passing few people but not discussing what had gone before, for fear of our conversation being overhead.

Once we'd passed the last of the town's buildings and were on the dark road home, I started to tell her everything and when I got to the part about Clarissa Wingfield she stopped. 'Samuel, her own father-in-law, doesn't know? How long has she been planning this?'

'Probably ever since she married into the family,' I guessed. 'Do *you* think she'll wait until the end of the war to try and get across to Amsterdam?'

Mary shook her head. 'If she realises Samuel knows, I think she's quite likely to make her escape much sooner.'

'So do we tell him, or do we just try and get the diamond from her ourselves?'

'I don't know, we need to think about it. We don't know if Samuel will stick to his word. If Clarissa can go back on hers as she did with Frank Markham, why wouldn't he?'

A sense of urgency transmitted itself from mind to feet, and we walked faster and faster. I felt the chill of her words creeping through me with each step that carried us towards our frightening deadline. Two days ... it wasn't enough, and yet if Clarissa left the country it would be two days too long, and then we would never be able to persuade Wingfield to release the information about Will.

We were almost at Oaklands when a sweep of light bathed the road ahead, and at the same time a car rumbled up behind us. I instinctively turned as I stepped to one side, and saw the driver was youngish and looked vaguely familiar, but as the car passed I saw its other occupants: Samuel Wingfield in the front, and a woman I assumed to be his wife Lydia in the back. My breath caught, but the car accelerated past us without incident.

Mary had seen him too. 'Dinner with Lady Creswell,' she reminded me. 'Don't worry, Lizzy, he's not going to stop us in the road and make demands. How would he explain that to his wife? We have another day yet.'

She was right, but just the sight of Samuel's face, even when it was fixed ahead and not turned to meet mine, was enough to make my stomach knot in fear.

We had just passed through the gates of Oaklands when I heard another car. For a terrified second I thought Samuel had driven around somehow and come up behind us again, but even before I turned I realised this car was different: older, rougher-sounding, and although I could see nothing beyond the brightness of its lights, I still recognised it.

The car stopped, the lights and engine on, and Mary caught at my arm. 'Don't just stand here!' She tried to pull me into a run but I shook her off, my insides twisting for another reason altogether now.

'It's all right, it's Jack!'

'It's not all right!'

Jack got out of the car and raised his hands to show he carried nothing with which to hurt us. I spared a second to puzzle over this before I remembered how we'd ended our last meeting; he couldn't have known my feelings towards him had deepened despite what he'd told me then.

Before I could call out to him he spoke, raising his voice above the noise of the engine. 'I'm not going to hurt you, I promise. Please, Lizzy, just let me talk to you.'

I walked back down the avenue towards him, stopping shy of where he stood but holding out my hand to him. He stepped forward and took it, drawing me closer.

I looked at our linked fingers, it was easier than looking into his face. 'Why are you here?' He didn't answer, so I glanced up. He was looking past me at Mary with a frown, but I shook my head. 'She knows,' I said. 'She's not happy about it, but she knows. Now why *are* you here?'

'I could ask you the same question, out here like this,' he said, gesturing at the darkness, held at bay by the lights of his car. 'I'm here for dinner with Lily. She's lined up yet another "eligible young lady" for me—' He broke off as headlights swept over the front of the house ahead, and Samuel's car began moving back down the avenue. So Jack was the 'one other person' who'd been invited to dinner then? Mary had clearly taken my refusal to speak of him quite literally, but I thought she might at least have prepared me for the chance of seeing him.

'Damn, I'll have to move the car,' Jack muttered. 'Lily won't appreciate Wingfield having to drive all over her grass.' The emphasis he put on the name told me there was a real enmity between these two men, and I remembered Samuel's evident disgust when he'd mentioned Jack in the summer house ... was that only last night?

He stepped away from me and back towards his car, and I turned to go back to Mary, who was moving towards me, but we all froze in shock as Samuel's car accelerated.

'Move!' Jack shouted. I heard his feet on the road behind me but in the split second in which I had time to think, Samuel's car had skidded to a stop right next to Mary and the passenger door had opened.

The two cars' combined headlights created a pool of illumination, like the spotlights in some terrible play in which Mary and I played the lead, and in that light I saw something that stopped my heart mid-beat: Samuel Wingfield was holding a gun.

It was a great, hulking thing, dwarfing even his hand, and it was pointing at my chest.

'Stop exactly where you are, Carlisle.'

I glanced over my shoulder and saw Jack had reached into his own car but now stood, hands raised as before. 'Leave them alone, Wingfield,' he said, and I was disturbed to note there was no shock or even surprise in his voice. 'These two can just go on their way, they have nothing to do with this.'

Nothing to do with it? What did Jack think was going on? But my horrified attention was locked on the gun, trying to imagine the sound it would make, my flesh burned where I imagined the bullet might take me, and all the strength I had could not subdue this crawling, suffocating terror.

'Right, now what have you two got for me?' Samuel said. Panicked, I glanced up towards the house, praying for some intervention, but all they would see from this distance would be two cars facing each other at the end of the drive; friends having a chat before moving on.

'We haven't got it,' Mary said, her voice shaking so much it was hard to understand her. 'And we have another day yet, you said so.'

'Another day for what? Wingfield, what the hell is all this?' Jack demanded. He took a step towards me but Samuel moved his thumb on his gun and, at the loud click, Jack stopped.

The driver climbed out of Samuel's car then, and as he moved into the pool of light I recognised him: David Wingfield.

'Mary's right!' I said with desperation. 'We have until tomorrow night.'

Samuel looked at me, his eyes narrowed, then from me to Jack. 'Nevertheless, I think I'll take out some extra insurance.' Keeping the gun on me, he grabbed Mary one-handed and pushed her towards his grandson. 'Put her in the car,' he said.

'Clarissa's got it!' I said quickly, as David hustled Mary towards Samuel's car. 'She's the one who ordered it to be stolen to begin with.'

'Don't lie to me, girl,' Samuel said, but his voice betrayed a sudden uncertainty.

'I'm not lying,' I said, and was struck with sudden inspiration. 'Where is she tonight then? Not joining you for dinner? I know she was invited.'

'She suffers from migraines,' he said.

'Or she's found out from someone,' I shot a meaningful glance at David, 'that you're taking matters into your own hands, and has decided not to wait any longer before taking the stone out of the country.'

'Get her in the car, boy!' Samuel repeated, and David obeyed.

I heard Mary call my name as she stumbled into Wingfield's car, and felt hot tears of fury; all she had done was try to help me.

'Wingfield, for God's sake!' Jack slammed his fist on to the bonnet of his car and the sound made me jump, my tears falling faster and mingling with the rain.

'Tomorrow evening, Shrewford Hall,' Samuel said to me, ignoring Jack's impotent fury, as he could well afford to. 'The two of you, and the Kalteng Star.'

'What?' Jack began, baffled, but Samuel turned, lowering the gun, and I felt as if someone had taken their foot off my chest and allowed me to breathe again.

Samuel took the two short steps to his car just as Jack reached through the window of his and, to my horror, withdrew a gun of his own. He turned back, raising it as Samuel slammed the door behind him. Jack lowered his arm with a curse; the risk to Mary was too great.

The clunk of the car door had an awful finality about it and seemed to hammer home suddenly the reality of what had happened. A bright flare of hatred, and of terror for my friend, exploded in my head. 'Mary!' I screamed, running at the car, but it rolled forward, drowning out my cry. For a second it seemed almost to hover in the air, then I felt a vicious thump against my right shoulder and crashed side-ways to the ground, falling half on the grass and half on the road. The horror of being knocked down brought on a wave of nausea and I gulped, waiting for the pain to hit me, but it never did.

Dazed, I lifted my head. Samuel's car had swerved to the left, carving deep tracks in the wet grass as it left the road and careered around Jack's stationary vehicle. It rejoined the drive on the far side, and then all that was left was a single car, the fast-falling drizzle lit up by its headlights ... and Jack's horribly still form, lying face down in the road.

Chapter 26

I found my feet and stumbled to where he lay. Dread turned my blood to ice water as I rolled him carefully on to his back; if he hadn't pushed me to the ground, my foolish and pointless charge might have killed me. Instead, the car had hit Jack's right side, and his clothing was ripped where something, probably the mascot on the bonnet, had caught him. There was a cut on his cheek, and a deeper scrape across his brow which the rain kept trying to wash clean, but which kept filling up with fresh blood.

My fault, all of it. Sick with fear I looked up at the house, wondering if I should leave him while I ran for help, but as I did so I heard his breathing change, and turned back to look at him.

To my relief his eyes were open, and he managed a low croak: 'Don't.'

'Don't what? What do you want me to do?'

'Don't tell anyone,' he said, sounding stronger now. 'Just get me somewhere out of sight.'

'But Lady Creswell could help—'

'Please!' The effort of speaking made him wince. 'Trust me, love. Please, just . . . I'll tell you later.'

That phrase again; I felt like screaming but there was no arguing with him. Desperation was clear on his face, and now that Samuel's car had gone there was nothing to block the view of the two of us from the house should someone glance out of the window.

We were far enough away to be indistinct, but we would make an intriguing picture as I somehow got my arm beneath Jack's shoulders and eased him to a sitting position. All I could do was pray no one's curiosity was aroused.

Jack reached out his right hand to grasp the axle on the front of his car, but immediately cried out and let go. He slowly flexed his fingers and I saw he couldn't clench them tightly at all. Instead, he reached across with his left hand, and I got a shoulder under him and we both pushed until he was able to get to his knees. From there I was able to grasp him around the waist and, keeping clear of his right side as best I could, I helped him to one foot while he dragged the other after it. Then he leaned against the car with his head down, breathing hard.

'Now where?' I said, looking around.

He raised his head, and swallowed a groan. 'Summer house. Feel sick, need to lie down. But we have to turn the engine off first.'

'The gun!' I exclaimed; knocked from his hand, it lay glistening by the side of the road.

'Help me round to the driver's side first,' he urged. I did so, then left him there while I ran back to pick up the gun. It was heavier than I'd expected, and I held it hanging down from my fingers as though it might explode at any moment. The wet metal felt somehow alive. I hated it.

Jack stopped the engine, and the sudden silence, and the darkness as the headlights also vanished, felt surprisingly like a huge, comforting cloak thrown over me. As I slipped my arm about his waist the night sharpened into pinpoints of heightened clarity. The breeze seemed to disturb every individual hair on my head in turn, the soft sound of the rain magnified as it fell on the leaves all around. I absorbed the warmth of Jack's body, the feeling of his arm around my shoulder.

'I think we've been here before,' I said.

He hugged me closer. 'I'm just glad it's this way round now.' His other hand came across and pressed against his side, and he took a couple of shallow, experimental breaths. 'Right, I'm ready.'

We made our way, as quickly as we could in our hobbled state, across the lush lawns towards the far side of the garden and the shelter of the summer house. I thought back to my first day here. It was as if it had happened to someone else, which I suppose in a way it had. I had walked up this seemingly endless avenue, the house in the distance, my eyes everywhere, taking everything in, including the summer house.

I remember thinking it was big enough to house my entire family, and if someone had told me that one day I'd be going there in the dark with the man I loved, my romantic and innocent mind would have thought of a scenario far different from this one.

Amazingly, the thought actually made me laugh, and I felt

Jack twitch in surprise as he instinctively turned his head at the sound. 'Nothing,' I said. 'I'll tell you later.'

'Touché,' he murmured.

Once inside the summer house I left him holding on to the door jamb for support while I felt my way to where I remembered seeing a paraffin lamp the previous night. To my relief there was a box of matches on the small table next to it, and soon a flickering light was pooling in the corner, gradually widening as the flame steadied.

I offered to help Jack lie down, but he shook his head.

'Changed my mind,' he said grimly. 'I'd never get up again.'

Instead he stood very still for a few minutes, breathing slowly, letting the nausea roll away. As I pulled the curtains across and checked no light was shining through, I told him a shortened version of the encounter with Samuel in this very place, about Will, and finally about Frank's story that Clarissa now had the Kalteng Star.

'Someone will notice Mary's missing if her work's not done,' he said. 'And you too, of course. If they call the police things could get very tricky for us.'

'They won't, not until tomorrow at least,' I said, relieved to have good news for once. 'I've finished my duties for the day, and Mary has her own reasons for being absent for a while, which Lady Creswell won't argue with.'

Jack had shed his coat while I talked, and I looked more closely at the torn waistcoat beneath. It glistened in the lamplight and I realised there was a great deal of blood there. He saw me looking and touched my face gently. 'It's all right, don't worry. Tell me about Mary.'

'Only if you'll let me clean you up while I talk.' I couldn't shake the worry that Wingfields' car might have wounded him more deeply than we'd thought at first, but Jack seemed confident it was otherwise, so, as I unbuttoned his waistcoat, I told him how Mary had offered her notice, and that Lady Creswell would probably simply be glad she hadn't yet made good on that offer.

'I expect she'll be hoping Mary is off thinking about it, and will change her mind,' I said.

'Well, we know she'll be all right, at least until tomorrow night,' he said. I eased his waistcoat down over his shoulders and laid it on the table with the instinctive neatness of a lady's maid.

'Wingfield won't risk hurting her,' he went on, 'he doesn't seem to believe Clarissa really has the diamond, but if I know him, and her, he'll play it safe and keep a close eye on his household.'

His words dispelled the worst of my fears. Mary was valuable to Wingfield as a hostage as long as he believed we would bring him what he wanted.

Jack had begun to open his shirt, but his right wrist had started to tighten and swell. I had to help him with the last few buttons, then I spread the material and turned him towards the light in order to examine the gash. It was quite deep, but although there was obviously going to be bruising as well, he was right, it was nothing more sinister than a flesh wound. I pulled the handkerchief from my coat pocket again, once more silently thanking Ma, and wadded it against the wound.

'Hold that tight,' I told him, 'and keep pressing.'

The white cotton soon soaked through, but the bleeding would ease off if he kept up the pressure. What worried me more was the reddened area immediately above, at the bottom of his ribcage, and it was with great trepidation that I touched it, keeping my eyes on his face as I did so.

His eyes were closed, but the muscles in his jaw tightened and I immediately took my hand away. 'You've damaged some ribs there,' I said.

'Damn, how careless of me,' he said, trying to make me smile.

I gave him a flicker, it was all I could manage.' Very,' I said. 'We'll have to bind them as best we can.'

'What about the cut?'

I frowned, returning my attention to the bloodied area. 'It looks nasty. Does it hurt a lot?'

'Not too much, no. The bleeding's already easing up, I think.'

'But we need to find something for your ribs,' I said, looking helplessly around.

Jack, supporting himself on the mantle shelf, did the same. 'Curtain?' he suggested. 'It's only got to last me a few hours and make sure I can drive.'

So he was leaving again. This time the pain sank deep enough to make me catch my breath, and I swallowed hard as I made my way over to the smallest window, the only one out of view of the house.

'Why, where are you going?' I had tried very hard to keep the tremor out of my voice, but he'd heard it, and when I turned back he was looking at me with such affection I could have cried all over again.

'I'm going to get Mary back,' he said, 'and you're coming with me, daft girl.'

There was a brief pause while I let the relief sink in. 'Well, I should think so,' I said, trying to disguise my feelings under a veil of briskness. 'You couldn't have stopped me anyway.'

He chuckled. 'I wouldn't dare try! All right, let's get cracking. Those curtains will do, but we're going to have to be quick: Lily is going to start wondering why all her dinner guests are going missing, and if she sees my car out there on the drive she'll be sending Dodsworth down with a big stick.'

His humour was helping to calm me. 'Poor Mrs Hannah,' I said, 'trying to keep the food hot while all the people who should be eating it are gallivanting around the countryside, kidnapping and knocking each other down.'

'Very poor manners,' he agreed.

I set to work making him as comfortable as I could. His wrist was too sore to help me tear the dark-green material, but my hands were strong from years of hard labour, both at Oaklands and in Holloway, and I soon had two sufficiently wide strips.

I tied them together to make one long bandage, then began wrapping the lengths around Jack's body and under his shirt, trying to ignore the way he tensed whenever I made a pass over his right side. He didn't make a sound, though, and I finished by making the final pass lower, covering the cotton-wadded cut before tucking the end in.

'There,' I said, stepping back and looking critically at the result. I glanced up to make some comment about how he could now thank me for my handiwork, but the words died on my lips. Jack's face had gone dead white, his eyes were closed again and his breathing was shallow and ragged. His swollen right hand hung limp by his side but his left gripped the mantle tightly enough to turn the knuckles white. He turned away to press his head against that forearm while I stood looking on helplessly. His struggle was such a personal thing, there was nothing I could do or say. So I kept quiet, wishing I could bear the pain for him.

Gradually his breathing eased and he straightened up. He opened his eyes again and gave me a shaky smile. 'Well, *that* wasn't pleasant.'

It was the last straw. 'Right, we have to get help,' I said. 'Never mind Wingfield, I'm going up to the house to call for a doctor and there's nothing he can—'

'No.'

'Why?' I demanded, furious all over again. 'You've been knocked down by a car, you probably have broken ribs and goodness only knows what else broken in there.' I gestured at his gruesomely bloody midsection. 'I'm not a nurse, I can't take care of you properly.'

'Listen a minute,' Jack said, his left arm coming down to rest across my shoulder. 'It's all right, there *is* someone I can go to, probably the only one I should ask, but it's a bit of a drive. I need to be able to do that, can you help me?'

'Of course I can,' I said crossly. 'But I want to know why you won't let me fetch someone who can help *now*.'

'I know, sweetheart, and I'm sorry,' he said, and kissed my temple. Suddenly that too angered me.

'I'm not a child,' I snapped. 'I'm a fully grown woman, in case you'd forgotten, so stop treating me like a wayward four-year-old!'

'Sorry,' he said again, and I heard the smile in his voice. 'I've had to try and train myself not to think about how much of a woman you really are.'

His good hand traced a gentle line along the side of my face and I felt the terror-fuelled anger ebbing away under his touch, and the next time he kissed me it was my lips he brought to willing surrender. For a long, blissful moment there was no fear, no pain, no worry over friends in danger, there was just Jack and me, and the feeling of closeness that no degree of physical attraction could entirely account for; it was so much more than our lips that touched, it was a linking of two souls that needed only each other in order to find a fleeting peace amidst the chaos of the night.

When the kiss ended we remained standing very close together, our breath mingling in the chilly air. His hand slid beneath the heavy curtain of my hair and drew me closer still, tucking my head against his shoulder, and when my hands went to his waist they encountered bare skin beneath his open shirt.

Despite the fact I had touched him throughout the binding of his ribs, this was different and we both tensed at the unexpected sensation. His breathing shortened for an altogether different reason and neither of us wanted to move, but time and danger soon staked their claims. After a moment I kissed his shoulder through his shirt, and stepped back. Reluctant to let go of him completely, I reached up to touch the scar at his throat.

'What did that?'

'Pom-pom.'

I looked up with a smile, thinking he was joking again, but

he wasn't. 'That doesn't sound very dangerous,' I said, 'but it clearly is. Or was.'

'The Boers liked them well enough, I will say that. One of our gun emplacements was hit, there was an almighty flash and a roar, and I got in the way and afterwards spent a bit of time in the field hospital.' Now he did smile, and squeezed my arm. 'It looked worse than it was, don't worry. It didn't hold me up for long.'

'No, I imagine not,' I said drily. It seemed there was very little that could.

I remembered something else that had been bothering me, and bit my lip, watching his expression carefully in the flickering lamplight. 'Jack ... Wingfield told me he and the boys had arranged my release from prison.'

Jack's eyes widened slightly. 'He didn't. He certainly took advantage of the situation, and I'd even go so far as to say he helped David decide to own up. I couldn't work out why until you two started blathering on about that blessed diamond. He was clearly trying to shake your faith in me by saying he intervened on your behalf.'

'Well, he hasn't.' I wanted to hug Jack again in relief, but noticed the goose bumps on his chest. 'I'd say the first thing we need to do is get you properly dressed,' I said. Then pulled a face. 'And I wish I had something to clean off that blood with.'

He glanced down. 'Doesn't look very good, does it?' he agreed. 'But at least we know that's not as bad as it looks.'

'The cut isn't. Does it hurt anywhere else?'

'No, just the ribs, and a general overall ache. But I can drive and that's what matters.'

'Which brings me to my next question,' I said. 'Where are we going, and who are we going to see?'

He hesitated, clearly reluctant to give me one of his cryptic answers and raise me to anger all over again. 'There's someone, a doctor, down in London. We'll get going, and on the way I'll tell you about him. And about me, and ... everything,' he finished rather lamely. Then he took a deep breath. 'And, most importantly, about Henry Creswell.'

Chapter 27

The rain had stopped again, and the clouds were blowing quickly across the thin sliver of moon in a brisk breeze, welcomed by us both as we made our awkward, shuffling way across the grass. Twice we had to stop, the first time to let Jack catch his breath, the second time to let me catch mine. My stature had never been sturdy, and although I had strong arms and was used to tiring work, Jack was a tall man, strongly built, and in enough pain to make leaning on me a necessity.

His hand, gripping my right shoulder, clenched in apology every time he felt me tighten my grip on him, and I kept up a steady stream of inane, though quiet, chatter as we went, to try and distract him. Once he leaned closer and kissed my temple again, with a firm pressure of his lips that tried to convey his gratitude, and this time I was far from annoyed. I reminded him how he had become injured in the first place, and that if he hadn't done what he did the story might have had a very different ending.

'God, don't say that, Lizzy, please, I couldn't bear it . . .' He broke off and I realised he was struggling for composure. For the first time I fully grasped the fact that we stood equal in our feelings for one another, and in our mutual dread of harm befalling the other. It was at once thrilling and terrifying, and the surge of complicated emotions that swept through me then almost robbed me of the strength I needed to keep him upright.

Eventually we reached the car at the end of the drive. Jack rested against it while I opened the door, and together we got him settled in behind the wheel.

He looked up at me, just an outline in the faint light. 'You're going to have to start her up,' he said apologetically.

I nodded, although I had absolutely no idea how to do that. It had always looked simple enough, but it seemed there was a bit more to it than I'd thought. 'Right,' I said when he'd finished explaining, 'let's get on with it then.'

'Don't grab the starter tight,' Jack warned, 'just rest your hand under it. That way if it kicks back it'll still hurt, but you won't break your thumb.'

'Oh, good, that's all right then,' I muttered as I made my way around to the front of the car.

I located the choke wire by feel, and pulled it, then put the palm of my hand beneath the cold, wet crank handle and took a deep breath. I could do this . . . I gave the crank a slow turn as Jack had instructed, then pulled it rapidly, feeling a great thrill as the engine coughed into life.

'Well done, love,' he said as I climbed into the car and closed the door, immediately feeling safer, as if one flimsy half-door between myself and the world could keep all the horrors out. Reluctant to drive up to the house and use the circle to turn, Jack followed Wingfield's example and drove across the grass; I felt the thin tyres slide in the newly made mud and clutched at the wooden dashboard, only relaxing when we rejoined solid ground.

As we turned on to the main Breckenhall road Jack reached across and brushed a wet curl away from my cheek. 'You're incredible,' he said, returning his good hand to the wheel. I blushed, glad he couldn't see me in the dark, but warmth coiled through me at his touch and his words.

'You know, this car might have been named after you,' he went on. 'She's called the Tin Lizzie. Several steps down from the Silver Ghost I had before, but she's exactly what I need now.'

I couldn't help myself. 'So I'm the Tin Lizzie, and Constance Wingfield was the socially elevated Silver Ghost?'

There was a silence, broken only by my namesake's hard-working engine as she carried us through the night towards London. I cursed myself for spoiling the moment.

'Quite possibly, yes,' Jack said at last. 'The Silver Ghost was beautiful, smooth . . . and utterly boring.'

I felt a smile on my lips despite a niggling sense of guilt at making fun of my future employer. 'And the Tin Lizzie? Small, rattly and sometimes kicks back?'

'The Tin Lizzie is also beautiful, extremely so,' Jack said, laughing through his words, 'but more importantly, she's coura-geous, strong, steady, and has saved my life in more ways than one.' I felt him looking at me, and turned to see him still smil-ing. 'Unfortunately she rarely does as she's told, and stops whenever and wherever the mood takes her.'

357

'Lucky for you the mood took her tonight,' I said pointedly, 'or you might still be back at Oaklands trying to explain a lot of things to your hostess.'

'Lucky for me,' he agreed. Then he renewed his grip on the steering wheel and straightened his shoulders, and I knew he was finally going to tell me everything. I waited, saying nothing, suddenly unsure whether I wanted to hear it.

Eventually he cleared his throat. 'It's true, I killed Henry Creswell in 1902. I had no choice.'

'I know you didn't.'

He sighed. 'No, you don't. How could you?'

'Because I trust you,' I said, 'surely you know that by now? Whatever happened, I believe you would have done what *you* saw as right at the time.'

I jumped as his hand struck the steering wheel. 'It *was* right,' he said harshly. 'Part of me is still glad I did it, and I would do it again if I had to. Without hesitation.'

A little trickle of ice water pooled in my heart at his words. I had been ready to hear that they had perhaps been involved in some kind of accident, or even another fight where emotions had taken over. But this sounded more like a cool-headed, deliberate act, and one for which he did not suffer the kind of remorse I'd assumed.

But I was beginning to understand a little about the way women could become embroiled in destructive relationships. In Holloway a timid-looking girl named Susan had told us how she'd come to be arrested along with her lover when he'd beaten a doctor to death. The doctor in question had objected to the man being outrageously drunk and refused him treatment, paying the heaviest price imaginable.

Susan had been a bright young thing with a shining future ahead of her as a talented stage actress, but instead she'd become hopelessly attached to a man who had dragged her down and seen her thrown into jail as an accomplice to murder. Still she wouldn't hear a word said against him, swearing love and fierce devotion right up until the moment she took her own life.

Was I like Susan now? The man I loved had committed murder, and had also abandoned me when I needed him ... I glanced sideways at him, his profile tight with tension as he searched for the best place to start the story.

'We were serving together in South Africa, at a place called Tweebosch,' he said. 'Henry was a brilliant man, a good soldier, and my closest friend.'

His voice shook and I wanted to reach out to him then but I kept my distance, and my silence, and he continued, his voice sounding stronger as his tale took him further into the past. 'We were part of the British forces on the Little Harts River when the Lord Methuen was taken.'

Jack negotiated a tight turn in the road before continuing. 'Someone had passed information to the Boer Commander De la Rey, who'd led the attack. We had no clue who could have done it, only that there was obviously a traitor in our company.'

I suddenly realised where this story was going, and held my breath as he went on, 'A few weeks later, in April, we were operating under a man called Ian Hamilton. It's a long story, and the details don't matter, but we ended up dug in at a place called Rooiwal. The Boers had scouted the area earlier and believed it wasn't well defended. Which it hadn't been, at the time.'

'Your spy tried to get word out to the Boers to warn them,' I said quietly, 'and by then you knew who he was.'

Jack nodded. 'Henry was good, but he and I were close and I noticed things other people had no opportunity to see.' He was silent while the car ate up the distance, speeding us towards the mysterious doctor. Jack's face was a pale, indistinct shape in the almost total darkness, and I knew his pallor wasn't only due to the ache in his side; he was reaching the most painful part of his story.

'I had no choice but to go to Hamilton,' he said eventually, his voice quieter than before, 'and he issued the order.' I felt a chill at his calm words even though I had been expecting them; this was Evie's *father* . . .

I heard the breath catch in Jack's throat. 'Henry left the camp in the early morning, while it was still dark. I followed him, and even then, right up until the last minute, I wanted to be wrong so badly that I held off. In the end, though . . .' He shrugged. 'In the end he went exactly where I knew he was going. Kommandant Potgieter was waiting, it was obvious this was a prearranged meeting. Henry must have sent a runner as soon as we arrived. I don't like to think what happened to that runner once his message was delivered.'

I felt sick. 'But it was so dangerous to follow him alone.'

'More dangerous to involve anyone else. One person can stay hidden reasonably well. And I was well known for my abilities with a long range rifle in those days.'

'Oh, no . . .'

'I left it 'til the last second, just to be sure, but I shot him, Lizzy. Had to do it, before he could open his mouth and tell Potgieter where our strengths lay. If I hadn't, hundreds of our men would have died.'

'Why didn't you shoot the Kommandant instead?'

'I wanted to, and came frighteningly close to doing it. But it would have been pointless. Potgieter would have ensured he was covered by marksmen as good, if not better, than myself. If I'd chosen to shoot him instead of Henry, I wouldn't have taken another breath, and Henry would still have passed on the information.'

There was silence between us as he drove, the sounds of the engine and the rain drowned out by imagined gunshots and cries.

'Potgieter didn't wait around to find out what had happened, he ran,' Jack said after a while. 'I couldn't even go to Henry. I knew he was dead, it was a clean shot, but I had to leave him lying there.' He let out a shaky breath and I realised this might have been the first time he had spoken of it aloud, except to report to his commanding officer that the mission had been accomplished.

'Stop the car,' I said.

He looked startled. 'What? I would never do any—'

'I know. I'm not scared. Just . . . stop the car.'

He did so, and I leaned towards him and slipped my hands around the back of his neck, bringing his head to my shoulder. He rested there willingly and I felt the tension drain out of him, his hands relaxing until they slipped off the wheel, and his relieved sigh against my neck spreading a pool of warmth against my skin.

The car rocked in the wind, and the rain lashed against it as we sat quiet and contemplative, both of us lost in a past we could not change, heading for a future we could not imagine.

Chapter 28

We needed to start moving again. Jack was clearly in a great deal of discomfort; the way his hand constantly stole to his side told me the effectiveness of the tight bandaging was wearing off.

'We have to get you to that doctor,' I said.

'In a minute,' he agreed, 'but I'd rather just finish this now I've started.'

I learned how he'd returned to England to impart the news of Lord Henry's death. He had insisted there was no gain to be had by telling the Creswells the ugly truth, and so the army assisted with the cover-up. A story of heroic sacrifice was concocted, leaving Lily distraught but proud, and the children with an image of their father they could keep unsullied.

'It seemed the right thing to do,' Jack said. 'He wasn't an experienced spy, had only just been turned.'

'That doesn't excuse treason!' I said, appalled.

'No, it doesn't. But there was no watertight proof to support our strong suspicions and it would have destroyed an entire family if we'd spoken out. Besides, it seemed prudent to let whoever he was working for believe we hadn't suspected him at all.'

'The Boers? But they must have known, when you shot him?'

He shook his head. 'No, not them. Henry had been turned a lot closer to home than that.'

After the death of Lord Henry Creswell, when his reputation had been polished to a neat, respectable shine, Jack had been approached by the aide to a man named William Melville, director of a new organisation known as MO3, an intelligence section in the War Office.

'He offered me the chance to work in counter-espionage. And the more I thought about the damage Henry might have done, and the fact that whoever had been pulling his strings was still out there, the more I knew I wanted to do it.'

And so he had accepted the offer, casting aside any thoughts of settling down at the end of the war and creating a conventional life for himself. His work had taken him overseas for months at a time, making maintaining a home a pointless luxury, hence the hotel room paid for by the department now known as the Directorate of Military Intelligence, or MI6. Of all the jobs I'd considered that might have carried Jack to warmer climes, none of them had been half so exciting, nor so tragic, as the truth.

'Does Evie know?' I said suddenly.

'That I'm a spy?'

But I could tell he knew what I meant. 'That you killed her father,' I said softly. 'She doesn't, does she?'

'No,' he said. He tapped his hand hard against the steering wheel and another heavy sigh escaped him. 'Are you going to tell her?'

I thought of Evie's utter devotion to Jack and how it would crumble if she knew what he'd done, and felt my heart splinter. 'She's one of my closest friends,' I said. 'I love and respect her and would never want to lie to her.' I put my hand on his arm. 'But I would never want to hurt her either, and this would kill her.'

He nodded, and I wondered how he'd managed to maintain the close relationship the two of them had with this dark secret eating away at him. No wonder he had sometimes seemed distant enough to feed those rumours of a guilty secret, although who had started them remained a mystery.

'This answers so many questions,' I said, to break the tension and dispel the shadow that hung over us.

'What questions?'

'Why no one knew anything about you, why you were skulking around Lord Henry's study when—'

'When you were setting fire to the Creswells' finest linen?' he said with a tiny smile.

'Thank you! I was going to say the day Evie played that trick on Ruth. And the other time,' I reminded him, with a rush of pleasure at the memory of our first kiss. 'And it would explain why you would disappear for weeks at a time.'

'You noticed my disappearances?' He sounded pleased.

'Well, mostly you were just someone who came to dinner simply to annoy Mrs Cavendish,' I teased. Then I leaned towards him, lowering my voice, suddenly shy at speaking my heart. 'But when you went away it was like someone suddenly blowing out a candle I never even realised had been lit.'

He gave me a slow, beautiful smile and brushed his thumb across my lower lip, following it with his own lips in a gentle kiss that left tingling warmth on mine. Then he sat back and I sensed the recommencing of the story for which I'd waited what felt like half a lifetime.

'You remember I said Henry had been turned at the start of the Africa campaign?'

'Yes, I didn't know what you meant, though.'

'Usually an older, more experienced agent will spot some potential, or more often a weakness, that can be used to their advantage. Henry was a good man but he had that weakness. He also had wealth, and that made him an even more attractive proposition, so this particular agent had been working on him for some time. Feeding him the kind of lies that would eventually eat away at what he believed; convincing him we're a corrupt nation and mustn't be allowed to win the campaign against the Boers; confusing his national pride until he believed he'd been misled by government and felt the need to redress the wrong he'd done under their orders and guidance.'

'Poor Henry,' I said, surprising myself.

'Exactly. Well, it wasn't until after the war that intelligence finally surfaced and we were able to pinpoint the likely suspect. Largely because by then he'd transferred his allegiance to the German Empire.'

'And you were sent after him,' I guessed.

Jack nodded. 'What made it easier was that the man in question was connected to Henry through family ties as well as through the military. It was Samuel Wingfield.'

I shouldn't have been surprised; the man was cold, cruel and prepared to take any risk to get what he wanted, or at least to ensure his family would take the risks for him. I understood now what he'd meant about his connections in Europe.

'Henry's brother Charles was a high-ranking Naval officer at that time,' Jack went on. 'Part of Wingfield's success has always stemmed from his knack of working on the vulnerability of others. Charles had just been passed over for a command and Wingfield knew this. All it took was a few generous measures of the best whisky in the house, and a sympathetic ear, and he had names, numbers and ship's capacity just ready to pour into the ear of a man named Steinhauer.'

'But you got there first?'

Jack nodded. 'I'd been told he was to make contact on New Year's Eve, with the equipment he had set up for Henry years ago, in the attic at Oaklands.'

'Didn't he have his own?'

'He has a wireless at Shrewford, I've heard him use it. I suppose it just made sense to use the cover of the party rather than travelling back there and having to answer awkward questions. Anyway, I had to intercept the information without Wingfield knowing, but . . .' he gave me a crooked smile '. . . things didn't exactly work out the way I'd hoped.'

'Because of me.'

'You didn't ask me to stop and help you,' he pointed out. 'But yes, it was the disturbance on the lawn that put things out of kilter. I had to make a choice between stealth or speed. I could still stop the information getting through but destroy my cover in front of Samuel, or I could remain hidden and risk the intelligence falling into the hands of someone who'd use it against us if it came to war. Judging by the way things have turned out, I think it's fair to say I made the right choice.'

Jack told me all that had happened that night; how he'd made sure enough people saw him leave, then had parked the car at Breckenhall station where he habitually left it when he'd claimed to be returning to Liverpool.

I understood now that Liverpool had never, or rarely, been his destination at all – his home was in London, his contacts there too, but it suited him that everyone believed him to have been visiting family or attending to some supposed business in his home town. The timetable he had given me on the day we met was added window-dressing; I remembered how much-folded and creased it was, with a flicker of admiration for the detail.

He had not caught the train, of course, to Liverpool or to London, but several people who knew him would have been at the station after the party, and would have seen and recognised the distinctive red and black Silver Ghost.

Jack had cut across the fields back to Oaklands and made his way up through the garden, keeping to the hedges and away from the wide path that led to the front door. It was then that he'd seen the shadowy shape of David Wingfield, crushing the life from me on the wet grass – his hand crept out to hold mine as he told the story – and had made his choice and interceded.

The intention had been to secrete himself in the attic before Samuel Wingfield arrived, and apprehend him as he came through the door. But, arriving later than planned and finding Wingfield already in the process of setting up the radio transmitter, he had immediately realised the luxury of maintaining his cover was out of the question.

Wingfield had turned at the sound of Jack's entrance, his open code book falling from his hands. Jack had launched himself at him, and both men had tumbled to the floor as each fought for control; they were equal in size and Wingfield was in excellent physical condition, but Jack had youth and fury on his side. It was a short battle; after only a couple of minutes Wingfield lay unconscious. Jack had picked up the code book, studied the transmitter for a moment, and five minutes later the coded message was sent.

'I'm sure they found the numbers I sent them cause for concern,' he said with a wry smile. 'Either way, the intention was that they could never trust Wingfield again.'

'And what happened when he woke up? I mean, he knew about you by now.'

'Yes, he knew.' Jack said. 'But what could he do? To reveal my identity as an agent would mean revealing his own. We were equal on that score. He lost some credibility that night but . . .' Jack paused, just for a second, and a shadow crossed his face '. . . he clawed it back the next. He's still active in Europe, and has some influential connections there which I've been . . .' He shifted slightly in his seat and, for the first time since climbing behind the wheel, gave an involuntary gasp.

'We'll talk more later,' I said, 'but for now we *have* to get to that doctor.'

To my relief, he agreed. I was silent as he drove, turning over in my mind all he'd said, picturing it. He must have returned to me directly after the confrontation with Wingfield, I realised. So while I'd been sitting in the outhouse feeling mightily sorry for myself and half-convinced he was a murderer coming back to finish me off, Jack had been in the attic, fighting a traitor and sending misleading, coded messages to Europe. I stole a glance at his strong profile, felt the phantom touch of his lips, and surreptitiously pinched the skin on the back of my hand. It hurt, and I looked out at the night and smiled.

Chapter 29

The journey seemed to take forever; too often Jack felt the need to pull to a stop and let waves of dizziness pass. As we drew close to London we halted outside an inn, and he gave me a piece of paper on which he'd scribbled a number.

'You'll have to do this, I'll attract the wrong kind of attention,' he said. 'Call the operator and ask for this number. Don't, whatever you do, leave the paper beside the phone. Don't even put it down. When the man answers, no matter what he says, you just say *Goshawk*. He will then give you an address. Memorise it but don't repeat it back to him. That's important. Just hang up.'

Trembling with a mixture of excitement and terror of making a mistake, I did as he'd instructed, locating the pay phone in the back hallway of the inn, and was surprised when the man answering introduced himself as a florist. I told him Jack's code-word, grateful it was so short, and memorised the house number and street name he gave me in return.

The property turned out to be a squat, two-storey house with a set of wide, semi-circular steps leading to a plain-looking front door. We sat outside for a moment while Jack assured himself we were not being observed.

'Why are you called Goshawk?' I asked, to fill the silence.

'It's to do with Africa, I think. I didn't choose it myself, I'd have chosen something far more dashing and exciting.' He turned to me, his face worryingly pale in the darkness despite the humour in his voice. 'I'm sorry you can't come in, love. It's for your safety as much as his.'

I shook my head, dismissing the obvious. 'I'm coming round to help you out of the car, though,' I said. 'Are you ready?'

'I think so,' he muttered, and started taking slow, steady breaths as I pushed open my door and stepped out into the night.

Watching Jack making his way alone up the wide steps to the front door was one of the hardest things I'd ever had to do. Every part of me ached to be at his side, helping him. He leaned heavily on the railing with his right elbow – he couldn't bear any pressure on his hand or wrist – and his left hand was pressed against his right side, his head low as he concentrated on putting one foot in front of the other. Eventually he reached the top and, to my relief, turned and gave me a circled thumb and finger signal to show all was as well as it could be under the circumstances.

I have no idea how long I waited there after he was admit-ted, but, as uncomfortable as I was, I realised I'd been dozing. A half-dream had been rattling around in my head; something to do with Frank Markham and his baby daughter.

Odd, how we misjudge people, I thought as I struggled to sit upright. Markham had seemed such a simple character to me all this time, mocking, ambitious and even slightly cruel, yet he was the one who'd been wronged, first by his family, then by the mother of his child.

I looked at the closed front door of the terraced house into which Jack had gone. He'd been misjudged too, and I wondered if Mary had realised it yet. She must have known he had held off shooting at Wingfield because of her, and that he had saved me from potentially fatal injuries by incurring some on his own account. She didn't even know he'd survived, so surely she couldn't still believe him to be a coward.

At the thought of her kind, beloved face I felt a despair so fierce it stopped my breath for a moment. Jack was right; they would be unlikely to hurt her straight away, but she must be absolutely terrified and I would have given anything to have spared her that. She might be older than me, and she might be the one who always knew things about people and places, but still she was just a girl who'd been snatched away into the night with no idea when, or if, she would ever see her home and friends again.

My train of thought, of regret and guilt, was cut off as the doctor's door opened, and despite the blackout I could immediately see the Jack who negotiated the steps this time was a different man. Or, more accurately, back to his old self. He walked upright, his head high, only a bandage around his right wrist indicating any obvious injury. His bloodied shirt had been exchanged for a new one, likewise his torn waistcoat, and the cut across his brow now sported a small clean dressing.

I had been ready to leap out and help when he emerged

from his mysterious doctor's premises, but he clearly had no need of it. He moved a little stiffly as he bent his tall frame to get into the car, but I could see the colour had returned to his face and his eyes were no longer hooded and squinting with pain.

'Is he a magician?' I asked, laughing with relief.

'Sort of,' Jack agreed. He leaned across and kissed me, thoroughly and with enthusiasm, and I kissed him back, matching and then exceeding both; my hands captured his jaw and this time it was my lips that led, hungry for the taste of him, and his that responded. When we parted, his smile was surprised and gratified, and I had to resist the urge to kiss him again, to prove the depth of my relief.

'Now,' he said, sitting back and wincing only slightly, 'we're going to need a good night's sleep for what's in store for us. Are we agreed?'

'We are,' I said, and at the mere thought of lying down and closing my eyes it suddenly seemed all I could do to keep them open.

'Right then, we'll stay in London for the rest of the night. Then we'll get a good breakfast and head back up to Shrewford Hall.'

'What if Clarissa's already left?'

'She probably meant to, but her delightful father-in-law would have scuppered that by returning earlier than she expected last night. The chances are she'll only have got as far as packing, and I should think Wingfield will have her under close scrutiny downstairs this evening.'

'Which means we'll have to get to her things, rather than her.' I felt immeasurably happier about that; the memory of

373

her tall, spare frame and commanding voice gave me shivers, even now.

'That's the idea,' he said. 'Mary's our first priority, and we'll work out the details when we're less tired, but I think I can distract Samuel and Clarissa while you two look for the necklace. Now,' he gave me another apologetic look, 'do you feel up to cranking your namesake into life again?'

Walking through the lobby of Jack's hotel felt strange; it was well into the small hours of the morning yet the lights were still on and a receptionist sat attentively behind the polished counter. His eyebrows went up a fraction as we passed, but professionalism kept him from doing more than nodding to each of us in turn.

When Jack had carried me through here not so long ago, at least one other set of eyes had assessed us and made the same calculations based on what they saw. It made me cold to think of Wingfield watching us from a distance for all that time, and I knew now why Jack was constantly looking around him, although he had clearly missed the observer at the prison. It explained his shady behaviour in Breckenhall that day too.

Back in his room there was a new awkwardness between us. He closed the door, and the click of the latch sounded loud enough to wake everyone in the hotel. We stood in exhausted silence for a moment, not looking at one another.

Then Jack came to, with a little shake of his head. 'I'll leave you to it then.'

'Where are you going?' I was surprised by my sudden, panicky reaction to his leaving me.

'I'll sleep downstairs in the lounge, like I did last time,' he said. 'You need the comfort of the bed, and I'm used to it. I'll take a blanket down.'

'Jack, please ...' I could feel my skin burning, but his eyes suddenly fixed on mine and their clear, steady gaze helped calm me, so that my voice shook less. 'Stay here, with me. I don't mean ...' I gestured helplessly, but he knew what I meant. 'Just lie down next to me?'

He came over and took my hands and I looked up at him, struggling with the frighteningly strong emotions his touch ignited.

'Are you sure?'

I nodded. 'Please,' I whispered again, and he drew me to him, resting his hands only lightly on my back so I could pull away if I wanted to. I didn't.

After a while he turned the light out and I slipped out of my coat and dress in the darkness. Clad only in my petticoat I lay down on the bed and he settled, fully clothed, next to me and took my hand. In the silence, with only the distant sound of an occasional car outside, we lay wide awake – I could tell he was as tense as I was. His breathing was not the slow, steady sound of one drifting towards sleep.

It seemed easier to talk in the dark, and I had to know now, before I wondered any more about it. 'Where were you, all that time?'

There was a long pause. Maybe I'd been mistaken about his wakefulness, I thought, but then he spoke, and for the first time I heard bitterness in his voice. 'All that time, almost all of it anyway, I was every bit as much a prisoner as you were.'

I listened with steadily increasing dismay as he told me

what had happened immediately after we'd left the outhouse: a genuine journey to London this time, to report to Melville's aides the following morning. Then the plan had been to spend some time in Europe, in particular Serbia, where the Black Hand partisan academy had recently recruited a young Bosnian Serb by the name of Gavrilo Princip.

I remembered the name with a chill. 'He's the one who shot the Archduke and his wife.'

'Yes, that's him. A sickly kid by all accounts, although a deadly shot with an automatic pistol as we later discovered. But I didn't manage to get that far.'

I lifted my head; Jack's voice had taken on a new, tighter note and I strained through the dark to see his face but couldn't. 'What happened?'

'Wingfield had managed to get word to someone in MI6, I never found out who, and when I arrived for the debrief I was knocked unconscious. That was the last I knew of it until I woke up in a crate, in the hold of a steam packet to Hamburg.'

I was shocked. My hand tightened convulsively on his. 'How long were you a prisoner?'

'Until a few months ago. April. They let me write some bland letters now and again, just so people would know I was alive and wouldn't raise the alarm. Despite that I was able to get word past the censors to Melville and he sent out his best people, on two separate occasions, but they were both killed.'

'So they just abandoned you?' I was growing more horrified with every word he spoke.

'Not exactly. Melville had known about Steinhauer's operation for a year but they deliberately left it in place. That way they were able to come down on them in one fell swoop at the outset of the war. As I understand it he'd thought I'd be released at that point, but Wingfield got wind of it and made sure I wasn't there at the collapse of the network. Melville assumed I'd been killed, my file was archived, and that was it until April this year.'

'But why weren't you . . .' My mouth dried at the words, but I forced them out. 'Why weren't you killed? Wouldn't it have been easier for Wingfield to make sure you were?'

'I suspect, if he'd had his way, I would have been. But Steinhauer knew I'd be a good bargaining tool. Your own situation was always infinitely more dangerous than mine.'

I doubted it, but before I could think what to say I sensed him turning with difficulty to face me, and as I felt the warmth of his breath stir my hair I moved closer. He curled one arm around my shoulder and I draped mine across his hip to ensure I didn't accidentally brush his ribs, and we were both quiet for a long time.

Just as I was slipping into the beckoning peace of sleep, Jack spoke again, his quiet voice floating out of the darkness to fill me with warmth. 'I have loved you a long time, Lizzy Parker. I suspected it when we first talked properly, in Henry's study, and by the time we met in the garden I was sure of it.'

'It's the same for me,' I said softly. 'Although our first meeting was the starting point, I think.'

'Even though I'm so much older than you?' he said, and I heard the nervousness in his voice.

'I don't even think of that,' I said truthfully, and his arm tightened around me, seemingly in relief. Knowing myself and how much I loved him, that he should ever have been in any doubt was a strange thought to me, but clearly he had been.

'It was killing me, being so near you and not being able to tell you how deeply you'd affected me,' he said. 'I made more and more excuses to stay at Oaklands, but every time I wished I hadn't. It was too painful for words.'

'Well, I'm glad you did,' I said with a little laugh. 'I wouldn't have missed those political spats for anything.'

He laughed too, I felt his body shake, but then he gasped and shifted slightly, and we fell quiet again. At last he let out a deep, contented sigh and cupped the back of my head, seeking my lips with his in the darkness. There was no demanding hunger in that kiss, but the tenderness brought tears to my eyes and when our mouths released each other I moved closer, resting my head in the hollow of his shoulder. The gentle rise and fall of his chest was like life being breathed into my body, and as we both surrendered to our separate dreams I felt my heart swell with gratitude for this precious time, this chance to be with him, and to forgive him at last.

When I awoke it was to more rain. I found I had an appetite like a horse. Jack was in the bathroom; I could hear the sounds of water running and splashing, and then the gurgle of it running away down the drain as the door opened. I assessed him carefully through half-closed eyes as he came back in with just a towel around his hips: I didn't want him to know I was awake just yet, and to put on any act of bravery for my benefit.

The mysterious doctor had done a thorough job of binding and bandaging, and Jack sported a wide, clean tape around his lower ribs and a fresh dressing immediately below it. He walked a little stiffly, but without that awful, hunched posture of yesterday. Even bending to pick out clean trousers from his cupboard produced nothing more than a wince and a small hiss of discomfort.

As the cupboard door closed he turned quickly, realising he might have woken me. I blinked, feigning sleepy surprise. 'Oh, what time is it?'

'Seven,' he said. 'Sorry, I was trying to let you sleep a little longer. How are you feeling?'

'Almost as well as you, by the looks of it,' I said, smiling. He came over to the bed, and I found my eyes drawn to the smoothly muscled contours of his chest and stomach as he sat down next to me and took my hand. A little flustered, I concentrated instead on his rapid recovery. 'That doctor worked miracles,' I said. 'Is he a ...' I hesitated, not liking the word '... a spy too? Or a friend?'

'Not a friend, I've never met him before last night. But we're given that number knowing we'll see someone good who'll behave with absolute discretion.'

He took my chin in his other hand and looked squarely into my eyes. 'It's a dangerous business I'm in, Lizzy,' he said quietly. 'That man has to be on call to deal with emergencies at a moment's notice. The phone call you made only told him he needed to go to that place, his surgery, to treat an injured agent. Might have been anything wrong, from a broken toe to a gunshot wound.'

I understood now why he was staring at me so hard. 'It's all right,' I whispered, meeting his eyes without flinching. 'I know, and I'll try not to worry.'

'This life, it's unpredictable. Takes me away for long stretches of time. Constance couldn't bear it.'

'She didn't know why you went away, though, did she?'

'No, but—'

'Well then, I do.' I hesitated, then decided to say it. 'Henry would forgive you, you know.'

Jack's eyes darkened, the already deep blue seeming almost black for a moment. 'But what about Evie?' he said bleakly.

I had no answer for that; some things were his alone to put right.

After a light breakfast we were ready to go again. Suddenly every passing minute mattered and I could hardly believe I'd slept at all, not with two friends whose lives depended on what happened in the next few hours.

There had been too many people at breakfast in the hotel for us to talk through any kind of plan, so before we began the drive to Shrewford Hall Jack took me to an all-but-deserted park where we sat in a shelter watching the rain. He put his coat around my shoulders and I felt the last of his body heat seeping through my clothes as I drew it closer around me, relishing the warmth. That it was his, particularly.

'The gardens at Shrewford aren't like Oaklands,' he cautioned. 'There are no trees, no bushes for cover, and no summer house as a midway point. There's a very high wall that goes all the way around, no gate at the back, and no one can approach the house without being in plain sight of someone casually glancing out of a window. Which suits Samuel perfectly, of course.'

'So how are we going to get in?'

'Well, that high wall is a bit unusual,' he said. 'It actually joins on to the house in one place, through a short connecting piece.' He drew an instantly vanishing impression of it on the cloth of his trousers, but I saw what he meant: it was like a staggered '7' with the shorter line coming to the side of the house.

'Wingfield had that wall modified years ago, and the extra part added, but as well as that linking piece you'll see the wall has another characteristic: it's uncommonly wide, for a garden wall.'

Jack looked at me and smiled. 'You're going to have an easier time of it than he does, I'm sure.'

'Easier time of what?'

'The wall is our way into the house without being seen,' he explained. 'It's hollow.'

I gaped. 'Why on earth would someone build a hollow wall?'

'With Wingfield's activities, what better way to come and go, without the likes of me watching his every move?'

'In that case, you're right,' I conceded, looking down at my skinny frame. 'If it's built for someone Samuel Wingfield's size, I could probably do cartwheels down it.'

'That I should love to see,' Jack grinned. He looked much better now, with the colour back in his face, only the faint shadows beneath his eyes betraying a night of discomfort and too little sleep.

'How will we know where to find Mary?' I asked. If Shrewford was anything like Oaklands it might be impossible to locate her without being seen.

'From what I've learned over the years, Wingfield has a liking for attic spaces,' Jack said. 'The one at Shrewford is large, like the one at Oaklands, and houses three separate rooms. Only one of these has a lock.'

'You know an awful lot about this house.'

381

'I've been watching him a long time,' he said simply. 'Besides, I was engaged to a Wingfield once and spent a good deal of time there.' He frowned, realising that might have sounded insensitive, but it didn't matter to me at all and I waved away the apology I could see him contemplating.

'The wall will bring us right up into the house, inside the coal cellar,' he went on, with a quick, grateful squeeze of my hand. 'We'll have to be utterly silent; most of the servants have been let go, but there is still a small staff and we'll come out very close to the kitchens. Besides, fewer people means less background noise and we're probably more likely to be noticed.'

I nodded, trying to picture it all as he explained it. 'I assume we take the servants' staircase up to the attic?'

'Exactly right. As we come out of the cellar we'll be in the back corridor. To the left lie the kitchens, and on the right is the staircase. We go to the very top, and the locked door is the last one in the row of three. I'm sure that's where they'll be keeping Mary.'

'What if she's being guarded?'

He shrugged, but his eyes cut away from mine and I felt a tiny coil of chilly unease; he seemed like a different person for a moment. 'That's why I'm going with you, instead of heading straight for Clarissa.'

I chose not to pursue his plans for dealing with anyone who might pose an obstacle. 'How will we open the door?'

At this, Jack produced from his pocket an odd-looking key; very plain with only a small intricately shaped tip. 'This is known as a skeleton key, it'll open any basic lock. Since Wingfield believes he has little need of anything more

complex, it should work as easily on his door as it does on . . .'
He hesitated, but I finished it for him.

'On a linen room, or Henry's study door?'

He shrugged. 'Yes. You have to understand, Lizzy, it was my—'

'I know, you don't have to explain,' I said. 'There are more important things to worry about now, in any case.'

Our eyes met in shared understanding, and he nodded. 'Here, you take this, I'll need to keep my hands free.'

I took the key, slipping it into my own pocket and feeling the cool weight of it like a magical talisman. If it was the saving of Mary that would be magic enough for me.

'Right, when you and Mary come out of the attic you'll have to try and find the Star, then get back down to the coal cellar yourselves, into the wall and out of that house quickly and as quietly as you can. I'll leave the car a short distance from the house. Just get in and wait for me if I'm not there already.'

'What if we can't find the diamond?'

'Then we'll have to take more direct action to get Will back. I don't care what happens to that bloody stone! Evie was right, it's a curse, always has been. If you can't find it I'm going to have to turn the tables on Wingfield while I have the chance.'

I took a long, deep breath, trying not to sound too excited. 'It seems as if it might work,' I said.

Jack looked at me, his face grim. 'I hope so, for Will's sake.'

Chapter 30

When we eventually drove slowly past the entrance to Shrewford Hall on the outskirts of Nantwich, I compared the Wingfields' home with that of the Creswells. The two buildings weren't much different in size; the grounds at Oaklands were more extensive certainly, but Shrewford's gardens were austerely impressive, with a wide sweep of driveway leading to the imposing front door.

Despite this it all seemed a little shabbier than I had expected, and I could well imagine the family who lived here envying the affluence of the Creswells, and believing that possession of the Kalteng Star would make them more alike in status. But according to Mary the stone had been in the Wingfield family for around forty years; they'd had their chance and this was the result – something about the starkness of the building suggested it matched the family ethos very accurately, and no amount of money would change that.

Jack drove a few hundred yards beyond the entrance, down

the hill to a wooded copse. He parked in amongst the trees, and as the engine died into silence the full enormity of what we were about to do hit me. I started to tremble. Jack's warm hand on mine stilled the tremors somewhat, but there was still a sick churning in my stomach and I could feel my limbs tensing.

'Sweetheart, you don't have to do this. I can try and get to Mary by myself without alerting Wingfield, and still keep the advantage of surprise.'

'But it's less likely,' I reminded him. 'You have to distract them, or all he has to do is make a single telephone call and Will's in front of a firing squad.'

He paused – we both knew there was no option but to go in together – but the depth of my fear worried him. Seeing this I tried to push it aside, and drew the necessary strength from his touch, from the calm in his eyes, and from the memory of Mary's terrified face at the window of Wingfield's car.

'Come on then,' I said, with a confidence I hoped I would soon begin to feel.

The entrance was very well concealed, as it would need to be. We had to walk beyond an angle in the wall separating Shrewford from the rest of the world, and then double back so we were facing the road again. Only then, ankle deep in marshy grasses that brushed my knees, did I see the double thickness and the tiny, dark entrance.

Immediately fear came rushing back and I felt my hands curl into tight, painful fists. I don't know what I had expected; some kind of hidden doorway maybe, some sign that this was a well-travelled secret passage, but this . . .

I felt Jack's hand, firm against my back, and his breath tickled my ear as he leaned in close. 'I have a flashlight,' he said quietly. 'I'll go first, but I won't be able to hold your hand, there's no room.'

'A flashlight?'

'Very useful for this kind of skulking around,' he said, and without looking at him I knew his face would be lit by a smile. 'Unfortunately it lives up to its name: the bulb needs to be rested now and again so I can only use it in short bursts.'

'Anything at all will be welcome,' I said with a shudder, eyeing the cobwebby entrance.

'Come on then,' he said as he eased past me. 'And no cartwheels.'

I was surprised into a laugh, and with fresh courage I gripped the back of his coat, taking comfort from that small contact. But he had to turn sideways to squeeze into the entrance, and duck his head to avoid cracking it on the stone above, and I had to let go. I was less constrained, but as my own body blocked out the last of the meagre daylight behind us, and I smelled the mustiness of wet moss, I had to fight the urge to turn back; the wet, grey afternoon beyond suddenly held all the appeal of a warm summer evening by the sea.

Jack's flashlight illuminated a tiny portion of the way ahead for just a moment, then he shut it off. It was enough to show me that our surroundings would not improve in the next few minutes, and then as we were plunged into blackness I held tight to his coat again, and to the image of him, and strained my ears for the sound of his breathing.

The space afforded by the cunning doubling of the wall was even smaller than I'd imagined. The next time Jack turned on the flashlight I realised his shoulders brushed the sides all the way. It must be nearly impossible for a man of Samuel Wingfield's girth – I recalled his tall, stout frame with a flare of hatred – to make regular use of this without injuring himself, and I assumed it must be only on rare occasions he would have to do so. Meeting someone coming the other way would mean one of them either retreating to the opening at their end, or else knocking the other down and stepping on them to get past.

Now and again along the wall, a gap in the stones provided us with a pinprick of daylight and a breath of cleaner air, but these were few and far between. Soon I had to let go of Jack's coat again as he constantly needed to twist his way past obstacles, and it was easy to believe I was on my own but for the sound of his feet scuffing the ground now and then as the path rose unevenly underfoot. When this happened he would have to duck down further, I realised; the stone ceiling was not far above my own head so must be a constant hazard for anyone even slightly taller.

He had taken to trailing his left hand along the stones above his head, to avoid cracking his skull, but there were larger stones that would lie flat from the outside, yet protruded into the already limited space, causing Jack to grunt and curse when one of them dug into his exposed left side.

Whenever the flashlight came on during our slow progress through the passage I tried to see more of our surroundings, but all I could make out was a glimpse of the low, rocky ceiling and Jack. Walking slightly stooped over, he kept his injured wrist tight against his side to avoid knocking it, holding the flashlight in the same hand. Now and again he softly asked if

I was all right and I told him I was, answering in a whisper so he couldn't hear the tremor in my voice.

When it seemed we had been stumbling along in the darkness for hours, and I could barely recall what a proper lungful of fresh air tasted like, he stopped moving. I bumped into him and he turned the flashlight on again, now transferred to his left hand and held close to his body. This position gave me a strange view of his face, rather than our surroundings, making him seem like some ghostly, disembodied head floating in the otherwise dark tunnel; I was relieved to hear his familiar voice.

'Right, from here we keep as silent as we can, and I'll have to save the light for you to use on the way back. There's a sharp turn to the left here that will take us right up to the house.'

I felt a tingle of renewed fear now we were so close to our destination. Mingled with it, though, a healthy dose of relief that we would soon be out of this musty, damp darkness and able to move freely again.

Sure enough, ahead of us the passage ended abruptly, where the wall became just the ordinary thickness again, running the length of the Shrewford parkland. To our left lay an even smaller passage, and now Jack had to move sideways to negotiate it.

Without any source of light, as even the tiny gaps between stones we had taken for granted in the main tunnel were absent here, it was a hazardous final few yards; the ground beneath us was strewn with roots and stones; once I tripped and fell against Jack, and he drew a sharp breath as my arm connected with his injured wrist. I squeezed his upper arm in mute apology and can only assume he knew what I was trying to say.

At last his outstretched left hand met the wood of the door to the coal cellar. Jack pulled it open and I shifted from foot to foot, desperate to move forward, but before we did Jack made a slow sweep with the light to make sure no one was lurking in wait for us. The temptation to push forward was strong, but I gritted my teeth and stayed still; he knew what he was doing, after all.

When he was satisfied we were alone he stepped into the cellar, and I followed as if glued to his heels. The cellar was indeed dark, but after the complete blackness of the tunnel it didn't take long for my eyes to adjust, and I quickly made out the steps into the house.

There was a wooden hatch high up where the wall met the ceiling, that led out to the yard – the coal chute – and around its edges glowed the faint light of day. I fixed my eyes on it, wondering how long it would be until I was back out in the fresh air, and promised myself never to take freedom for granted again. Then I remembered how I'd believed the same thing when the doors had first closed on me at Holloway, and knew that of course I would take it for granted, accepting it as a fundamental right. By that very acceptance I would be embracing it.

Jack moved towards the steps, but at the foot of them turned to me. I could see the tilt of his head but not his features, and reached up to brush his cheek with my chilled fingers. He leaned his head against my hand for a brief, intimate moment, then turned to kiss my palm.

'Are you sure?'

I nodded, but realised he might not be able to see with the light behind him. 'Absolutely.'

He smiled suddenly, I could see the gleam of his teeth. 'I asked you that question last night, I believe?'

I couldn't help smiling back. 'I'll keep my clothes on this time, though, don't worry.'

His sudden, surprised laugh made us both glance automatically wards to the top of the steps, but we heard no sound and he took my hand.

'At the top we take a sharp turn to the right,' he said. 'Follow the back staircase to the very top.' He handed me the flashlight. 'I need my good hand free so you take this, but try not to use it until you absolutely have to. Then you'll have it for when you and Mary come back down here.'

I gave an involuntary shudder at the thought of going back into the passage in the wall, but at least next time I would be with Mary, and we would be making our way out to daylight and safety. Hopefully with the Kalteng Star and Will's salvation.

We started up the steps and I felt my heart give a little lurch as Jack reached into his coat and withdrew his gun. Although I understood the necessity of that grotesque thing, seeing it in a hand that had previously touched me with such tenderness made me feel sick.

I tried not to think of him using it on another human being, and focused instead on how he was prepared to risk everything, including his life, to help both Mary and Will. As the door opened my thoughts flashed briefly to my other friend, and I wondered what Evie would think if she could see me now – as exciting as her life had been, I was certain she had never crept around a stranger's house with an armed secret agent, but how she would love it if she did! She probably wouldn't be nearly as scared as I was either.

The back staircase was surprisingly well lit, from small but regularly placed windows set high in the wall. Not nearly as bright as the rest of the house would be, with its many, multi-paned windows and skylights, but at least we could see to walk without using more of the precious battery.

We passed the first floor where Samuel, Clarissa and her sons were doubtless even now sitting down to afternoon tea, and continued in silence up three more flights, past the family rooms, then the servants' quarters, finally emerging on the uppermost landing of the house. By now Jack was flagging again and I was short of breath myself, but the nearness of our goal gave us both a resurgence of energy and we exchanged relieved glances, again perfectly in tune with one another.

It was much darker here, there being only one skylight on this side of the house. Presumably there would be windows that let light into the rooms themselves, but here the dimness stretched from one end of the corridor to the other. We could still see the three doors quite clearly however, and Jack made his way without hesitation to the third one along.

I followed close behind, wondering how many hours he had spent here, watching and listening while Samuel carried out his treacherous activities. Once I had acknowledged my growing longing for him I had conjured up his image so often, but always in my mind he had been either dining with some beautiful woman, or working in a stuffy office in Whitehall. Never in my wildest imaginings had I ever pictured him crouching, muddy, sore and tired, in a hidden corner of an attic.

Outside the third door, Jack stopped and looked back at me, at the same time leaning his ear close to the wood. His hand shifted slightly on the gun, and I realised he was going to have to shoot left-handed if he had to shoot at all. I wondered how much his other injuries were paining him but beyond a quickened breath when he moved awkwardly he gave little sign of discomfort.

He raised his eyebrows, and mouthed, *Are you ready?*

I nodded, gripping the flashlight in the same manner with which he'd reinforced his grip on the gun, and felt inside my pocket for the skeleton key.

There was no sound from inside the attic room, and I began to hope for a swift end to this after all. Jack stepped back to let me insert the key into the lock. He held the gun high, supporting his left hand with his injured right, and the sight of it so close made my fingers tremble. The key slipped as I broke into a sweat.

'Easy, love,' Jack whispered, but there was new tension in his voice.

I took a deep breath, wiped my fingers and tried again. This time the plain barrel slipped into the lock and I heard the click of the tumbler inside. Immediately from within there came the sound of a pair of feet hitting the floor, as if they had been resting on a bed.

No one spoke but I imagined Mary on the other side of the door, perhaps the other side of the room, dreading who she might see come through it. I pictured her stunned relief when she saw me, and, bracing myself, I pushed open the door, but just before I stepped through Jack pulled me to one side.

He slid in front of me and through the doorway, and I instantly realised Mary was not alone; a figure moved across my field of vision, striking at Jack as he stepped into the room, but Jack was ready and ducked, then turned and swung his left hand around to smash the gun against the head of his assailant.

The figure dropped like a stone and in the blur of fast-breathing panic that had taken me over I recognised David Wingfield. His fingers were still thrust through the handle of a heavy-looking pitcher, although the hand that had wielded it was now limp, and a stain of dark blood bloomed over the top of his ear, matting his hair to his head.

I swallowed an exclamation, and turned to see Mary staring at us both with her mouth open. She sat huddled on a tiny chair in the corner, and I guessed David had commandeered the narrow bed once he had taken up guardianship of her, but she didn't appear hurt.

'Quick!' I urged. 'Come with me.'

She slid off the chair and crossed the room to where we stood, then flung her arms around me as if she had only just accepted the truth of my presence.

'Oh, Lizzy!' She held me tight, then pulled back and looked at Jack. 'I thought you might have been killed,' she said, and to my astonishment she burst into tears and put her arms around him too.

He closed his eyes briefly in pain but hugged her back, and between them there seemed to be a great deal more to say, though neither of them knew how. After a moment they released each other, and he took her hand. 'Mary, I'm just so, so sorry. For everything. Arthur—'

'It's past,' she said, sniffing and suddenly brisk. 'I'm sorry too. I made it very hard for you to acknowledge me at Oaklands. But there'll be time enough later on for us to talk. I'm glad you're not dead, that's all.'

393

'So am I,' Jack said solemnly, and was rewarded with a watery smile from Mary and a grateful one from me. Though whether I too was grateful he wasn't dead, or simply that he was still able to joke, I couldn't decide.

Jack stooped and fished in David's pockets for the key. 'Right,' he said, turning to me. 'Clarissa and Matthew's room is on the next floor down. As you come out of the servants' stairs it's directly under here; third door along. Go quickly . . . but for God's sake be careful, and don't waste too much time. If you don't find the Star in five minutes, get out.'

I swallowed hard. 'You'll be careful too, won't you?'

He raised his bandaged hand to brush a curl away from my eye with swollen but gentle fingers. 'I'm not going to risk anything, sweetheart,' he said. 'But I have to try.'

'I love you, Jack' I said, and felt tears start to my eyes at the enormity of the feeling that rushed through me then. It was only Mary's hand on my arm that held it all in check. There would be time enough for tears, for the relief of tension, when we were all out of this horrible house, but for now I couldn't give Jack the added worry that I might fall apart.

'I love you too, Just Lizzy,' he said in a voice that barely rose above a whisper. The immediate three-way connection with Evie actually made me smile, and I saw it reflected in the curve of his own lips, and in the gaze that steadied and strengthened me.

'Hurry, won't you?' I urged, and he nodded. Then the three of us left the attic room and I locked the door once more, securing David Wingfield where he could do the least damage.

I watched Jack descend the stairs quickly and silently, gun

still clutched in his left hand, and tried to fight down the awful feeling he might be walking into grave danger for the sake of a young soldier he barely knew.

'You were right,' Mary said softly, as if reading my thoughts. 'For all he was a troubled boy, he's turned into something very, very good.'

I didn't want to be reminded of his past, not when his future was in doubt, but I took Mary's hand, acknowledging her change of opinion with a brief squeeze, and led her down the stairs.

We stopped outside Clarissa Wingfield's room, and listened carefully at the door while Mary kept watch by the staircase. I saw her head cocked at an angle to detect any approaching footsteps but there was no sound, either from the stairs or from the room, and so I carefully turned the handle. My grip tightened on the flashlight, although I didn't know if I'd have the courage or strength to use it if Clarissa should prove to be in here after all.

I was relieved to discover I didn't have to find out. The room was deserted. Mary joined me, and when the door had closed we stood looking at each other, sharing wordless gratitude at being together again and, momentarily at least, safe.

'What are we looking for?' Mary asked, turning to survey the room. There wasn't much to see; the bed was extremely neat, there were no clothes left out and few knick-knacks on the dresser ... it was more like a guest bedroom. The one sign that a married couple shared it was a photograph hanging on the wall: a family portrait showing Clarissa, a pleasant-looking man in his mid-forties, and their two sons. Matthew Wingfield was currently away fighting, but I wished he was here to help now; from what I'd heard he'd have come firmly down on the side of right, despite his name.

'Lizzy?' Mary said.

'We're looking for any sign she's been packing,' I said, and told my friend in a few short sentences what had happened after Wingfield had driven away, leaving Jack and me lying in the road. She said nothing but her touch on my arm told me she was glad I hadn't been hurt. I didn't have to speak either, to tell her I felt the same about her.

We turned our attention to searching the room, but I could already see it was going to be pointless. There were no trunks or hat-boxes, no travelling or vanity cases except for one small, plain one that lay open on the dressing table.

I crossed to it, unwilling to leave any stone unturned, but it yielded nothing. A terrible thumping noise from above our heads made us both look up with a start.

'Robert! Damn you, man, where are you?'

Mary's eyes widened as she turned back to me. 'David?'

'Yes,' I whispered, my heart crashing so hard I could almost believe I heard it above the rattle of the attic door. 'We have to go!'

I grabbed the flashlight and Mary seized my hand and we ran from the room, not bothering to stop and check the corridor first. Our hands were sweaty with fear and we kept losing our grip on each other, but I stayed close on Mary's heels as we thundered down the stairs, heedless for the moment of the noise.

As we drew level with the ground floor, a glance to my right showed me the short corridor leading to the large front hall. A sudden thought struck me and I felt again the weight of the talisman in my pocket.

I pulled Mary back into the shadows. 'Down the stairs, turn left into the coal cellar,' I said, breathless and urgent. 'Once you're in there you'll see a small wooden door. Go through it, use the light sparingly and try not to panic.'

'Lizzy!' Mary hissed, instinctively taking the flashlight I pushed at her. 'What are you doing?'

'I must try something,' I said. 'Listen: once you're through the door you'll be in a very narrow tunnel. Just follow it. There's a right turn a short way down, then a long straight bit which will bring you out at the bottom of the garden. When you come out, go down the hill, and you'll see a copse with two large trees at the entrance, like an archway. Through there you'll see Jack's motor.' I closed my eyes briefly, wondering if I was being reckless in giving up that chance of freedom for myself. 'I'll meet you there as soon as I can.'

Without waiting for a response, or to see if my instructions had been noted, I took a deep breath and started down the hallway to the main house.

Chapter 31

There were voices, I heard them immediately I stepped out into the entrance hall. They seemed to be coming from a room diagonally opposite where I stood, one of the two closed doors I could distinguish leading off the hall.

The other doors in the large, square, plainly decorated space were standing open; one, I could see, led through to a games room of some kind, the billiard table set neatly for a game I could never imagine happening. The remaining door was the one I had just come through and I closed it carefully behind me, mindful of the noise and holding my breath.

The voices continued, raised and defensive-sounding; Jack was in there with Samuel Wingfield. The urge to be sure he had the upper hand was so strong it almost overcame my resolve, but the thought of Will, and of Evie's grief if the worst happened, pressed me to ignore them and fix my attention on the remaining closed door, hoping it led to the room I sought; if I couldn't find the necklace I would try to do the next best thing.

With a glance towards the billiard room in case someone should be in there after all, I chose boldness as my disguise and marched across the hall to my target. I tried the handle and found the door locked. While this was frustrating and slowed me down somewhat, I felt it was a good indication that this was in fact Wingfield's study, so I slipped the key from my pocket and fitted it into the lock. Magic . . .

Once inside, with the door locked behind me, I breathed more easily and turned my attention to Samuel's desk. It was fanatically neat, with only a pen stand, a stack of paper and a small notebook in view – I picked this up with faint hope, but a riffle through the pages revealed nothing more than a running total of household accounts, a summary taken from the housekeeper's records. The desk had a single drawer but this time the key failed me. Frustrated, aware of a third voice joining the men next door – a woman – I jiggled the key as hard as I dared, but with no luck.

Apart from the desk, a tall cupboard in the corner and a sparsely stacked bookshelf, there was nothing in the room to lead me to believe anything of value was hidden here; no metal safe, no padlocks, no chains. I started with the bookcase; luckily Wingfield was no great reader, and it was the work of a few minutes to open each book on the shelf and shake it, hoping to see a loose leaf floating free from the pages. Nothing.

Every time the voices fell silent next door I felt my own heartbeat pound to fill the void. But no one came in. I bit my lip in frustration, looking around for inspiration: he *had* to keep his important papers in here . . . all I was looking for was an address, but where would he keep it? I looked again at the notebook. Something niggled at me about the way it lay there, filled with the same neat, close writing I remembered from the letter he had sent Mary by mistake.

Once again I looked through it; rows and rows of figures, and of names of local merchants and larger suppliers, of staff wages and fines levied for breakages or disobedience. I felt a frustrated growl building inside me, and put the book down.

The cupboard then . . . I stepped towards it, my hand raised to draw back the bolt, only realising at the last second that I had mistaken a narrow connecting door to the next room for a simple cupboard. This must lead through to where Jack held Samuel and, I guessed, Clarissa.

Their voices were louder here, though the words were muffled by the thick wall and the snug fit of the door. My hand froze a mere inch from the handle. My hairline prickled with sweat as I realised how close I had come to barging in on what might be a very delicate negotiation. But Jack clearly had doubts about Samuel's willingness to surrender any information, and it seemed those doubts were justified.

My gaze was drawn back to the notebook and I picked it up. This time when I opened it I studied not the addresses, but the names of the staff and tradesmen. It was only once I'd gone through four tightly written pages that I saw it, and the breath caught in my throat.

*Stentiford, G.: Butcher. Grassmore St – £2 for poultry purch'd 17
   Oct'r 1916*
*Smithaleigh, R.: Fuel Merchant. Grant St – negotiations ongoing
   for new coal supply*

Carling, S.: Fruiterer. Wicket Ln – 14d for oranges purch'd 22 Oct'r 1916.

Davies, W.: Butcher. 50-00-43 and 2-46-21 – negotiations ongoing.

I stared at the odd numbers next to Will's name and my heart turned slowly over. As an entry it did not stand out from the others in any obvious way apart from those, and the fact it had nothing to identify it as a household expense other than the qualification 'Butcher'. Highly unlikely a household would use two different butchers, and the 'negotiations ongoing' were clearly our own.

But what of those numbers? I searched frantically for another entry, one which might give some indication of an address, but there was nothing. I was just turning to the very back of the book to see if any pages had been glued together to conceal more information, a code key perhaps, when the door handle turned.

My heart in my mouth, I shoved the book deep into my coat pocket before remembering that the door was locked, and then I heard an unfamiliar voice.

'Grandfather? Are you in there? I must use your telephone.'

I froze, one hand clutching at the key in my pocket as if by the tightness of my grip I could ensure I had made proper use of it.

'Grandfather! If you're in there, please unlock the door. This is urgent! David has been attacked, his head's badly cut, we need to use your telephone to call for a doctor!'

'I'm in the library with your mother, Robert. Come in here,' Samuel's voice called from the next room, and I experienced a moment of the purest relief, letting out a shaky breath and releasing my hand from its sweaty grip on the key.

But that moment was short-lived. From the library I heard another voice, this one achingly familiar, and it shouted: 'Robert, no!' An instant later an horrifically loud bang echoed through the connected rooms and my head rang with it even as my heart pounded against my ribs.

Dazed with shock, I fumbled at the bolt, then pulled open the connecting door and stumbled into the library on feet that felt disconnected from the ground. I saw Samuel Wingfield standing beside the main door, Evie's necklace wrapped around his fingers and his arm tight about his younger grandson's neck.

I had time to note a deep crimson stain on the forearm of his jacket before another crack split the air and I felt something strike me, brutally heavy and white hot, above my right breast. The blow sent me staggering backwards, and I felt a scream rise but it remained locked in my throat. Time slowed, my heart struggled with sudden, breathless panic, and I crashed to the carpeted floor, the one clear part of my mind wondering if it would hurt terribly before it was over ... the last thing I saw before darkness swept in was Wingfield pushing his grandson away from him, and a single drop of his blood splashing on to the brilliantly faceted surface of the Kalteng Star.

There was light, it returned in flashes of white and dark red, and I hadn't even opened my eyes yet. Apart from that strange, disturbing vision there was also, gradually, sensation. But I didn't want it, couldn't bear it ...

Something warm on my cheek, a hand I realised dimly, snatched my attention from the deep, burning agony in my chest, but only for a second. A low voice choked my name over and over again, and then I did manage to open my eyes. Even that small effort was something I instantly regretted, and the relief of knowing Jack was alive was all but eclipsed by the complete terror of knowing I could not go on with him.

I felt new pressure against my chest, he was trying to staunch the flow of blood. I blinked up at him, pleading soundlessly for him to help me, but the grief in his face frightened me still more. I tried to talk, to ask him if I would live, but he shook his head.

'Shhh, love, don't try to speak,' he said, and his voice broke on the last word.

It terrified me to think he had given up already, and I struggled once again to form the words. This time I managed to part my lips and speak his name in a whisper. I thought I might be able to communicate this way and took a deep breath to try again, but the pain clawed harder, ripping right through me, and instead I heard my own weak voice give a cry. I faded a little bit, feeling his arms tighten around me, and only then realised I was cradled in his lap.

When I came back I found myself desperate to see his eyes, to read my future there, but when I found them I couldn't see anything, not even the rich, dark blue that had sustained me through the worst years of my life, for the glittering wash of his unshed tears.

I started to cry too, in fear and regret and pain, at the dreadful prospect of losing a life I had just begun to embrace. I wept for my mother, my sister and my brothers, but most of all I wept for Jack. His tears fell too then, I felt them splashing on to my cheek and mingling with my own, and his hand pressed harder on my chest, holding me close to him and telling me help was coming, help was coming, help was coming ...

Chapter 32

The next time I woke he was gone. But help had indeed come. I found myself in a hospital bed, numb all over and with the sense that I had weights tied to my limbs. I knew it was a hospital by the smell, but other than that my vision was restricted to a few blurry shapes and a bright overhead light.

The first shape resolved itself as it leaned in closer, and I saw a tired-looking nurse who nevertheless smiled at me. 'Welcome back, pet,' she said. I tried to smile at her, but my lips were as numb as the rest of me and she patted my arm. I saw her do it, but couldn't feel it.

The second of the forms I sensed hovering waited until the nurse had moved aside, and then took my hand. I recognised Mary and began to feel the warmth of her touch.

'The first time I saw you, I said you'd be one to watch,' she said, and in her eyes I saw the same crystalline brightness I had seen in Jack's as he'd cradled me on the library floor. 'It seems I was right. You were very lucky, you know.'

I licked my lips. Feeling was starting to creep back into various parts of my body now, and I knew it would only be a very short time before pain followed and quite possibly robbed me once more of the power to speak. 'Who shot me?'

Mary looked around but the nurse had left, so quietly we hadn't noticed. 'Clarissa,' she said. 'Evidently she was getting ready to shoot Jack, but you distracted her. Daft girl.' She spoke with affection but a chill raced through me as I considered how close I had come to losing Jack after all.

'How is he?' I was desperate to see him, to touch him, to know that he was whole.

'He's well. Had to make himself scarce, though,' she said. 'He managed to arrange this room for you, to keep you away from prying eyes. You're quite famous locally at the moment.' With so many war casualties returning every day, it must have taken a great deal of persuasion and I felt a surge of guilt at the privilege.

Mary went on with her explanation. 'The story is you were having a job interview with Clarissa when Samuel came in. They argued and you tried to protect her, but he shot you both and scarpered.'

So Clarissa was dead? Much as I'd disliked her, it was a shock. 'How long have I been here?' I mumbled.

'It's been two days since you arrived. Jack was called to London yesterday. He came to tell me he had to leave for a while, and to explain . . . things.'

'Then you know—'

'Yes.'

'So you understand he's not a coward or a traitor,' I said. My hand turned in hers and gripped her fingers tightly. It was so important to me that she should think well of him.

'Lizzy love,' she said gently, 'I was wrong about him. I know that now, and not just because he saved your life, and possibly mine too.'

'How then?'

'Remember you told me once about the tree he planted for Lord Creswell?' I nodded. 'Well, the day after you were shot, I went down to see it. I think it was to try and understand him a bit better, to see it for myself. You were right. The photo he left there was one of him and Lord Creswell. I never saw the one in the study, but from your description it's the same one. You must have prompted him to put it there when you noticed it.'

'So, you see? He did care for him, and he cared for your dad too,' I said, feeling a little weepy through shock and relief, and the almost overwhelming need to see Jack again.

'I know he did.' Mary's smile wavered and she clutched my hand tighter still. 'There was another tree there too. A newer one, with a stone in front of it, propped up and painted with three letters: A. J. D.'

For a moment I didn't understand, then it came to me. 'Arthur and Jean Deegan,' I said. 'Oh, Mary...'

'That's what he was planting that day you saw him, after you'd told him about my mother,' she said wretchedly. 'I got him completely wrong, didn't I?'

'It wasn't your fault,' I said. 'You didn't know then.'

'Neither did you,' she pointed out, 'but you believed in him.'

'Not all the time.'

'No, which was sensible. But you kept your mind and your heart open, and you loved him anyway.'

I had. I had loved him for so long now he was part of what made my heart beat. So strong was my longing for him that when I saw the door open just a few minutes later, and his tall form standing there, I half-believed I was imagining it.

Mary stood up. 'I'll leave you to talk,' she said, and as my eyes followed her across the small recovery room, I saw her stop beside Jack and the two of them embraced. Friends at last, after all these years.

When the door had closed behind Mary, Jack looked at me and I breathed in the sight of him like oxygen. He looked exhausted, pale and rumpled, as if he hadn't slept in a good long while, and before that had rested on the floor of a barn somewhere.

I felt a smile curve my lips. 'Come here,' I whispered.

'I don't want to hurt you,' he said as he sat down on my bed, tracing the line of my jaw with one finger, a wondering look on his face, as if unable to believe I was still here.

'Nor I you,' I reminded him, and although my arms ached to hold him I shied away from any movement. Seeing it, he leaned forward and gently kissed the corner of my mouth, moving to claim my lips only when I turned my head to offer them.

My hand lay on his collarbone, thumb resting at the side of his neck where I felt his pulse quicken as we kissed. My own heart strove to match it and for a while I was able to ignore the insistent, probing pain of my wound. But soon it became too much and, sensing it, Jack broke the kiss and instead held my face pressed to his. I felt the tenseness of his jaw under my cheek.

'I'm sorry,' he said. 'I don't want to hurt you, but I can't believe I can still touch you. I always knew you were stronger than you looked, but now you've proved it. Tin Lizzie has turned out to be Iron Lizzy.'

I smiled. 'Just let anyone try and hurt you and see what they get back, that's all. How are your battle wounds holding up?'

'I can hardly compare them to yours,' he said, neatly side-stepping the question. 'Do you want me to call the nurse back?'

'No,' I said. 'She'll send you away and I want to know what happened in that room. I'm going to close my eyes now, but don't worry, I'm not going to sleep.'

In truth, the glare of the overhead light was giving me a vicious headache, and my chest had begun to burn unbearably, but I didn't want him to see it in my face and stop talking. His voice soothed me, and his hand never left mine as he told me how it had been in that room where so many lives had been shattered.

'I found Wingfield in the library. He'd already managed to get the necklace off Clarissa, presumably by threatening her. They were both horrified when I walked in, but that told me we'd been successful in keeping ourselves unnoticed, and I knew *you* would be all right.' At this he shook my hand and I opened my eyes to see him giving me a stern glare. I smiled and blew him a kiss, then closed them again.

'Anyway, when I stepped into the library I saw that Wingfield was armed, and Clarissa was over by his desk looking furious. She had a suitcase by her feet that had been pulled to pieces, and I guessed that was where she had hidden the diamond.

'I held the gun on Wingfield. His was down by his side and he didn't dare raise it. I told him he could keep the necklace, I just wanted to know where Will was. He refused to tell me. He also pointed out that if I killed him the ensuing investigation would expose us both as spies.'

Jack paused but I didn't open my eyes. I was picturing it all as if it were happening right in front of me, and I didn't want to distract myself. 'That was when we heard Robert looking for his grandfather,' he went on. 'He's home on leave for two weeks. We heard him rattling the study door, and I realise now you were in there at the time, silly girl.'

'I do wish people wouldn't keep calling me names,' I murmured, and heard him laugh softly. He raised my hand to his lips and I felt a brief, warm pressure on my skin before he went on.

'Robert had obviously heard David shouting and had freed him from the attic, but David must have lied about what had happened. As far as I know Robert had no idea about any of this, and when he shouted for his grandfather, Wingfield gave me such a look ... Lizzy, I could have killed him right there and then.'

'Look?'

'It was a look that said he'd do whatever it took. To whoever he needed to. Then he shouted back, as you heard, and the next thing Robert was at the door. I could see what Wingfield was planning, why he had drawn the boy to us.'

'But why would he want to hurt his own grandson?'

'He knew Robert would piece it all together eventually. This way he could blame it on me. I yelled, hoping to distract him. It didn't work so I shot him.'

'In the arm,' I supplied, through rapidly numbing lips. I was so tired.

'You saw?'

'I saw his blood on the stone.'

I felt myself growing heavier and heavier, only the burning

pain in my chest keeping me from slipping under the weight of exhausted sleep.

'Well, he dropped the gun, but grabbed Robert anyway and dragged him across his own body as a shield. The next thing I knew Clarissa had scooped up Wingfield's gun and was pointing it at me. That is until you came bursting through the connecting door from the study.'

'And the resht is ... hist'ry,' I mumbled.

'Yes,' he whispered, placing my hand gently back on the covers. 'I was so mad with grief I turned on Clarissa.'

At this my eyes snapped open again, everything suddenly back in sharp focus. '*You* shot her?'

'I'm not proud of it,' Jack said. 'But I don't regret it either; she was armed, she'd shot you and I was next.'

'You could be sentenced to death!' I said in horror. My wound flared white-hot and I clutched at it. 'Jack, you have to go ...'

He immediately bent closer. 'It's all right,' he said. 'Listen to me, sweetheart. Robert will swear it was his grandfather who killed her, and the actions of Wingfield himself will reinforce that. He's taken that damned rock and gone. Probably to Germany.'

I drew in a couple of deep breaths and tried to calm my panic as Jack told me how he and Robert had talked, how Robert had known about his mother's planned flit but not about the diamond or Will.

'I was going to try and search the study, but I was called back to London for debriefing. I had to explain how Wingfield had slipped through my fingers. That means I still have no idea where Will might be,' he added. 'And since David has taken over as head of the family while his father is away, I can't get in to search the house for any clues.' He sighed, regret showing in every line of his face. 'I'm worried that by the time I do find anything it'll be too late.'

A fuzzy memory occurred to me. 'Jack, my coat pocket,' I said. 'I found something . . . a book. I'm sure it makes mention of Will though it makes no sense to me. I can't find an address. It must be him.'

Jack's face went blank with astonishment, and if my chest hadn't been hurting so badly I might have laughed at his expression. 'We'll make a secret agent out of you yet, Lizzy Parker,' he said, then became businesslike. 'Right, your clothes were taken for cleaning and mending. I'll find out where they've put them and see if I can find anything hidden in the book.'

'It's just numbers,' I said, shifting position in the bed and trying not to wince too obviously.

'They must be decipherable in some way,' Jack said. He leaned over to kiss me, and straightened up again. His own expression showed the same determined restraint as mine, but his lips had tightened slightly.

He saw my raised eyebrows. 'Two cracked ribs, some internal bruising and a fractured bone in my wrist,' he said. 'I was lucky.'

'Except you haven't had time or chance to let the healing begin,' I reminded him softly. He shrugged and smiled. 'There'll be time for that once we get young Davies home safe,' he said, and left me alone to sleep.

*

412

I drifted in and out of a bizarre dream-world for several hours. Once or twice a nurse came in to check on me, and the surgeon who had operated on me paid a visit and declared me to be mending nicely. I wished I shared some of his optimism; my chest felt as if it had been gouged raw and the inside filled with hot coals. Every breath was torture, and every beat of my heart found its echo in the throbbing sensation I felt from my neck to my waist.

But I was alive, and likely to remain so, and the pain would fade, eventually, even though I couldn't imagine it yet. During one of my more wakeful moments I let my thoughts settle on Jack, on what our future together would hold, and what he was doing right now – hopefully locating the book had been easy enough and he was working on deciphering those numbers next to Will's name.

I was just drifting away again when there was a timid knock at the door. It opened before I'd had chance to say anything. When I saw who stood there my eyes filled with tears and my arms lifted themselves from the bed and beckoned her to me.

'Hush, Just Lizzy,' Evie whispered, bending to hug me with the utmost care. 'Don't cry, darling!'

'Oh, Evie!' The shudder I gave hurt me but the relief of seeing her again was blissful. 'I'm so glad you're here. Anyway you're crying too, so don't you dare tell me to stop!'

When our emotions allowed us breathing space, Evie told me how Jack had made contact with her in France, through an acquaintance of his who was stationed there. 'He just introduced himself as Archie, and I had no idea who he was, but he knew Jack, and he knew about Will, and most importantly he passed on Jack's message that you needed me.'

'And you left immediately? Won't you get into trouble?'

'Not at all,' she said. 'Besides, someone had to come back to collect an ambulance that's been donated so I volunteered. I told them about you, and said you'd been adopted by my family and that we were sisters.'

'We sort of are,' I said. 'Or maybe cousins, at least. Evie, I have to tell you something . . .'

'I know about you and Jack,' she said, and relief swept over me as she smiled. 'Mary and I have had quite a talk. I was shocked at first, of course, but I can't think of two better-suited people.'

'Except you and Will,' I pointed out. 'And if fate smiles on us just a little longer we'll soon find out where he is.'

Watching her tremble more with every word, I told her about Wingfield's book and how Jack had gone to look for it and would soon return. When he came back into the room their mutual pleasure at seeing each other was evident. But this time I didn't feel uncomfortable or if I were intruding on their reunion. They embraced, then Jack looked at me questioningly.

I nodded. 'I've told Evie about the book. Did you find it?'

He sat down beside me and took my hand in his bandaged one, holding his good hand out to clasp Evie's and bring her close again. 'I know where he is,' he said, and Evie gasped and turned pale.

'Are you sure?' she said in a whisper filled with desperate hope.

'The numbers are co-ordinates. Will is sheltering in a farm just to the north-west of a village called Montauban-de-Picardie in the north of France. He must have wandered south after the battle at Bazentin-le-Petit, missed the patrols by some miracle, and not regained his memory.' He looked at Evie, clearly troubled. 'He may never regain it, sweetheart. Are you prepared for that?'

'He's still my husband,' she said. 'Better to have to start over and win his heart again than to hear that he is dead.'

Jack squeezed my hand though it must have hurt him to do so, and I could tell what he was thinking because I was thinking the same: anything rather than lose each other. 'I've sent Archie to the farm. He's carrying a note from me, a photograph of you, and orders that Will must return with his escort or face a firing squad. We can't risk losing him again now.'

He gave me a long, searching look and then stood up, pulling on Evie's hand. She smiled up at him, but the smile faded as she saw the intense expression in his eyes.

'What is it, Uncle Jack?'

'Please – you're too old to call me that now,' he said. 'And you may no longer want to in any case. I have to talk to you about something, and it must be now.'

'What on earth do you mean?' She tried for a teasing tone but it didn't work.

'Not here,' he said. He gave me a last look, filled with pain that had nothing to do with bruises and sprains, and I tried to smile for him but it was hard, knowing this might be the end of his relationship with the girl he regarded as a daughter.

They were gone a long time, during which a nurse gave me an injection and, despite everything, I slept. In my dreams I battled monsters inside hollow walls, masked assailants in attic rooms and dragons in prison cells, but I would have taken any

415

one of them on in my real, flesh-and-blood life, if it meant I could save Jack from telling Evie the truth about her father. But tell her he must, and all I could do was wait.

When Evie came back into the room she was sheet-white but composed. She sat on the bed and studied me intently. 'Can you still love him?' she said.

I didn't hesitate in my reply, and she nodded slowly. 'Good,' she said. 'He'll need that.'

'And you?' It mattered so much it hurt all the way through me as I waited for her answer.

She closed her eyes for a moment and took a deep breath. 'Yes, I can,' she said at last. 'It kills me to say it but my father knew what he was doing, and made his choice. Jack did what he had to do to save lives.'

She looked at the heavy white bandage beneath my nightgown, that covered the slope of my breast to my collarbone, and her voice hardened slightly. 'But he has let harm come to you, Lizzy, and that's different.'

'He was trying to help Will. And he saved me from Wingfield's car,' I reminded her.

Evie nodded, her expression still grim. 'As you saved him. And you'll continue to save each other because you'll both continue to need saving,' she said. She leaned over and put her arms around me, mellowing but still worried. 'Be careful, Lizzy, he leads a very dangerous life. He always will.'

I raised an eyebrow as she sat back again. 'Look who's talking!'

Evie laughed at that, and I saw the spark flare in her again. 'He still won't let me drive him anywhere.'

'Can you blame him?'

'When you're better I'll take you out in his car, and prove that neither of you has anything to worry about!'

The door opened then and Mary poked her head around. Evie waved her in, and the three of us relished the feeling of being back together. I asked Evie if she regretted the loss of her birthright, and her reply was an expletive I guessed she must have picked up from her time at the Front.

'So, no loss then?'

'Not even the slightest glimmer,' she said firmly. 'I always told you that stone was a curse, and now hopefully it'll bring equally shocking bad luck to the greedy soul who has given up everything to hold it in his hot, grasping hand.'

'Hear hear,' Mary and I said together.

I touched Mary's arm, wincing at the movement. 'Have you told Lady Creswell you want your job back yet?'

'Oh, don't worry,' Evie put in. 'She wants you back, Mary, she told me so. You can start whenever you like. She's most horribly sorry, especially after what happened with Lizzy.'

'It was my choice to leave,' Mary reminded her, 'I wasn't dismissed. And anyway I don't want to go back. I've decided I am going to train to be a nurse after all.'

'That'll be useful, with Jack around,' Evie said, looking pointedly at me.

'I was thinking more of tending the heart attacks *you* keep giving people,' Mary returned smartly.

Evie chuckled. 'Very well, I'll tell Mother she must find someone else.' She looked at me. 'I don't suppose you would like the job, when you're better?'

'I would, of course, but then *I* don't suppose I'd be her first choice,' I said with a tired smile.

She winked. 'Well, we all know what happens to Mother's first choices, don't we?'

I watched her and Mary as they fell to talking about the Red Cross, and what it was like for a nurse in the field, and felt my eyes drifting shut. A comforting weight settled on the bed next to me; I knew who it was without opening my eyes, and my smile deepened. His hand brushed my hair with the gentleness of a father with his newborn.

'Sleep now, love,' he said softly. 'You've earned it.'

Epilogue

It was a perfect day for a winter wedding. Snow had been falling steadily since before we had woken, and the small garden of the crooked, two-up-two-down house looked every bit as beautiful as those at Oaklands Manor, with drifts blown by the stiff December wind into smooth, graceful shapes. Only the rich, dark green of the holly bush showed up against the white mantle.

As bridesmaid, Evie fussed over the folds of the white wool dress, smoothing silk brocade panels at the upper arms the way I had done for her in another life, and straightening the veil until it was exactly right. I closed my eyes and pictured Jack, my heart swelling as I heard his low voice telling me he loved me, and that he would be at my side for ever, no matter what. I knew it couldn't be as idyllic as he'd promised, but to know he wished it as deeply as I did made his words all the more precious.

'Shall we have a glass of champagne? Let's have a glass of

champagne!' Evie said, as excited as if it were her own wedding. I supposed this was closer than she herself had come to a traditional day, and that she had thrown herself so heartily into its organisation was to be welcomed; her life was difficult enough, she deserved this chance to be joyful, even if that joy was for someone else.

'I'd say that was the bride's decision, wouldn't you?' I teased.

Evie huffed in mock impatience, 'Well, what does the bride say?'

Mary smiled and picked up her bouquet of fresh winter honeysuckle. 'I say: what are we waiting for?'

The simple service took place in Breckenhall's parish church, and was attended by a small number of Mary and Martin's closest friends. The butcher's boy's mother was looking as proud as she had every right to be, but there was a certain poignancy to the affair as we counted those who could not be there; those away fighting and those already lost. Jack caught my eye as Evie and I walked up the aisle behind Mary, and the look on his face was matched only by Martin's as he saw his bride. His smile seemed to light the furthest, darkest corners of the church.

Afterwards, while the newlyweds were chatting to Alice Peters, Jack and I were able to slip quietly away to stand in the thickly falling snow, enjoying the cold, crisp air. In the distance I could see Evie and Will, her arm determinedly hooked through his despite his still having no recollection of her as his wife. He glanced around and quickly pulled away; to him she was still the Creswell heiress. He had no memory of anything immediately prior to the war, including their marriage.

'It's a good thing, in a way,' Jack said, reading my mind as he followed the direction of my troubled gaze. 'The court martial actually heard his medical evidence, they don't always.'

'It was only thanks to you that they did,' I reminded him.

'It was all I could do, though. No amount of string-pulling afterwards would have made any difference, not when the penalty is death.'

'So they might still have sentenced Will . . .' I couldn't bring myself to say it, not after everything we had been through to save him, the thought was too awful.

'Possibly,' said Jack. 'It happens more often than you'd think.'

I hadn't realised Will had come quite so close; I think we had all assumed, except Jack, that once the doctors had confirmed shell shock and memory loss, all would be well.

'Poor Evie,' I said, and Jack put his arms around me from behind, holding me tight.

'She'll bring him back around. He loved her a long time before the war, and deep down he loves her still. But too much has happened, it'll take a while.'

'It's such a shame. But I'm so happy for Mary,' I added, reluctant to dwell too much on something we couldn't change. Evie knew we were here for her to lean on, that was all we could do. She had resolutely brushed aside our sympathy until we had learned not to offer it. Aloud, at least.

'Mary makes a lovely bride,' Jack said. 'I wish Jean and Arthur were here to see it.'

'So do I.'

He cleared his throat. 'Lizzy?'

I twisted in his arms to look up at him and he hugged me tighter, his gaze passing over the top of my head as if afraid to meet my eyes. 'I wanted to ... I mean, I know it's ... I'm too ... but times are ...' He threw up his hands in frustration and turned me to face him. 'Oh, for heaven's sake! Will you marry me?'

There was a long pause while I gave my galloping heart its head, and tamed the smile that wanted to turn into a blaze of joy. 'Well,' I said at length, and very calmly. 'And here's me thinking you would never ask.'

Later, we waved the happy couple off on their two-day honeymoon, and when the butcher's van had rattled out of sight the four of us stood together, reluctant to part company yet.

'So, today Miss Mary Deegan becomes Mrs Martin Barrow,' I mused.

'And Miss Evangeline Creswell is happy to be plain Mrs Evie Davies,' Jack added.

'I'll thank you not to refer to me as plain, Uncle Jack,' she said primly, and that brought a rare smile to Will's gaunt face, and a surge of hope to us all.

'It's odd how a name can mean so much, yet matter so little,' I said. 'I've had three names in four years.'

'And what do we call you now?' Jack asked, his hand finding mine. 'Are you ever going to be known as Mary Elizabeth Parker again? Or perhaps you'll just go straight to being Mrs Jack Carlisle?'

I heard Evie's delighted exclamation, and Will's murmured congratulations, but my attention was focused solely on the man in front of me, with snow melting on his eyelashes and a smile that warmed me from the inside out.

Our breath mingled on the frigid air as I reached up and pulled his face down to meet mine. 'Really, Mr Carlisle,' I said, just before our lips touched. 'you know perfectly well ... I'm just Lizzy.'

Acknowledgements

My thanks to my first editor and long-time friend Neil Marr for all his patience and advice over the years, and for getting my short stories into print. Also to everyone who has given me the encouragement and determination I have needed to move into novel-length fiction, especially Anne and Eddie Deegan, Tony and Shirley Steer, and my tireless and constantly supportive beta-reader Tonya Rittenhouse. Huge thanks to my fabulous sons Rob and Dominic, for being brilliant and basically letting me get on with it.

My gratitude also to editor Caroline Kirkpatrick, for taking the chance and pushing me on, and to my agent Kate Nash, who has already gone above and beyond to guide me during this exciting – but rather nerve-racking – time.

Lastly, many thanks to Edwin Cheers and the RCHS (Railway and Canal Historical Society) for their invaluable help with details of rail links and timetabling during the 1912–16 time period.